Sadistic Pattern

Sadistic Pattern

by

Michael J. Molloy

Gypsy Shadow Publishing

Sadistic Pattern
by
Michael J. Molloy

Gypsy Shadow Publishing, LLC.
Lockhart, TX
www.gypsyshadow.com

Library of Congress Control Number: 2015957921

eBook ISBN: 978-1-61950-270-3
Print ISBN: 978-1-61950-275-8

Published in the United States of America

First eBook Edition: November 1, 2015
First Print Edition: November 20, 2015

Dedication

I dedicate this book to my friends, Alojz and Joe. They always favor a good suspense novel. I hope I didn't disappoint.

Acknowledgements

To Gypsy Shadow Publishing, I thank Charlotte Holley and Denise Bartlett for backing me once again on my second book with them. To my new editor, Kathleen Marusak: great job! And to all my friends, family members, and allies with the RWANYC writing chapter, I'd like to express my appreciation toward you all. Thanks again for your support and encouragement.

Prologue

The bearded man was sweating bullets. He could feel every muscle in his body tighten. His throat was constricting as he asked the gentleman sitting next to him if he could drink the water in the other man's glass. The second man gave his blessing to do so.

His hand was trembling as perspiration continued to run from the pores of his skin. The bearded man took measured, small sips, but he was desperate in his intake, and it seemed if a full pitcher of ice water were in front of him, he'd guzzle it down. Conserving his consumption with the limited amount of water before him was prudent. He reached for the knot in his necktie and began to loosen it in order to unbutton the top of his white dress shirt.

Opposite the man sat a smartly dressed woman. She was behind a long desk, similar to the one where the bearded man and his water angel had stationed themselves. Thanks to an abundant amount of hairspray, the dyed dark red strands of her hair held together in place as if they were molded in plastic. Caked-on makeup failed to camouflage her age, the dead giveaway being the thick reading glasses she was wearing to peruse the sheaves of paper before her. Her appearance was authoritative as she continued to gloss over page after page.

In front of them all was an elevated wooden structure that dominated the room, with intricate and ornate designs carved along the top. Behind it, sitting like a queen was a black-robed woman, whose silvery blonde hairstyle could have allowed her to pass as a sister to the other woman. She was busy scribbling down a few esoteric notes, much like a finals contestant on Jeopardy.

Sitting in front of the structure was a young, plain-looking woman wearing a dowdy ensemble. She was positioned in front of a device that looked slightly bigger than a

desk phone and had various levers laid out in an arrangement perfectly understood by the woman, but not by a layman.

A formidable, tall man, without a trace of hair atop his
head, walked into the room from a side door. He wore a
neatly pressed white shirt, adorned with a gold metal badge
over his left breast and a patch in the form of a shield sewn
on his upper right sleeve. Black pants, with shoes and socks
to match, completed his ensemble. The man possessed a
holstered firearm on his right hip, an indication that he was
someone to be reckoned with.

Marching behind were thirteen individuals of mixed
race, ethnicity, age and gender—a harmonious hodgepodge
of humanity. Each person in cadence assumed his or her
pre-assigned chair. Once all were settled, the bald man
orated.

"All parties are present, Your Honor. All jurors are as-
sembled, including the lone alternate."

"Very well," the silvery blonde woman responded matter-of-factly in her role as judge. Gathering a few sheets of
paper from in front of her, she addressed the jury.

"Mister Foreman, has the jury reached a verdict?"

A man with thinning white hair rose from the group.
He seemed better suited to play checkers with friends at
a senior home with his red-and-black plaid flannel shirt
and khaki trousers. But the man was wise in his years, no
doubt the reason he'd been elected as the spokesman. He
cleared his throat for all to hear.

"Yes, we have, Your Honor," the foreman replied.

"What say you?"

"In the case of the People of Rhode Island versus Roger
Lavoie of murder in the first degree of Darren Haber, we
find the defendant not guilty."

A hush of astonishment silenced the room. The bearded man, Roger Lavoie, closed his eyes and released a great
sigh of relief. He leaned back in his chair as the burden of
such an enormous crime was lifted off his shoulders. The
man sitting next to him, attorney Vance Beckwith, slapped
his meaty right hand on Roger's left shoulder in a show of
victory. Roger thanked his hired suit for exonerating him.

At the other table, assistant district attorney Claire
Torelli pounded the oak top with a thud that resounded

throughout the room. If one were next to her, one could detect the mumbling of an expletive from her mouth. Behind closed doors, Claire had told associates and friends alike that the case was airtight. Apparently the jurors didn't get the message.

A woman from the back of the gallery bolted up from her seat upon hearing the verdict. She screamed, "No! You fucking murderer! You killed my brother!" The twenties-something woman then turned to the members of the jury with tears streaming down her face. "How could you! How could you let him get away with this?" Judge Sylvia McCormack banged her gavel several times.

"That's enough, Mrs. Doyle! I will not tolerate such behavior in my courtroom!" Judge McCormack motioned for a few of the court officers to physically remove the distraught young woman. Chloe Haber-Doyle continued to kick and scream as she was manhandled by the guards. When she was safely escorted out of the courtroom, Judge McCormack gestured for the foreman to continue.

"In the case of the People of Rhode Island versus Roger Lavoie of aggravated assault, harassment and torment of Margaret Lavoie, we find the defendant not guilty."

Claire flung her arms into the air as if looking for divine intervention. She then glared at the jury and shook her head in disgust. Unlike Chloe, Claire had more emotional restraint. But that was due in part to her use of proper protocol and comportment as a professional. But she was just as livid as Chloe on both counts.

Meanwhile, Roger and Vance were glad-handing each other at evading the second charge. His ordeal with the courts was over.

But there was yet another woman who sat in the gallery. She was fairly attractive, her age falling somewhere between that of Chloe and Roger. When the second verdict was announced, she tilted her head upward. Her emotionless countenance didn't change, except for the slight rise of her eyebrows. Siobhan O'Mara then closed her eyes and folded her hands on her lap. She sat there unwavering while learning that her tormented sister Margaret was going to be taking up space in a mental institution for doctors and psychiatrists to find a way to restore her sanity. Unlike the frantic Chloe, Siobhan calmly rose from her seat and exited through the rear of the courtroom. One of the guards politely opened a door facilitating her egress. Siobhan didn't speak. She simply nodded at him as a token of her appreciation at the ability to leave without touching the doors.

"This case has now ended," Judge McCormack affirmed. "The defendant is free to leave. The state thanks the jury for their services." And with one swift bang of the gavel, the lead court officer instructed everyone present to stand as the adjudicator retreated to her chambers with her entourage. Claire quickly gathered the papers on her desk and proceeded to march after Judge McCormack, perhaps to vent her own disgust privately, not only on how the verdict was reached, but also on the allowed elements that may have swayed the jurors' decision.

Roger and Vance engaged in another exchange of hearty handshakes.

"Thanks, Vance. You were brilliant!"

"That and the fact that Torelli didn't have all her ducks lined up."

"Please have your office bill me for whatever I still owe you."

As Vance nodded in consent, stuffing papers into his attaché case, Roger looked back at the departing members of the gallery. He was keenly interested in one particular individual. His eyes darted back and forth as if watching a heated tennis match, but the object of his search appeared to have already left. Roger sighed briefly and shrugged his shoulders.

Vance had finished packing up his gear. He grabbed Roger by the arm and advised his client to walk with him as they left the courthouse. "There's an army of newspaper, radio and TV journalists out there, Roger, including CNN. You'll want me by your side to dodge the barrage of questions you're going to face."

Roger wasn't going to question his lawyer; the legal beagle's advice made a heck of a lot of sense. Both men headed toward a private side door. But before he was about to exit, Roger took one more glance at the back of the courtroom. Now only the officers and two or three other people remained. But not the one Roger sought. Frustrated but unbowed, Roger vacated the scene.

Chapter 1

Roger Lavoie sprang up from his bed. The look of fright was etched upon his face.

"I did not kill Darren Haber!" Roger shouted while sitting up.

Roger continued to tremble. It had been twenty years since the trial, but the ordeal continued to haunt him like a menacing specter. His heart was racing and his gasps of terror were almost in step with his pulmonary beat. Finally his wife Beth woke out of her sleep after the commotion Roger had created. She turned on the light atop an adjacent nightstand. Beth had to snap Lavoie out of it or she feared she would need to call 911 to prevent a heart attack.

"Roger! Roger!"

Beth's cries finally reached Roger, as the fifty-eight-year-old Lavoie came to his senses. He suddenly looked around his bedroom as though he didn't recognize it. With fear still written across his face, Roger turned to Beth. It took him a few seconds, but he was finally able to identify her, even without his glasses.

"I," Roger spurted, "I'm sorry, Beth. I . . . I must have had a terrible nightmare. I'm sorry if I disturbed you."

When she attempted to comfort Roger, Beth noticed that his pajama top was soaked, presumably from perspiration. She quickly removed her arms and began to question her husband on the reason for his excessive sweating.

"I remember about a month ago you had a similar bad dream," Beth said. "You almost threw me off the bed."

Roger's head was still reeling. He didn't know what to make of it himself. He was both worried and embarrassed by this latest episode. He rose from his side of the bed and headed to the bedroom window. He looked out at the quiet street below. The Pawtucket, Rhode Island, suburb of Central Falls was silent on this chilly autumn evening.

Beth was growing concerned over her husband's actions. She immediately got up and approached Roger from
behind, gently placing her hands over Roger's broad shoulders. She wanted so to allay his fears and nightmares.

"Maybe you ought to see that psychoanalyst Francine
MacKenzie suggested last week," Beth began. "What was
his name? Oh, I know. It was Dr. Mort Sonnenstein."

Roger gave his wife a hard look. He couldn't believe
Beth would suggest he see a shrink. And he couldn't believe
she would actually heed the recommendation of that flighty
Francine. Roger would only say that he would give it some
thought.

The bearded university professor walked out of the
room and proceeded down the short hall to the bathroom.
He opened the medicine cabinet and reached for a bottle
of low-dose aspirin. Expending a little energy to open the
confounded vial, Roger plopped a pill into the palm of his
left hand. He dropped the aspirin into his mouth and then
filled a paper cup with water from the sink to wash down
the medicine. After swallowing the pill, Roger then took a
long look at himself in the medicine cabinet mirror. He still
had visions of the nightmare that woke him up etched in
his brain. Roger closed his eyes as to make the remnants
of the frightening dream go away, but when he eventually
opened them, he could still see the disturbing images that
caused him to yell in his sleep.

Roger spent just a minute looking at himself, but for
Beth it seemed like an eternity. She became concerned over
the well-being of her husband, and so she walked to the
bathroom to join him. She could see that Roger was oblivious to her presence. He continued to stare into the mirror.
Beth came up from behind and hugged Roger, pressing the
side of her face against the top of Roger's back to show she
cared for him. Finally Roger came to realize that Beth was
there and acknowledged her by gently stroking one of her
hands. He then turned to face his wife. Beth was smiling at
him. But a closer look into her eyes and it appeared that
Beth was about to cry.

"Roger," Beth began pleading, "why don't you seek out
Sonnenstein's help?"

"What good is it?" Roger countered. "Do you think I really need to discuss my personal life with some . . . some stranger?"

"Oh, come now, you make it sound as though Sonnenstein is some sort of degenerate. God forbid, Roger, but if you suddenly became severely ill or even badly injured in an accident, you'd wind up seeing a doctor in the emergency ward. You'd have never met the doctor before, yet you would have confidence he was going to help you. Seeing Sonnenstein isn't all that different. He could help you get over these nightmares you've been having. Maybe there's something embedded in your subconscious that needs to be brought to the forefront. That's where Sonnenstein comes in."

Roger finally conceded and confirmed that he would make an appointment to visit Dr. Sonnenstein. He realized that Beth didn't bring up specifically what Roger had shouted, otherwise she would have wanted to know who Darren Haber was and why Roger stressed that he didn't murder him. Instead, Roger had to create a clever diversion for his wife. He brought up his son Mark and mentioned that he hoped Mark could teach at the same university he did, although in a different field of study. Beth was fully aware of this and assured Roger that Mark would be fine regardless of where he taught, once again pressing for him to get the help he needed to calm his anxiety. Roger offered a smile and patted Beth's right hand to assure her he would. Beth was satisfied with his affirmative gesture, so she smiled in return and proceeded back to the bedroom.

Beth was about to exit the bathroom completely, but she sensed that Roger was not trailing her. When she turned back toward her husband, who was still hunched over the sink, Beth asked Roger to come with her.

"I'll be right there, dear," Roger told her.

Beth smiled at Roger's response, but there was still that small element of doubt etched across her face that Roger's answer didn't dispel. Beth didn't see the need to beat a dead horse any further, so she left the bathroom.

Knowing he was alone, Roger studied his image in the medicine cabinet mirror. *I almost slipped,* he thought to himself. The ugly past that Roger didn't want to dredge up was relentless.

7

Chapter 2

Heeding the wishes of Beth, Roger had made an appointment to meet Dr. Mort Sonnenstein at the psychoanalyst's office in downtown Pawtucket. He didn't have classes on Tuesdays so Roger took the first available appointment.

Roger drove his late-model Nissan Maxima to the Sayles Avenue address that Dr. Sonnenstein listed as his physical locale. The professor noted it was a two-story beige wooden house, not that dissimilar from his own home. He wasn't sure if he had the right place and was ready to drive away. That was until he gave the building a second look and spotted a small shingle suspended from a metal post stuck in the middle of the front lawn. Satisfied with the verification, Roger parked the car and cut off the engine.

Roger climbed out of the Maxima and electronically locked it, all the while not breaking eye contact with the home. Even though he didn't have to teach anthropology that day at Winston College, Roger maintained the same wardrobe he usually wore when he taught. It was his gray tweed blazer, charcoal slacks, loafers, white dress shirt, bow tie, and, oh yes, a tan all-weather fedora. With a minor adjustment to his wire-framed glasses, Roger proceeded toward the house.

The professor went up to the wooden porch and rang the doorbell. He looked around the neighborhood to see if anyone was watching him. He still felt shame about meeting Sonnenstein. He had his pride, and began to wonder if there was anyone in the area who might recognize him from the college. For good measure, Roger lowered his hat to just above his glasses and turned up the lapel of his blazer. There was no answer at the door, so Roger rang the bell one more time.

Finally the mocha-colored wooden front door opened. A gentleman, similar in age to Roger, stood in the doorway. He was quite tall and had a full head of dark hair, flowing just above his ears and across the back of his neck, with streaks of gray mixed in. The gentleman looked professorial, with a royal-blue cardigan over his light-blue open collar dress shirt, and tan slacks, but oddly worn sneakers, which clashed with the rest of the ensemble. With tortoise shell glasses precariously balanced over the bridge of his nose, the man addressed the visitor.

"Ah," he began, "you must be Professor Roger Lavoie! I'm Dr. Sonnenstein. Welcome! And please come in!"

"Thank you," Roger responded in kind. The two shook hands as Roger entered the domicile. At least he was pleased to hear that Sonnenstein said his name correctly in its proper three-syllable French pronunciation, instead of *Lavoy,* which always made Roger cringe.

As he walked inside, Roger took in the interior. He noticed the cherry wood split-level staircase to the left leading to the second floor. Roger spotted a traditional grandfather clock as he waltzed past the parlor and down a hallway. There was a musty smell to the place. Roger was amazed that Sonnenstein didn't at least use room deodorizer to freshen up the scent, especially knowing he was expecting a client.

Sonnenstein led Roger to a private room in the back of the house. It was the doctor's *office,* if you will, although it appeared to be nothing more than an oversized study. Several bookshelves were filled with various texts in Sonnenstein's field of expertise. Roger also spotted a few diplomas on one of the walls, which as an academician, he appreciated.

"Please, have a seat," Sonnenstein instructed his patient.

Roger looked behind him and found a large leather upholstered high-back chair. As he sat down, Roger saw Sonnenstein doing the same in a chair exactly the same as Roger's. Sonnenstein made a mention of the chairs to say that the two of them were equals and that the psychoanalyst didn't wish to appear condescending. Both men were a mere crumpled paper toss away from each other. A small Afghan rug separated the tips of their footwear.

"I'm sorry," began Sonnenstein. "I'm such a lousy host. Would you care for a cup of coffee?"

"No, thanks," replied Roger tacitly.

"You're a rather scholarly person. An anthropology professor over at Winston, is that correct?"

"That's right, Doctor."

"Oh, please. The one rule I have is to drop titles and surnames. Those diplomas you see on the wall are just to substantiate my credentials, not to impress anyone. Besides, you and I share similar academia and intellectual levels. So during our sessions, do call me Mort. And may I call you Roger?"

Roger agreed, if not for any reason but to clear a hurdle and get this meeting over with.

They began the session very informally. It was just small talk, but it was Mort's way of feeling out his patients. But Roger was also reciprocating by asking a few questions. Perhaps Mort wasn't aware of it, maybe because he was too engrossed in the workings of his profession, but he, too, was being scrutinized by his patient.

With the ancillary talk out of the way, Mort wanted to get at the root of the problems Roger had experienced, necessitating his visit with the psychoanalyst. To his questioning, Roger simply replied that it was just a recurring dream. Mort seemed to become more curious. His forehead furrowed, his eyes narrowed, and the doctor gripped his pen tighter as if he wanted to get Roger's every word. Mort probed Roger for the nature of these nightmares. Just as he had done with Beth that evening, Roger had to think of a diversion before revealing his secret. His brain had become numb. Roger was tapping an index finger on the armrest of his chair. Mort noticed the gesture, but wasn't too sure whether to dismiss is as a nervous twitch or as a compulsive disorder when Roger was confronted with a harsh and direct question.

"Okay," Roger began hesitantly, "if you must know, it's . . . it's . . . it's about my son, Mark."

Mort leaned forward even further. The psychoanalyst asked Roger point blank what it was that had Roger so obsessed about Mark. That was when the professor opened up to say he had been trying to get Mark, a well-qualified math teacher, also to teach at Winston.

"And this is what's causing you these *nightmares,* waking you up in the middle of the night?"

"Basically," Roger responded, "yes."

Mort leaned back in his chair as if he were satisfied with Roger's assessment. But in actuality he wasn't. There was silence in the room for a few seconds, which for Roger seemed like an eternity. Then Mort leaned forward again to give his take on the matter.

"You haven't told me Mark's age," Mort began, "but if I were to take a guess, I'd say he's in his mid-to-late twenties, perhaps thirty, am I right?"

"A fairly good guess. He's twenty-seven."

Mort reclined again. He was scribbling copious notes on his pad. All along Roger had been playing the game very well with his host, but now it had reached the point where the professor was getting peevish at the detailed notes Mort was jotting down.

Mort's brow furrowed. He was studying his own notes to make sure his observation was accurate. Feeling confident in his own summation, the psychoanalyst leaned forward once again to give Roger his assessment.

"Have you always been overprotective of your son?"

"I wouldn't say overprotective. I'm just a little concerned, that's all. There's nothing unusual about that, is there?"

Mort shrugged his shoulders, as if Roger's question was just the normal reaction of a parent. He began to scribble down more notes when suddenly the grandfather clock in the living room belted out a tone at the quarter hour. The series of chimes didn't faze Mort in the least because he was used to it. But it did pique Roger's curiosity. The psychoanalyst's relaxed attitude did allay any trepidation Roger might have had about the intoning chimes.

After a few more gyrations with his pen to paper, Mort began to probe Roger's relationship with Mark. Perhaps there was some hidden rationale for the elder Lavoie's worries in seeing that his son got the job.

"Has your relationship with Mark always been a good one, and by that I mean one in which his life and yours are strongly intertwined?"

"We've been that way ever since Mark was a little boy. But probably more so since Mark turned seven."

Mort scratched the back of his head. Roger thought perhaps it was a nervous tic of his. But it actually was a result of having leaned his head back against the headrest

11

portion of his chair. It affected his scalp to the degree it caused the reaction.

Mort wanted to get to the bottom of what significance Mark's age had to do with the solid bonding between father and son.

Mort leaned in closer. His eyes seemed to be piercing Roger's. The professor felt he was being intimidated, under the impression he was viewed more as a lab specimen than as a patient. Mort finally came to the point of his inquiry. He asked the bearded Lavoie what was so important at this time concerning Mark. Roger finally laid his cards on the table.

"When Mark was seven, his mother, Margaret—that was my first wife—fell victim to a severe degree of mental illness."

"How so?"

"She had to be institutionalized. To this day, twenty years later, Margaret still is being treated there. By there I mean Crenshaw. Are you familiar with the place?"

"Yes," Mort answered, "that's over in Johnston. But tell me, Roger, do you know to what the psychiatrists there have subjected Margaret?"

"You name it, she has undergone it. Electroshock therapy, psychiatric medication of just about every kind. They diagnosed her illness as schizophrenia. But she's beyond hope. That's why I had to step in at that time and become both parents to Mark. And let me assure you, until Mark came to an age where he could handle himself alone before I came home, it was a struggle. But I made the sacrifice."

Now Mort was puzzled. He figured that Roger had divorced Margaret in order to marry Beth. But Mort was wondering to what degree Margaret's condition had progressed, so dreadful that it compelled Roger to go through with the divorce, and if Roger had any conscience to begin with, to do it. Roger bristled at Mort's suggestion of callousness.

"I find your remark to be repulsive!"

With that Roger was about to rise from his chair and storm out of Mort's office. The clever psychoanalyst didn't want his patient to leave so abruptly. Instead he came up with a subtle, yet effective remark.

"Is this how you resolve your conflicts, Roger?"

Mort's volume was as soft as a whisper, yet his question resounded in ear-shattering decibels. The psychoanalyst sat calmly in his chair with his right elbow planted firmly on an armrest while the rest of the arm supported his head. Mort didn't say another word. He allowed his eyes to follow Roger, who had risen from his seat at this point and was ready to make a beeline toward the front door. But Roger froze in his tracks at Mort's understated but powerful point.

Roger and Mort engaged in a staring contest for seconds until the college professor retreated back to his chair. The bearded anthropology educator thought it best not to run away from a disagreement. He sat down and decided to attempt to iron out his differences with the psychoanalyst.

"Let me tell you something," Roger began. "Margaret was totally withdrawn back then and still is to this day. How the hell can anyone sustain a relationship when a spouse runs away from you, and others, for that matter?"

Mort sat back to absorb Roger's question. He pressed his hands together and touched the tips of his index fingers to his lips to give the situation some thought. Mort was beginning to believe that Roger had his own self-interests in mind and wondered if the professor was being selfish in not wanting to be with his wife any longer because his physical, emotional and sexual needs weren't being addressed.

But the psychoanalyst was curious as to how Margaret had arrived at Crenshaw in the first place. Mort posed that question to Roger, to which the professor was once again perturbed by the analyst's query.

"How the hell should I know? Her mind suddenly snapped one day, that's all! Must I have a reason for Margaret's spiral downward? You ought to know in your line of work that these things can occur without any rhyme or reason!"

"Why are you so defensive, Roger? All I did was ask a simple question."

For the second time in his session with Mort, Roger was ready to bolt from the room and leave. Deep inside he knew the real reason why his first wife went berserk. But the college professor wasn't about to show his hand to his questioner. Roger just kept telling himself to remain composed and relaxed and not to allow any outward signs of the deep secret tucked away in his brain. But he felt he owed Mort an answer. After giving the psychoanalyst's inquisition some careful thought, Roger released a short sigh. He then rubbed his eyes as if to erase a bad vision he had seen from long ago.

"You'll have to please forgive me, Mort. The experience with Margaret was quite taxing. It put a horrible strain on me. And on Mark, too. To think, as a child, Mark had to see his mother locked away in that godforsaken place. It wasn't agreeable with him either. To be frank, the whole situation troubles me to this day. It's caused me a lot of sleepless nights, especially at the beginning."

"Perhaps those horrific images still plague you. Are you sure, Roger, that it's Mark's inability to get a teaching job at Winston that's caused your recent nightmares and not Margaret's being locked up at Crenshaw?"

"I am quite sure. Margaret's tragedy occurred twenty years ago. Mark's problem is more current. While I still carry those vivid memories of Margaret in that maddening state of hers, there is nothing I—or anyone—can do for her at this point. She's beyond help. But I can help Mark now. It's my current battle with the chancellor to get Mark in that has caused me this angst."

Mort continued to scribble notes. But his writing was in cryptic form such that if Roger were to have looked over the psychoanalyst's shoulder, he would not be able to decipher the code. What Mort was writing was a note to himself. He was somewhat incredulous toward his patient and his story surrounding the terrible predicament of Margaret's.

While Mort continued to write, Roger sat there like one of his students. He was waiting for the session to come to a conclusion. Or perhaps Roger was waiting for the other shoe to drop. He was contemplating Mort's next question. Was there going to be more grilling on the situation concerning Margaret, or would Mort finally move on to other issues?

Whatever hieroglyphics Mort had put down on paper suddenly came to a stop, when Mort glanced at his notation and studied it briefly. Then he looked up at Roger and smiled.

"I think we've made some progress today," Mort began, "but you'll have to agree with me that Rome wasn't built in a day. I would like for us to get together again, Roger. That is, of course, if it's all right with you."

Roger hesitated before giving a response. Did he really want to return to Mort's office for another consultation? He gave it careful thought and then assured Mort that he would make another appointment. Mort was pleased, and it wasn't simply because the psychoanalyst was going to make more money on Roger. No, Mort was still quite curious about the circumstances surrounding Margaret's plight. Perhaps with a little more subtle interrogation, Mort might coax a bit more vital information from Roger in the next session.

The two men rose from their chairs. There was a cordial exchange of handshakes between the two. But, whereas Mort's offering was very sincere, Roger's was not. The professor put up a good front to exhibit a tepid expression. Inside Roger's mind was a different story. This was supposed to be a skull session. But for the Winston College educator, in this session he was given the third degree, similar in distress to the recent nightmare he had experienced, and the devilish reason for his being in Mort's presence.

Roger was about to leave the room and head to the front door of the house. But not before he gave Mort's degrees another eyeful. Ever the academic, Roger was.

"I hope you have an umbrella with you," Mort concluded as he opened the front door. "That storm system they kept chirping about on TV and radio appears to be on its way here, judging by the clouds."

Roger looked up at the skies and concurred with Mort's assessment. But he didn't say a word. The professor only offered a simple smile.

As Roger walked away from the property, Mort watched his latest patient. He wasn't too sure if Roger was going to come by again. But the issue involving Margaret was stuck in his craw. The psychoanalyst thought he might have to take matters into his own hands by investigating the problem himself. After looking at Roger's back advancing further away, Mort gave the situation more thought. He released a short burst of breath and then shook his head before retreating inside.

Just before he placed his hand on the driver's side door handle, Roger heard Mort's front door close. He then looked back at the house of the psychoanalyst and gave it a long stare. Roger was contemplating not returning to Mort's home. His appearance that day was just to appease Beth and assure her that he'd taken steps to resolve his series of wicked dreams.

And then something struck Roger. Just as Mort was profoundly inquisitive about Margaret's mind snapping, so was Roger's curiosity to see how far and where Mort was going with this. Maybe a second visit wouldn't be so bad after all. Only next time, Roger planned to be well-armed with rebuttals. After opening the door, Roger sat down in the driver's seat. He wanted to head home quickly to beat the impending rain.

Chapter 3

Roger was already at home by the time Beth arrived from her job as a nursing administrator at Rhode Island Hospital in Providence. She'd risen through the ranks at the medical center from a candy striper decades earlier while going to college, to become a nurse and then a registered nurse in the coronary care unit there, to finally reach her top position.

Beth was drenched from the soaking rain. She required immediate assistance from Roger, which her devoted husband was all too quick to offer. The professor peeled off the soaked raincoat, which clung to Beth like an extra layer of skin. Then he put away the umbrella in the stand near the front door, followed by Beth's drenched hat.

With his day off from lecturing at Winston, Roger found the time to prepare a broiled trout dinner with roasted potato wedges and creamed spinach. He told his exhausted wife to relax as he was fifteen minutes away from serving dinner.

"First," Roger told Beth, "we'll have some clam chowder before dinner. With this bone-chilling rain, I thought it was best to warm up the both of us."

"New England, of course?" asked a smiling Beth.

"Naturally."

Beth went upstairs to change out of her soggy business attire and slip into warm, dry casual clothing. While she was doing that, Roger was putting the finishing touches on the meal. He checked on the fish and wedges in the oven and noticed they were just about done, while the spinach was complete. A little spoonful taste of the chowder atop the stove told him that, too, was ready to eat.

By the time Beth came down, Roger was placing everything on the dining room table. He later decanted some Sauvignon Blanc into the pair of wine goblets by their place settings. He remembered reading somewhere that that particular wine went well with trout.

When she arrived at the table, Beth looked at the marvelous dinner Roger had prepared and was quite impressed.

"You spoil me!"

"Well, you do the same for me," Roger reasoned. "It's only fair."

Beth was being treated like a queen, though she was exhausted. After Roger served himself, it was time for the couple to sup on the sumptuous meal. Beth complimented her husband on how well the trout was prepared and tasted. Not too fishy. Roger only offered a slight smile and an appreciative thanks in return.

As they continued dining, Roger engaged in small talk, asking Beth how her day was, although he could easily tell how stressful it was just by looking at her. Beth sighed and lamented that the hospital was running dangerously low on certain medications, the medical equipment had seen better days, and a snag in the negotiations with the nursing staff, the very group she oversaw, could force a possible work stoppage, looming in the near future.

The subject then switched to Roger and his appointment with Dr. Mort Sonnenstein. Beth was curious about how the session went between the two. Roger was reluctant to give a full explanation, but he did give her a terse comment, stating that it was fair. Now Beth was even more inquisitive.

"What do you mean by that, dear? Wasn't Dr. Sonnenstein helpful in trying to get to the source of those dreams you've been having lately?"

Roger just gave her a stare. He then broke his gaze and slammed the fork he gripped down atop the maple dining room table.

"Why couldn't you just accept the answer I gave you, Beth, without further instigation?"

"Why do you have to be so testy? All I asked was a simple question. Judging by your reaction, I'd say the meeting with Sonnenstein didn't go very well."

As before, Roger simply glared at Beth without saying a word. That lasted for about five seconds. Meanwhile, Beth sat quietly, waiting for her husband to say something. Finally Roger broke his silence. Staring at his dinner plate as if the answer were there, Roger came out with a confession.

"I'm sorry for the way I just acted, Beth. I do apologize. And you're right. My session with Mort, as he likes to refer to himself, didn't go as well as I had hoped. He wants me back for another session. I'm beginning to have second thoughts."

Although she didn't say it, Beth accepted Roger's apology for his outburst in reaction to her line of questioning, by offering a smile. But Beth also wanted to encourage her husband to continue to seek out the psychoanalyst's help.

"I think you should go back, at least once more. After all, Roger, you don't expect a full answer from a physician from one visit. He's going to want you to take tests and then review them with you. It's not that much different with Sonn . . . excuse me . . . Mort."

Roger gave Beth's rational line of reasoning some serious thought. He then concurred with Beth's logic by stating he would return. The rest of the dinner continued without further incident.

Chapter 4

"Mister Collins! Can you repeat what I had just said to the rest of the class on Sir James George Frazier's theory on magic versus religion?"

Roger had cornered one of his students. He knew Collins couldn't come up with the correct answer. It was just the professor's way to get your attention if you were dozing off in class or exchanging loving glances with a coed, which was the case with the blond-headed Collins.

When Collins got his act together, Lavoie then felt compelled to go on with the lecture. But the moment Lavoie was about to say another word, the bell sounded from the hallway outside the classroom. His anthropology lecture for the day was over and the students were happy to move on to their next agenda. Roger reminded the departing students that there would be an exam the following Tuesday on the subject matter covered in class over the last few weeks.

One by one, each student made his or her way to the exit. Not a one would give Lavoie eye contact, although it really didn't matter much. But Roger looked at each student with contempt. *What a waste of my time it is in trying to educate these ungrateful ne'er-do-wells!* This was especially true when he saw Collins engaging in conversation with the pretty coed he'd eyed in class. That irked Lavoie to no end. But rather than dwell on the subject any further, Roger decided to pack up his teaching materials and vacate the classroom.

The lecture concluded a string of three classes Roger had taught for the day. Although the classes were interspersed with lengthy breaks in between, Roger still had stood and droned on in front of the students for over four hours. He was totally exhausted and felt compelled to head straight home and relax with a glass of wine. But there was one person he had to see before putting the Winston College campus in his car's rearview mirror.

Roger left Danforth Hall, the building that housed his classes, and raced across the acreage of Winston. Despite the sunny skies, the temperature was only in the mid-40s. The trees were devoid of foliage and whatever crimson and gold leaves that had remained strewn across the vast lawn were scattered far and few between by the brisk autumnal winds.

Roger arrived at his destination. It was Chase Hall, the oldest building on the campus, whose stone spires atop its dual towers gave it a regal appearance. Laceworks of ivy partially covered its venerated exterior. One could designate the structure for landmark status, a place revered as hallowed.

With his teaching assignments completed for the day, Roger was seeking out a particular office, not a classroom. He climbed the two long flights of stairs and then walked thirty feet down a corridor lined with oak doors and beveled window panes to conceal the occupants behind them. The whiff of a coat of fresh paint wafted through the hallway. He came to a stop when he spotted a notable shingle outside one of the doors: *Professor Edward Asmundsson, Dean of Mathematics.*

Roger opened the door and immediately spotted a woman in her mid-twenties with shoulder-grazing dark hair striking keys on the keyboard connected to her PC. But she was the only one present in the office. Although she was intent upon completing what she was typing, the woman did sense that someone was in her presence. She stopped what she was doing and looked up. She smiled at Roger, having recognized him from previous encounters.

"Hello, Professor Lavoie," the woman greeted.

"Hello, Heather. Is Professor Asmundsson in?"

"No, I'm afraid not. But I'll bet you just might catch him in the faculty lounge."

Roger thanked the fetching brunette. But the anthropology lecturer wasn't pleased that he had to trudge across the Winston campus once again. The Shelton Building that housed the lounge was off in a different direction, much farther than the distance he had to walk from Danforth Hall to Chase Hall. But there was a very important matter that Roger had to discuss with Asmundsson that had to be addressed as soon as possible. He couldn't wait for a communiqué from the math dean via phone or email. And so Roger tipped his gray flannel bucket hat and wished Heather a good day.

Chapter 5

Mort Sonnenstein had just completed his session with another one of his patients, Andrea Thorpe. She was in her late thirties and was seeking treatment from Mort because of social hang-ups she had, having been rejected by friends and family members many times over. For Andrea, this caused her to become withdrawn, though not to the point where it affected her job as a data technician. Still, just as he had dealt with Roger on the day before, Mort handled his patient with the utmost care.

Mort escorted Andrea to the front door. He graciously wished her a good day and said he was looking forward to their next session. Feeling appreciated, Andrea smiled back at the psychoanalyst and thanked him for his keen insight and the special attention he gave her.

The good analyst kept his smile even after he had closed the door on the now departed client. He thought fondly of the good he was doing in helping another person. There was nothing like a little self-gratification to boost one's morale.

Mort walked back to his office in the rear of the house. Sitting down in his executive-style leather chair, he began to peruse his appointment book. Mort was making an entry for Andrea's next visit when he happened to stumble upon the appointment written in for the session he had with Roger the day before. He gave Roger's name a long studious look. Mort then brought his elbow to the top of his desk and rested his chin on the widened crook between his thumb and ring finger. His forehead began to furrow. Some issues still had to be addressed, and Mort wasn't going to wait for the next meeting to get the answers, if there were to be a next meeting, judging from Roger's lukewarm agreement to see him again.

The encounter with Roger required deeper contemplation. Mort reclined in his chair. He was looking up into space as if to seek out the answers there. And then it dawned on

Mort to review the copious notes he'd made during the session.

Mort began to sift through the notes, coming across the mention of the first Mrs. Lavoie taking up residence at Crenshaw. Mort immediately pulled his Rolodex on the corner of his desk closer. He thumbed through the *C* portion of the small card holder and came across the name of the institution, complete with address and phone number. In his line of work, Mort had consulted with those running Crenshaw, but it had not been for quite some time. He noticed a handwritten name on the card. Mort gave it some study and tried to recall the individual in question. But that was where it got a little fuzzy for the psychoanalyst. No matter, Mort's quest for finding the truth and his voracious curiosity got the better of him, and he decided to follow up.

Mort dialed the listed number. After going through a series of pre-recorded greetings and menus, Mort was able to connect with a live voice.

"Hello, this is Dr. Mort Sonnenstein. I'm trying to see if Dr. Oswald Borshevsky is in, please."

The person on the other end told Mort that Dr. Borshevsky had already left for the day. Mort was puzzled. He looked at his watch, which read three-forty-nine. *This man has hours like a banker,* Mort thought. The person asked Mort if he wanted to leave a message, but the psychoanalyst politely declined and said he would try to reach Dr. Borshevsky in the morning. Mort thanked the operator and hung up the receiver.

Now the wait to get at the truth was beginning to gnaw at Mort, but there was nothing he could do without speaking to Borshevsky. Filled with frustration, he made the return call in the morning a number one priority.

Chapter 6

Roger made the trek to the faculty lounge. He scanned the tables of the professorial oasis and spotted the same tired faces he would normally encounter on any given day.

There was Suzanne Hensley, dean of the English Department. She was perusing a stack of papers, attempting to give out grades on short stories written by her students as part of the curriculum. As usual, Suzanne held a pen in her right hand with a cup of coffee in her left. About the only things that held up the English scholar were coffee and cigarettes, the latter of which she was not allowed to light up inside the lounge. The diet of caffeine and nicotine might have accounted for her thin figure, since she hardly ate.

Dirk Sorgaard, dean of the Political Science Department, was busy giving his opinions on just about any subject to other professors and adjuncts sitting near him. Despite being the effusive orator that he was, Sorgaard never made the law into a successful career, nor did he achieve any heights when he ran twice for political office. Those who can't progress well in public life wind up teaching. That was the conventional wisdom of most everyone, although Dirk would argue the point. Such was the normal reaction of a closet lawyer/politician, although Dirk would make a valid case that someone had to teach the future attorneys and lawmakers of tomorrow. Roger was always amused by Sorgaard's first name: Dirk. To Roger it sounded as though Dirk should have been a bricklayer or steelworker, or perhaps a motion picture action figure. Perhaps his first name made others disbelieve Dirk could give credence to his legal points.

Professor Harold Washington had his head buried in that day's edition of the Providence Journal. The distinguished lecturer of African studies at the university often argued with the institution's chancellor about creating a department devoted to such criteria. But the chancellor argued it was too esoteric to establish itself on its own and so the subject was relegated to being part of the Social Studies Department. Harold never gave up and often would bring up the subject whenever he crossed the chancellor's path.

And then there was Edward Asmundsson, the Mathematics Department's dean, and the subject of Roger's search. He resembled Peter O'Toole's scholarly character Mr. Chips with his drooping mustache, gaunt and weathered face and horn-rimmed glasses. Edward was studiously poring over the lesson plans for his classes the next day and the day after that. That was Edward for you. He was always planning well ahead to get the chore out of the way. As he liked to put it, one can never tell when a surprise may pop up, causing an otherwise carefully thought-out plan to go awry. Edward was meticulous in that regard. Whereas he always made sure he looked proper in front of the students and that his suit looked crisp and his necktie properly knotted, Edward would loosen the tie knot and open the top button of his dress shirt when here. After all, the time spent in the lounge was his, not the college's, even though Edward spent it on planning his teaching assignments. As was his custom, Edward was slowly sipping his afternoon cup of Earl Grey tea, with just a small twist of lemon.

Roger walked over to the spot adjacent to where Edward continued to peruse his lesson plan. But the math dean was oblivious to Roger's presence. The anthropology professor rolled his eyes because he couldn't believe Edward didn't notice him, despite the fact that Roger was practically on top of him. Finally Roger had to resort to clearing his throat to get Edward's attention. The sound finally broke the math dean's fixated gaze on the printed matter before him, and caused him to look up. He recognized Roger immediately.

"Oh, hello, Roger," Edward said and smiled. "I'm sorry for being unmindful. Come, have a seat."

"I'm glad you finally noticed me," Roger replied. "I was afraid I might have to do a drum roll on the table to get your attention."

"Well, I would've acknowledged your presence eventually. You're one of the few professors on campus who wears a damn bowtie to work. And then there's your gray beard."

"At least I keep my beard properly trimmed, unlike that soup strainer of an excuse for a mustache that you wear. I can't tell what you're hiding underneath that brush. Do you still have a mouth? Honestly, Edward, the only way I can tell you're smiling at me is by looking at your eyes."

And with that Edward's cheeks expanded upward, causing his eyes to squint. Each enjoyed the other's cutting humor. Roger accepted Edward's invitation to sit across from him.

They began to engage in idle banter, mainly on how each other's families were coming along and lamenting on the college's students and how the class of today wasn't as it once was twenty or thirty years ago. To Roger, the students seemed to show up in the classrooms just to satisfy their tuition-paying parents or the government, for those receiving Pell grants. Edward echoed the sentiments of his fellow educator. Of course, as Roger had pointed out, one couldn't see Edward's mouth move under his hirsute upper lip. Only a subtle movement of the math dean's chin and slight vibrations of his bristles were indications of his speaking; that and his vocalization. Edward also had a tendency to smack his lips when he's finished voicing his train of thought.

But Roger wanted to discuss with Edward the real reason why he'd sought out his colleague. He wasted no further time in mentioning his purpose, but Edward beat him to the punch for he'd heard the story before.

"I know why you're here, Roger. Let's not beat around the bush. It's because of your son, Mark, isn't it?"

Roger was at first reluctant to concede that Edward had hit the nail on the head. But there were no two ways about it, so Lavoie acquiesced.

"Yes, it is about Mark."

"How is he doing? Is he still working as a departmental manager at the Best Buy place?"

"Yes, he's still there. But you know as well as I do, Edward, Mark doesn't belong there. He's a fish out of water. A square peg in a round hole. A—"

"Please," Edward politely interrupted, "spare me the analogies and metaphors. I know where you're coming from with all this."

"Then you know Mark is highly qualified. He could easily teach high school algebra, geometry and trigonometry. But Mark's heart lies here. You always marveled at his skills, saying he was one of the best students you ever had, Edward."

"I do recall his passion for learning and dedication to detail."

"The chancellor won't listen to me anymore. He feels I have a bias."

"Oh, dear, I can't understand why."

Roger didn't appreciate the sarcasm. Growing more and more frustrated over the chancellor's unwillingness to hire Mark as a math professor, Roger had to vent more steam.

"I don't understand the chancellor's thinking, Edward. My Mark is more than capable of teaching here. I think he could teach at the University of Rhode Island, perhaps even Providence College. Hell, I think he could even teach at Brown. But at Winston College, he can't even hold the chalk to the blackboard."

"You're worrying yourself to death, Roger. Let me see what I can do for Mark when I talk to the chancellor this evening."

"I appreciate all your efforts, my friend. Thank you."

With that Roger stood up from his seat to give Edward a warm and firm handshake. But the math dean didn't promise he was going to overturn the chancellor's thinking; just throw paint on the wall and see if the university leader considered it art.

Roger was confident Edward would go to bat for him and his son. But the anthropology professor was a realist. There was only so much Edward could say or do when he was to meet with the chancellor later. This would be the last chance for Mark to get his foot in the door of the college. Roger was only hoping the door wouldn't slam shut on it.

Chapter 7

The Lavoies decided on a little adventure that evening when Roger and Beth made tacos for dinner. Each collaborated on the meal. Roger focused on preparing the chopped sirloin with his special spicy seasoning mix while Beth was responsible for slicing and dicing the tomatoes and lettuce.

After the meal and the huge cleanup that followed, Beth relaxed by watching a theatrical film on HBO. Roger, in the meantime, sat in his study and cranked up the classical sounds of Bach in his headphones. As was his wont, Roger listened with his eyes shut while motioning with his arms as if he were John Williams conducting an orchestra.

At a critical point in the movie, the house phone suddenly rang. Beth wasn't too pleased about the timing of the call. She was still glued to the tube as she scowled after the first ring. And Beth really became annoyed after the second ring. She was hoping her significant other would pick up one of the other receivers scattered throughout the home. Beth even called Roger's name, but that didn't seem to work. If Beth was in a zone watching the film, Roger was in his man cave listening to the concerto.

The phone rang a third time. Beth drew a deep sigh and conceded she would have to answer it. With great reluctance and a deep sigh of angst, she rose from her comfy corner of the living room divan and walked over to the receiver at the other side of the room. After the traditional hello, Beth recognized it was Roger's son, Mark, on the other end. She rolled her eyes and thought, *Is this the reason I had to interrupt my movie?* Nevertheless, ever the gracious stepmom, Beth bit the bullet and exchanged a few pleasantries with Mark. But the hospital administrator wanted to get back to her film. She immediately went to the study. Without further ado Beth knocked once, but saw that her husband was deeply engrossed in the classical piece. She had to remove one of the padded headphone pieces and speak into Roger's free ear to tell him that Mark was on the phone. That got the professor's attention. He immediately apologized to Beth, turned off the music and then took the receiver from his wife. Beth was relieved because now she could get back to watching the movie, hopefully not having missed any critical points.

Roger watched as Beth hightailed it back to the living room couch. When she was out of hearing range, Roger began to speak with his son. After a few quick exchanges about Mark's job at the Best Buy store and a few additional, ancillary subjects, they came to the purpose for the young Lavoie's call.

"Did you hear anything about what might be happening about getting a teaching job at Winston, Dad?"

"I spoke with Asmundsson again over at the lounge this afternoon. He said he was going to meet with the chancellor this evening, or at least talk with him over the phone."

"I hope it's soon. I may have to resort to accepting that teaching job at the high school. Not that it's bad, but it doesn't carry as much weight as teaching at the university level."

"Listen, Mark, are you free tomorrow night?"

"Yeah, why?"

"Why don't you and I take in a hockey game tomorrow night in Providence? The Bruins are playing. Perhaps I might have an answer from Asmundsson then, and we can discuss it in person. It'll do both of us good to get out together for the evening. We haven't done that in a while, you know."

Mark agreed to Roger's invitation to attend the minor league hockey game. Roger said he would pick up Mark from his Providence apartment at about five o'clock. That would give the two of them time to grab a quick bite together before heading to the arena. They then ended their conversation.

Roger returned the living room receiver back to its resting place. He saw Beth riveted to the film she was watching, but she wasn't oblivious to his presence.

"What did your son want?"

"He was just curious on what was happening with Asmundsson about the possible position at Winston for him. I told him I may get an answer tomorrow from Asmundsson since he's seeing the chancellor this evening. Oh, and Mark and I are going to take in a Bruins game tomorrow night in Providence, if that's okay with you. It'll do Mark good to get out and enjoy a good game. And maybe, just maybe, I might have good news for him."

"A little male bonding, huh? That sounds good. Have fun."

"Thank you, Beth. But I like to look at it as just a father and son get-together."

Beth accepted Roger's interpretation of his upcoming meeting with Mark. Hopefully the anthropology professor would have something of relevance for his son.

Chapter 8

As was his usual morning custom, Mort Sonnenstein read that day's copy of the Providence Journal and then watched CNN and MSNBC for the latest developing news stories. He then checked online briefly to see how his modest portfolio was doing in the financial markets. Satisfied with his fill of information, the psychoanalyst retreated to his back office to review the log of patients he would be seeing that day.

As he was about to open his appointment book, Mort noticed a piece of paper sticking out from it. He opened the book and on the slip was the name, along with a phone number, of Dr. Oswald Borshevsky over at Crenshaw. As a person who analyzes the human mind regularly, even Mort needed reminders of what he had to do on a daily basis to keep his brain alert.

Beside Borshevsky's name was a little blurb about Roger Lavoie. Again this was another reminder to Mort of the reason to contact the head of the mental facility. Mort did recall that Borshevsky's assistant told him her boss was going to be in that morning. With a quick check of his watch, which read 9:18, Mort picked up the receiver of his desk phone and began to punch in the sequence of numbers.

Mort had to go through the ritual of endless automated greetings to get to Borshevsky's office. After a few rings, the psychoanalyst reached the admin of his intended target. Mort identified himself, just as he had done the previous afternoon. The assistant both recognized his name and his voice and asked the psychoanalyst to wait while she spoke with Borshevsky. A few moments later, the two medical professionals finally hooked up.

In a cordial exchange of banter between Mort and Borshevsky, each recalled knowledge of the other through mutual relationships. But the administrator of the mental health facility was a busy man with a work schedule to match. Whatever Mort's reasoning for wanting to see Borshevsky would have to be conveyed in a terse and to-the-point manner. The psychoanalyst didn't pull any punches.

"This has something to do with one your patients," Mort said. "Margaret Lavoie."

At only hearing silence at first, Mort wanted to make sure Borshevsky was still there. Borshevsky acknowledged that he was, but there was an eerie pause before he responded to Mort's urging. Mort couldn't see Borshevsky's reaction, but he knew the mere mention of Roger's ex-wife didn't sit well with the head of Crenshaw. Borshevsky wanted to know why Mort was interested in Margaret. That was when he mentioned the connection.

"I have begun seeing her ex-husband, Roger Lavoie. He's a patient of mine and in our session he brought up Margaret."

Again Borshevsky did not utter a word, giving Mort the further impression that the entire affair surrounding the former husband and wife made the Crenshaw leader uncomfortable. Borshevsky seemed reluctant to discuss the matter and was just about to hang up the phone. That was when Mort had to beg Borshevsky for just one minute longer of his valuable time.

"As a fellow medical professional, you can relate to the scientific curiosity I have regarding Margaret. I am due to see Roger again very soon, but before I do I need to satisfy my pique of interest involving his ex-wife. I was wondering when you might have a few minutes to spare so we can meet in person."

Finally Borshevsky conceded and agreed to have Mort come by the next day and see him. Mort was delighted that Borshevsky capitulated as the two doctors agreed upon 11:00 the following morning. The two concluded their conversation, and Mort hung up his line.

Mort continued to smile for a few seconds longer, knowing that he had achieved his desired goal with Borshevsky granting Mort his audience. The psychoanalyst was eager to see for himself the circumstances regarding Margaret. It was vital that he did before he scheduled another session for Roger.

Chapter 9

Right on cue, Roger picked up his son Mark at five o'clock that evening. They ate at the Capital Grille restaurant where both dined on a tender New York sirloin steak dinner done to perfection. The manly atmosphere of dark wooden walls and subtle lighting added to the hearty ambience of the robust repast. The father and son shared an ice-cold pitcher of Sam Adams Lager.

After the meal, it was on to the arena known as the Dunkin Donuts Center, where the Providence Bruins were to play host to their archrival Worcester Sharks. It was a fifteen-minute walk from the restaurant to the arena as both Roger and Mark made it in time to hear the National Anthem.

Whereas Roger was a rather taciturn individual, not wanting to mingle at social gatherings, Mark was more outgoing. This was a trait the younger Lavoie inherited from his mother Margaret before she went over the deep end. While Roger's hair up top was thinning and gray to match his neatly trimmed beard, Mark sported dark blond hair, in more abundance than his father's. The younger man did not have any facial hair whatsoever and was an avid jogger. Altogether, Mark's features and youth made for a handsome package.

The game was midway through the first period with neither team able to make a point through the opposing goalie. Then one of the Sharks, defenseman Ty Levantin, rammed Bruins forward Keith Brinkman heavily into the far side boards. The crowd screamed at the officials immediately for a penalty, and the referees were right on it. As soon as another Worcester player touched the puck, play was called as Referee Niles Redmond signaled Levantin to the penalty box.

The crowd was frenzied with the Bruins on the power play. Just after the face-off to the right of the Worcester goaltender, Sharks right winger Evan Luwoczyk high-sticked Timo Aaro. The partisan faithful was clamoring for another penalty. They got their wish when Redmond whistled for the call once one of the Worcester players touched the puck. Luwoczyk headed to the sin bin while the crowd whooped and blaring rock music streamed through the arena's loud speakers.

The house organist led the charge, and the puck was dropped by one of the linesman, thus resuming play. The Bruins were cycling down low for one of their players to get a clear shot toward the goal. The puck was centered out to Troy Burton, who released a one-timer. The shot whistled past Worcester goalie Patrik Bergstrom. Suddenly a loud foghorn sounded as the fans erupted in jubilation. The Bruins took an early 1-0 lead.

Roger and Mark celebrated the power play tally, like just about everyone else in the crowd. When order was restored, the two of them began to talk shop about Mark's teaching prospects at Winston. They had purposely refrained from such talk until the time was right to promote the exchange.

"So," Mark began, "did you hear anything from Asmundsson and his talk with the chancellor?"

"He told me they had a pleasant conversation last night. Edward sounded extremely positive, Mark. I feel you might be offered the job in time for the spring semester in January."

"But that's still more than two months away. It's not even Halloween yet."

"Patience is a virtue, Mark. Besides, I'm sure Best Buy will appreciate your presence with them through the holidays. That also might spike your commissions."

Mark let out a short burst of air as he smiled at his father's reference to bonuses the younger Lavoie could look to win by staying on through Christmas. But it was a sarcastic chortle. Mark's number one priority was to get the teaching job he had long coveted at Winston. And Roger knew that full well. The problem was that Roger could do nothing more until the chancellor decided upon hiring Mark.

But Mark wasn't about to drop the subject entirely. He just shook his head at the situation.

"I don't know what's stalling the chancellor, Dad. Is it nepotism?"

"Perhaps, but that hasn't been a key issue here, believe it or not. And let me tell you, I've tried all I could, short of installing a bright neon sign on the chancellor's front lawn to highlight my beseeching him. But I haven't given up on it, son. Let me probe Edward again for a better fix on the subject."

Mark wasn't totally satisfied with Roger's explanation, but neither was Roger thrilled with the reluctance of the chancellor. There was no sense in harping on the issue. But Roger did indicate that he would fight tooth and nail to get Mark the job at Winston, which was why he had asked his son to meet with him that night for dinner and the game. It was Roger's way of showing moral support for his son.

The rest of the game was a tight defensive battle with Providence winning by a narrow three-to-two margin. It was then time for Roger to drop Mark off at the latter's apartment before he would return home to Beth. And just as he had done earlier, Roger encouraged Mark not to lose faith and assured him that he would continue the fight. The younger Lavoie wanted to believe his father, but he knew that Roger had intervened as much as he could. Now it was up to the chancellor.

Chapter 10

It was a delightful autumn morning. The sun was shining brilliantly with not a cloud in the sky. A very comfortable fifty-two degrees was the reading at eight-fifteen, which by Pawtucket standards, given the hour and the fact Halloween was just a day away, made it feel downright refreshing.

Mort Sonnenstein was whistling a happy tune as he drove his Lexus along Route 6 West. Mort was listening to the Providence news station, so there was no catchy music to latch onto, unless you call commercial jingles worthy of the top 40 hits. But then again, that was Mort's persona. He was always cheerful and optimistic on life in general. Perhaps this was his way to deal with the garbage he had to put up with day to day with patients suffering from one form of neuroses or another. You need to have an optimistic bent on life if it's your job to get people out of a deep funk.

Then again, Mort was curious to learn more about the condition of Roger Lavoie's first wife, and he allowed his inquisitiveness to serve as his own intoxicating drink. The thirst for knowledge gave Mort his high.

Mort finally arrived at the gated entrance at Crenshaw. It had been several years since he last visited the facility. Under normal circumstances there was no need for Mort to be there. Crenshaw was reserved for those who had gone over the deep end where a series of cocktails containing mind-altering drugs were the norm. Mort's clientele consisted of people who had hang-ups of some sort, and it was his obligation to make sure that these problems didn't mushroom into such a state that his patients could eventually become candidates for the institution. But Mort was happy to note that only a handful of former patients were worthy of such high maintenance needs, and thus his visits to Crenshaw were few and far between. Besides, the purpose of his visit wasn't about his patients. It was only about the ex-wife of one of them.

His last visit at the sanitarium was a few summers ago, and Mort vividly recalled the beautiful arrangement of lovely flowers and well-maintained shrubbery that festooned either side of the eight-foot-high brick pillars. But the autumn climate had taken a toll on the magnificent splendor of botany. The landscape was now stark and foreboding. Tree branches were naked as they awaited another harsh New England winter only weeks away. But Mort still kept his cheerful disposition, despite the lack of a bucolic setting.

Mort drove the Lexus just past the front gate to a nearby security guard check point. The guard, who had all the flamboyance of a state trooper, looked down on Mort. He had to amble slowly because of his ample girth, in order to greet the visitor officially.

"Yes," the guard tacitly began, "can I help you?"

"My name is Dr. Mort Sonnenstein," Mort kindly responded. "I have an appointment at eleven o'clock to see Dr. Oswald Borshevsky."

The guard told Mort to wait while he made a phone call, but the guard was also multi-tasking. Unbeknownst to Mort, the guard was chatting with another party while performing another function. Underneath the console of his booth, the guard pressed a secret button. There a special camera was strategically hidden and angled to capture a snapshot of the license plate of any visitor's vehicle. Perhaps this was the sanitarium's way of keeping track of potential undesirables or curiosity seekers, as if they had something to hide. Mort was being spied upon. But there was no way for the analyst to conceal himself. Mort just wanted to get to the bottom of the Margaret Lavoie case.

After a nominal pause, the guard finally sauntered back to Mort. He told the visitor where to park, although Mort had a good enough memory to recall where the lot was located. Mort smiled and began to head to the closest vacant space he could find to the institution's front entrance.

Chapter 11

Roger had just concluded his early morning anthropology lecture. As the students began to file out of the room, Roger sat behind the front desk to go over the material he had just covered and to prepare to administer an exam the next time his students met.

The bearded professor was about to stand up and exit the room when his cell phone, which he kept on his belt off his right hip, began to vibrate. Roger scanned the ID reader on his phone and saw the name of the chancellor on display. Without hesitation, Roger dropped the papers and notebook he held to devote all his energy and attention to answering the call.

Roger pretended he wasn't expecting the call, but who was he kidding? He knew the reason for the chancellor to phone him was about the potential employment of Mark at Winston College.

After an exchange of pleasantries, the chancellor asked Roger if he had a moment to see him in his office at 11:30 in the morning. Without hesitation, Roger accepted the invitation. With that agreement, Roger signed off with the chancellor and closed his phone.

Knowing that his summoning by the chancellor was the portent of a good omen for Mark, Roger stared off into the distance, deep in contemplation. Like the cat that ate the canary, Roger had a satisfied grin. He knew the upcoming employment of his son was a foregone conclusion, although Roger wasn't about to call his son just yet. That would have to wait until after the meeting. It was one thing to tell Mark the job at the university was in the bag. It was another thing entirely to dwell on the details that went with it, and so Roger decided to bide his time until he had all the facts ironed out.

Roger placed his personal papers into his briefcase. He then turned toward the open door of the classroom. In a pleasant surprise, Roger spotted a familiar figure standing in the doorway. It was none other than the man who had played a huge part in convincing the chancellor that Mark was worthy of teaching timber at the college.

"Edward! I'm so glad to see you!"

Professor Edward Asmundsson was smiling through that thick brush of a mustache of his as he stood there waiting for a reaction from his colleague.

"Did you hear," Roger continued with enthusiasm, "that the chancellor called me just as my lecture concluded?"

"Well," Edward replied, "he knows your schedule, which was why he called you when he did. And I found that out, too, but through your department. That's why I've shown up just now. I wanted to get firsthand your reaction to the invite by the chancellor."

"I know it's going to be about Mark. And I have you to thank, dear friend."

Edward held up the palm of his hand to Roger. The math dean didn't want to take any credit in greasing the wheels for Mark's potential employment. And he also cautioned Roger that nothing was ironclad until both Roger and the chancellor came to an agreement, with Mark signing on the dotted line. But the anthropology professor knew that if it weren't for Edward's influence, the chances of Mark teaching at Winston would've been very slim.

The two educators warmly shook hands. As he was about to head off, Edward asked Roger to let him know afterward how the meeting with the chancellor went. With zeal Roger promised Edward he would. And with that the math dean left. Roger had another class at twelve-thirty, and if ever a lecture would be extra special it would be that one, for Roger had a gut feeling that the chancellor was going to offer a position for his son well before the class.

Chapter 12

Mort Sonnenstein waited by the front desk patiently for Dr. Oswald Borshevsky's admin to arrive. He bided his time by looking over things in his small briefcase just so that he wouldn't become a candidate for the institution himself. When he didn't have his head buried in his work, Mort did take the notice of the antiseptic entrance to the facility. Plain and ordinary off-white sheetrock walls surrounded him, graced only by a few potted ferns and pictures of prominent past donors to Crenshaw. The seats were a charcoal-gray, hard molded plastic. This wasn't a lounge, and Mort dismissed the stark decor as just what the chairs were designed for: temporary seating to keep one relaxed until summoned. Of course, the seats were cheap as opposed to cushioned chairs or sofas, which were much more expensive. That and the fact that given the nature of the place, it was wise to have seating that wasn't prone to vandalism or destruction by the patients there.

As he continued to wait, Mort spotted two ward orderlies, a fortyish male and a female about ten years younger, leaving the facility for refuge outside. They were dressed in their sterile white uniforms, and Mort guessed the pair went outside to drag on their cigarettes during a break. Mort released a short laugh under his breath and mused on the illogical connection of a facility that promotes health, albeit on the psychiatric level, and allows its employees to ruin and abuse their bodies. But to each his or her own, and Mort was sure the institution didn't want to invoke the threat of civil liberties being expunged and catch the wrath of the ACLU.

As the orderlies continued with their irritating habit, Mort picked up a magazine. He had begun to leaf through it when he heard his name called. Mort looked up and saw a wholesome young woman of mixed race. With her black hair styled in a frizz, the woman greeted Mort with a broad smile highlighted by shimmering scarlet lip gloss. She was smartly attired in proper business clothing, which consisted of a golden-yellow button-down blouse and a burgundy knee-length skirt as part of the season's autumnal motif. With hooped earrings and a gaggle of dangling oversized bracelets on her wrists, the woman addressed him.

"Hello," she greeted, "I'm Crystal Cambridge, Dr. Borshevsky's assistant. Won't you follow me, please?"

With briefcase in tow, Mort followed Crystal down one of the adjacent hallways. Their journey was a brief one, for the head of Crenshaw held court only two doors down on the right. Mort spotted the wooden door and recognized it to be Borshevsky's office immediately. But, then again, how could one not spot it with Borshevsky's name emblazed in raised plastic lettering against the wooden door? Crystal opened the door and didn't hesitate to announce the visitor to her boss, who was sitting in the adjacent room.

Mort waited for Borshevsky to enter. He had met the Crenshaw head before, but still had to re-familiarize himself with Oswald's appearance. Borshevsky reminded Mort of the actor Jason Alexander of Seinfeld fame with his ring of black hair around the back of his head and bald pate and spectacles. He also sported a full black beard to match what strands on the head he had left.

"Dr. Sonnenstein? I'm Dr. Borshevsky. How are you?"

"I'm fine, thank you. I believe we've met a couple of times now. As I recall, you and I attended a conference down in New York City two years ago, and I also attended a symposium that you helped chair up in Boston back in July."

"Ah, yes. That was before I extended my trip up to Maine for a little R&R. That and a few fresh lobster dinners."

"There's nothing wrong with a little indulgence every now and then."

Crystal interjected politely, "Would you care for some coffee, Dr. Sonnenstein?"

"That would be wonderful, Crystal, thank you. I prefer a little milk in it and please, no sugar."

Crystal smiled as she left to prepare the cup of joe for Mort. In the meantime Oswald welcomed the visitor into his office.

Mort looked around and was impressed by the interior. Light teal-colored walls, in order to give a sense of tranquility, surrounded Mort as he admired several paintings adorning the space. Mort was pleased that Oswald was an art collector like himself and had a tasteful eye in the choices selected. What was that? It was an actual model of the USS Constitution, that permanent bastion of the Boston Harbor, festooned on the mantel above a fireplace that had not seen activity in decades. And then he noted the huge windows with floor-length velvet blue drapes and matching satin swags holding them back.

As Oswald seated himself in his high leather chair behind a huge mahogany desk, Mort also noted the glistening wooden floor with a magnificent Persian rug positioned in the middle. Oswald extended a hand, gesturing for Mort to sit in one of the leather upholstered wooden chairs opposite him. Just as Mort was about to sit down, Crystal entered with his coffee. Mort appreciated that Crystal served it in a ceramic mug and not a Styrofoam cup. Mort thanked the admin for her hospitality. Crystal smiled and gave him a simple, "You're welcome," as she then retreated to her desk to tend to her other pressing duties.

Mort took a sip of the piping-hot beverage. Then he and Oswald traded a few war stories from their field of expertise. They even dropped their professional monikers and addressed each other on a first-name basis. And then came time for the real purpose of the visit.

"As I made clear the other day, Oswald, my chief reason for being here is Margaret Lavoie, the ex-wife of Roger Lavoie."

Whatever affable visage Oswald sported before quickly evaporated. It was a subject that was as welcome as an IRS audit, but Oswald knew he had to satisfy Mort's curiosity. The Crenshaw director leaned forward with his hands folded and gave Mort a stern look. Even though Oswald was well aware of the reason for Mort seeing him, even the mere mention of Roger's name made him bristle.

"Let me explain something to you, Mort. Just for a moment I'm going to step away from the psychiatric professional side of the matter, and give you my personal opinion of that piece of shit, Roger Lavoie. Twenty years ago we had

43

a huge story here in the Providence area about the situation involving Lavoie. I don't know if you recall it."

Mort was trying to remember this, attempting to find the connection between Roger and some nefarious event.

"When I first heard of Roger's name as a potential patient of mine, I began to wonder where I had heard it before. But I just couldn't place it. Please refresh my memory."

"Lavoie heard that his wife at the time, Margaret Lavoie, whom, by the way, now goes under her maiden last name of O'Mara, had an affair with some guy. I believe his name was Haber, if I remember correctly. Anyway, Haber went missing after that. He did show up eventually, in various stages and at different times."

"I'm not sure I follow you, Oswald."

Oswald drew a deep breath. "Haber's body parts were sent to Margaret, one by one. It frightened her to the point that she couldn't recover. And she has been a permanent resident here at Crenshaw ever since."

Mort was shaken by Oswald's revelation. He placed his hand over his open mouth. Mort looked absently around Oswald's office as he tried to further absorb all that was being thrown at him. After releasing an, "Oh, my God," Mort turned his attention back to Oswald.

"Now that you've mentioned this, I do recall some of the details of that case. The police suspected Lavoie, if I'm not mistaken."

"Bingo. Lavoie had a very good criminal attorney working for him at the time. The jury acquitted him on account of insufficient evidence. You know, the so-called *reasonable doubt*. Perhaps the prosecution lawyers didn't conduct themselves in a manner commensurate with the nature of the crime."

"The way you put it, Oswald, it sounds as though the higher the degree of the crime, the better the DA people should represent the office."

"In a way, that's precisely what I'm saying. The ADAs didn't live up to their billing. Lavoie went scot free. And Haber's murder still remains a cold case to this day. But I think the vast majority, including this doctor, believe that Lavoie orchestrated Haber's murder and scared the wits out of his wife to the point of no return."

Mort took a sip of his coffee, but he was drinking in all that Oswald threw at him. Somehow his mind refused to accept Oswald's opinion. Maybe he was thinking now of Roger as his patient. Wasn't that what the legal system was all about? Mort just wanted to allow Roger his due process, at least in Mort's own version of a psychiatric tribunal. He cross-examined Oswald on what medications Margaret was taking. The Crenshaw director mentioned clozapine and Xanax to deal with Margaret's schizophrenia and severe psychological trauma. Oswald said Margaret could not cope with society and had been kept institutionalized for the last two decades.

"From findings I have read and been told by other doctors who treated Margaret O'Mara, they say she was an outgoing individual and liked to mingle. According to previous reports found in her file, Margaret's family members often said how effusive she was and that she would strike up a conversation with just about anyone. That was until the chain of events involving Haber's body parts came into play. Now Margaret is totally withdrawn, hardly speaks at all, suffers from severe mental anguish and anxiety, and is often delusional. No one can get near her. She is so far gone that it would be impossible for me or anyone to release her back into society in her present state. And, quite frankly, I don't see any cure for Margaret's mental well-being any time soon."

This disturbing information warranted another sip of coffee. Unfortunately, there was just enough left in the cup for a small swallow. Mort drained the last drop and decided he still wanted to see Margaret for himself, if for no other reason than to ease his own mind. Oswald warned him that the scene would not be pretty. Nonetheless, Mort asked the Crenshaw director to lead the way.

Chapter 13

Roger wasted no time when he learned the chancellor wanted to see him immediately. He raced across campus to get to Vernon Hall, the building that housed the chief administrative office and bursar of Winston College. And, yes, that was where the chancellor's office was located.

Normally a summoning by the chancellor would cause one to cringe, for that person knew the reason for the visit wouldn't be good. But Roger was aware that the news could be positive and so he made the trek with alacrity and purpose.

Despite his eagerness to see the chancellor, Roger opened the door to his office slowly and carefully. After all, you just don't barge in to see the head of the learning institution with a loud scream of, "Here I am!" Roger popped his head in and gave the office a cursory look. He soon noticed the chancellor's secretary, Ruth Wojteka, clicking away at her computer keyboard. Roger was amazed that Ruth was still working. She was fast approaching seventy. But then it dawned on Roger that Ruth was a widow and her children and grandchildren likely only saw her on some weekends and holidays. Being that she was still of able mind and body to get up every morning and go to work, Ruth did just that, rather than stay home and vegetate in front of a TV or fill out endless crossword puzzles.

Roger approached Ruth's desk in measured steps so as not to be too intrusive. The veteran admin did sense Roger's presence, despite being engrossed in her key stroking.

"The chancellor will be right with you, Professor Lavoie. Please have a seat."

There was nothing much else for Roger to do but bide his time. He took a seat and promptly placed his attaché case on his lap in an upright position, much like a prospective employee would while waiting to be interviewed.

As Ruth continued to click away on her keyboard while juggling the occasional call for the chancellor, Roger looked at his watch. It read eleven-twenty-six. He had just finished his morning class clear across the campus and there wasn't much time he could devote to lunch, not with another lecture at twelve-thirty. The anthropology professor decided to take the initiative and rose from his seat. It was at this point Roger heard a buzzer go off on Ruth's desk. The admin picked up the phone and gave the person on the other end a simple compliance.

"The chancellor will see you now, Professor Lavoie," Ruth said without emotion. "Please go in."

Roger accorded Ruth the same level of sincerity in his gratitude. He headed toward the open door of the chancellor's office. Upon entering, Roger looked around the office. It was expansive with books lined up along the glistening oak walls, much like a library. A huge globe of the world dominated its center. And a heavy mahogany desk gave one the sense of who's in charge.

Roger was still looking for the chancellor. Somewhat puzzled by the chancellor's whereabouts, he offered a soft hello to let his host know he was present in the room.

"Welcome, Professor Lavoie," a voice emanated from a silhouetted figure by one of the large windows. "Do take a seat, please."

Roger sat, as he was told, in one of the chairs in front of the chancellor's desk. As he did, he kept his eyes on the figure until the person moved away from the bright sunshine obscuring his appearance. Once the figure was away from the dazzling window with its long gold chenille drapes, his features became more apparent.

It was indeed the chancellor. He was tall and handsome—certainly someone who was attractive to most women, although he was devoted to his wife. And not one strand of his black hair was out of place. The chancellor looked more like a Wall Street banker with his black pinstripe Armani suit, white shirt, onyx cufflinks, royal-blue necktie and sparkling black designer shoes. He was also a health and fitness nut and muscular, a far cry from Roger's weak physique.

The chancellor sat down in his leather executive chair, a seat so big it resembled a regal throne. Once seated, the chancellor looked directly at Roger. On his desk was a name plate. It read Valen Pagano in large gold letters against a black background, with the title Chancellor in smaller lettering underneath. The Valen part was short for Valentino, but the chancellor preferred the shortened version. He also made it a point that Valen, when spoken, rhymed with the long *A* sound, as in the rock band Van Halen. It was his way of impressing others with his aristocratic airs. But nobody at Winston dared to call him Mr. Pagano or Dr. Pagano, or the totally disrespectful Valen. No, Valen was referred to as Mr. Chancellor, much the same as the leader of the United States is called Mr. President.

Roger sat in silence while Valen reviewed some papers on his desk. Valen took his gold-plated pen and inserted its back end into his mouth as he continued to peruse the pages. He raised his eyebrows as he was finally about to speak.

"Top third in his class here at Winston," Valen remarked. "Very impressive."

Roger knew Valen was referring to Mark. He was grateful for Valen's impression, but didn't dare say much beyond that.

"Of course, that doesn't automatically warrant a golden pass to work here."

"Yes, I'm well aware of that, Mr. Chancellor. But Mark does have very good credentials . . . as you've so graciously pointed out."

Valen released a short laugh. He glanced once more at the papers before continuing.

"As you are well aware, Professor Lavoie, Winston does hold high standards in academics. You more than anyone know what we expect from our faculty. And I'm sure Mark knows this from his own experience, with what you've gone through over the years. This isn't some fifth grade class he's about to teach in some inner city school. This is Winston! And we expect—no, *I* expect—a high level of excellence. Do you think Mark can handle the pressure of maintaining our high standards?"

"I know he can," Roger professed. "He's been waiting for this moment for a very long time, Mr. Chancellor."

Valen reclined in his chair. He gave Roger a studious stare.

"I do hope Mark doesn't go through a similar ordeal to what you went through twenty years ago."

Roger stiffened at Valen's reference to when he was put on trial for the murder of Darren Haber in retaliation for Haber's affair with Margaret.

"Let me tell you something, Mr. Chancellor," Roger countered with anger in his voice. "Never in my life was I ever so humiliated, so ashamed, that I could hardly show my face in public without someone pointing at me saying, 'Look! There's the guy who killed that Haber fellow!' I had to take a year's sabbatical just to recover from that horrific experience. Thank goodness this institution stood by me through those difficult times."

"I'm well aware of what happened twenty years ago. I do review everyone's file occasionally. Of course, if I were around back then, perhaps you and I wouldn't be having this conversation. I would have denied your return to these hallowed halls. The one thing I do not tolerate is unscrupulous behavior, whether on or off this campus."

"But I was acquitted of that—"

"Let me make myself clear," Valen interrupted. "I am putting you and everyone else who is employed by this institution on notice that I will not accept anything that smacks of suspicious acts or questionable deeds. However, I see your son does have a clean slate, and I firmly believe that one shouldn't be held accountable for the sins of his or her father. Being that November is upon us, it would be rather impractical to hire Mark immediately. Therefore, I will be looking toward the beginning of the spring semester in January to start his career here. Of course, I still want to interview him nonetheless. But, if everything goes according to plan, I believe the start of his professorship will be in less than three months and our chat together will be a fait accompli. Please have Mark get in touch with Ruth to set up a meeting between us. And, once again, Professor Lavoie, congratulations on behalf of your son."

The way that Valen conducted himself made it appear Roger should kiss his ring, much like the pope's. But the anthropology professor offered a simple smile and a slight nod of appreciation. Valen offered the same in response.

Yet, as Roger rose from his seat to vacate the room, Valen's benevolent visage quickly morphed into one of deep concern. If it were truly up to him, Valen would have had Roger on a Providence street corner selling pencils. *Damn those long-term trustees of the university!* But he was only helping Mark for Mark's sake, certainly not from any obligation toward Roger. Valen sat back in his leather chair and began to reach for a pen. It was time to execute the other functions of his capacity as chancellor.

While Roger was thrilled the path to Mark's career at Winston appeared to be paved, he still didn't take too kindly to Valen's disposition. Roger sought out Edward to thank the mathematics dean for laying down the ground work for Mark . . . and to inquire if he knew of Valen's condemnation.

Chapter 14

Mort allowed Oswald to lead the way through the complexity of hallways. If he had to guess the path on his own, Mort would've been lost. He was trying to make mental notes of all the turns, stairwells, and doorways, but he lost track after the fourth maneuver.

The orderlies performed their tasks with care—sometimes with muscle, but always with tact. But whenever the big man patrolled the halls, the orderlies ratcheted it up a notch as if to make a lasting impression for praise and a raise.

Crenshaw was the abyss where all of Rhode Island humanity that divested itself of pride, sensibility, and logic found their final destination. Maintenance personnel should have received combat pay for all the herculean tasks they had to perform. The heavy air of pine-scented disinfectant suffocated one's lungs, but it was necessary to saturate the wards with the cleaning solution, if only to mask the overwhelming acrid stench of urine and regurgitation. Once in a while pieces of excrement would lie scattered across the floors. Crenshaw was not the place for the faint of heart and those with a weak stomach. You needed strong intestinal fortitude as a pre-requisite for employment.

The walls were in constant disrepair. There were numerous punched holes and gashes in the sheetrock, created by the residents from time to time, requiring habitual spackling. And some residents would occasionally get hold of markers and pens and stake out their claim by inscribing their signatures or disjointed poems. Perchance, one might suspect the board of directors of Crenshaw had stock in Home Depot, what with the countless number of times that a patch here and a coat there were required.

And there were the residents who routinely paraded up and down the hallways, more so than the staff. One of them, a foppish fellow by the name of Colin, had a tendency to look oddly at anyone who was not familiar to him. Having not fully outgrown an autistic childhood, the mid-twenties man presumed the stranger that was Mort to be the one to finally spring him from the wretched confines of captivity that Crenshaw represented. Colin walked with a limp, but this was not as a direct result of a born impediment or injury. It was his way to draw attention to himself. Mort was taken aback by Colin's forwardness.

"Excuse me," Colin began, "but are you the man who . . . who is supposed to rel . . . release me from here?"

Oswald snapped his fingers at two orderlies and then pointed at Colin. Not a word was uttered by the director, as the orderlies knew exactly what to do. One of them, a giant of a man who was completely bald, approached the resident. Rather than use brute force, which the orderly was able to execute without any effort, he politely soothed Colin while his partner stood by, prepared to do whatever was necessary to control the situation.

"Now, c'mon, Colin," the giant began, "you need to leave this gentleman alone. Why don't you come with me and Willie back to your room?"

"Leave me a . . . alone, Rocco. Don't you s-s-see I'm talking to the man who can get me out of here?"

"Hey, I told Rocco that you showed me some interesting drawings you made," Willie countered. "How 'bout sharin' them with the rest of us?"

Rocco and Willie escorted Colin to his private room. Mort was amazed at the way the orderlies had defused a potentially awkward problem without having to act like barroom bouncers. Their work was of neatness with the stealth of a deft magician's handiwork. Oswald took pride in the way it was handled, but didn't seem to obsess over it.

"The one thing we strive for here at Crenshaw, Mort, is that our staff exerts psychological tact when dealing with the residents, as opposed to applying muscle. Oh, there may be an occasion from time to time when that's needed, but only when absolutely necessary. Thankfully those incidents are few and far between. Our goal is to avoid confrontation if at all possible."

"And avoid lawsuits from the families of these residents," Mort slyly responded.

Oswald simply offered a wry smile at Mort's cutting remark. The journey continued.

They were now into the backstretch of the tour. As they turned a corner, Mort suddenly spotted another one of the patients in their path. She was a small and frail elderly woman whose whitish-gray hair was a cross between a dust mop and straw, the length of which went down to her waist. The long hair would have looked attractive on a twenty-year-old coed, but on a woman nearly four times that age, it made her look like an old hag. Her face was wrinkled and read like a history book. Her hands, probably soft and delicate decades earlier, were darkened by age spots. Veins popped out and appeared like ripples in a pond. As soon as she saw Oswald, her time-ravaged eyes lit up.

"Dr. B, it's so nice to see you," the woman exclaimed.

Oswald grinned to placate the resident. "Same here, Melanie. You're looking wonderful as ever."

Melanie waved dismissively and smiled as if embarrassed. "Oh, go on, Dr. B. You say that to all the gals. I see how you go after the aides and nurses!"

"You have a vivid imagination."

Melanie then turned her attention to Mort. She offered the same enthusiasm for the guest. "And who might this distinguished gentleman be?"

Mort chuckled. He introduced himself, not waiting for Oswald to jump in. "I'm Dr. Mort Sonnenstein, Melanie. It's a pleasure to meet you."

Mort then delicately held Melanie's hand. He was fearful that he might accidentally pulverize it with only minimal strength. The haggard woman beamed with delight at the attention that Mort was dealing her. Melanie took her hand back and held it close to her ragtag bathrobe, as if never intending to wash it.

Although she was not quite altogether like the vast majority of the residents, Melanie was able to decipher why Oswald and Mort were paying a visit to her ward. As the self-appointed queen of the section, Melanie made it a habit to check on all that was going on. She was hip to the fact that the only reason Oswald bothered to make his presence known to her was to check on a particular resident of the ward who remained secluded.

"I know why you're here, Dr. B," said Melanie, sounding every bit like the brightest girl in a grade school class. "You're here to check in on that nutty woman in 429, aren't you?"

Talk about calling the kettle black, Mort was stunned at the remark. Oswald disapproved if any outsider referred to any of the residents as a bottle short of a six-pack. But he was deeply disturbed if a patient gave his or her fellow resident a similarly unflattering title. The director politely asked Melanie to allow them privacy while they conducted business.

"Okay," Melanie answered. "Goodbye, Dr. S. You're so cute!"

Mort coyly grinned in appreciation of Melanie's comment. Now it was on to his sole purpose for being there.

With a little trepidation Oswald grabbed hold of the doorknob to Room 429, their destination. Before he rotated it, Oswald looked back at Mort and asked him to prepare for a striking revelation. Mort modestly nodded in compliance. Oswald then reverted his attention to the knob. He released a small sigh as he turned it.

Oswald gently opened the door so as not to startle its resident. As it swung open, the room came into full view for Mort to see. Suddenly his face was ashen and a look of stunned disbelief overwhelmed him. His jaw dropped a couple of inches as his eyes widened like saucers. He was shocked by what he saw.

"Oh . . . my . . . God!"

Chapter 15

Heather was taking a break from her clerical duties by talking up a storm on her cell phone with one of her friends. While she was allowing the other party to join in the conversation, Heather was admiring the artistic care her manicurist Yang Li did on her nails the other day. The subtle shade of fuchsia was the backdrop to carefully painted yellow roses on her cuticles. If her renderings were displayed on canvas, they would fetch a handsome sum for Yang's masterful strokes. For the admin it was money well spent.

Roger walked in and approached Heather to see if Edward Asmundsson was in. Without saying a word she pointed at her boss's office door as if Roger were already expected. Roger was nonplussed by Heather's lack of protocol. She should have at least interrupted her phone chat to give Roger his proper due, but discovering her friend's shopping tastes, recent nightlife excitement and current boyfriend were more important to her. Roger shrugged off Heather's indifference and moved on.

After a light rap on Edward's door signaling his arrival, Roger stepped into the math dean's office. A towering stack of papers and periodicals almost concealed him from view. Roger was beginning to wonder if Edward was there at all.

"Edward, are you hiding?"

The math dean popped up like a prairie dog behind his excuse for bonfire fuel. His aged eyes expressed welcome. One would have to surmise that he was grinning behind that scrub brush underneath his nose.

"Roger! Delighted you were able to stop by! So, how did everything go with the chancellor?"

Roger didn't say a word at first. He just glared at Edward with a look that said as if you didn't know. But he felt he owed an answer to the man who'd helped push Mark to the front of Valen's agenda. However, talking through paraphernalia worthy of the recycling bin wasn't going to do for the anthropology professor. He pulled up a seat and stationed himself to Edward's right. Roger needed to discharge the venom created by Valen's badgering.

"Why didn't you tell me the chancellor was going to dredge up that incident of twenty years ago?"

Edward slumped in his chair. The level of exuberance he'd demonstrated for his colleague earlier was wiped off as if by a blackboard eraser. He was at a loss to explain the actions of Valen and why the chancellor seized an opportunity for condemning Roger instead of lauding praise for Mark. The math dean scanned the interior, like the windows, walls, pictures and bookcase were a source for plausible answers. Finally he had to come clean with Roger.

"I'm sorry, Roger. I do apologize if the chancellor's character assassination of you caused you discomfort."

"So, you knew he was going to throw that trash at me! You knew it all along!"

"No! No! No!" Edward was near tears as he pleaded for mercy. He lowered his head a few times in his petition for clemency. "I mean . . . how in the world was I to know he was going to mention it? He didn't say anything to me when I initially brought up the subject with him. Nor did he discuss your past with me in the other chats we've had together since. You've got to believe me, Roger! Why would I do this to you? How could I do this to you? What do I have to gain by it?"

Roger just sat in his chair and allowed Edward's confession to speak for itself. He saw a shadow of a man in his visage. Edward had demeaned himself to the level of a school kid allowing the class bullies to pummel him for his lunch money. Roger was convinced. There was no motivation for Edward to betray his colleague by having him walk into a trap. Now Roger was starting to feel ashamed for his boorish behavior. He tilted his head forward and began to massage the bridge of his nose. Now he was the one displaying an act of contrition.

"I apologize, Edward," Roger humbly began. "I shouldn't have doubted you for one minute. You have been very helpful and instrumental in getting Mark to this point. For that I am eternally grateful. It's just that . . ." Roger winced as if it were too painful for him to bring up the subject. "It's the sheer vindictiveness of the chancellor that got to me. God-damn it! Why can't he let sleeping dogs lie?"

Only moments before, it seemed as though Edward's head was going to be at the end of a lance wielded by Roger. But now the math dean began to feel a little compassion for his colleague. As Roger held his head between his hands, Edward reached over to console him. He placed his hand on Roger's shoulder.

"I wish I could alter the chancellor's way of thinking, but I can't. And neither can you. I'll tell you what, Roger. What say you and I stroll over to Brennan's Ale House for a pint and forget the chancellor's barbs and innuendos? After your afternoon class? Besides, it's time we celebrate a new beginning for Mark, rather than dwell on any hostility the chancellor may harbor toward you."

Roger looked up at Edward and displayed a slight smile. He quietly answered his true friend with a polite thanks, but no thanks. He then stood from his seat and extended a hand to Edward, who nearly rose from his chair at the same time. The math dean was relieved to see that Roger had regained his composure and was beginning to put Valen's scathing attack behind him.

"I think once Mark signs the contract with the university, we'll take the time to celebrate. Speaking of which, I need to call him so that he can arrange the meeting. But mark my word, Edward. Once Mark is signed there will be a bash at my place the likes of which you've never seen."

Edward exhibited his pleasure once more now that Roger was back to his old self. He escorted his fellow teacher to the front door of his office, but not before offering further assistance in whatever capacity it took to help Roger's son. The anthropology professor calmly exited.

Chapter 16

He had been watching his every step as he made his way back to Oswald's office. It wasn't so much that the hallways of Crenshaw were littered with debris or cluttered with obstacles. It was because Mort still had a difficult time trying to comprehend the transformation of a vibrant woman two decades earlier—as Oswald had put it—into a horrifying mere shell of a person.

Oswald entered his office first. He turned around and saw Mort, still with his head down. The facility director offered a small smile and gestured for his guest to have a seat. With the grotesque image indelibly etched in his brain, Mort had trouble understanding Oswald's command. Or perhaps he had shut out his host's request because of what he had just seen. Oswald paced over and gently helped Mort into the chair on the other side of his desk. He allowed the visitor as much time as he needed to regain his composure. But even when Mort seemed comfortable, there was still that lingering doubt nagging at him.

Mort remained silent, as he was at a loss for words. Oswald observed the stupefied expression on his visitor. He had seen it before. Not necessarily from those who might have paid Margaret a visit, but on others who had visited poor souls like her; and if not at Crenshaw, then elsewhere. With an eye on Mort's unchanged visage, Oswald waltzed around his desk. He took a key from his left front pants pocket and was about to unlock the bottom right-hand drawer of the credenza. Oswald stabbed the cylinder with the serrated metal piece. But before he was about to make the necessary one-quarter right turn to open the drawer, Oswald gave one more glance to Mort. With eyes squinted, he scrutinized the visitor. Oswald subtly nodded to confirm that what he was about to do was the right decision.

As Oswald began to open the drawer, Mort continued to sit in the chair without making eye contact with the host.

In fact, he was oblivious to Oswald's earlier stare as well, still having trouble putting two words together, let alone a sentence.

Oswald brought forth the contents that were under lock and key. It was a bottle of Remy Martin VSOP brandy, reserved for those occasions when it was necessary to retrieve a guest from the depths of stunned disbelief. This was definitely one such instance. Oswald placed the bottle atop his desk with authority. He then slammed an accompanying shot glass next to it, making a sound that resonated in the room. Yet despite the deliberate creation of such a stirring noise, he didn't capture one ounce of attention from Mort. So Oswald just sat and scrutinized Mort for several seconds. Perhaps much more intervention was going to be needed to break the spell. But Oswald proceeded as if he had Mort's unmitigated consideration. He elicited two fingers of the potent libation into the glass. With a pout of frustration the director then stood up, picked up the jigger of brandy and offered it to Mort.

"Here, take this," commanded Oswald as he extended his hand, holding the glass. Mort didn't flinch. Oswald drew a deep sigh and reiterated the order. "C'mon, Mort. I don't do this as a routine, you know. Please, drink this. It'll do you good."

His hand was trembling, but Mort graciously accepted the drink from his host. Afraid that he might spill its contents across Oswald's office floor, Mort didn't hesitate for one second to down the potent liquid. He grimaced as the liquor began to tighten his throat. His eyelids shut to the point that a crowbar couldn't open them. Yet Mort allowed the brandy to flow down his esophagus and invade the lining of his stomach. Once accomplished, Mort released two huge gasps for air. His eyes opened once again as he slammed the glass on Oswald's desk. Mort was coming back to his senses as the ferocity of his breathing was abating. Oswald was pleased his guest was returning to his old self.

Mort rubbed his face. His hand, which was convulsing just moments before, was steady. The alcohol was taking its effect. Oswald recognized that Mort wanted to say something. But the visitor was still too upset to utter a word. Instead, Mort just kept shaking his head. Oswald pressed him to speak. Finally, Mort complied with the director's wishes.

"Never," Mort began, "never in my entire career have I seen anything as disturbing as what I saw in that room! I still can't believe it! How? How could something like that happen to transform anyone into such a . . . such a . . . God! I can't even describe what I saw!"

"I told you the answer," Oswald smugly replied. "It's your patient, Lavoie."

Mort looked across Oswald's desk in search of answers to his other questions. He then looked up at Oswald. "How could you allow this to continue?"

"Do you think for one minute I enjoy seeing this go on and on? What, I like to get my rocks off at seeing such desperate misery, as if I'm running some sort of freakish sideshow?" Filled with anger, Oswald formally addressed his guest. "Let me remind you, Dr. Sonnenstein, my number one goal is to ensure our residents get the proper care and the help they need to better themselves so they can assimilate into society again! I would like nothing more than to have Margaret get her life back! But I can't! At least, not in her present state, as she continues to self-destruct."

"Surely you could've administered some sort of treatment?"

"As I've explained, we have done all that we could for her. All we can do now is watch her in whatever years she has left. Did I mention that she's also bipolar and has had suicidal tendencies?"

Mort had figured that out for himself, but allowed Oswald to elaborate.

"Did you ever wonder why Margaret has short hair? One night, several years ago, a nurse and an aide went into her room to administer medication. At the time Margaret wore her hair well below her shoulders. They caught Margaret trying to strangle herself by taking several bunches of her hair and tying them around her neck. Fortunately, we prevented her from following through with it. That's when I ordered Margaret's hair cut to stop that from happening again. Trust me, caring for Margaret has been no picnic."

"What about her son, Mark? How does he feel about all this, seeing his mother in such a deplorable condition?"

"He does visit on occasion. You know, for her birthday, Mother's Day, the holidays. But from what I've observed, he just shakes his head and goes about his merry way. I guess he feels there isn't much we can do for her. But I also believe that Mark's been spoon-fed whatever shit his father has been giving him through the years. Don't forget, Mort. This all happened when Mark was seven years old, a very impressionable age. I'm sure Lavoie instilled in his son some cockamamie story long ago so that he has more or less filtered out the truth, although I still can't see how, if he just researched the case on the internet."

Mort thought hard before continuing. "What about other close relatives?"

"Margaret's father died when she was twenty. As for her mother, she passed away a few years ago. She has cousins, but after she'd been here for the first few years, they sort of drifted away. Margaret has this friend, Cynthia Magnuson, I believe is her name, who used to come by every so often, but even as devoted as she is to Margaret, I think she's also given up."

"Margaret doesn't have any siblings?"

Oswald didn't answer Mort immediately. There was some deliberate hesitation. He puckered his lips as he began to twirl his executive-style pen, searching for the right words. Oswald finally decided to provide an answer.

"Let me tell you about Margaret's sister," Oswald began. "Her name is Siobhan O'Mara. But she's a strange character."

"In what way?"

"Well, she . . ." Oswald offered a grin, but it was because he was perplexed in describing Siobhan to Mort. "She has an aloof attitude about her. No feelings. No hatred. Kind of cold, I'd say. It's as if she's as content that Margaret remains here as is Lavoie. I mean, in my dealings with her, it's been more like a . . . a business transaction. Yes. No. Okay. She's very laconic. Even when I try to stir up any emotions within her when I bring up the subject of her ex-brother-in-law, Siobhan just avoids the issue entirely and wishes rather to focus on the matter at hand."

"It may be too painful a subject for her to discuss. Did you ever consider that?"

"Well, here's the kicker. When I mention Lavoie to Siobhan, you would think there might be some fire in her eyes or some nervous twitch about her. After all, we're talking about the bastard that most people still believe to this day was responsible for putting her sister in here, perhaps permanently. But Siobhan never even flinches. I don't know. Even I can't figure her out."

Mort pawed at his chin, in search of any explanation to describe Siobhan's disposition. He began to chuckle at a thought that crossed his mind. Oswald gave him a strange look, but Mort quickly offered the explanation for his amusement.

"I'm wondering how long Lavoie has been married to his current wife."

"What's that got to do with anything?"

"Well, Margaret's sister sounds very much like Lavoie. I was just thinking that perhaps the two of them are happy that Margaret's here because they wanted to have a relationship."

"But Lavoie married someone else. Your theory doesn't hold water."

Mort shrugged his shoulders. "Just a thought."

And with that Mort smiled at his host and elevated himself erect. He offered Oswald a firm handshake and a sincere thanks for allowing him to see for himself the sorry state that Margaret was in. Oswald countered by extending an open invitation to drop by again, so long as he was available to speak with Mort.

Before leaving Oswald's outer office, Mort once again thanked Crystal for the coffee earlier and politely bade her a good day. The admin grinned and offered the same in return.

Once he vacated the Crenshaw halls, the smile Mort had sported earlier quickly vanished. His head was spinning as ideas and thoughts danced in his head, some ignited by Oswald's opinion and others by his own whimsy. Mort couldn't yet make a clear study of everything. But one thing was certain. Mort had to arrange another appointment with Roger as soon as possible. He needed to get direct answers from his patient.

A chilly gusty wind greeted Mort when he stepped outside. The skies were even murkier than when he entered

Crenshaw an hour before. The barren tree limbs were do-ing a rhumba as they were ensnared by the strong breezes. Perhaps they were saying goodbye to Mort. Or perhaps they were issuing him a stern warning to beware of ominous portents to come.

Chapter 17

Roger was smacked in the face by brisk gusts and a foreboding sky as late October clenched its grip throughout all New England. He paced just a few steps from Chase Hall when he reached for his mobile phone. Roger's primary concern was to get in touch with Mark as soon as he could.

He fumbled for his phone as he had to wrestle with his tweed blazer and the off-white Irish knit wool sweater underneath to get at the darn instrument. By the time he succeeded, Roger was stunned to learn that it was suddenly ringing. He glanced at the ID reader and recognized it was Mort calling him. Deep frustration set in as Roger was dead set on calling his son, only to be interrupted by Mort's signal. At first Roger was inclined not to bother answering Mort's call. But then he realized that he could deliver a bit of good news to the psychoanalyst. Hell, Roger would have shouted from the steeple of the campus chapel if he could, to announce Mark's impending hiring. He therefore decided to accept Mort's invitation to chat.

"Well, well, Mort," Roger began while feigning a smile. "To what do I owe the pleasure of this call?"

"It's been a while since we had our initial session, Roger." Mort hesitated for a moment. He didn't want to discuss his discovery of Roger's ex-wife and her condition at Crenshaw for fear of scaring off the anthropology professor. "I was hoping you could set up a time for a follow-up. I'd like to track our progress."

Roger thought about the invitation for a second or two, and then conceded to Mort's wishes.

"Very well. I don't have classes on Friday morning. How about we meet this Friday?"

"Why, that's splendid! Let's say ten o'clock. Is that okay?"

"Fine. I'll be there. Oh, and by the way, my son Mark, I'll have you know, is on the fast track to landing a teaching position here at Winston."

"That's excellent, Roger! I'm happy for you and Mark. And that's a great way to begin our discussion! I'll see you then. Good day."

Roger ended the conversation. He gazed off into the distance along the paved concrete walkway of the campus. He was curious about why Mort was so eager to engage in another skull session with him. But Roger wasn't going to allow Mort's insistence for an immediate meeting to get the better of him. His primary focus was to reach Mark and instruct him to get hold of Ruth as soon as possible.

After a few short strides, Roger resumed his attempt to call Mark. He was glad that he was able to get through to his son. The concerned father told Mark to make the arrangements to see Valen at his first chance. But he also wanted to prepare his son for what could be a hard line of questioning, possibly about Roger. When Mark asked him to expand on the thought, Roger simply told him they'd meet the next morning for an early breakfast at a restaurant they both frequented. Mark agreed. Roger wished him a pleasant afternoon and ended the chat.

As he put away his mobile phone, Roger was musing over various dangling thoughts. While some had to do with the possible interrogation Valen might unleash upon Mark at their eventual meeting, Roger was more concerned with the prior phone call with Mort. Just why was it so important for them to meet that Friday morning? Even the professor knew it had to be more than just sucking a few dollar bills out of his wallet.

A few people crossed Roger's path as he continued to walk along the campus. Some were fellow faculty members, others students. And while he reciprocated each greeting with cheerful pleasantries, in the back of his mind was that lingering question of the reason to see Mort so soon.

Chapter 18

He was sipping his piping-hot coffee, careful not to take a big swallow for fear of scalding his mouth and throat. All the while Roger periodically gazed through the adjacent window of the Modern Diner on East Avenue in Pawtucket. He was seeking his son Mark, who was habitually late. Roger sighed as he took another sip of the caffeine-laced beverage.

To pass the time Roger scanned the décor of the bistro. It harkened back to the days when diners were truly diners with its mocha-and-ivory parquet-tiled floor and green padded counter stools. Its shell resembled a train car to give the patrons a sense of dining in one of those old Pullman cars of yesterday.

While the diner was noted for its patented stick-to-your ribs, artery-clogging breakfasts, Roger ate sensibly with a bowl of wheat flakes in front of him and a side order of fresh strawberries and blueberries, which he scattered over the flakes. The trouble was that Roger was waiting so long for his son that the flakes were getting soggy. But the professor wasn't too concerned about the wilting cereal. He was more concerned that Mark was all right and didn't get caught up in one of those notorious traffic delays on I-95 for which the Providence area was famous.

Roger was becoming more worried as time progressed and Mark didn't appear. He reached for his phone and was about to call his son when he heard a familiar voice.

"Sorry I'm late, Dad. You know how that traffic is at rush hour."

Roger looked up in the direction of the voice and smiled. He knew right away it was Mark, but he didn't expect to see his son in a smart navy-blue business suit with a crisp, clean white shirt underneath, accented by a conservative two-tone blue silk tie. He didn't have to look down, but Roger could have guessed Mark also sported black dress shoes to round things out. This was not the dress code required to work at Best Buy. Roger was taken aback to see Mark dressed like he worked for a brokerage house.

"I'm very impressed with your taste in clothing, Mark."

"Well, the moment you told me to call Ruth at the chancellor's office yesterday, that's exactly what I did. I'm meeting him at ten this morning. Don't worry about my job at the store. I don't work until four this afternoon. That'll give me enough time to change."

For someone who had avoided him like the plague when Roger attempted to discuss his son's employment, Valen had surprised Roger by quickly finding time to interview Mark. Perhaps there was a lull in Valen's workload to afford the young Lavoie an audience. Or maybe it was the fact that Valen wanted to fill the void immediately so that he could devote the rest of the fall semester to more pressing needs. At any rate, Roger was grateful that Mark could see Valen so soon in order to facilitate the almost-certain anointing of the young man to teach there.

A waitress came by to ask what Mark wanted for breakfast. He began with a simple glass of orange juice along with a cup of coffee. Mark was almost tempted to order eggs and bacon. Unlike his father, Mark was better suited to handle a heavy breakfast. At twenty-seven, one didn't always worry about the caloric and cholesterol intake of such a repast. But in a show of solidarity with his health-conscious dad, Mark opted for a simple buttered croissant.

With the waitress on her way, Roger wanted to devote his time with Mark to strategizing on the forthcoming interview with Valen. Although Roger wasn't finished with his cereal and fruit, he pushed both off to the side in order to stress the importance of their meeting.

"I'm going to lay all the cards on the table," Roger began. "The chancellor is a sneaky fucking bastard, who I think gets his jollies off by irking everyone. He likes to bring up things that happened in the past; things that shame you, regardless if they were true or not." Roger paused briefly. He looked down at the tabletop in search of the proper way to delicately put his thoughts up for discussion. "If you must know, the chancellor was talking about your mother."

Mark stared at his father for several seconds. What broke his concentration was when the waitress placed his

67

juice and coffee on the table. Mark snapped out of his trance to thank her. Then he refocused his attention on Roger.

"What did he say about Mom?"

"Oh, he brought up the accusation that I was responsible for the situation your mother is in. The same tired Pablum that the whole world was convinced I conspired to bring about. No one knows the ordeal I was put through, and the difficulty of raising you while you were so young. It was just a vortex of problems that were piling up in her head that drove her mad. I've told you this time and again through the years."

"Yeah, I know," Mark responded while looking down at the glass of OJ, but not imbibing. He then looked up at his father. "Dad, I'm going to ask you a direct question and I want a direct answer. You never did explain to me why you divorced Mom while she was already committed at Crenshaw. I mean, if you still loved her and cared about her, you wouldn't have done that."

"I did it for my own sanity," Roger argued. "Hell, would you have liked for me to go insane like her and join her at Crenshaw, not knowing what the real world was like anymore? Is that what you wanted?"

"No. I didn't mean it that way. But I'm beginning to wonder if that was because you had to satisfy your sexual urges, which you couldn't when not having a woman."

Roger was beginning to believe that his own son, the last person on earth he would suspect to betray him, was being influenced by trash he heard about or read. He was getting pissed.

"When I first met and married your mother nearly thirty years ago, no other woman came between us. But five years after she was committed to Crenshaw, I met Beth. She was and still is my only source of support, love and trust. I am devoted to her just as she is to me. And believe me, she has had to endure a lot of shit being flung our way because of the case surrounding Haber's disappearance and Mom's condition. She even helped you in your adolescent years. Beth is my lifeline, and I don't know where I'd be without her. Maybe you'll find a special woman someday, Mark, and experience firsthand what I'm talking about."

"And you don't know the crap I had to—" Mark was interrupted by the waitress serving his croissant. He thanked her and continued his talk with Roger, although he decided wisely to lower the volume. "I had to take shit when I was a kid. I'd get fingered by classmates who were aware that Mom was sent away. How would you like to be ridiculed, Dad? I was laughed at and got into a few fights. You remember those times when you had to go to my school and straighten things out with the principal. It was no bargain for me either. So, I have every right to say what's on my mind."

Roger released a short burst of air as if to laugh, but there was nothing humorous in his countenance. Instead his eyelids narrowed as he zeroed in on his train of thought.

"We've both been through hell over the years, son. That's something that can't be undone. We can only hope it just dies out." Roger sighed briefly. "But getting back to the chancellor, I can guarantee he will bring all this up, too. And he'll lay down the law of the code of ethics and the proper conduct all faculty members must comply with. Just appease him. And be as terse as possible. Good luck. I'm confident you'll do well if you heed my advice."

Mark nodded. He bit into his croissant. He would have no need for Roger to further coach him on what to expect and what to say. Now it would be up to Mark to do well.

Chapter 19

His watch read nine-forty-nine, but Mark was compelled to show up at the chancellor's office with time to spare. This could very well be the last job interview he would ever have for the rest of his life, and Mark surely was not going to blow it by being tardy. After all, for someone as renowned as Valen and the power he wielded, one ought to be more than just punctual.

He entered the reception area with great caution. Mark monitored his every step as if he were prey for some predator lurking behind the tall reeds of the jungle. He approached Ruth carefully. She was engrossed in keystroking a letter for Valen on her desktop, but she sensed his presence and halted her work to devote her attention to him.

"Hello, Mark." Ruth smiled at the visitor.

"You recognize me?"

"Well, aside from the fact that you're the only scheduled visitor for the chancellor at this hour, I do see a lot of your father in you. You're, of course, much younger, more handsome, you don't have a beard, and you've got more hair on top."

"Give me thirty years and I may look exactly like him," Mark returned with a smirk.

Ruth laughed. "Have a seat, please. I'll let him know you've arrived."

If Mark didn't know any better, he would have sworn Ruth was flirting with him. But, then again, it might have been the fact that Mark was a little more outgoing and gregarious than his stoic dad. That was a social trait he'd inherited from Margaret before her life-changing experience turned her world upside down.

As Ruth went inside to announce his visit, Mark sat quiet as a church mouse, biding his time. He nervously rubbed his hands in anticipation of his meeting with Valen. A minute passed before Ruth emerged from Valen's office.

"He'll see you now, Mark."

Mark offered a polite nod as he rose from his chair. He grabbed the knot in his necktie to make certain it was both straight and up against his Adam's apple without choking him. He cleared his throat and carefully paced his steps toward the open door. Even though he was summoned, Mark, out of courtesy, knocked on the doorframe to announce his presence officially. Valen looked up at his guest and welcomed the young Lavoie. The chancellor asked the visitor to close the door behind him so the two of them could have a sequestered chat. To confirm the need for privacy, Valen called Ruth on the intercom to hold all calls.

Mark sat in his seat like a prisoner awaiting execution. Valen couldn't see from his vantage point that Mark was obsessively rolling his thumbs over each other. His throat constricted and his muscles tightened as he girded himself up for what was to come. Meanwhile, Valen toyed with one of his gilded pens from his desk set. He was studying a couple of sheets on his blotter. A slight grin upturned the ends of his lips. Whereas this might have been a good sign for Mark, what curbed his enthusiasm was the chancellor's furrowed brow, indicating a hint of incredulousness on Valen's part. Mark focused his stare at Valen. That was in part due to his pent-up anxiety, but also because he didn't want to appear rude by looking around the room distractedly.

The chancellor appeared satisfied with what he had just read. He dropped his pen on the blotter and lifted his head to focus on his guest. Valen targeted his sight on Mark's eyes.

"Professor Asmundsson gave you high praise, stating you were one of his best students. Your GPA here was 3.61, and you did very well in presenting your lesson to our screening committee a couple of months ago. Impressive, Mr. Lavoie, but it's not satisfying enough. What do you bring to the table?"

"Well, I bring my youth, my vigor, and my enthusiasm." Mark thought hard for what to say next. "You see, Mr. Chancellor, teaching runs in my family. It's been that way for the last four generations. You might say it's in my blood."

"In your blood." Valen had a wry smile. "I had a very interesting chat the other day with your father. Did he tell you about it?"

"Yes. We had a discussion about that this morning in detail."

"No doubt. He was wise to brief you on the finer points that I hold dear in someone of academia representing this institution."

Mark replied with a soft yes. Then there was utter silence in the room. Valen rose from his chair. He deliberately treaded the area away from his desk as he turned his face away from Mark. Valen looked out one of the two huge windows behind him as if to embrace the world. But all the while the wheels were turning in his brain as he methodically reduced Mark to sweating in uncertainty. Mark rubbed his hands more purposefully in his nervous disorderly state. Intimidation was becoming a predominant factor in the interview, as the younger Lavoie didn't know what to expect next. Finally Valen cleared his throat to break the tension.

"Tell me something, Mr. Lavoie. That horrible situation surrounding your mother and that poor fellow who was murdered twenty years ago, how do you feel about the accusations leveled at your father?"

"I feel bad for Mom. I wish she wasn't where she is. But my father gave me a straightforward answer concerning her and all the things that led up to it. As for that guy who was killed, Dad was acquitted. There was the rumor that the guy was in love with Mom, but that was just it . . . a rumor."

"Was this your father's version of the story?"

"Well, if it'll convince you, sir, even my Aunt Siobhan, that's Mom's sister, corroborated the story."

"And you believe them?"

"My dad has guided me through some terrible moments in my young life. He has embodied everything I needed from a father. And to this day he still is very much concerned about what happens to me. That's why he fought hard to get me this interview with you."

Valen continued to peer out the window before asking another question. "Do I frighten you?"

Mark was flummoxed. His eyes went left to right. He wasn't sure how to answer.

"Excuse me, sir, but I don't see the relevance of your question."

Valen was taken aback by Mark's response. His eyebrows shifted, and his face reflected a look of disdain. Valen pirouetted to face Mark dead on and sharpened his edge.

"I am probably the most despised person on this campus. No doubt your father has either mentioned this or at the very least intimated it. And as part of your preparation for this interview, I'm certain you've been guided by him to show a steely reserve. But I am not one to be trifled with. Besides expecting a high degree of decorum and professionalism in your teaching skills, I also command—no, *demand*—respect. I don't care if you loathe and revile me. Quite frankly, I would take that as a compliment. I can put you on a pedestal, but I'll also be the first to knock you off. All it takes is just one misstep, one act out of character and your house will come down. Have I made myself clear?"

Mark nodded meekly. He didn't utter a word. He didn't have to. Valen gave Mark permission to leave his office. He told the young Lavoie to see Ruth on the way out to begin the paper process for employment. The chancellor extended his right hand and welcomed Mark to the faculty fraternity at Winston. Mark was hesitant to shake it after Valen's bullying. But he clamped down on the chancellor's hand and gave it a move of gyration.

Ruth warmly handed Mark a few forms, including a W-9, to fill out. As he was gathering the material, Mark glanced over his left shoulder back at Valen's office door. There stood the chancellor, his arms folded, looking directly at him. The scrutinizing had already begun, even though Mark had yet to sign the contract.

Chapter 20

The very moment he left Valen's office, Mark sent a text message to Roger letting him know that the interview with the chancellor had concluded and that it seemed to go well. What Mark didn't reveal was the interrogation to which Valen had subjected him. But Roger didn't have to guess. He knew the iron-fisted leader of the institution too well to think otherwise.

Mark and Roger got together at Edward's office to celebrate the announcement. Heather was happy to greet them. While she warmly welcomed Roger once more, Heather kept her eyes on Mark, both of whom were of similar age. She gently stroked her throat as if to allure Mark, direct his attention to her open blouse. Mark just offered a grin in appreciation of her hospitality, but offered nothing else.

Fresh off three classes, Edward walked in happily to meet with his colleague and new protégé. He apologized for his tardiness, but Roger held up the palm of his hand. The anthropology professor had lectured two classes of his own that day and knew all too well the struggles of putting together a lesson plan and standing in front of coeds for hours.

Edward showed the two men into his office. "I'm sorry if I can't offer anything more stimulating than a bottle of ginger ale," Edward confessed. "I suppose we can pretend it's fine French champagne of exquisite vintage. You know the rules of the university when it comes to alcohol, although that hasn't stopped some members of the student body, particularly the fraternities and sororities."

"Quite all right," Roger countered, "we'll just save our libations for a party I'd like to throw at my house a week from Saturday."

Heather couldn't help but overhear. "Ooh, could I come, Professor Lavoie?" She directed her question at Roger, but was ogling Mark. The younger Lavoie smiled back, but knew that wasn't his decision. He quickly turned to his father.

"How 'bout it, Dad? You already told me it was okay to invite Lane and Hunter to the party. I'm sure you wouldn't mind if Heather comes, too." Mark then turned his head and said sweetly, "I'm sure Heather has a few friends of her own who'd like to tag along."

Heather was hoping to be the young female star of attention, but agreed to ask a few of her people to come. Roger was suddenly placed in an awkward position. He couldn't say no. He raised his eyebrows and his arms to the ceiling. "Okay. Sure. Why not?" Roger then dropped his arms, his hands making a loud clap against the sides of his legs.

Edward turned to Mark to address the subject for the gathering. "So, how did the vetting go at the chancellor's office?"

"A little too intimidating, if you ask me."

His eyes were a dead giveaway that Edward was smiling under his soup strainer of a mustache. He assured Mark that both he and Roger knew of Valen's tactics and instructed him to quickly dismiss the interrogation.

Speaking of dismissal, Mark glanced at his watch. He didn't want to appear rude, but he had to excuse himself politely so that he could get ready for his present job at Best Buy. Roger and Edward understood and permitted Mark to leave.

As Mark was about to exit, Heather wished him a pleasant day and told him she was looking forward to the party. Mark smiled as he left the office, a little flattered by Heather's flirting.

Chapter 21

It was an exhausting, but self-gratifying day, knowing that his son was going to be joining the faculty at Winston in January. For Roger, all he wanted to do was lie down on the sofa with his shoes off and relax. Just five minutes into his nap, Beth stumbled in, looking spent, just like her husband.

She saw Roger and gave him a smirk. Beth would've preferred to have been occupying the divan after her arduous day at the hospital. Well, maybe she could share it with him. But Beth didn't want to startle Roger. She murmured a few words of surrender to see if dear hubby would react. Roger, who was still cognizant of his surroundings, opened his right eye to spot Beth. He wiped away the cobwebs from his head to address his wife.

"Hello, Dear. You look about as perky as I am."

Beth chortled. "Let's face it, Love. We're both getting older. How about making some room for me?"

Roger sat up. Beth eased herself next to him, the back of her head resting against Roger's shoulder. She released a huge sigh after a day of hearing of Dr. Malcolm Neiderman's successful surgery a week after it was performed, Corinne Kuiper's boasting of her daughter Marisa getting accepted into Harvard, Max Stoller's lament over the shaky ground the fiscal operations of the medical center seemed to be precariously treading, and Doreen Marlowe's showcasing pictures she took on the fabulous European trip her husband Ted gave her last summer. Beth looked to her husband as an escape from the nonsense and strife that was the hospital.

Although the office had already taken its shots at her that day, the alluring fragrance of Beth's seductive perfume still lingered. Roger adored the sweet aroma. If they both weren't already tuckered out, he might have suggested to Beth they head upstairs to the bedroom. But fatigue had worn down both of them. He was resigned just to holding her in his arms and allowing his body to be her pillow.

"What say we just order Chinese takeout this evening?"

"That suits me," Beth answered. "I was in the mood for some vegetable lo mein anyway."

"And the steamed chicken dumplings?"

"Oh, how can we forget that?"

Roger gently rubbed Beth's upper arm. As much as they both were in agreement on that night's dinner menu, neither was in any rush to speed dial one of their favorite haunts for delivery. A few more minutes of cuddling were more important than satiating their hunger.

Beth broke the silence. "So," she hesitated before continuing, "are you going to tell me what happened with Mark, or are you going to keep it a secret?"

"I wanted to tell you earlier, but that hospital of yours forbids cell phone usage and I couldn't leave a message on your office voice mail. Gee, when was the last time you cleaned out your inbox?"

"Never mind. You could've emailed, you know."

"You know how I hate those absurd smart phones. A phone is a phone. It's made for calling. Period."

"Oh, you've got a lot to learn, Roger. But enough of that. Tell me. What happened?"

Roger couldn't contain himself. Like any proud father, he told Beth that Mark passed the litmus test with Valen and that he would begin as an adjunct come January. Beth squealed with delight. She was happy for Roger and her stepson and accented her feelings with a rapid sequence of clapping her hands. He thanked his wife by bussing her lips.

Roger caressed Beth once more. He looked up at the off-white ceiling with wistful eyes. "I think it would be a great idea if we were to host a party in Mark's honor here a week from Saturday."

"Hmmm. Sounds as though this was a directive rather than an inquiry."

"Let's face it, Beth, when was the last time we hosted anything here?"

"Four years ago, remember? Your twenty-fifth anniversary of teaching at Winston, I remember. Quite vividly, I might add. That was when Stu Billingsley got totally plastered. I still don't know how Sherry got him home."

"Well, he won't be coming this time. Not after that terrible stroke that nearly killed him two years back."

Beth shook her head sadly at the thought of their friend, now a shadow of his former self. She suddenly shot up and moved away from Roger. Beth suggested they invite her friend Francine MacKenzie. Roger rolled his eyes because it was that same person who put the bug in Beth's ear to prod her husband to seek psychiatric help from Mort Sonnenstein.

Suddenly the house phone began to ring. Neither Roger nor Beth had any strong desire, let alone energy, to answer it. After hearing Beth's terse but pleasant greeting and subsequent high-pitched beep, the next voice was Mort's. He wanted to remind Roger of their 11 o'clock appointment the next morning at the psychoanalyst's office. *Terrific,* Roger thought, as if he had to be reminded of it. He cursed Francine's name under his breath, blaming the mere mentioning of her as having caused Mort to call him.

Meanwhile, Beth took the call in stride. In fact, she exclaimed that Mark's recent hiring by the college could be something positive to discuss with Mort. If only Roger shared the same enthusiasm over the upcoming session.

Chapter 22

A cold, drizzling rain swept through much of New England the next day. An umbrella was useless, for the ferocious winds would blow the precipitation into one's face, like a deckhand facing the omnipotent salty spray of the sea rocked by whitecaps.

Roger's eyeglasses were the only protection he had from the piercing wet needles. With great effort he trudged up the modest front steps to Mort's residence/business and rang the doorbell several times so that the host got the message to open it ASAP. As Roger waited, he turned around to look at the street. On a normal weekday you could find at least three or four people parading the sidewalks and a vehicle or two roaming up and down the macadam. But on a day fit for ducks . . . As Roger winced from the biting weather, he wondered if he was the only one dumb enough to come out here on a day like this, when to him it was a non-essential.

Ten seconds had passed and Roger grew frustrated. He was about to unleash his wrath at the bell once more when suddenly the door opened. Mort was happy to see Roger not only made it, but was also a little early. Without further hesitation, Mort rushed Roger in from the inclement weather.

After helping Roger remove his top coat, Mort offered his client a cup of orange pekoe tea. He told Roger that the beverage was his choice on a dreary day like this one. Roger would have refused the drink under normal circumstances. But he was chilled to his bones and his pants and galoshes were soaked. The tea would indeed hit the spot. Mort's noble gesture was accepted.

Mort kindly asked Roger to have a seat in his office while he retrieved the tea. The professor noticed not much had changed since his last visit. The exception being a few more journals might have been added, lying on top of each other like layers of meat, cheese and garnishment in a sandwich. Surprisingly, the stack of papers and magazines held up to the load, without toppling over. Dust was beginning to accumulate over other sections of Mort's humongous desk that hadn't seen the light of day in God knows how long.

Two minutes passed before Mort reemerged with the tea. "I hope this is how you like it."

Roger graciously accepted the hot beverage. Carefully he took a small sip, careful not to burn his mouth. But that sample alone was enough to relax and warm his insides. Roger even allowed a small grin to exhibit his gratification. Mort was pleased that his patient was soothed by the tea, thus allowing the harshness of the day and all inner turmoil to melt away. This was an opportune time to begin the session, and perhaps get Roger to open up.

"So," Mort began, "how have you been since our last meeting?"

Roger still had his eyes closed when Mort asked the question. His mind was elsewhere. The comforting beverage was taking the professor to a faraway island in the middle of the ocean with pristine white sand and majestic palm trees, their frayed long branches gently swaying in the tropical sea breezes. Mort had to clear his throat in order to snap his patient out of his self-induced trance. Finally Roger came back to face reality.

"Oh, I'm sorry, Mort." He placed his cup on an adjacent stand as a sign of devoting his full attention to the psychoanalyst.

"I asked, how have you been since we met last?"

Roger was at first reticent to share. But then he mused over the idea that the revelation of Mark's employment at Winston might put a halt to further sessions with Mort. "Well, I'm happy to announce that Mark will start his teaching career at Winston come the spring semester in January."

Mort was floored. His jaw dropped, but he bubbled over with elation. "Why, that's fantastic news! Congratulations, Roger! I'm so happy for you and your son! My, this has to be a cause for celebration!"

"As a matter of fact, Beth and I are going to host a party to honor Mark's acceptance a week from tomorrow at seven o'clock."

"That's next Saturday evening, November ninth?"

"That's right." Roger was a bit reluctant to invite Mort, but then he felt awkward telling the psychoanalyst of the soiree and not extending a free pass. He scanned the floor to summon the nerve but then swiftly raised his head. "Would you like to come?"

"That's awfully kind of you, Roger, but I have tickets that night to attend the Rhode Island Philharmonic with an old college classmate I once had a crush on back then. Now that I'm a widower and she's a widow, I guess that makes us eligible. But thank you just the same."

This was great news for the professor. The weighty stone of etiquette had lifted off his shoulders as the burden of obligation took wing. In the same light, Roger was convinced that his son's spectacular ascendancy to academia would call a halt to the need to meet with Mort in the future. In fact, he felt compelled to exit on the spot.

There was almost a stillness of breath for nearly a half minute. Rather than engage in a staring contest, Roger slapped the sides of his torso, a clear indication that he had had enough of the mano a mano.

"I guess we have nothing much more to say then, Mort. It has been a short but very productive two-visit stint. I wish you well."

Roger was making motions to bolt from the house. But Mort raised his right hand and softly uttered, "Please." The professor froze in his stance then retreated to his chair. Roger was a sack of mixed feelings. There was anger at the doctor for forbidding his getaway, but also confusion over what rationale Mort had conceived to clamp on the iron chains. Curiosity got the better of Roger as he again ensconced himself in the seat.

"You've only been here for ten minutes, Roger. Use up your hour. My next appointment is not until one o'clock. But, listen, if you're worried about remuneration for the session, don't worry about it. I'm more intrigued that you're here than you are. Besides, I have to admit, I did summon *you* here, not the other way around. So, today it's on me."

Roger gave Mort a strange look. He softly brushed his neatly trimmed whiskers; all the while his mind was racing to ferret out just what the reasoning behind Mort's altruistic gesture might be. His eyebrows gathered in his confusion. Mort couldn't care less about Roger's reaction. He was just pleased that Roger decided to stay. Now it was time to deliver the message.

"I was at Crenshaw the other day," Mort began. Roger started fidgeting in his seat on hearing the news. The jubilant flush over Mark's rise to teaching was now so old you could wrap fish in it. As uncomfortable as he was, Roger sat with narrowed eyes to see where Mort was taking this. "I met with Dr. Oswald Borshevsky. He runs the place. Anyway, Dr. Borshevsky was kind enough to allow me to see the current state your ex-wife Margaret was in. After twenty years I find it extremely difficult to fathom that her condition never improved, even slightly. She's totally withdrawn and disturbed. I won't go into detail. Besides, I'm sure you're familiar with her condition already. But it did leave me shaken, frightening even for this old man who thought he had seen it all."

"You didn't believe me when I discussed the matter with you last time?"

"It's not a question of disbelieving. We people of the medical and scientific field are a curious lot. Someone of your background can appreciate that. But there was something else Dr. Borshevsky discussed. He didn't have a high regard of you concerning the circumstances surrounding the development of your ex-wife's condition and the murder of one Darren Haber."

Roger glared back. "You dragged me all the way here for this! You sound just like my university's chancellor, badgering me about old wounds that never seem to heal because people like you, the chancellor and that doctor at Crenshaw just love to bring it up! I've had just about as much of this as I can take!"

The professor was about to race out of Mort's office, repeating a similar moment in his last session. But as before, Mort had to think quickly.

"Please, Roger. I'm just the reporter here. I'm not expressing any feelings of my own; instead, I maintain neutrality. Stay a little longer?"

The kettle was about to boil over, but Roger lowered the flame. He remained in the chair and granted Mort a further audience. The psychoanalyst ruminated over what to say next. He chose his words carefully.

"It is of my humble opinion, however, that the cause behind those nightmares you have been experiencing has more to do with what happened back then than they had to do with your son finding a teaching job. If I'm mistaken, please let me know."

Roger closed his eyes and nodded gently. Now Mort was getting somewhere.

"Let me assure you, Roger, that I have no hidden tape recorder lying around or video camera filming this session, so there won't be anything to submit as evidence of any possible confession to a crime that happened two decades ago. I only tape my notations for my own usage, and that's after my sessions. Think of me as a priest or minister you can confide in without any repercussions."

"Hmm, even the priests in my own parish are not exactly thrilled to see me because of all the innuendo. How bad is that? To be cast aside by your own church! Nobody wants to listen to what I have to say. I can talk until I'm blue in the face, and people still have their doubts about me! They think I'm the same as that former football player . . . OJ Simpson. They're never satisfied that I've been exonerated by my peers. How do you think that makes me feel?"

Mort drew a deep sigh. He scribbled notes on his legal pad. Mort brought the back end of the pen to his mouth to gather his thoughts. But then, he reasoned, it was better to devote time to his subject and engage in conversation than to continue jotting down a few ramblings.

"I really do feel for your predicament, Roger. But let me ask you. What have you done to suppress these recurrences, or what have you done to release the stress they have caused?"

Roger was at a loss. He merely responded by muttering, "Not much." He had kept it all inside. Mort suggested a few activities, including jogging or walking long distances, painting, reading, and even writing; anything to unshackle himself from the torments of demons from his past. The professor conceded he would take up the matter in advisement.

Mort didn't want to interrogate the man any further. In just two sessions he had already formulated the volatility of Roger's persona and rationalized it wasn't worth the risk of infuriating his patient. The psychoanalyst wanted to keep the relationship amiable, for he was certain there was something Roger was withholding—perhaps the truth—but that would have to wait for another time.

Each man slowly rose from his seat and made the measured trek toward the front door. Mort did throw out one last observation.

"I think the fact that you're hosting a party next week to celebrate Mark's new teaching job at Winston can certainly be construed as one of those stress relievers we talked about. I think it's grand, Roger, that you're doing this. You're focusing your attention on your son and not the problems that seem to haunt you. And I certainly encourage this. It's all critical to building a positive mental attitude. Things like this will go a long way in your recovery."

"Thanks, Mort. Are you sure you can't come?"

"I've got the tickets to spend a night with the harmonious violin strings and horns. Besides, I think Jacqueline, that's my date, is looking forward to it, too."

"Well, maybe some other time."

"Of course. And do let me know how things went, perhaps at our next session."

They shook hands. Roger smiled, but it was only superficial. He was actually elated the session was over. Mort's warmth was more genuine. He opened the front door for Roger, who was struggling to get his umbrella open as the harsh, wet conditions continued to pelt the community unmercifully. Mort wished Roger a safe journey home as he comforted the professor with a gentle pat on the shoulder.

As Roger left the property, Mort flashed the visitor one more smile and a benevolent wave. The psychoanalyst drew a deep sigh and silently shut the door.

Mort was now in solitude. He kept thinking about Oswald's opinion of Roger and began to entertain thoughts of his patient as a murderer and a twisted, deviant individual, after all. But nothing came out of the session to prove that, although the door was left wide open to ponder such possibilities.

The psychoanalyst suddenly darted his eyes back to his office. With alacrity Mort paced himself to his desk phone. He punched in a series of numbers without giving it much thought, as if the digits were committed to memory. After a few rings, a familiar voice came on the other end.

"Hello, Crystal? Hi, this is Dr. Mort Sonnenstein." A nominal pause ensued. "I'm fine, thank you. Listen, is Dr. Borshevsky in?" Again Mort allowed the other party to speak. "Oh, I see. Well, can you do me a favor, please? Can you have him call me when he gets a chance? Great! He has my number. I'll be here the rest of the day. If I don't answer him immediately, it's because I'm with a client." A few seconds passed. "Thank you, Crystal. Stay dry!"

Mort was disappointed Oswald wasn't there, but given the latter's responsibilities and hectic schedule, it was understandable. Mort would have to wait until later to discuss Roger's session with Oswald, and oh, what interesting tidbits that would reveal.

Chapter 23

The chilly but clear early November evening did not deter the partygoers from attending the soiree hosted by Roger and Beth Lavoie. Although the overnight temperatures were expected to drop to near the freezing point, many of the guests were dressed as though it were a month earlier, allowing the heat of their vehicles of choice to warm the frost in the air out of their bones. The back seats of cars, SUVs, and minivans became racks for their topcoats.

Attending, of course, was the man of the hour, Mark Lavoie. Much like Roger, Mark was sporting a blazer over an open-collared Van Heusen dress shirt, with a burgundy tee shirt underneath. Mark wanted to express his gratitude for Winston by at least boasting one of the school's colors—harvest gold was the other. He spent the first two hours shaking a hand here, getting a soft peck on the cheek there from well-wishers attending the soiree.

The party hosts, Roger and Beth Lavoie, were more enthusiastic than Mark as they welcomed familiar guests as though they hadn't seen them in decades.

Not many neighbors, though, were present. Beth's good friend Francine MacKenzie and her husband Cal showed up, as well as Roger's pal from two doors down, Burt Petruszka, and his wife Kate. Francine and Burt were happy to be present. The same could not be said for their respective spouses. At least there were plenty of food and spirits available.

Math dean Edward Asmundsson was present, along with his Russian-born wife Svetlana. Like her husband, Svetlana also taught at the college level, but over at Ivy League Brown. Her background in Russian history and government had earned Svetlana distinction as a contributing commentator on MSNBC. When on the air, she went by her maiden name, and the title Dr. Svetlana Nikiforova, to add authenticity to her role as an authority on the subject.

Political science dean Dirk Sorgaard and his wife Stacy attended. As usual, they made a grand entrance to let the world know when they arrived. The dean of English, Suzanne Hensley, came unescorted. She probably would not have come, had it not been for her long professional association with Roger. Suzanne owed Roger that much. And then there was African studies professor Harold Washington and his elegant wife Gloria. Harold's demeanor was understated and down-to-earth, whereas Gloria was the epitome of Eliza Doolittle, flaunting her status as a professor's wife as she spoke eloquently, masking the humble beginnings of her upbringing.

Beth invited only one friend from work, Camille Demos. Accompanied by her husband Bart, Camille was about the only person at the hospital who wasn't full of herself.

Roger's younger brother Don and his wife Delores were there, but not their sister Gerri. She and her family had become snowbirds and all lived down in the Fort Meyers area in Florida.

These were all associates and friends of Mark's parents. But, just so the night's honoree wasn't bored, Roger and Beth allowed Mark's best friends, Hunter Morales and Lane Pascale, to attend. Hunter worked as a tour guide at the Providence Museum of Natural History and Planetarium while he continued his studies toward his doctorate in geology. Hunter also had the makings of a college professor himself, and Roger had already made overtures to him to pursue a career at Winston. The trouble was that Hunter already had numerous other advances from the other prominent learning institutions in the region, as well as from a growing number of universities from around the country and abroad. Despite his ambition for a highbrow career, Hunter's great looks, jet-black hair and athletic 6'2" frame, made him desirable to many young women. Lane didn't possess Hunter's chiseled features or eclectic intellect, but he was an IT technician and computer whiz. If you had a problem with your laptop or wanted advice on what new technological gizmo to buy, Lane was the man to consult.

On the other end of the room, Heather Karinski was huddling with her girlfriends by the liquor table. She'd received the invite courtesy of Mark, but no one expected the posse coat-tailing her. Although she had a boyfriend, Heather wanted to keep her options open. That, and the offer of downing a few shots of tequila for free, were enticing enough for her to attend.

Tamiqua Barnstable worked in the bookkeeping department of a major plumbing supply company. When she wasn't tabbing things away on a desktop calculator, Tamiqua would spend money on all the latest designer clothes. She loved to dangle her hooped bracelets, the constant clinking noise always alerting you she was nearby. Her skin was as dark as ebony, but she would date any guy regardless of his race, so long as he had a fat wallet.

Kayla Ling, a graphics illustrator by trade, was even wilder. She bore the features of her grandparents, both of whom were born and raised in China, but had not continued their rich cultural traditions. Kayla eschewed the customs of her ancestors in favor of the narcissistic and self-indulging pleasures of modern Western society.

Amanda Leipzig was between jobs, a casualty of the recent depressed economic times after her first job out of college became defunct. She was the least attractive of the group and therefore her needs were different from the others. Although looking to hook up with a guy wasn't off the table, Amanda didn't make it a priority. Whereas the other women would've settled with just about any strapping young man to satisfy their own desires and urges, Amanda preferred the idea of a long-term relationship. To her, substance and character were far more important than Adonis looks.

And then there was Rebecca Dyer. She was a very attractive twenty-six-year-old blonde, although not cute enough to prevent her long-time boyfriend from dumping her recently. The loss depressed Rebecca greatly, and it was at the strong urging of Heather and the others that she come to try her luck. When she wasn't trying to get over her ex, Rebecca made a living working as an analyst in the accounting department of a regional retail department store chain.

Mark looked around the crowded living room and dining room. He saw his Uncle Don there and realized Aunt Gerri couldn't be there because of the great distance. But Mark was hoping that someone else was going to be there too, someone who, like the others, was his direct blood relative. Disappointment shadowed him. He needed an explanation for the absence of a certain individual. Mark saw his father and approached him. Roger, who was engaged in a lively discussion with Burt, Dirk and Harold, felt someone tapping his shoulder. He immediately excused himself from the others to see who wanted his attention. With raised eyebrows, Roger turned and saw Mark before him. With a puzzled visage, the anthropology professor asked, "What's the matter, Mark? Do you need anything? Is everything all right?"

Mark looked away from his father as if to recheck the house for the missing person. "I was a bit curious, Dad. I see Uncle Don here with Aunt Delores, and I know Aunt Gerri and Uncle Bob and my cousins are in Florida. But I was wondering why Aunt Siobhan isn't here?"

Roger stared at his son as if he had two heads. The elder Lavoie had to respond, and fast. "Well, she was offered an invitation to come. She . . . had a previous engagement. I'm sorry."

Mark folded his arms unhappily. He wanted to believe his father, but there was something holding him back. Perhaps it was the way Roger delivered his answer. But this was not the time to ask twenty questions. The focus was on merriment, and Mark decided to bury his concern . . . at least for the time being.

As he reconvened with Hunter and Lane, Mark looked across the living room and spotted Heather and the other girls. She gave him a flirtatious smile and waved. The others joined in, too. Somewhat surprised by the advances the women made, Mark coyly grinned and waved back. He then turned to his male comrades.

"So, Hunter," Mark began, "how's the job at the museum, and tell me, how are your studies coming along?"

"Great! I was able to obtain a special grant through the museum for an expedition in February to Brazil. It'll be the basis for my thesis."

"Oh, wow," Lane chimed in. "Brazil, huh? Sounds exotic."

"It's an exploration of the rain forests of the Amazon, not Rio de Janeiro."

"Oh, well," Lane replied. "Oh, Mark, tell your parents I'll stop by Tuesday to take a look at your dad's laptop. I'll try to determine what's slowing it down."

"Thanks, he'll appreciate that."

Mark took another sip of his Bacardi and Coke combo. He turned to his side and saw the five women giggling and laughing. Mark was about to discuss the young ladies with his friends, but Roger appeared and addressed Hunter, taking Mark's attention.

"I do hope you'll consider Winston after you receive your doctorate, Hunter. It would be an honor to have both you and Mark teaching there."

"I'll certainly take it under consideration, professor. But I have to confess to having other options I'm not ruling out."

"Well, I'll put in a good word with Dr. Krausse. He'll easily get you an audience with the chancellor."

"I'm surprised you didn't invite him to the party, Dad."

Roger rotated to Mark. "Just because you and I had to deal with the devil, Mark, to get you in, doesn't mean we have to hold his pitchfork. Besides, the main goal has been achieved. I'm sure the chancellor has other things to occupy himself with on a Saturday evening, hmm?"

Roger returned to friends closer to his age. Mark just shook his head, noticing a second individual suspiciously absent. He decided to let it go and resumed chatting with Hunter and Lane.

In the meantime, the women were cackling like hens. Then Kayla salaciously glanced over at Mark and the others. Heather was observing Kayla's keen interest.

"If you'd like, Kayla," Heather began, "I'll help you get to know Mark a lot better."

"Oh, he's okay," Kayla replied. "But what I've really got the ribs for is that sexy hunk with the dark hair! Ooh, I'll bet he can hit my G-spot! What was his name? Hector?"

"Girl," Tamiqua piped in, "if you're gonna have him fuck y'all, at least get his name right." Tamiqua looked in Hunter's direction and to emphasize her point, she instructed, "It's Henry."

Amanda felt awkward to mention it, but she had to correct the corrector. "Um, I believe he said his name was Hunter."

"Well, he can hunt me down anytime!" Kayla exclaimed.

Heather glanced at Rebecca. She appeared the least excited of the girls when talking about the guys. It seemed that Rebecca was still having difficulty trying to purge thoughts of her now former boyfriend from her mind. Heather decided to assist this sullen member of the sisterhood.

"Hey," Heather began, "aren't you interested in those guys? If anyone needs to rebound amongst us, it's you."

"I'm sorry, Heather," Rebecca responded. "I'm doing my best to get Logan out of my head. I mean . . . he dumped me!" Rebecca paused for a moment and then snorted. "I always thought it was the other way around. You know, we get rid of the men. I hate to say this, but I think my ego was bruised."

"Get over it! Logan Galwyn is a loser! He threw away the best thing that's ever happened to him. And when Logan's sixty years old and gray with a pot belly, he's going to rue the day he said goodbye to the best lover he ever had."

Rebecca smiled at Heather's endorsement of her. "I appreciate your making me feel better." She swished around her drink a couple of times before continuing. "I don't know, Heather. It's like . . . part of me wants to let go, while the other part is saying, 'No. You'll never find a guy like Logan again.'" Rebecca sighed as she contemplated the overhead track lighting in the ceiling.

Heather draped her arm over Rebecca's shoulder. "Hey, just remember. You and I can sit at a bar and, by just flicking our hair back and holding our drinks in the air with a little panache, we'll have at least five or six men offering to buy us another. We hold all the cards, my dear! And someone as attractive as you will have no trouble finding a man when you're ready."

Rebecca glanced over at Mark and his friends. She nodded in their direction. "What about those guys?"

Heather grinned. "Well, apparently Kayla has dibs on Hunter there, but Mark and the other one are fair game. Come. Let's go." Rebecca was at first apprehensive. "Don't be shy! It's bad enough that Logan blew a good thing when he had one, in you. Don't follow in his footsteps!"

Rebecca conceded as she and Heather broke away from the others. Kayla noticed the two women walking over and decided to join them, just in case they intended to stake a claim on the geologist. To affirm her position, Kayla practically elbowed Rebecca out of the way to get to Hunter. Finding his back turned to her Kayla tapped Hunter on his shoulder. He broke away from the other two men to have a look-see at who was trying to get his attention.

"Oh, hi," Hunter said with a grin.

"Hey," Kayla responded, flashing her pearly whites. She then pointed to him with a question mark written on her face. "Hunter, right?"

"Yeah. That's right. And you are . . ."

"Kayla Ling." She hooked her arm around Hunter's and pulled him away from the pack. "So, what do you do for a living?"

"I'm a geologist."

"Cool! Dealing with rocks and fossils! Wow!"

Heather gave Kayla a perplexed look, as it seemed her friend was actually into Hunter's occupation and not his boxers. She then turned toward Mark and Lane and smiled.

"Professor Asmundsson and I can't wait until January when you start working in our department, Mark."

"I'm really looking forward to it."

She looked around at everyone. "It's a nice party."

"Oh, it's okay. I think my father and stepmother are enjoying it more than I am."

Heather was noticing the way Rebecca was ogling Mark. Apparently whatever inhibitions she'd had quickly evaporated. Seeing there was some chemistry brewing, Heather asked Lane to come with her to mingle with Tamiqua and Amanda. As Lane was being tugged by Heather, he looked back at Mark for moral support. Mark smirked and threw up his hands. Mark and Rebecca were left behind like two shipwrecked castaways. But that didn't seem to bother them.

The silence was awkward between the two while the others around the house were chewing the fat and laughing loudly. Each of the nervous couple was feeling the other out like two prize fighters in the ring, waiting for the other to flinch first. Finally Mark blinked.

"So, how do you know Heather?"

"We went to high school together," Rebecca replied. "Then we went to Roger Williams University. Sorry!" Mark smiled and waved his had dismissively, as if to forgive her for not attending Winston. "Anyway, I finished my degree, but Heather dropped out after her sophomore year."

"From what I understand from Professor Asmundsson, Heather's taking courses here and there at Winston."

"Yeah, she wants to get her degree in nursing. Maybe even continue toward a Master's."

"I'll have her talk to my stepmom. Beth knows enough people over at the hospital to get her in if she wants."

Rebecca smiled and took a sip of what was left of her mixed drink. After downing it, she continued.

"Are you getting psyched about the new job?"

"Oh, I can't wait! I've always wanted it. With my father well established at Winston, you might say it's in the genes."

"I guess you'll be moving out of your dad's house once you start at Winston. I mean, now that you'll be making more money, I presume."

"Oh, I don't live here. I moved out a couple of years ago. I have my own place on Westminster Street, just outside Downtown Providence."

Rebecca was impressed that Mark had sprouted wings and left the nest. She raised her eyebrows and nodded approvingly as a sign of how enthused she was to learn this. But now Rebecca wanted to go a step further. She noticed Mark wasn't wearing any jewelry, which would have been a sure sign of a woman's influence if he had. Rebecca didn't want to be too forward in her attempt to see if Mark had any current love interest. She gave it careful consideration and deemed a backdoor approach was the best.

"I'll bet your girlfriend must be excited at what's happening."

"Well," Mark responded, "I'm not seeing anyone now. I mean, I had a girlfriend, but we broke up a while ago."

"Oh, I see," said a smiling Rebecca. Then she realized she had to put on an act of contrition for Mark's breakup. She sucked in her lips. "I mean, I'm sorry that you broke up and all."

"Yeah . . . well." Mark gulped the last of his beer. He gave Rebecca a quick glance up and down. "What about you? Do you have a boyfriend?"

Rebecca hesitated before answering. In the back of her mind—no, the back of her heart—she was still holding a candle out for Logan Galwyn. She looked away for a brief moment. Perhaps she was ashamed to mention his name. But then she remembered what Heather had told her earlier. Rebecca needed to move on with her life and expunge Logan from her life. She quickly recovered as she looked up at Mark with a smile.

"No! Well, that is to say, not anymore!"

Mark beamed like a contest winner. He then offered to get Rebecca another drink, which she gladly accepted. The party was to extend only a few more hours at the Lavoie house. But for Mark and Rebecca it had all the makings of an extended evening.

Chapter 24

It was near midnight, and the festivity at Roger and Beth's house was over by nearly an hour. The hired help Roger employed had already begun the big clean-up after the partygoers. The host and hostess had thanked everyone for attending and making the celebration of Mark's new position a memorable one.

Mark's Downtown Providence apartment was pitch-black. They swung the front door open with as much ferocity as a hurricane. The sound the doorknob made in contact against the opposite wall resonated like a gunshot. Mark and Rebecca stood as silhouettes against the garish light of the hallway. They ravenously kissed each other up and down their faces and necks.

Instinctively Mark reached for the wall light switch. He flicked it on to illuminate the darkened space. Once light was on the subject, the couple resumed their salacious exchange. Rebecca jumped up and wrapped her legs and arms around Mark's body. With a hard kick, Mark closed the front door behind him, not to allow his neighbors a free show. He supported Rebecca with his right arm around her back and his left hand on her ass from underneath. And all the while the two continued their heated lip-and-tongue fusion.

Fueled by an intoxicating combination of mind-altering libations of every conceivable kind imaginable, Rebecca was unshackled of whatever inhibitions might try to stop this coupling. It was a losing battle for the mores instilled in Rebecca since she was a little girl. Lust, triggered by alcohol, was in charge. Logan? Logan who? Yes, even the image of Logan Galwyn, seemingly seared on Rebecca's heart by a branding iron, was beginning to fade like last week's suntan. Logan was becoming a quick afterthought, as Mark was proving to be the hot stud she had sought after the breakup.

Rebecca gasped and tapped Mark's left shoulder repeatedly. As much as he wanted to continue the oral trading of body fluids, Mark gently released Rebecca until she was back on her own two feet. She was struggling for air, as if choking. Rebecca quickly began removing his clothing. Once Mark was bare-chested, Rebecca unbuckled his belt and groped inside his pants until she felt the shape of his genitalia. She peeled down his trousers like a banana. Mark reciprocated by reaching behind Rebecca and unzipping her crimson dress. She allowed him to slip the top over her shoulders and arms, dropping the garment to the floor. Mark fumbled, trying to unhook her bra. Exasperated by his inability to unstrap her, Rebecca threw out her arms and closed her eyes.

"Fuck it! Just rip it off! Rip it off!"

Mark was hesitant. He was caught between the fine line of a direct command and upholding the dignity of sacred principles.

"I," Mark responded with a nervous chuckle, "I just can't do it. I feel . . . I feel terrible doing this. I mean, I just don't go around ripping a woman's bra off."

Rebecca was becoming furious that Mark held such guilt, even after she gave him permission. She had to sever his altar-boy ties.

"Damn it! Stop being such a wuss! I told you to rip the shit off! Now!"

Rebecca's order was heard throughout half of Rhode Island. Now Mark's masculine pride was wounded. He was beginning to wonder if this night of lust was worth it. Mark was full of rage as he decided to take Rebecca up on her offer. Venting his anger, Mark reached for the middle of Rebecca's bra. With a grip like a vise, Mark yanked it off her so hard she nearly stumbled to the floor. But Rebecca regained her footing. She began to breathe heavily as if she had just finished a marathon. Rebecca gazed at Mark with wanton eyes. And he saw the prize that was revealed there. Whatever bitterness he had felt earlier over his damaged self-esteem was now vanquished. The heat of passion was burning inside him. His temperature was rising. The soul wanted more. This was true for her, too.

Mark's mouth sucked in Rebecca's lips once more. Their tongues wrapped around each other like climbing ivy vines. Mark unhitched himself, although Rebecca wanted him to keep going. But there was something else she wanted, and for that she had to concede and allow him to break away.

Mark's lips paid another visit to Rebecca's slender body. He first perched them on her neck, just below her chin. Using his tongue like an out-of-control windshield wiper, Mark slowly descended down Rebecca's silken, scented flesh. He stopped briefly when he arrived at a point between her breasts. She wrapped her hands tightly around Mark's head, clutching the strands of his hair and yanking at them. Mark was in pain as a result, but the fire of the moment overcame the discomfort.

All the while Rebecca tilted her head toward the ceiling. With closed eyes, she began to sensually moan while still clinging to his head like barnacles to a ship. Mark continued to move his mouth downward, swishing his tongue around her belly button. He stretched his fingers around her hips and began inserting them inside her pantyhose and briefs. Slowly and seductively he pulled down her undergarments until they dropped to the floor. Mark knelt down to continue his lips' journey southward. But when he was about to move toward her most sensitive area, Rebecca stopped him.

"Take me to your bed," she panted. "Now! I want you to fuck my brains out!"

Mark obliged by lifting Rebecca up and carrying her to his bedroom down the modest hall. He delicately placed her down on the sheets as if she were an infant he was placing in a crib. Staring at Rebecca's inviting body greatly aroused Mark. He knelt down at her feet and began to assert himself on her. Mark grunted with every plunge as Rebecca's whines grew louder and louder each time he penetrated. Finally Mark climaxed as Rebecca achieved orgasm. She groaned like a great weight had been lifted. And Mark exhaled as if he'd just run a 100-yard dash.

The carnal activity had drained them both. They were even too exhausted to kiss. Instead Mark and Rebecca lay side by side and held each other. The indulgence in alcohol, especially on Rebecca's part, contributed mightily to their lethargy. Not long after that they dozed off.

Chapter 25

The low-angled morning sun burned through the faded and tattered curtains in Mark's room, turning the drab yellow panels to a fiery orange. Mark remained in a dead sleep. Even a passing truck in the street, which rattled the window with its sound, didn't wake the newly appointed teacher.

Rebecca, on the other hand, was stirred by the echoing vibration. She began to open her eyelids and shake the cobwebs from her head. Rebecca scanned the room she found herself in. Her forehead furrowed deeper with every glance, her memory banks unfamiliar with the surroundings. The mystery deepened until her pupils focused on Mark's bare back to her left. The presence of the slumbering sex partner startled her. And then she looked down at herself and noticed her exposed shoulders and arms, with a woolen blanket covering the rest of her naked body. All Rebecca could think was, *Oh, shit!* The over-indulgence in alcohol had compromised her normal morality the night before.

Mark continued to snooze away. This was Rebecca's chance to escape without being noticed and forget the evening of drunken lust altogether. With the stealth of a burglar, Rebecca gingerly peeled back the blanket, all the while spying on Mark to make sure he wasn't awakened. Satisfied she had removed enough of the covering to swing her legs, Rebecca carefully boosted herself off the bed. She slowly stood until fully erect. Without looking back, Rebecca assumed she was in the clear.

The problem was that Mark's lumpy mattress was very unforgiving. With the loss of Rebecca's weight on the bed, although there wasn't much to begin with given her slender frame, Mark sensed a shift in the comfort of the mattress. It was enough to rouse him.

He blinked his eyes twice to adjust to the bright daylight. What he saw at first pleased him. It was a rose tattoo

Rebecca sported on her lower back. Mark immediately recalled staring at it the night before when they were making love. His smile widened twofold, cherishing the memory.

Perhaps out of curiosity, Rebecca decided to look back one more time to make certain Mark was still in dreamland. She turned her head and much to her surprise she saw Mark admiring her. Rebecca gasped and quickly covered her frontal private areas with a shirt Mark had left on a chair nearby.

"I'm sorry," Mark said, changing his visage to one of concern. "I didn't mean to alarm you."

"No," Rebecca replied, still catching her breath. "I . . . I just didn't expect you to be up."

"Then why did you look back?"

Rebecca had no answer for him. She searched for the proper words, but they never came. Meanwhile, the ends of Mark's lips dropped downward. He was starting to show empathy for the poor woman.

"In that closet to your left, you'll find a blue terrycloth bathrobe. Please put it on." Rebecca glanced in that direction. She was hesitant. The only thing she wanted to do was make a beeline out of Mark's flat. The host pouted at seeing his guest's reluctance. "Please," he insisted softly.

Rebecca gave thought to Mark's request. He appeared to be mild-mannered, and at least Mark showed concern for her. Rebecca decided to take him up on his offer. She darted over to the closet, while continuing to clutch his shirt to her, but she was still feeling uncomfortable with Mark gaping at her.

"If you don't mind, please," Rebecca imposed, twirling her index finger in a circular motion.

Mark smiled and snorted. He threw up his hands and complied with Rebecca's wishes. He focused on the radiant window shade, but his thoughts were about her.

"Listen," Mark began, "I don't want you to think that I was taking advantage of you or something."

Rebecca tossed Mark's shirt back on the chair and donned his robe. Obviously oversized to match Mark's tall frame, the cover allowed only Rebecca's fingertips to show through the sleeves. She tied the sash to secure the garment. But all the while, Rebecca heard what Mark had to say and responded in kind.

"Hey, it's okay. Let's just forget this ever happened. Oh, by the way, you can turn around now."

Mark looked at Rebecca. And despite her hair being totally out of place and her small form wearing something three sizes too big, her youth and beauty were apparent, as he admired her. He certainly didn't want her to leave so readily.

"I at least owe you a decent breakfast before you leave. I mean, if you're that much in a rush, I understand. But I make a mean dish of bacon and eggs and a robust cup of coffee. But I leave the OJ to the Florida guys. What d'ya say?"

"No. I really must be going."

"Hey, c'mon. It's the least I can do for you. I'll even drive you home instead of your having to wait for a taxi."

Rebecca gave it further thought. On the one hand, she wanted to file Mark in the recycling bin of one-night stands, but on the other she was attracted to his genuine hospitality and his offer of a safe ride home. A college teacher, eh? At least it was a noble profession, educating young minds and molding their future. Rebecca eyed her host and nodded in agreement.

Satisfied that he had won over Rebecca's commitment to breakfast, Mark rose from the bed to start his task. Unlike Rebecca, who'd acted more like a prude when finding herself without clothing, Mark wasn't shy about revealing his naked body to her. And the strange thing about it was that Rebecca stared at him with interest, perhaps channeling the voyeuristic curiosity of her subconscious. She intently studied Mark's masculine attributes. And whereas his nudity didn't compel her to disrobe and join him, Rebecca was still captivated by his well-proportioned features. Perhaps the darker side of Rebecca's conscience was taking over her mind and soul, engaging her to ogle Mark greedily.

But the free show quickly came to an end. Mark reached into the top drawer of his dresser and pulled out a pair of maroon jogging pants. From the same space he grabbed a dark-colored tee shirt. Mark donned the garments in order to present a more decent appearance.

With Rebecca in tow like Mary's little lamb, Mark paraded to his modest kitchen and began getting things in order for the morning feast. In the meanwhile, Rebecca sat herself down at one of the two vinyl chairs in front of what could be excused as the kitchen table, although it was only as big as an end table for a lamp. With Mark continuing to dart to and fro for coffee, eggs, bacon, juice and a frying pan, Rebecca eyeballed her surroundings. She noticed that the place could use a little dusting and certainly needed a makeover. Oh, well. Chalk that up to one of the many drawbacks of a bachelor's pad.

Rebecca remained non-talkative, perhaps still apprehensive about being in Mark's home. She looked down at the bathrobe she wore. In a weird display of appreciation, Rebecca began to sniff various sections of it. She was looking for traces of Mark's masculine scent in the robe. At first she tried the sleeves. But that wasn't enough. She then reached for the inside of the left chest area. Voila! The scant levels of testosterone were alive and well. Rebecca inhaled deeply to get a more vivid appreciation of the enticing musk aroma of Mark's body scent.

In between his various tasks, Mark took a glance at Rebecca. He thought she was acting weird with her head buried in the inside of the robe. His eyebrows shifted in wonder as he was stymied by Rebecca's odd behavior. Sensing she was being spied upon, Rebecca halted her peculiar act and cast her eyes up at Mark. She dropped her hands to her side like a dead weight, then sat erect. Rebecca cleared her throat and began to brush back the strands of her hair as if nothing out of the ordinary had transpired. Mark just gave her a quizzical smile before dismissing the episode.

"So," Mark opened, "how do you like your eggs? Scrambled? Over easy?"

"Scrambled is fine," Rebecca replied. "No cheese, please. I can't tolerate a lot of dairy products."

"Lactose intolerant?"

"Yeah, it sort of runs in the family. My mother has the same problem."

Mark poured a glass of orange juice for Rebecca and one for himself. She thanked her host modestly as he plugged in the coffee percolator. Mark then threw several strips of bacon in a pan and turned on the jets underneath the burner.

Feeling useless, not to mention guilty for just sitting there idle, Rebecca responded by asking, "Listen, I feel as though I need to assist you. I mean, I'm just sitting here like a lump and there you are like a whirling dervish."

With a spatula in hand, Mark raised his arms up expansively. "Hey, don't worry. You're the guest here." He dropped his arms, but began to wonder if Rebecca could be of some use after all. At the very least he wanted to give her a sense of contribution. "Okay. Could you please pull out the egg carton from the refrigerator?"

Rebecca smiled and rose from her chair. She opened the refrigerator door and began her search. Although it didn't take long for her to come across the carton, another item in the fridge had caught her eye. It was a tomato on which mold had begun to form. At first she winced at the sight. But then she began to laugh at the idea of anyone keeping something so far past the date of freshness. The mere thought of it had Rebecca chuckling.

"What's so funny?"

"Do you . . .?" Rebecca couldn't complete the sentence due to her uncontrollable giggles. "Do you?" Again she burst out into more laughter. She leaned against the far wall and began to slide down, eyes closed and her mouth open to more laughter. Once she slumped to the floor, she regained her composure enough to continue her thought. "Do you always keep lab experiments in your refrigerator?"

Mark gave her a strange look. He then peeked inside the fridge to discover the rotten tomato. Embarrassed, he reached in and disposed of the spoiled fruit. Meanwhile, Rebecca was now roaring. Mark glared at her.

"Okay, okay. Show's over."

But Rebecca continued to giggle. At that, Mark also fell prey to finding the amusement over the incident. At first his face bore the trace of smile. Then he emitted a short burst of breath through his nose. And in short order he began to laugh with her. He then sat next to her on the floor.

"Do you always make fun of people when they do stupid things?"

"Not really," Rebecca replied, her chortles subsiding. She looked at him with an admiring gaze. Perhaps Mark was the best thing that had happened to her in a long time, especially in light of her break-up with Logan. And because of that, she was remorseful and wanted to offer Mark her apology as an act of contrition. "I'm sorry. I didn't mean to offend you. But you have to admit, it was funny."

"Yeah, I'll agree. But making light at my expense?"

Rebecca realized she had to soothe Mark's bruised ego. She hooked her arm around his and then leaned her head against his shoulder. As an added level of comfort, Rebecca stroked his chest.

"Oh, c'mon," Rebecca cooed. "I promise not to do it again . . . at least this morning."

Both Mark and Rebecca laughed at her remark. "Well," he said, "let's get past breakfast at least."

Rebecca sniffed the air. "Speaking of which . . ."

She nodded toward the stove. Mark catapulted to tend to the bacon. Just in time. The strips were well-done on one side. Mark swiftly turned them over. He then turned to his guest, still sitting comfortably on the floor. He offered her his hand to help her up. Between her own power and Mark's strength, Rebecca rose. There would be no more inspections of his refrigerator. Rebecca again took her seat as she allowed Mark to pamper her with a hearty meal.

Chapter 26

Mark and Rebecca took separate showers before they left his apartment. As he had promised, Mark drove Rebecca home in nearby Cranston. But oddly she told him to pull up by a strip mall.

"Do you need to do some shopping?" Mark was curious.

"No," Rebecca replied. "This is where you can leave me."

He considered the weird location and posed a question. "Let me guess. You live in the back of a store, right?"

Rebecca laughed and told him no. "I help out on Sundays working at the donut shop. It belongs to my mom's best friend. It's a little extra spending money."

"A bit overdressed with that party dress, don't you think?"

"I don't have time to go home and change. Besides, it'll add style."

Mark smiled; his focus on her baby-blue eyes. "So, when can I see you again?"

Sucking in her lower lip, Rebecca reevaluated her situation. Although she was attracted to Mark's good looks and charm, she didn't feel right about jumping into a new relationship so soon after losing Logan. She was having second thoughts on the whole entanglement thing, and felt the need to pull back on the throttle. She began to cast about in search of the proper response to Mark without damaging his feelings.

"Look," Rebecca replied, fumbling the words along the way. "You're a terrific guy and all, but . . . I mean . . . damn! What happened last night was just a big mistake. You do realize that, don't you?"

Mark leaned his head back against his car window. Stunned by her comment, Mark had difficulty digesting Rebecca's words. He'd heard them before from previous relationships gone sour. He was very much attracted to Rebecca and he wanted to let her know of his feelings about the escapade the prior evening.

"You don't know how beautiful you were last night," Mark countered. "That was the best night I've had in a long time . . . a very long time. From the party right on through when we made passionate love together. Nothing else can compare to that. And you were the best part. And now you want to take that away, as if it never happened. How can you? How could you?"

"We didn't make passionate love, we had sex. There's a difference. I don't even remember all the details. That's what happens when you down a couple of screwdrivers, rum and Cokes, and gin and tonics. I was compromised."

"And what about the way you were sidling up to me back at the apartment? I suppose you were compromised back there, too?"

"I was showing compassion for you after criticizing you about that rotten tomato," Rebecca pleaded. "I'm just getting over a break-up. I need time before I immerse myself in another relationship."

His face was reddening. "What's the matter? I wasn't *man* enough for you?"

Rebecca sucked her teeth and rolled her eyes. "God, what is it about you men? One little ounce of rejection and you roll out the *I'm Mr. Macho!* carpet. You make it sound like your ego is deflated." She drew a deep sigh. "Look, I'm sorry. Maybe we can be friends."

That wasn't going to cut it with Mark. He was developing deep feelings for Rebecca. He truly felt that she just might be his soul mate. But Rebecca's expressed thoughts said otherwise. Suddenly disenchanted, Mark gave her a sendoff. He gestured toward the bakery.

"There's probably an overweight truck driver in there in need of a couple of jelly rolls and a cup of coffee. Why don't you go tend to him?"

With eyes squinted and lips puckered, it was easy to discern Rebecca's anger at Mark's barb. After releasing a disapproving grunt, she quickly exited Mark's car and slammed the passenger door in her wake. Realizing he had to get ready for work himself, Mark disengaged the car from park to drive, and sped away to return home and change into his work uniform.

Chapter 27

Roger and Beth had an uneventful day after the party the night before. Thanks to the clean-up team they'd hired, there wasn't much for them to do except to relax. For Beth that meant going out and doing some preliminary Christmas shopping with the holiday less than two months away. For Roger it was grading some papers while listening to Mozart.

As he was going over one such set of papers, Roger heard the doorbell ring. Even one entrenched in the vigorous sounding of the horns of classical music would have been able to hear it clearly. Knowing that Beth had her keys, Roger was perplexed as to who could be there. With a furrowed brow of suspicion, he lowered the music from the stereo and gimped his way to the front door. Upon opening it, Roger was stunned to see who was on the other side.

"Why, hello, Mark. This is certainly unexpected."

He didn't say anything to his father. Mark offered a hint of a grin and held up his hand, to stop a barrage of questioning. He politely asked Roger if he could come in, to which the elder Lavoie extended an open arm, allowing his son to enter.

Mark looked around the living room. He scanned the walls, floor and furniture and was amazed by how immaculate everything was. One would never know that a party was held here the night before.

"The cleaning people you hired did a great job," said Mark.

"Isn't it fantastic? Excellent work! They were worth every penny. Can I get you anything?"

"No . . . I'm . . . I'm good."

"Come sit down. The sofa should be dry by now."

The obedient son respected his father's wish. He sat down with his hands folded, almost withdrawn. Roger inherently knew there was something troubling Mark, but he didn't want to bring it up; at least, not right away.

"Are you working at Best Buy today?"

"Yeah. I have to be there by one. I'm there till closing. It's less than an hour away. I'll make it."

Roger flashed a smile, but he could no longer fight the need to pry into the reason for Mark's sudden appearance. "You've come because you need something, Mark. And it isn't to check on how well the place has been cleaned up. What's on your mind?"

Mark was a little embarrassed to discuss the issue at first. But then he reasoned he'd made the trip to see Roger, not the other way around. "When I left last night, I took a girl with me. Her name's Rebecca. She's a friend of Heather's, you know, Professor Asmundsson's admin?" Roger nodded. "Well, anyway, I took her back to my place last night. We had sex. But to me it was more than that. I felt a solid connection between us, you know? I mean, there was some synergy going on. Then, after making her breakfast, I drove her over to a bakery shop in a strip mall down in Cranston. And she just flipped me. I don't know, Dad. Maybe it's just me. Maybe I'm sending the wrong vibes to women. I mean, considering how many I have dated?"

"And you came to me for a little fatherly advice," responded a smiling Roger. "Son, maybe this Rebecca girl wasn't meant for you. Her rejection might be a blessing in disguise. Perhaps you might not be ready to settle down yet."

"I've considered that idea for a while now. But since I'm going to be teaching at Winston, I thought it just might be the right time. And I thought Rebecca just might be the girl."

Roger extended his hand to rest on Mark's shoulder. "There's still a whole lifetime ahead of you. Besides, women are as unpredictable as the weather. Just when you figure them out, they throw you a curve. Don't let it floor you."

Mark appreciated the pearls of wisdom from Roger. They shook hands as the younger Lavoie rose to proceed to his current position, now counting the days to his retirement there.

107

Chapter 28

Her car was in front of the Cranston Victorian house where she had an apartment on the third floor. But it didn't do Rebecca any good there when she got off from work at the donut shop at seven. Fortunately for Rebecca, it was no more than a good half-hour walking distance. Although the evening was dark with a brisk chilly mid-autumn wind kicking up, there was no rain and the area was fairly safe. Her first order of business was to feed her little orange tabby cat, Feisty.

When Rebecca flipped on the front light switch, Feisty greeted her with a heartfelt meow. Rebecca gave the cat a sympathetic grin.

"Aw, don't worry. Mommy's going to feed you right now."

She finished feeding the ravenous little kitty when suddenly her cell phone began to ring. The ID registered it was her mom, Sheryl. While she had maintained a good relationship with her mother, Rebecca wasn't in the mood to talk with her. But like the respectful daughter that she was, Rebecca accepted the call. Unfortunately, after a cordial greeting, she got an earful from Sheryl.

"I had a call from Rachel a little while ago," Sheryl began. "She was upset over the way you were dressed at her store today. A party dress? And she noticed you weren't wearing a bra! Rebecca, you practically had your boobs hanging out in front of the customers! I raised you better! Do you know how embarrassing it was for me to hear all this from her?"

"Oh, Mom, please! I wasn't trying to be provocative. Rachel likes to exaggerate."

"Rachel's my good friend. I've known her a very long time, longer than you've been around. And if there's one thing I know about her it's that she doesn't lie. She runs a respectable donut shop. And here you were dressing like you were tending bar in a seedy joint on the wrong side of town!"

"I'm . . . I'm sorry. I didn't have time to go home and change."

"It's that Logan guy you've been dating, isn't it?"

"No." There was a little hesitation. "We're through. If you must know, I went to a party last night at the request of my friend Heather. It was for some guy who's going to become a teacher for Heather's boss at Winston. He was cute, and I was drunk. The next thing I knew I went with him to his apartment later and then . . . well . . ."

Rebecca didn't complete the sentence. She didn't have to. Sheryl deduced what had happened next.

"I suppose you didn't protect yourself either. What the hell has gotten into you, Rebecca?"

Rebecca rolled her eyes. She'd had her fill of Sheryl's lecture. With a sarcastic final sendoff, Rebecca then clicked the phone off and flung it toward her sofa, scaring Feisty in the process. After seeing the cat scamper away in fear because of her own pent-up disgust, Rebecca felt even more miserable. Feisty was in hiding until his owner cooled her heels.

She trudged over to the refrigerator and opened the freezer portion. There waiting for her was a gallon of rocky road ice cream she had bought when the weather was still quite warm for lower New England. It had already been opened, but there wasn't much taken out. For someone critical over keeping a rotten tomato in the fridge, Rebecca was one to talk, holding on to a nearly full gallon of indulgence that was three months old.

After removing the lid, Rebecca looked at the frozen dairy treat with ambivalence. She really didn't need to put on a few inches and spoil her hourglass figure, but she did want to wallow in self-pity. Rebecca curled her lips downward, furrowed her forehead, still absorbed in the vortex of forsaking her petite frame for the panacea to extinguish her anxiety. *Oh, what the heck.* She grabbed a huge tablespoon from her utensils drawer and began to excavate the rectangular box for a bit of oasis from a society full of disdain toward her.

It seemed no one understood the plight of poor Rebecca—not even her own mother. And when you can't gain the sympathy from dear old mom, who can you turn to?

She portioned a huge amount of the frozen delicacy into a large bowl. *Screw it! I'll get fat and fuck everybody!* Satisfied with the *healthy* portion, she pranced over to her living room couch and used the nearby remote to turn on the TV. She began to channel surf. She wasn't in pursuit of any particular program. She could have watched a test pattern and remained glued to it. Clearly her mind wasn't focused on what was on the screen. It was just a reason to pass the time before going to bed; that is, if her brain was sufficiently numbed to all that had been happening to her.

Rebecca was normally a slave to romantic movies and books of the same. But watching or reading about love connections, even if between fictional characters, was not in the offing, given her present state of mind. Instead, she was viewing a program that wouldn't normally be on her must-see list. Guys collecting junk was not one of her interests. But Rebecca's mind was elsewhere as she forklifted one shovelful of ice cream after the other.

Just as she devoured another spoonful, her cell phone rang. Without expending much energy, she reached over to see the caller ID. Rebecca was praying that it wasn't Sheryl trying to continue to lecture her. Perhaps she might have been hoping for Logan to call her, with a bouquet of roses in his voice, asking for forgiveness. But probably even better, it was Heather calling her, and for Rebecca, that was the one person she needed to reach out to above anyone else, for comfort in her behavioral malfunction. She immediately plopped the bowl on the adjacent coffee table and muted the TV.

"Hey, what's up?"

"I didn't get a chance to say goodbye to you after you left last night," Heather replied. "I tried texting you, but you didn't reply. Damn, you were all over Mark by night's end. My God, what did you two do afterwards, as if I didn't know?"

"Well, if you must know, we went over to his place and screwed each other's brains out."

"Oooh! Awesome! I always wondered how big he was. Is he?"

"Heather, I was wasted last night. I don't fucking remember." She paused for a moment. Rebecca vividly recalled the sight of Mark's endowment. But it was from that morning when he rose from his bed to don some clothing, not from the night before. And that picture of him was so etched in Rebecca's mind, that it was as if Mark was in the room with her at that moment. But she wanted to downplay the entire incident. "Besides, what matter is it anyway?"

"Gee, I'm sorry! You don't have to jump down my throat! I was only teasing."

Rebecca drew a deep sigh. Her brief experience with Mark was unpleasant. She was so depressed about it that she failed to see the humor in Heather's ribbing. Scratching her forehead, Rebecca became more conciliatory.

"I apologize for getting on your case, Heather. You know how those one-night stands work. They don't. I tried to pacify Mark, you know, like a 'let's be friends' type of deal. But that didn't wash with him. I guess he wanted something more intimate."

"You know, if I were a man, I'd jump at you, too. You're very pretty."

Rebecca took comfort in the compliment, certain that Heather had no lesbian love fantasies about her. "I see where you're going with this. So, you think I made a mistake dissing him, huh?"

"Let's just call it a misstep. I've talked with Mark a few times. He really is down-to-earth. I think you should give him another try. Delete Logan from your brain. He's not coming back. I know you'd like to take a breather, but guys like Mark don't come around too often. Trust me. He's the answer to all your problems."

And as Heather made her case for Mark, Rebecca looked over at the corner of her living room. She visualized him standing there, like a trophy waiting to be taken. Suddenly that awkward moment in the strip mall parking lot became a distant memory and only Mark's wholesome qualities emerged. A smile creased her lips as Rebecca saw the merits of Heather's suggestion.

"Okay. You've sold me."

Chapter 29

That Monday evening, Mark returned home from working at the electronics store. He was totally drained and wanted to do nothing else than to flick on the TV and watch the remainder of the Monday Night Football game between the Chargers and Steelers. He reached over to the refrigerator for a cold beer and popped it open as he shuffled to an armchair.

He was fortunate when he turned on the set. The game was only one quarter in and he'd only missed one scoring play. He was now counting the days when he could watch the NFL every autumn Sunday and Monday night when his days at Best Buy were over.

Mark took one swig of the fermented beverage. He allowed the brine to slosh around his gums as if it were mouthwash. A few spins inside his cheeks and Mark gulped the high malt and hops concoction, which made its descent down his throat. He then released a satisfied burp as his body was giving its approval of the brewski.

He wanted to pace his intake and so he decided to set the brown bottle on the nearby table. Mark was watching Pittsburgh lining up for a field goal when his phone began to ring. He wanted to relax and watch the remaining portion of the game in private and thought about ignoring the call altogether, but Mark took a glance at the caller ID on the phone display and noticed it was his good friend Hunter Morales. As much as he was looking forward to seeing the rest of the football game, Mark muted the set and took Hunter's call.

"Hey, fossil man," Mark greeted. "What's happening?"

"Nothing much. I figured you wouldn't be home until about now with that crazy schedule you keep."

"Perfect timing. How are things at the museum?"

"Great. That grant will be coming soon. Brazil, here I come!"

"Awesome! Just watch out for those anacondas. They can be pretty big."

"Tell me about it. Listen, Mark. I've got to tell you about that chick Kayla I met at your party. Whoa! Dude, I had trouble keeping up with her! Man, we were doing it in the bedroom, on the kitchen table, on the floor. Check this out. One time, when we were doing it in the bathroom, she introduced me to a new position there."

"Sounds like you two had a blast."

"That's only the beginning. I'm taking her out after work tomorrow night. You know, the usual. Dinner. Maybe a movie. And then back to her place to finish where we left off. Would you believe she's pierced down there?"

"That's a little too much information."

There was a moment of silence before Hunter continued.

"So, what about you and that blonde you were with?"

"Rebecca? Oh, she's all right. But there's nothing going on between us. I guess the chemistry wasn't there."

It pained Mark to say this. It was far from the truth. What he didn't want to convey to Hunter was his heartbroken response to her rejection. Mark was glad Hunter wasn't talking to him through Skype. His friend would have noticed a tear running down his cheek. Rebecca touched his heart like no one else had. And now she'd wrenched the love out of him and tossed it away.

He was about to continue his talk when suddenly the buzzer from the entrance to the building resonated. The crackly irritating noise sounded like the one signifying a wrong answer on a quiz show. Furthermore, the ring wasn't consistent. Its sporadic sound gave one the impression of a Morse code sequence.

Mark asked Hunter to hold the line while he buzzed in the supposed guest. All the while his mind was curious about who could be paying him a visit at nearly ten o'clock at night. It wasn't soon after that Mark heard a rap on the door.

"Who is it?"

"Pizza delivery!"

Mark noticed the voice was that of a woman. Thank goodness for the fisheye peephole so he could see who was on the other side of the door. At a quick glance, Mark saw

Rebecca dressed in a woolen brown coat and sporting a red-and-white striped ski cap to protect her against the chilly evening. She was holding a flat, square pizza box in her hands. Mark's heart began to thaw, but it wasn't until he unlatched the two deadbolts and opened the door to see Rebecca in full view that his disposition changed entirely.

Still holding the pizza box in her arms, Rebecca smiled.

"I've got one with fresh mozzarella, tomato and basil. Would you like some?"

Before taking the pizza from Rebecca, Mark had to bid goodbye to his friend. "Hunter? You'll never guess who just showed up at my door. I've got to go, dude."

With a smile as broad as New England, Mark took the box from Rebecca as he relished the visit from the attractive blonde. It wasn't hunger for pizza that lit up Mark. It was hunger for love.

Chapter 30

Except for one beer to wash down her pizza, Rebecca refrained from imbibing any alcoholic beverages. The result was a more intimate conversation with Mark, where the two got to know each other better. Mark learned that Rebecca worked for the Templeton's Department store chain in their main office in Downtown Providence in accounting. She also had a mother who was self-determined, especially after her alcoholic father had left the family two decades earlier. Rebecca had a younger sister and a younger brother.

When it came to discussing his family, Mark was fairly laconic. Rebecca already knew of his father and learned that Beth worked in an administrative capacity at a hospital. But when it came time to mentioning his mother, he was extremely reticent to visit that part of his life. He simply said that Margaret was institutionalized for a nervous breakdown that seemed to have no possibility of reversal. Much in the same way that Rebecca didn't want to elaborate on her abusive dad, Mark was reluctant to discuss Margaret. But that was okay with Rebecca. As Mark had respected her wishes not to probe the inner workings of the Dyer patriarch, Rebecca allowed Mark to keep his deep thoughts of his helpless mother to himself. And that worked out best for both. Each had dirty laundry that neither wanted to bring out concerning a parent.

Unlike her initial intimate encounter with Mark, Rebecca made this meeting more personal. There was no wild sex fling like that of two nights earlier. They had a long chat about their families, their likes, their dislikes. And after the pizza was gone, they relaxed on his couch and smothered each other with long sensuous kisses.

Realizing the lateness of the hour, Mark insisted that Rebecca remain there for the night, instead of driving back home in the impending severe rainstorm. She agreed to stay until morning when she would then return home and prepare for another day at the office. And so they snuggled together in Mark's bed and caressed affectionately. No fornication. No heated passion. And that seemed to work.

The next morning Mark saw to it that Rebecca didn't leave without something substantial in her system. He poured her orange juice, brewed a huge pot of coffee, and prepared a bowl of piping-hot instant oatmeal. To enhance the hearty cereal, Mark folded blueberries into her portion. In self-deprecating humor, Mark joked that he did check the expiration of the fruit before adding the berries, to which Rebecca answered with a teasing smile as she pointed her tablespoon at him.

As was the case two mornings earlier, Rebecca donned Mark's oversized terrycloth bathrobe to wear at the kitchen table. She had grown to like wearing the garment. Rebecca was fond of the association it held and the sensual mental images it evoked of Mark's masculinity. She conjured up tender thoughts of Mark holding his arms around her amorously much in the same way as the bathrobe was enveloping her.

Soon after breakfast was over, Rebecca slapped on her sweatshirt, jeans and sneakers, along with her coat and ski cap. It was time to head home, shower, and pick out the appropriate attire she'd wear to work.

Mark didn't want Rebecca to leave. But even he had to respect and honor her need to dress adequately and be punctual for her job, even though he wasn't due in at work until nearly eleven.

He was seeing her through her clothing. All Mark could think of was Rebecca's shapely hourglass figure and her silky smooth skin. He wanted more of it, but he was a gentleman and allowed Rebecca to make her own decisions, uninfluenced by intoxication that is, hoping she'd carry their newfound romance to a more lustful level.

As she was gathering her handbag, Rebecca marched to the front door where Mark was waiting for her.

"Thanks for breakfast," Rebecca said with a smile.

"Thank you for the pizza, even if it meant chewing on an antacid tablet last night."

"Oh, I'm sorry."

"Hey, I was only kidding."

Rebecca giggled at Mark's comical reply. She then plopped down her handbag on the counter nearest the door. Rebecca pulled out a pen and began to scribble her name and mobile number down on a slip of paper. She was about to hand it to Mark when she teased him by pulling the paper back before he could clutch it. While sporting a smile with her lower lip sucked in, Rebecca gazed at Mark with bedroom eyes.

"I'll give it to you on one condition."

"Shoot."

"You come over to my place next time. Deal?"

"Deal!"

"Oh, and bring some wine. I'm a sucker for chardonnay."

Rebecca draped her arms around Mark's muscular neck. He in turn slipped his hands around her slender waist. They gazed deep into each other's eyes. Slowly they moved their lips together. At first there was a soft peck, but immediately their mouths welded together and their tongues entwined.

Realizing the time, Rebecca broke away. She looked at the crumpled paper she still held and gave it to Mark.

"Here you go," she admonished, "call me."

She flashed a coquettish smile to him that said *You'd better call me.* And with that Rebecca sashayed down the hallway to the staircase. All the while Mark watched the flirt lustfully as she moved away from him. As she turned around to head to the street below, Rebecca gave Mark one more wave as she wiggled her fingers at him. Mark grinned and simply held up his hand to wave back in appreciation.

With Rebecca out of sight, Mark looked down at the slip of paper as if it were a cherished prize he had won. He leaned back against the door and looked up at the hallway ceiling with glazed eyes. He was fantasizing about the next time he would be with her.

Just then Tommy McManus, Mark's fifty-something neighbor down the hall, popped out of his apartment. Sensing that Tommy was nearby, Mark snapped out of his trance and offered a gentle, "Good morning," to him. Tommy gave Mark a strange look and replied the same. *Tommy wouldn't understand,* Mark thought to himself. *Or if he did, it isn't any of his business.* But for Mark, all he could think about was that Rebecca was beginning to show the love for him that he had for her.

Chapter 31

Roger had finished his classes for the day. He was still walking on cloud nine with the knowledge that Mark was going to be teaching at the institute soon. And Roger had even received word from Mark that his son's love life had taken a turn for the better with Rebecca's visit the night before. The tenured professor was delighted to learn of it.

The moment he opened the front door, Roger heard the phone ring. Not pleased that he had to drop everything to answer it, he hurriedly picked up the receiver. When he learned who was on the other end, Roger cursed under his breath. *I nearly broke my neck in dashing across the room, only to discover Mort is calling me!*

"Hello, Roger. How did the party go for your son the other night?"

"It was great," Roger replied. "So, how was the concert with that lady friend of yours?"

"Oh, you mean Jacqueline? It was splendid. We had a wonderful evening. But nothing much went on between us, I'm afraid. She did tell me she thought the concert was spectacular. By the way, how has your son been since he received the confirmation?"

"Mark is quite well. He also just met a young woman at the party. I suspect it may lead to something serious between them."

"That's great news, Roger. Why don't you stop by my office so we can discuss all the details? I'll even have some Earl Grey tea ready for you."

"Really, Mort, I don't see the purpose of us getting together again. My principal source of anxiety was worry over Mark getting a job teaching at Winston, and that has been resolved. I see no reason to further discuss the condition of my ex-wife. Her case is regrettably unchanged. I think this physician/patient matter is closed. Now, if you don't mind, Mort, I'd like to focus on the positive aspects of my life, especially with Mark landing the teaching job and perhaps resolving his more personal matter. I wish you all the best and I'd be happy to recommend anyone to you who may be in need of psychological assistance. Goodbye, Mort."

Roger didn't allow Mort to get in another word. And why should he? The only thing Mort would bring up would be some contrived need to continue the therapy sessions in order to exorcize Roger's inner demons entirely. That and perhaps his need to raid Roger's bank account.

But Mort's expertise didn't excoriate those subconscious monsters. If anything, thanks to Mort's probing, they were now more energized and had become larger than life. And all Roger could think of was the nightmare from twenty years earlier.

In a flashback he remembered the vivid details of the trial and the accusations thrown at him by Chloe Haber-Doyle and the ruthless attacks by ADA Claire Torelli. Roger was beginning to sweat profusely just thinking about that dark area of his history, reliving the mental anguish as if it had only happened the day before. Plus, Roger recalled the money he had to outlay for his lawyer, Vance Beckwith, and how he almost lost his position at Winston as a young professor back then.

The disturbing recollections prompted Roger to head to the refrigerator where a cold bottle of cabernet sauvignon awaited him. He had trouble holding onto the carafe of the wine. The ghosts of his past tormenting him caused his hands to tremble.

Roger took a deep breath to regain his composure. At this point he was only interested in making sure he wasn't going to spill the wine all over the place. Once he decanted the right amount, he placed the rest of the fermented beverage back in the icebox, double-checking where it sat in case of the need for an emergency refueling.

With his nerves still shot from the horrifying images, Roger took one huge sip and guzzled the rest down as though the wine were water. He gently placed his glass on the adjacent counter, which he used to support his weak legs. Roger closed his eyes and allowed the alcohol do its trick in soothing his anguish. He felt a little giddiness, but that was a good thing. *Erase all these specters!* He commanded his subconscious.

Roger was tempted to imbibe even more. *Oh, what the heck. Why not?* He was well-stocked with a few bottles as it was. Roger and Beth had an affinity for wines of all sorts, particularly the red variety. They would buy bottles by a case of twelve. And once in a while they would save a bottle or two and place them down in the basement. It wasn't as if the Lavoie household had a proverbial wine cellar down there, but they did stock a good number of bottles, especially if the years were of a great vintage.

Although he was more composed, Roger couldn't resist another sip of the cabernet sauvignon. But he had to be reasonable. He only drew two fingers this time. And just as he had done with the first glass, Roger knocked it back as if he were still living his days as a college student nearly forty years earlier, consuming shot after shot, like in a contest with his school buddies in a bar.

If the first glass didn't totally comfort Roger, the mini shot did. He was beginning to feel much better and even forgot what his thoughts were centered on altogether.

The wall clock in the kitchen read four-eleven. Darkness was beginning to creep in as twilight was sweeping across the land. This was typical with the changing of the clocks back to standard time. And given Rhode Island's longitudinal location, night would come in earlier than in, say, Cincinnati.

It was a little early to prepare dinner, as Beth wasn't due home for at least another ninety minutes. Besides, tonight only veggie burgers were on the menu. Fairly simple.

The wine was taking effect, but Roger was not about to snooze the drink off. It was only meant to erase some horrid memories, at least for the time being. He needed a diversion to further ease his mind. So Roger decided to go on the internet, something he was not obsessive about, to pass the time.

He noticed there was a ton of emails for him. Beth was more of the web junkie and checked her email daily. For Roger, looking at it once a week was a lot to ask.

Most of the material was pretty standard. There were notices of Lasik surgery, e-cigarettes, work-at-home schemes, raising one's testosterone levels and finding a sexy date. The more personal emails were from those thanking both him and Beth for the wonderful party the other evening.

And then there was one email that stunned Roger. The more he looked at it, the more shocked he was. A sense of fright overcame him. His hands began to shake. Roger couldn't believe the name of the sender. It read *fairmaiden58*. He didn't have to open the message for Roger knew the sender's identity. A simple *Hello, Roger* was typed on the subject line, but the professor knew the greeting wasn't cordial.

Still suffering from his shock of disbelief, Roger sat back in the executive-style chair in front of the PC, trying to drink it all in. He didn't know what to make of the inquiry at first, and he was hesitant to open it. Perhaps there might be a virus attached to it, thus rendering his hard drive useless. No, perhaps not. He hadn't heard from the sender in ages, and he was hoping to keep it that way. But that wishful thinking had apparently gone by the wayside. All Roger could do was to stare at the email in terror.

She found me!

Chapter 32

Siobhan O'Mara. It was Margaret's sister who had sent Roger the email. He hadn't heard from her in ages, and he was hoping to keep it that way. But the jig was up. She had somehow discovered Roger's new email address and sent him a message. Not just any message. It was to inform him that she was still around and wasn't planning to go anywhere else soon.

This was the same woman Roger had to explain away to Mark with a lame excuse about why she wasn't at the party the other night. The real reason was that Roger had no intention of inviting her. He wanted to keep a safe distance from her. *Well, that's not going to happen soon. Maybe if I changed my address again with my ISP,* Roger thought. But then that would mean informing colleagues, friends, neighbors, and family members of the new address, and he decided it was too much hassle to do it. It might be best to simply ignore Siobhan's request to open dialogue.

But then his curious side got hold of him. For as much as he wanted to avoid Siobhan like the plague, he was inquisitive as to why she wanted to barge into his life once more. Was it to make him feel uncomfortable? That certainly was a possibility. But there was no way of knowing without reading the message. And so Roger bit the bullet and decided to open it anyway.

He was delighted that there were no attachments in the message. He wouldn't have opened them anyway. But at least there was no malice connected with the missive. Not yet anyway. Roger read on.

Hey,

I don't know why you continue to shun me. It's been like this now for over twenty years. I suppose that weekend on Cape Cod back in the summer of '92 meant nothing to you. Symposium in Boston?

Hah! That was your cute excuse to my dumbass sister, wasn't it? We had something magical going on, Roger. What happened?

I know you got pissed when I didn't hide our affair from Maggie. But that was the master plan, wasn't it? That's what drove her to Darren Haber. And then after you took care of poor old Darren in an act of so-called revenge, you sent his body parts one by one to Maggie. You and I were hoping she might have committed suicide. But that just drove her crazy instead. Just as well. You and I know she's incurable over there at Crenshaw.

And then that jury acquitted you on Darren's murder and driving Maggie insane. Deep inside I thought you might be cleared of the charges. The prosecution didn't have all the facts. Your decision to secure a very clever lawyer also helped. And, after hearing the verdict myself that day, I thought for sure that maybe we might be together at last. I guess you felt it wasn't appropriate. My family would have felt the same way.

Strange, isn't it? How the rest of my family would've liked to see you hanged from the highest tree, but I felt differently. Oh, I put up a good front for them. But all the while I was still holding a torch for you.

Then, after you got that divorce from Maggie, I thought for sure you'd be with me. But then along came that former nurse. Her name is Elizabeth, right? Gee, you must have a thing for nurses. First Maggie, now Elizabeth. I think her nickname is Beth, no? You broke my heart again. Maybe I'm a little crazy, but I still have a thing for you. Sure, you've got a lot of gray in that beard of yours. And you don't have as much hair as you once did. Plus you must have a few extra pounds now that you're heading toward your senior years. What the heck. I don't have the same hourglass figure from thirty years ago anymore, and I've hit menopause. But that means I don't menstruate anymore. I know you always complained to Maggie years ago when she had her periods or cramps. She told me.

I know you had a party for Mark for landing the teaching job at Winston the other night. And I wasn't invited! I was pretty miffed about that. He is still my sister's son and I deserved that much. Don't ask me how I know these things or else I'd have to kill the messenger. Killing. Hmmm. That's really your department, isn't it?

Well, I've said enough. I'm sure you got the point. Don't wimp out on me, Roger. Let's at least get together for a lunch someday. Hey, that's a start. Where it goes from there will entirely depend upon you. C'mon, we need to resolve a few matters between us and reminisce on all the old times. More importantly, we need to look to the future . . . *our future!*

Ciao,
Siobhan

Siobhan left a phone number at the end of the message, as if inviting Roger to take the bait and call. Instead, Roger just reclined in his chair. He was wondering if Siobhan was twisted. But then he recalled that magical weekend she mentioned. It was Friday, July the tenth, right through that Sunday the twelfth, a spectacular weekend, Roger remembered. The temperature was in the low 80s, but the onshore breezes off the Atlantic made it pleasant. And there wasn't any rain.

And then there were the times when they made love. Roger fondly remembered how soft Siobhan's skin felt next to his and how he had compared her impassioned orgasmic cries to those of Margaret's. Imagine that. Deciphering which sister was better in bed.

But then Roger's inner soul got the better of him. His angelic conscience was pleading with him to ditch Siobhan and ignore her sexual advances toward him. And Roger had done the right thing by telling Siobhan it was a fling that would be best soon forgotten. But Siobhan would have none of that. She'd always had a crush on Roger, mainly because Margaret would titillate her sister with wild stories of lovemaking sessions between her and her husband. That fueled the inner erotic fantasies Siobhan held secretly. But

125

she hadn't been able to keep it hidden any longer. No, Siobhan had wanted a taste to see what Margaret always raved about. She needed to experience the sensual pleasures for herself. That's how it all began.

Roger remembered how he became a party in every man's fantasy of loving a woman on the side while still married to another. But eventually, his guilt-ridden inner self had snapped him to his senses.

Siobhan didn't take Roger's rejection well. In fact, she dismissed it as a hiccup in love's journeys. *He'll come back to me. I know he will,* she'd decided. But it became apparent that Roger's deferment was final. That was when Siobhan took matters into her own hands and tattled to Margaret about the lustful Cape Cod weekend. She wanted to drive a wedge between her sister and Roger.

But she also knew of Roger's jealous tendencies. So when Margaret repaid Roger's sin by cheating of her own with Haber, her husband reacted accordingly.

And then came the law. Roger went through hell with the pursuit of the police on the Haber case as well as the matter of Margaret's madness. And then the prosecution went after him and Roger had been forced to hire Beckwith and shell out to get the best defense counsel possible. No help from Siobhan came. She just stood on the sidelines as a spectator.

And then there was his job at Winston, which was on thin ice over the episode. Indeed, if Torelli had presented a more compelling argument to persuade the jury, Roger would be in prison right now. Is that how someone should be treated by a so-called admirer? No, Roger was about to delete the message.

But just as he was about to depress the button on his keyboard, Roger looked at Siobhan's inquiry one last time. He had second thoughts. Perhaps there were some things he needed to get off his chest with her. Maybe it was time to air that dirty laundry and lay out his grievances with her. Yes, that might make this situation a little better, or at the very least, tolerable.

Roger picked up his cell phone as he decided to take up Siobhan's invitation to call her.

Chapter 33

Roger had called Siobhan later that afternoon. He kept his conversation with her brief and to the point. He didn't want to go into sordid details, rehashing old stories and their past history. That was something reserved for a chat over a cup of coffee. And Siobhan agreed. Just how can you truthfully go over various subject matters by just instant messaging over the internet, or worse, exchanging email, which could meander for quite a while before getting to the point? The bistro was the solution. The Dunkin' Donuts on Division Street was the mutually agreed upon meeting venue.

He had finished his morning lectures and had one more class for the day at three. Roger still had well over two hours before his next session, but he was growing impatient waiting. He began to trace the patterns on his ceramic mug while occasionally glancing around at the various patrons. Roger took small, unsatisfying sips of the coffee, and even worse, was nibbling at his blueberry scone like a pilfering mouse.

Although time was still on his side, Roger didn't like the fact that Siobhan didn't show up on time. Just like his son, Roger thought. Maybe that's where Mark got his lack of punctuality.

Roger approached the counterperson again. She began to pour him a refill while he slipped her two Georges without looking for change. Roger would be wired for his afternoon lecture, and thus keep his students on the edge of their seats. But no sooner had Roger left the counter than Siobhan decided to make her entrance.

A slightly rumpled beige raincoat cloaked her frame. Underneath she wore a smart navy-blue blazer with matching skirt and a white silk blouse peeking through it. A simple necklace with what appeared to be sapphire beads, but in reality was nothing more than costume jewelry, graced her top. With her high heels clicking along the tiled floor, Siobhan made her way to plop herself down at his table.

"Sorry I'm late."

Roger hadn't seen Siobhan for years. In her facial features, she hadn't changed much since the last time he saw her. But she was honest and correct from her email message to him that she did add a couple of pounds. But they weren't enough to turn away the men nearby from gawking at her.

Roger wasn't impressed. He was committed to Beth and nothing was going to get in the way of that, not even Siobhan. Still, he was there to meet her. If nothing else, Roger wanted to appease Siobhan and move on with his life.

Just at the moment Roger was about to open up the conversation, Siobhan's cell phone began to ring. Embarrassed by the interruption, Siobhan held up her index finger at Roger. She murmured that she had to take the call. Inasmuch as she wanted to discuss all matters relevant, Siobhan was a slave to her phone. It played an integral part in her business as a real estate agent, a field in which she had become quite successful. The last time Roger had seen Siobhan, she had discussed with him the possibility of entering that field on a whim. Now it appeared that the lark had blossomed into a full-time profession. He was amused by her demeanor and comportment while talking to a potential buyer. *Maybe she's changed after all,* Roger thought. *Perhaps the flighty exterior from years ago has galvanized into that of a serious and disciplined businesswoman.* Siobhan ended her conversation and put her smart phone away. The rest of the time was to be devoted to speaking with the professor.

"I apologize for the call," Siobhan began. "That was a client who wants to see a property again that I showed her over in Fall River."

"Massachusetts?" Roger pawed at his beard. "You now have a license to sell in that state, too?"

"Oh, I've had that for the past five years now. I also have a license to sell in Connecticut. I've sold property over in Mystic. It's very nice over there. Not just for the summer, either. You should take you wife there someday. I was right in my email. It is Beth, isn't it?"

"Yes, her name is Beth. And, yes, we have gone down to Mystic a few times during summers past."

Siobhan noted that she was without a cup of coffee and something to nosh on. She excused herself while leaving Roger to his devices.

While waiting for her, Roger began to postulate the reasoning why Siobhan wanted to meet. They were last together when Mark graduated with his Bachelor's from Winston five and a half years earlier. Siobhan wasn't invited when Mark received his Master's degree in mathematics. But then again, Mark didn't make a big production of it, either. Still, Roger preferred not having Siobhan's company. Not just because she was his ex-sister-in-law, but because of her fanatical infatuation with him. Imagine that, a man whose looks perhaps only Beth could appreciate, still catching the eye of another, successful and attractive woman.

But was there an ulterior motive for Siobhan's seeking out Roger? Certainly it wasn't a scheme to get her sister to become a permanent resident in an insane asylum. She had already played a role in making that happen. So what was it then?

Roger still wasn't comfortable about accepting Siobhan's invite. But there was that sliver of lingering doubt, that suspicion of something Siobhan might have been keeping a secret that was weighing heavily on him. It wasn't just a cat's curiosity. No, Roger was intrigued by it. It was more like a deadly car crash. You might not stomach the corpses being hauled out from the wreckage, yet the full magnanimity of the horrific accident draws you like a sports spectator to a rousing game.

Siobhan paid the cashier for her chicken Panini sandwich and soft drink. It was a good portion and enough to sustain her through to dinner, after she closed another successful deal. It was time to get down to business.

"It's so nice to see you again, Roger."

"Really?" Roger sized her up. "I'm very curious. Just how were you able to find my new email address?"

"I can't reveal my sources. But what difference does it make? I know where you live anyway. I'm sure you may have changed your home phone number, but you haven't changed your location."

"Don't you dare go near my home! I have told Beth about you. She wouldn't stand for it. She wants me to get on with my life and doesn't want you anywhere near our place."

"You tell that precious lady of yours to tie a huge rock to her ankles and go jump in a lake. No one tells me I can't see my nephew!"

Roger reclined in his seat. He squinted slightly at her with one eyebrow raised.

"So that's what this is all about."

"Why wasn't I invited to that party the other night for Mark?"

"For the very reason I told you earlier. Beth doesn't want—"

Roger stopped in mid-sentence. His countenance changed, forehead creasing. There was anger in his eyes. Roger demanded an explanation how Siobhan knew of Mark's celebration. But the realtor cleverly responded with her pat answer of not mentioning the name of her informant.

"It was bad enough I wasn't included in congratulating Mark on receiving his Master's degree."

"You didn't miss anything, unless you call eating sausage-and-pepper subs over a couple of beers at Angelo's your idea of fine dining and a great time. I paid dearly with heartburn that night. But that's the way Mark wanted it. No hoopla. The other night was my idea because I was so proud of him. He deserved that much."

Siobhan pushed her lips up in agreeing with Roger. She took a bite of her sandwich and remarked on how tasty it was. Having eaten something else entirely, Roger just sat there in silence with no opinion of his own on the food, and no certainty on where this conversation was going. He finally brought up a point Siobhan made in her email that he wanted to clarify.

"By the way," Roger began, "just what did you mean by *our future* in that email you sent?"

"Oh, that," she responded with a slight chuckle. "I know your weakness, Roger. You never had the self-control to contain yourself if a woman flirted with you. But that was the only way to get your attention so that we could have this one-on-one chat together. My main goal was to voice my opinion about being involved with Mark's life a little more. And it worked. I'll admit, twenty some-odd years ago I had a little crush on you. And I needed to experience for myself what Maggie always bragged about. You were great in the sack."

"As I recall, you were pretty hot yourself back then."

"Ah, yes," Siobhan fondly remembered. "But that was many years ago. Once you cross the big five-oh threshold, your priorities change. I don't have time for men anymore. And unlike you, who has to consult with the other half to see if taking a vacation is a viable option, let alone when deciding where to go, I can go anywhere, anytime I damn well please. Plus, you're shackled to taking a vacation only when the school closes in May, and you must return in early August to start preparing for the new fall semester. Tell me something, Roger. Have you ever visited Paris in April for two whole weeks? Or gone down to Florida in October when it's not so oppressive that time of year? I have."

Roger was resenting Siobhan's comments. He'd like to do a lot of things if only he could. But even he came to the realization that he was not the same man as decades earlier, now having to rely on other means to stimulate himself besides having Beth wear a see-through negligee.

But there was another issue Roger wanted to get off his chest with his ex-sister-in-law. He wasn't going to beat around the bush. He had to confront her.

"That trial twenty years ago, I was nearly hanged, you know. You played a part in that, too. If things had gotten a little too edgy for me, I was going to rat on your involvement. You delivered most of Haber's body parts to Maggie."

"Moi? Au contraire, mon amie. I was just the distributor. Don't blame the mailperson for junk mail sent by some company. Besides, I would've denied everything. Also, I was your best ally because I didn't give the DA or the police any reason why you sliced up Haber. Or why you drove my darling sister to the booby hatch."

"I think you resented the fact that I eventually found Beth and married her without considering you. But, like you said in your email, your family would've disapproved."

"True indeed, but as I mentioned before, time changes everything. You're no more appealing to me now than that stop sign outside this place."

Roger had enough of Siobhan's talk. It was becoming irritating to listen to her. Plus, he needed to be back at the Winston campus for his next session.

"Well, if you'll excuse me, Siobhan, I must be getting back to the college. My next class is due soon. Besides, you have that deal in Fall River waiting for you to close. Good day."

Roger stood up from his seat and was ready to bolt. But Siobhan stopped him in his tracks by purposely sticking her right leg into his path.

"Not so fast, mister."

Roger was taken aback by Siobhan's determination to prevent him from leaving without resolving the matter surrounding her involvement with Mark.

"I want a straight answer—no, a promise—that you're not going to shield your son from me any longer. Christmas will be here next month and I want to start my holiday card writing early. How about his address and phone number? Maybe even his email address?"

"Well, speaking of email, why don't I give him your email address and allow him to communicate with you directly?"

"Oh, no, no, no! Do you think I was born yesterday? Fork it up, Roger."

"And have you corrupt him? I know how devious your mind can be."

"Roger," Siobhan responded with a wry smile while leaning back in her seat. "You can be so cruel. I think you've been reading too many James Patterson novels."

"I have my suspicions and reasons to back me up."

"I can still track you down, Roger. You're still living in that white colonial house on Westwood Road in Central Falls, right? You know, the one with the powder-blue shutters?"

Roger was glaring at Siobhan with a sliver of fear lodged in his brain. *Has she become some sick, perverted stalker?* The college professor was still hesitant to divulge any information about Mark. But then he weighed the negatives in not doing so. Scowling at the predicament, Roger reached into the breast pocket of his tweed blazer and whipped out a pen. He took a clean napkin from the table and scribbled Mark's cell number.

He looked at the number for the last time. His frown creased even deeper, so much so that his forehead rippled. With reluctance, Roger handed the napkin to Siobhan. Like the Cheshire cat, Siobhan smiled wickedly when receiving the number.

"There," Siobhan commented. "That wasn't so bad now, was it?"

Roger's eyes squinted even more. His nostrils flared, just thinking about what insidious ideas she planned to plant inside Mark's brain. Siobhan pursed her lips as she happily folded the napkin in quarters and discreetly slipped it into her purse. Her purpose for meeting Roger was accomplished.

Siobhan had won this round, but Roger made sure that she didn't escape without receiving one last body blow.

"So help me, you'd better watch yourself concerning Mark."

If Siobhan took Roger's attitude as some lethal warning, she wasn't letting on. Her satisfied grin widened as she gently patted Roger's clenched fist. Maybe it was her way of assuring Roger not to expect anything underhanded from her. Or maybe it was all a clever guise for some master plan she wasn't about to allow Roger in on.

And with that Siobhan stood up and gave Roger a soft peck on his cheek.

"It's been a pleasure seeing you again, Roger." She looked down at her sandwich, which was hardly touched. "Maybe you can give it to that collie/shepherd mix of yours. He might like it."

"Orion died two years ago."

"Oh," Siobhan responded forlornly, perhaps with a little heightened sarcastic frown. "I'm sorry to hear of it." She changed gears quickly and morphed her melancholy expression to a happy face. "Well, ta-ta. And let's not wait another five years to get together again, hmmm?" As if struck with an ingenious thought, Siobhan's mouth circled as her eyes widened. She touched Roger's chest with the tip of her index finger. "I know what we can do. Let's all meet for dinner one night. You, me, Mark, and Beth, too!" She looked around the Dunkin' Donuts establishment with a thoughtful expression. "I mean at a nice place, with tablecloths. Think about it."

But Roger didn't respond. He was still angry, and now leery. He watched Siobhan sashay out the front door. As she disappeared into the crowd, Roger wondered just who could have given Siobhan his email address. A number of people knew it, but it wasn't as if half the citizen of Rhode Island had their hands on it.

He took a quick glance at his watch. He had to return to the campus for the afternoon classes. But as he was about to leave, Roger looked at the sandwich Siobhan hardly touched. With deep hatred, Roger snatched up the edible and marched to the front of the store. He quickly noticed one of the workers mopping a portion of the floor. Roger shoved the sandwich into the midsection of the unwitting employee, who suddenly dropped the mop when receiving the tidbit.

"Here," Roger growled. "Give this to some homeless man!"

And with that Roger stormed out of the bistro, leaving the worker with a shocked look on his face as if uncertain what to make of the episode.

Chapter 34

Roger was still fuming over his meeting with Siobhan and how he had been coerced into relinquishing Mark's phone number to her. He preferred not to have his twisted ex-sister-in-law around. Of course, who was he to talk, what with his checkered past?

With his Bluetooth device in his ear, Roger called Beth while he was driving back to the campus. Much to his frustration, Roger learned from her secretary that Beth was in an administrative meeting. He then called Mark, wanting to warn him of Siobhan's call, unless she had made it the moment she left the restaurant. Further consternation settled in as all he could do was reach his voice mail. Just as he had explained to Beth's admin that the message wasn't that important, he explained in the recoding for Mark that there was nothing urgent.

The scowl of angst deepened. He even cursed at a few motorists, whose driving practices could have been in question. Under normal circumstances Roger wouldn't cuss at the world; at least, not this demonstratively. But Siobhan really got under his skin, and there was no other fitting recipient of his venting.

Well, not quite. There was one person Roger could turn to, but it was someone he preferred not to approach. Still, desperate times call for desperate measures. Through his dashboard console, Roger placed a call.

"Hello, Roger," the voice said. "This is a surprise, your calling me. Imagine that!"

"Yes, Mort. Fancy that. Listen, my last class ends at five this afternoon. Are you available to see me after that?"

There was silence on the other end as Mort told Roger to hang on while he checked his appointment schedule.

"Yes, I am. Can you make it at, say, five-thirty?"

"Yes, I can."

"Is there something else troubling you, Roger?"

"Let's discuss the matter when I get there, please."

Roger didn't want to rehash the sordid details with the psychoanalyst over the phone. He tersely ended the conversation by assuring Mort he'd be there.

Perhaps relieved that his meeting was secured, Roger drove the rest of the way without further incident. The idea that he could at least talk to someone, even if it had to come at some cost, calmed him. Waiting for Beth to return home or wondering if and when Mark would be available to chat were not options. As much as they were trusted confidants, Roger thought that perhaps Mort might be able to speculate on ulterior motives for Siobhan from a psychological perspective and possess insight that neither his wife nor son could offer.

Chapter 35

Nightfall embraced the late autumn sky, which was beginning to cover the Providence metropolitan area with flurries. The only saving grace from the ominous heavens was that nothing major by way of storms was coming. Providence had had a series of snowstorms even before Thanksgiving in the past. But there was nothing of great concern this night.

Even though seeing Mort was the only sensible thing to do, there was still that remaining hesitation on Roger's part keeping him from pressing the front doorbell. He removed his glove to get a better feel for the button, but still had little progress in moving toward reaching it. Tractor trailers had a quicker time backing into a cargo bay than Roger's fingertip connecting with the bell. Finally he worked up the nerve to press it.

A small snowflake came down from the purple ceiling. It landed on the shoulder of Roger's tweed jacket. The symmetrically hexagonal speck didn't last there for long. Roger's blazer was warm from the insulated heat of his car. The flake didn't have a chance as it soon evaporated.

Finally the front door opened before another flake could descend on Roger. There in the archway was Mort, reacting as if he was welcoming an old friend he hadn't seen in years.

"Roger," Mort beamed. "I'm so glad you took upon yourself to come down here! Please do come in."

Roger offered a faint smile to his host. He didn't want to make this sound like a revival meeting, and thus downplayed his visit.

Mort guided Roger through the Victorian house to the back office, but the college professor had been to the place twice before in the past month and knew the inner workings of the home almost as well as did Mort.

When they finally made it through the labyrinth, Roger was pleasantly surprised to see a cup of hot Earl Grey tea awaiting him, fixed just the way he liked it. Mort had an uncanny knack for remembering the small details of likes and dislikes of his patients. No, make that a dossier. The psychoanalyst scribbled tons of notes on his clientele, some of which read sideways and followed looping arrows to attach themselves to other pertinent criteria of insights into the mindsets of people like Roger.

Roger took a sip of the hot beverage. He raised his eyebrows in approval as he gently placed cup and saucer down on the adjacent table. Pleased with his patient's affirmation of approval, Mort proceeded with the session.

"As I said, Roger, I'm delighted you decided to come here of your own volition."

Roger gave Mort a dubious look. With his one eyebrow raised and his head slightly cocked, the professor wondered if it was just the money Mort would pocket from the session that made him so jovial, rather than the hope of something productive to be gained from all of it. Then he put aside his suspicions to get down to the real purpose for his being there. Still, Mort posed the question of why the sudden change. Roger cleared his throat . . . and his mind.

"Well," the professor began, "you know about Mark's new job coming about in January. And he appears to have a new woman in his life. I haven't officially met her yet. She came as a friend of my colleague's secretary to the party. I just saw her briefly."

"I'm happy for Mark on both counts. And I'm happy for you."

Roger began to rub his hands nervously. He didn't know how to broach the subject of Siobhan. But he also knew that if he didn't bring it up, then his sole purpose for being there was lost.

"After a few years of not hearing from her, I recently was contacted by Margaret's sister, Siobhan O'Mara."

Mort tried to put on his best poker face, but his face twitched a little and he released the grip on his pen. He apologized to Roger for being a little clumsy and quickly clutched the pen tightly in order to write more notes.

Roger squinted to get a better read on Mort's peculiar tic. But the psychoanalyst insisted to his patient that he was fine. Roger didn't totally buy it. He wondered who played the role of doctor and who portrayed the client in this exchange.

While there was a moment of silence, Mort did his best to hide facts he already knew about Siobhan, but couldn't reveal to Roger. The best defense is a good offense. Mort took back control of the session by initiating questions in order to divert Roger's attention away from Mort's awkward behavior.

"So, why do you feel so skittish about Siobhan?"

"Because she is evil! She wants to corrupt my son, and feed him a concoction she's made up of lies and deceptions!"

"Lies about what, Roger?"

Roger's face contorted. He was upset with Mort's persistent line of questioning and angry at Siobhan and the way she'd conducted herself. But while he needed to vent, Roger had to suppress the emergence of the many skeletons coming to the surface. He had to come up with some valid response for his beliefs.

"Ever since Margaret was institutionalized, Siobhan has resented me. And she has been hell-bent to cause a rift between me and Mark. I just want her to stay away and not bother me."

Mort scribbled down more notes. He then looked at the ceiling in search of the next question.

"Do you think it's fair to Mark to be kept from his aunt, even though he has minimal contact with his mother, given her present state?"

Roger glared at Mort, but there was also a visage of perplexity mixed in, too. The professor refused to answer Mort's question. The psychoanalyst just drew a deep sigh and nodded as he began to jot down more bits of minutia.

The session was over as far as Roger was concerned. He wasn't satisfied with the way it was handled. In fact, the professor was beginning to wonder whose side Mort was favoring: his or Siobhan's.

But Mort was just trying to come to a better understanding of Roger's state of angst. And if it meant that Roger was offended by it, well, too bad. In the long run, Mort wanted to help Roger and resolve his suspicions of and differences with Siobhan. As they say, sometimes the truth hurts.

Roger was about to rise from his seat and bolt for the door. Mort had seen this act before on their first visit and wasn't about to allow his patient to leave so readily. Some quick thinking was in order.

"If you think shielding Mark from your ex-sister-in-law is going to help any, Roger, you may be mistaken. Is it right to shield him from her? I mean, where does it go from here? You have to let Mark go. Let him make his own decisions. Certainly at his age he can think for himself."

"When it comes to overseeing his well-being, damn straight, I'm going to become involved!"

Mort sat back in his chair to absorb Roger's anger toward Siobhan. But rather than place emphasis on her, Mort shifted the conversation to Mark.

"I'm beginning to wonder if getting Mark that teaching job at Winston was less to further his goals and ambitions than it was for self-gratification on your part to see him do well."

"Yes, of course, I'm his father and I want to see Mark do well!" Roger scowled at Mort before continuing. "You're a parent, Mort. Don't you want to see your children do well?"

"There's a fine line between my wanting to be proud of what they do versus my making it an obsession to direct their lives to become successful."

It wasn't the answer Roger was looking for, but, just like before, the truth hurts. There was no way he was going to challenge Mort's rationale. Rather, the psychoanalyst was hoping for the opposite. The professor had to adjust and resign himself to the realization that he really had to let go of Mark. But that still didn't resolve his matter with Siobhan's meddling in his son's life.

Mort detected a bit of reluctance on Roger's part to accept Siobhan's embrace of Mark. The psychoanalyst deftly leaned forward and offered in a whisper, "Let it go!"

Stewing as he made every attempt to swallow Mort's advice, Roger finally conceded and nodded. Mort was satisfied he was finally getting through to his patient. The psychoanalyst sat back in his seat with a look of contentment as he folded his hands together over his lap.

Feeling very laconic, Roger decided to call a halt to the session. He rose slowly from his chair, not like he did earlier as if he were prodded by the protruding end of a cushion coil.

Mort helped Roger don his overcoat as it was time to head back out into the wintry night air. The professor offered a simple handshake to Mort, who reciprocated with a gentle smile.

"You're always welcome here, Roger. Please don't hesitate to call me again and let's have another chat soon, hmm? I'd love to hear how Mark settles into his new position. And if I don't see you until then, Merry Christmas and a Happy New Year to you and your family."

Roger offered a feigned smile to show appreciation for seeing him on such short notice. He had to get back home before the weather wreaked havoc on the roads. Besides, Beth would be home too, and he'd promised he would start dinner by the time she got off work.

With a simple pat on Roger's shoulder, Mort gave a final goodbye. As Roger made tracks to his car, Mort waved at him, regardless if Roger cared to look back. Once his patient was out of sight, Mort closed the front door.

He was now alone in his home and this gave Mort a chance to recount the session thought for thought. He leaned back against the front door and contemplated his next move. *Well, that was easy.* But it was the way to approach the step that gave him pause. *Oh, the heck with it, just make the call.*

With alacrity in his step, Mort shot back to his office desk. He glanced at a piece of paper nearby and began to replicate the sequence of numbers on the keypad. In just a few seconds Mort heard a familiar voice.

"This is Dr. Mort Sonnenstein. He was just here."

Mort paused to allow the other party to speak. An understanding ear of experience sent a subliminal message to conclude the abbreviated conversation.

" . . . and thanks again for coming over last week at my request. It's not like me to look for people to come to my office, but I needed to meet with you. We'll stay in touch."

He gently placed the phone back on its cradle, but all the while Mort's mind was running in circles. He was pitting Roger's interests against those of the person he'd just called. It was as if the psychoanalyst was conducting his own personal experiment. It was highly unethical. But there was a reason—no, a motivation—behind his purpose. He needed to resolve his own inner questions. And Margaret O'Mara was at the core of it all.

Chapter 36

Mark was invited by Roger and Beth over for Thanksgiving dinner. He accepted the invitation on the one condition that he could bring along Rebecca. There was no problem with the elder Lavoie, and so Rebecca was added to the very modest guest list.

Upon arrival, Mark was greeted with a hearty handshake and hug from Roger as Beth was standing nearby to give her stepson a smooch on the cheek. And in Mark's shadow stood Rebecca. The pretty blonde was a little nervous, and understandably so. Unlike the party nearly three weeks earlier where Rebecca was the third beer bottle in the fourth six-pack, she stood front and center for Roger and Beth to study. No longer the sixth member of the backdrop chorus, Rebecca was the star of this off-Broadway production. And she was aware that her every move, every word, every gesture, and every expression were being carefully scrutinized.

Although she had been to the house before, the Lavoie home seemed a little more intimate without the clusters of guests here and there, as was the case earlier that month. And that enabled her to better experience the quaint charm of the white colonial.

Mark felt a little awkward at not re-introducing his date to his father and stepmother.

"What a dummy I am," Mark began. "Dad, Beth. This is my new girlfriend, Rebecca Dyer."

Roger offered Rebecca a subdued smile and a half-hearted handshake. Beth, on the other hand, was quite the opposite. She spread her arms out like an eagle in flight, and sported a toothy grin.

"It's so nice to meet you," Beth said with a smile. "Come, sit down in the living room!"

Mark and Rebecca took up Beth's offer. Meanwhile, Roger asked his guests what was the beverage of their choice. Mark opted for a bottle of Newport Winter Porter while Rebecca asked for a glass of white wine. As Roger went to the kitchen for the drinks, Beth sat down in the recliner opposite the sofa where Mark and Rebecca perched. She wanted to open the conversation.

"So," Beth began, "do you prefer to be called Rebecca, or perhaps Becky?"

"Rebecca, please. I got called Becky from grade school through high school, and I hated it."

Beth cocked her head slightly and nodded while her lower lip protruded. By this time Roger had returned with the beverages.

After Mark thanked him for the brew, he looked to the dining room and saw a place setting for six. He then turned to his father with a puzzled look.

"Who else is coming, Dad?"

"Oh," Roger responded, his voice laced with a trace of reluctance. "Francine and Cal MacKenzie. They should be here shortly."

"Well," Beth piped in, "if you'll excuse me, I have to check on the bird and a couple of the vegetables."

"Let me help you," Rebecca replied.

"Thanks, but I'll be fine."

"No. No. I insist. Please."

"Why thank you, Rebecca. You are such an angel!"

The two women went into the kitchen to tend to a few items on the menu. Roger watched Mark's girlfriend until she was out of sight. He then turned toward his son with a face of approval.

"I like what I see, Mark. Sure beats some of those other women you've been with recently."

Mark smirked at his father's reference.

Roger turned on the 60-inch flat screen TV and quickly clicked on the traditional Detroit Lions game as they battled the visiting Denver Broncos. The volume was turned down so that the two of them could carry on a conversation without trying to yell over the announcers. Besides, Beth didn't care much for NFL football. The same could be said for Rebecca. Mark discovered soon enough that she was more into young Hollywood stars, rock musicians and fashion trends. Cold Play and Maroon Five were more her speed.

The father and son talked about Professor Edward Asmundsson and what he'd be expecting from young Mark once he began his Winston career come January. Roger encouraged Mark to spend a little time with Edward before the new term. The son promised he would, but added it all depended on his crazy schedule with Best Buy as he rode out his employment with the electronics retail giant. He'd promised his superiors that he would stay with them through the Christmas holiday shopping season. Roger admired Mark's dedication. There was no doubt that this characteristic, together with his father's influence and his own ability and qualifications, helped catapult Mark to his impending, lofty position.

Mark looked out toward the kitchen. It didn't appear that anytime within the next few minutes would either woman emerge from there. If the MacKenzies rang the bell, Roger could easily answer it. The timing was right to bring up an issue of concern.

"I, um," Mark began nervously, "I heard from Aunt Siobhan last week."

Now Roger was the one who appeared edgy. Although he was anticipating this would happen after Siobhan singlehandedly forced him to relinquish Mark's phone number, Roger was hoping that his former sister-in-law would have waited a while before pouncing on her nephew. After all, if Siobhan had waited this long, she could've held back just a bit before tracking him down. But then again, this was Siobhan. And to Roger she was a driven menace, like a shark in shallow waters.

To act surprised by Mark's announcement would have been a disservice. Roger had to come clean with his son regarding Mark's dear old auntie. He raised his eyebrows and sighed. With both hands clasped, Roger gazed into Mark's eyes.

"I'm sorry if her call to you made you a little uncomfortable. She somehow got hold of my email address and wrote to me about . . . nonsense." Answers to his inner turmoil were not going to come by his staring at the sofa arm covering. Eyes to the ceiling and a deep sigh. "She's up to something. I don't know, Mark. Maybe she's trying to shake me down, perhaps even using you as a means to do so."

145

Odd statement, Mark thought. "What makes you think that?"

"Isn't that why you brought up the subject rather nervously? I thought maybe you didn't want any part of her either."

Laughable idea. "Not really. I mean, I know she's Mom's sister and all. And I know you've had troubles dealing with her since . . . you know . . . Mom's mishap. That's the reason I mentioned it in a peculiar way. Actually, I was kind of surprised she sought me out."

Roger looked at the muted football game. The images alone were distracting him. Enough so, he decided to shut the flat screen off so that he could devote his full attention to Mark. *Hmm.* Beth and Rebecca were still busy in the kitchen with the finishing touches to the turkey. Good chance as any for Roger to continue, but with his guard up.

"Aunt Siobhan met with me for lunch two weeks back, shortly after that party Beth and I threw for you. She was determined to get your phone number from me. I didn't want to create a scene in the restaurant, so I relented. I think she's after something, possibly from me. Just watch your words with her, Mark. That's all."

Mark looked blankly at his dad in bewilderment. Pressure mounted on his temples as he tried to comprehend just what his dad meant by that remark.

Ding dong!

Francine and Cal had arrived. Roger slowly rose from his couch seat, but not before bellowing an "I'll get it!" for Beth. Before heading to the front door, Roger turned back toward Mark.

"Let's keep this chat to ourselves, hmm?"

Roger had a whole new game face. Like a quick-thinking actor, Roger slapped on a visage of elation as he opened the door. Francine one-upped the professor with a wide smile and a song in her voice. Cal was more natural with a subtle grin. Beth soon joined the group.

"Hi!" Beth cheerfully welcomed the couple with her arms extended outward.

"Hey!" Francine replied. "Thanks for inviting us!" She turned to Cal with an expression as if to cue him on what was to follow.

"Oh, Francine and I brought over a couple bottles of Pinot Grigio."

"You shouldn't have." Beth turned to Roger. "Dear, could you take the bottles from Cal, please?"

As Roger took the wine, Francine began to survey the living room. She immediately spotted Mark and said hello to him. But then she glanced to the left and spotted Rebecca in the distance. Her happy-go-lucky smile disappeared. In fact, Francine sported a curious look. Her eyebrows shifted as if she was trying to remember where she'd seen Rebecca before. She tugged at Beth's Irish knit sweater.

"Hey," Francine whispered. "Who's that young blonde over there? I swear I've seen her before, but I just can't remember where."

"Oh, that's Mark's new girlfriend. Her name is Rebecca. She's helping in the kitchen. Very sweet girl. You saw her at Mark's party a couple of weeks ago."

Francine appeared reserved, as though something was on her mind, but if there was, it was squelched.

Rebecca took a break from assisting Beth to join Mark. She tenderly placed her hand on Mark's shoulder, both as a sign of affection as well as to get his attention.

Mark looked at Rebecca's gesture with appreciation. He smiled at her and gathered her closer to him with his arm encircling her back and pulling her in at the waist. Rebecca grinned back at Mark, but then jerked her head slightly to the left as if wanting to discuss something.

"Hey," Mark whispered in a private corner. "What's the problem?"

Rebecca sucked her teeth. "It's that woman over there." She pointed. "The one with the beige turtleneck."

Mark took a quick glance around the room so as not to look suspicious. "Francine MacKenzie?"

"That's the one. She gives me the creeps. She's, like, giving me the third-degree by glaring at me. What did I ever do to her?"

Mark offered a soft chuckle as if to dismiss Francine's oddball behavior.

"Listen, babe. I've known Francine for the past ten years, ever since my dad married Beth. Francine is what you'd call a . . . busybody. I mean, I can walk around the house with this half bottle of beer in my hand for the next hour and she'll ask me several times whether I plan to finish it or not. Always curious about every little thing."

"Well, I'm not sure I like it."

"Unfortunately, that's the way she is. But, hey, don't let it upset you. Maybe you can strike up a conversation with her—you know, get to know her. She really is quite harmless. She just likes to talk a lot."

Rebecca's hint of a smile was an indication she was coming to terms with the situation. She strutted over to the sofa and gingerly perched on one of the cushions. Rebecca turned toward Mark and lightly patted the cushion next to her to invite him to sit. Mark glinted a smile and was about to do her bidding. That was until he felt a slight tug on his arm. He pivoted only to find his father in his face.

"What was that all about?" Roger asked.

Mark shrugged. "Oh, it's nothing, Dad. Rebecca was little nervous by the way Francine was looking at her. You know how Francine is."

"She's actually Beth's friend. I just came along when we married. But she does have a tendency to pry into one's affairs." Roger sighed and looked in Francine's direction. "She's the one who convinced Beth I should see this psychoanalyst she knows, Mort Sonnenstein. A fat lot of good it did me. I could've handled my own problems without Mort's help, thank you very much."

"Not to mention forking over hundreds of dollars to him during the visits."

"He didn't charge me on the last visit."

Suddenly Roger gave strong thought to what he had just said. Just why didn't Mort charge him for the last visit? He plopped himself down in one of the plush easy chairs. Random ideas concerning Mort began running through his brain. He pawed at his bearded chin.

Roger then reached into his front right pants pocket for his wallet. He opened it and proceeded to flip through a few photos and credit cards until he came across the compartment that held business cards. The professor wrenched the tightly packed group and began to fumble through them. Suddenly Roger stopped his search. There it was: Mort's professional card. Roger stared at it for several seconds. *Yes, just why did you invite me over on the house?* Roger was growing suspicious. He started to believe he was now visiting Mort not to be cured but to satisfy some underlying reason for which the psychoanalyst had beckoned him to return. Was he some sort of specimen in Mort's personal lab experiment? The idea of becoming a pawn didn't amuse Roger at all. He felt the need to mangle Mort's card and toss it in the trash.

Roger was about to do just that when suddenly he heard his name.

"Roger, could you be a dear and get something for Francine and Cal to drink, please?" Beth asked affectionately.

The professor complied with his wife's request, if for no other reason than to divert his attention away from Mort. But before doing so, Roger placed all the cards back in his wallet. He then gave Mort's card one more glance. A short chortle could be heard from him, but only if one stood next to Roger.

Roger was good at playing psychological games. And even the idea of going against a trained expert like Mort didn't faze him. He was up for the challenge if Mort should ever request his presence again.

"Roger?"

Oh, right. Drinks for the guests.

Chapter 37

Eight forty-five. Mark drove Rebecca back to her place after the Thanksgiving dinner at his father's home. There was no further discussion in the car about Francine MacKenzie's oddball behavior prior to the feast. Perhaps that was because Rebecca and Francine had a little chat at the dinner table. Their conversation was amiable enough to put aside any ill feelings either may have had toward the other.

Mark pulled his Chevy Equinox onto the driveway and placed the vehicle in park, but he continued to leave the motor running. Rebecca's face bore a questioning look.

"I thought you were going to come join me upstairs," Rebecca posed. "The Kozaks are away at their daughter's family's house for the holiday. Just me, you, and my cat."

Mark sighed. "I'd love to come up, Beautiful, but I have to get up in six hours. Tomorrow's Black Friday. The store opens at four am. Hopefully, this will be the last Friday after Thanksgiving when I'll have to get up early, now that I'll be starting my new career in January."

Rebecca slouched in her seat and peered at the dashboard. She folded her arms defensively. Her expression of frustration spoke volumes, even if she didn't utter a word.

Mark stared at his girlfriend. Yeah, this wasn't going to be easy for him to remedy. But he offered up a solution.

"Look, I get off at two in the afternoon and I'm not due back until 3 on Saturday. What do you say I come over after my shift tomorrow?"

Mark extended his arm around Rebecca's shoulders to console her. She was still looking ahead toward the front of the car. Continuing her pout, Rebecca gave him a glance from the corner of her left eye briefly, before resuming her focus again upfront.

"You'll be too exhausted to do anything with the lack of sleep and the hours you'll put in."

"Hey, haven't you heard of those quick-shot energy drinks?"

"You mean you're addicted to those things?"

"No, not really. I just take one once in a blue moon for special occasions." Mark gently brushed the strands of Rebecca's hair from her face. "And being with you is definitely one of them."

Rebecca turned her head slightly to the left to give Mark a better look. She offered up a half-hearted smirk. He realized this wasn't the answer his girlfriend was looking for, but this reaction was better than the down-in-the-mouth frown from moments ago. At least it was an improvement.

Mark at first chuckled, taking comfort that Rebecca was accepting his deferral of intense passion until the next evening. He then softly stroked the right side of her face. Her skin was smooth as velvet. Mark gazed amorously into Rebecca's soft eyes and she into his. He drew closer. They both closed their eyelids and opened their mouths to receive each other's tongues. The exchange of the oral bodily fluids wasn't enough for Rebecca, for she began to massage Mark's head of hair. But the newest addition to the Winston faculty knew when to call everything to a halt. His commitment to his current employer compelled him to quit. He broke away from Rebecca's seductive clutches, planting the white flag.

"I'll see you tomorrow," Mark repeated as he gently touched the tip of Rebecca's nose with his finger.

Rebecca offered a reluctant grin. "Don't forget the chardonnay."

"Oh, that's right. Your favorite."

She pointed at him. "Better make that two. You owe me big time."

Mark chuckled and nodded.

They lightly smacked each other on the lips before Rebecca left his car. She closed the door behind her, but not with the same ferocity with which she'd slammed the same door a couple of weeks earlier in the Cranston parking lot. While she might have been disappointed by Mark's postponement of passionate lovemaking, Rebecca was more understanding of his current situation and dismissed it as just a hiccup in the relationship.

Once she was safely inside, Mark shifted the Equinox into reverse. But even though he was visually concentrating on looking at what was behind him on the driveway, Mark's mind was on Rebecca. Oh, if only he didn't have to go to work the next morning. *Before the rooster crows, no less!*

Chapter 38

As he had promised, Mark arrived at Rebecca's place at 2:30 the next day. And thanks to the quick-energy shot, Mark was quite active for her.

Five-thirty rolled around. A soft light underneath a modest orange lampshade was all that illuminated Rebecca's bedroom, set against the darkened sky. The small light fixture rested its base atop an antique nightstand, with two semi-filled wine glasses keeping it company.

On the floor was a bottle of chardonnay. Most of its contents were gone. The vessel stood proud and tall like a lighthouse in the middle of a bay. But waves of water didn't surround it. No, it was erect in a sea of strewn clothing belonging to Mark and Rebecca.

They lay together in each other's arms. Rebecca's thick quilt covered most of their naked bodies. Their skin was only visible from the chest up.

Mark and Rebecca were engaged in a heated lip lock. It was impossible to determine what number kiss this was. If one had asked, each would have plainly answered ten-plus, for they'd lost track.

Their lips eventually parted company. Rebecca gave Mark an admiring gaze while he returned the favor. She then rested her face on his shoulder, giving his manly chest a massage in the process. Mark gently secured Rebecca, draping his ample muscular arm around the top of her back. She nuzzled her head against his neck, enchanted by the musky scent of his subtle but potent cologne. And he was captivated by the sweet fragrance of her golden hair. It reminded him of lilacs in a vast open meadow.

Rebecca's eyes were closed. She released a soft, sensual moan, her way of expressing sheer pleasure at being in Mark's company.

"This is wonderful," Rebecca uttered softly.

Mark hummed in agreement as he playfully stroked her back with his fingertips. He began to think about their first night in his apartment, comparing what happened then versus what had just occurred moments before.

"You know something?" Mark asked rhetorically. "I'm beginning to see what you meant by having sex as opposed to making love. You were definitely more into it today."

"A couple of weeks ago I had that wild concoction of various hard liquors sloshing through my head."

"Well, you had nearly two glasses of wine tonight. I'm sure that did something for you."

"It did, but in a nice way. Wine makes me feel mellow, more . . . sexy!" Rebecca giggled for a moment. "All that vodka, rum and shit fried my brain cells."

They engaged in another deep kiss. Gently breaking away from her, Mark commented on his sensual encounter with Rebecca.

"When you climaxed, your moan was loud, yet it sounded so beautiful. It was like a siren with the allure of desire."

"Oh, wow! I've never been told that before!"

"Well, it's true," Mark affirmed. "Last time you just grunted. That's why I stopped after just once. I was afraid I was hurting you."

"This time I was enjoying it!" Still under the covers, Rebecca got on all fours on top of him, pinning Mark down so he couldn't escape. "I hope you've still got something left in that tank of yours down there."

Mark smiled while giving her a wink. "Perhaps. I just hope we don't rile the neighbors."

"Ach, who the fuck cares! And my landlord and his wife are still staying at their daughter's house. Don't you worry, lover." Rebecca hesitated before continuing in a softer, more seductive voice, "Nothing's going to stop us."

Suddenly Rebecca's orange tabby cat entered the room quietly, except for his throaty meow. Rebecca's face morphed into a frown as her libido waned significantly.

"Nothing, that is, except Feisty's need to eat."

Mark gently rubbed Rebecca's exposed shoulder. He grinned and nodded his head in the direction of the kitty, as if giving her permission to leave.

As she rose from the bed, Rebecca turned toward Mark and pointed at him, also grinning. "You'd better stay where you are," she warned him. Mark held up the palms of his hands to her, signaling he wasn't going anywhere.

As Rebecca stood up, Mark couldn't help but admire her slender body. And unlike the morning after the party at his father's house, Rebecca wasn't ashamed of showcasing her nakedness in front of him, although she did quickly reach into her bedroom closet to don a soft-pink terrycloth bathrobe to keep her from catching a chill.

Mark was left by his lonesome as Rebecca tended to Feisty. He began thinking about women he had dated and was comparing them to Rebecca. In the back of his mind, Mark entertained the thought of marrying Rebecca. He felt ready to settle down, but he didn't know if she was. Time would tell if their relationship was going to rise to the next level. And then there was the notion of him becoming a father someday and making Roger a proud granddad. Of course, Margaret would never be able to appreciate becoming a grandmother, at least not in her present psychotic state.

Rebecca reentered the bedroom, now that the kitty was fed. She reached for the tied sash of her robe and asked, "Now, where were we?"

Just then, her cell phone on the nightstand began to ring. Rebecca lowered her head down in angst as Mark simply chortled and shook his head at yet another interruption to their racy rendezvous.

Rebecca saw the caller ID display on her android phone. Sheryl was calling.

"Ugh! I'm sorry, Mark. I've got to take this call. It's my mom. She gets into a hissy fit if I ignore her. Please forgive me." She cast her eyes toward the ceiling as she sat down beside Mark. Drawing a deep sigh, Rebecca answered, "Yes, Mom."

Mark noticed Rebecca's lips curling downward while she alternated her fixed stare between her closet and her manicured nails.

"I know, and I'm sorry again for not making it to Thanksgiving dinner yesterday, but I was invited by Mark's dad and stepmom to their place. I told you that a few days ago."

Sheryl yelled back so loud that Mark could hear her from his vantage point. Meanwhile, Rebecca held the phone away from her ear in a show of disapproval of her mother's high-decibel voice. Suddenly silence came, enabling Rebecca to respond.

"Look, I really can't talk right now, Mom. Mark is here with me."

Rebecca started to rub the back of her neck to relieve the tension of listening to Sheryl. Just then Mark sat up and took over the job, using both hands. Rebecca dropped her hand to her side and looked at Mark with a sensual smile and half-opened eyes to revel in the pleasure.

"I'm being careful, Mom, okay? Mark even brought over condoms. There, are you satisfied?"

Mark chuckled. Rebecca just looked back at him, shaking her head. She mouthed out, "I'm sorry," to him.

"I don't know if Mark can come by for Christmas dinner, Mom. Maybe he has plans to be with his family."

Mark waved expressively at Rebecca, giving her the green light that it would be fine for him to come over. He even nodded to her to seal the deal. But Rebecca didn't want to pressure her boyfriend.

"Are you sure it's okay, Love?" Rebecca asked softly, holding the phone close to her robe so as not to be heard by Sheryl. "I mean, I feel bad putting you through this."

"Hey," Mark whispered. "It's okay. Go ahead. You went to my father's place. It's only fair that I go to your mother's house."

"Okay, Mom. Mark said it's okay. We've got a whole month to discuss this. I've got to go now. Talk later. Bye."

As Rebecca tapped a button on her screen to end the conversation, she muttered an indecipherable snarl of frustration.

"You know," Rebecca began, facing Mark while shaking her smart phone. "I'm going to drop kick this thing into Greenwich Bay."

"Gosh, if you do that, how am I going to call you?"

Rebecca placed her phone in the top drawer of the adjacent nightstand and closed it up. She then turned to her lover.

"Try training homing pigeons to deliver notes."

Rebecca began the process of removing her bathrobe sash again. Then there was another phone ringing. But it wasn't her phone. Mark recognized the ringtone to be his and looked on the floor for his communicator. Now he was the one getting annoyed. He picked up the phone and read the ID. Mark didn't recognize the number so readily. After a few seconds of thought, he realized it belonged to his Aunt Siobhan. This call was not going to interrupt their salacious moment. He stared across the room at the phone, and said nothing.

"Something wrong?" Rebecca asked.

Mark snapped out of his trance to gaze into her eyes.

"Not a thing," Mark returned as he smiled.

Rebecca released two quick bursts of laughter. She finally got around to untying her sash and removing her robe. Mark allowed her back under the covers. The loving couple continued where they had left off.

Chapter 39

Mark had finally called Siobhan the Sunday morning following T-Day. Using his hectic work schedule at Best Buy due to the holiday shopping season as an excuse for the delay in calling her, Mark agreed to meet his aunt for dinner early Monday evening. He was enjoying a rare day off in the Christmas rush and felt that was the best day to get together.

Considering the calendar had turned to December, it was a rather balmy evening by Rhode Island standards. Temps were hovering in the lower 50s. Mark checked his watch. Seven-oh-three. He was a few minutes late.

Mark arrived at the front of the CAV Restaurant on Imperial Place. He hadn't recalled eating there before, but he knew of its reputation as one of the finest dining places in Providence. He was captivated by its exquisitely maintained brick exterior and its green awning protecting the front door. *But enough of that,* he mused. His benefactress for the sumptuous meal was no doubt waiting inside for him.

The din inside the bistro was almost deafening. Patrons at the bar were jockeying for position, either to grab another brew or to get a better glimpse of the Ravens-Dolphins pre-game. Power brokers were trading war stories of the day: some reveling in their coup of a market killing, others commiserating with fellow warriors on a day of frustration. It was a wonder how these veterans of the trade could find their way home and prepare themselves for the next round in the morning after the numerous shots of Johnny Walker.

Mark tried to peer through the forest of raised drinking glasses and darting figures. A comely brunette, clad in the professional attire of the establishment, approached him. Her hair was pulled back in a ponytail, allowing her perfectly shaped face to be highlighted among the other women there.

"Good evening," the woman began, "are you wanting a table for one?"

Mark responded, "I'm actually trying to meet my aunt. She's about in her early-to-mid fifties. Red hair, I believe.

The woman turned away from Mark. "Yes, I think I know to whom you're referring."

Suddenly an arm was waving back and forth in the crowd, the figure against the back wall.

"Never mind," Mark replied. "I think I see her."

Mark didn't need any further assistance from the hostess. He sucked in his breath and flashed a fraudulent smile as he made measured steps toward Siobhan. His aunt rose from her seat to offer a similar greeting. She raised her arms to the ceiling as if in celebration, and then opened them wide to receive Mark.

"Oh, how's my favorite nephew?"

"I'm you're only nephew, Aunt Siobhan."

Siobhan gasped as if making an egregious error.

"You're right!" And then she simply laughed it off and kissed Mark on the side of his face. Mark returned the favor, but was careful not to smudge her caked-on makeup or allow his dash of Hugo Boss cologne to clash with her overpowering application of Ralph Lauren perfume. Siobhan held out her right hand toward the opposite chair and motioned for Mark to sit down.

Once he took his seat, Mark looked around and marveled at the amazing finished brick interior, brought to prominence by charming suspended lanterns. Elegantly crafted chandeliers graced the ceilings, lending a little panache and style. And the appearance of hanging ferns from overhead trellises gave the restaurant a downhome ambiance.

"Is this your first time here?" Siobhan asked.

"Yeah." Mark continued to look around. "It's quite the place. I mean, I've heard of it, but I thought it was a little too classy for this beer-and-burger guy."

"Well, don't worry. This is my treat."

"Oh, c'mon, Aunt Siobhan. I should at least pay half."

Siobhan puckered her lips while looking skyward. "Tell you what. You can pay for the bar tab and tip. How's that?"

"Deal."

Mark was about to peruse the menu when a handsome young waiter approached and introduced himself as Keenan. He quickly rattled off the house specialties. Mark nodded.

"Would you care for something to drink, sir?" Keenan asked.

"I'll take a glass of merlot, thanks. Just give me some time to look at the menu."

"Excellent." Keenan turned toward Siobhan. "How are you doing with your drink, ma'am?"

Siobhan raised her glass with pride and moved it in a circular motion. The ice cubes performed a little tango.

"I'm still working on it." Siobhan smiled.

Keenan offered a slight bow before heading to the bar to retrieve Mark's wine.

"I'm sorry if I was a little late." Mark wasn't looking at Siobhan when he said this. He was scouring the menu. "What do you recommend?"

"I'm a sucker for seafood. I went with the pan-seared scallops and shrimp. But that's only if you're into it."

Mark snapped his menu shut and grinned. "Sold!"

Siobhan appeared pleased that Mark made up his mind so readily. She took a sip of her gin and tonic before offering up an unusual statement.

"You certainly don't kiss like your father."

Mark's forehead furrowed, wondering where his sweet aunt was going with this observation.

"Is that good or bad?"

Siobhan offered a sly smile. "You're going to have to ask him if you want to know what I mean."

Mark's gaze drifted off blankly into the crowded room. He snorted in frustration, succumbing to the notion that he'd never know what Siobhan meant, although a weird thought did a drive-by in his brain. Before he had a chance to think hard about it, Keenan came around with Mark's wine. Startled, he turned to the waiter.

"Oh, thanks," Mark said with a grin. "And if you're ready, I'll have scallops and shrimp."

With a slight bow Keenan took Mark's order and his menu and headed off to the kitchen.

Mark took a sip of the merlot before placing it back on the table. He offered an appreciative thanks to Siobhan for the dinner invite, but was still at a loss about where to direct the conversation. He focused on the tapping of his fingertips in the rhythmic motion of a caterpillar. Siobhan had to break the ice.

"Well, I'm happy you were able to make it this evening," Siobhan opened. "God, I've only left five messages with you over the holiday weekend."

"I'm sorry, Aunt Siobhan. I was with Dad and Beth for Thanksgiving and I was working at Best Buy the rest of the weekend. This is our busiest time, you know, with Black Friday and all."

Mark wasn't going to explain Rebecca to Siobhan. It was none of her business as far as he was concerned. Siobhan simply raised her eyebrows and pursed her lips as she glanced down at the linen tablecloth. For Mark it was a sign she was accepting his answer as gospel.

Siobhan began to massage the sides of her glass, formulating the words she was about to spew. There was no direct eye contact with Mark. But her spiel was enough to warrant his taking notice.

"You know, I haven't seen you since your graduation from Winston. That was what, five years ago? Make that five and a half. You did graduate in May, if I recall."

"I wanted you to come for my master's graduation, but Dad downplayed it."

"How does that make you feel, Mark? Knowing that your father shunned me and not making a big issue over that milestone?"

"I don't know," Mark answered with a sigh. He looked around the room for answers. But the explanation was inside his head. "I guess he overlooked it. Maybe he thought that was expected of me and trivialized it. But he did throw that party for me. That was awesome!" Again Mark never mentioned Rebecca, the bonus of that soiree.

"And I wasn't there for that either," Siobhan resonated. She cast her eyes back at her glass. "When was the last time you've seen your mother?"

"I saw her on her birthday back in July. But she . . ." Mark hesitated to continue. He frowned. Horrible images were flashing in his brain. "She didn't know I existed. In fact, she just runs away from me. Imagine that. Me. The boy she gave birth to twenty-seven years ago." Mark shook his head in dismay. "Realistically, I don't see the purpose of seeing her. It's as if she died years ago and there's this . . . woman, masquerading as Mom, but that's where the similarity ends. What about you? When was the last time you saw her?"

At that point Keenan brought over their salads with the house vinaigrette dressing. Siobhan flashed a muted smile at the young man by way of saying thanks. She began to twirl the cherry tomato in the center of the bowl, trying to absorb as much of the dressing as possible. But she didn't lose her focus and addressed Mark's query.

"I saw her in early October. She's a little better with me. She recognizes me because I'm there a lot. Facial recognition, you know."

"Is this some sort of dig at me because I haven't seen her as often?"

"Oh, no, Sweetie!" Siobhan's eyebrows lowered. She gently touched Mark's hand to reassure him. "To tell you the truth, in spite of what I just said, she does invoke in me a little anxiety every now and then. Of course, we all know why she's there . . ."

Siobhan paused to get a good look at Mark before continuing. He was in the middle of his first bite of the greens in front of him.

"It was because your father put her there."

Mark ceased chomping. He dropped his salad fork and glared at his aunt, trying to come to grips with what she actually said, what he thought he heard. He finished digesting the lettuce and decided to confront his aunt on her accusation.

"That's way off base, Aunt Siobhan, don't you think?"

Siobhan reclined in her chair. Her face was twisted, her mouth agape.

"I'm shocked by your response. But, then again, your father trained you well. Just how much do you know about why your mother became institutionalized?"

"Just what Dad has always told me. That Mom had some problems psychologically that were eating at her."

"I see." Siobhan looked down at what was left of her salad and it seemed she wanted to save what was left of her appetite for the main course. "Did anyone ever bring up all those stories surrounding your father and the trial?"

"Yeah, but he was acquitted. And I believe him. He brought me up, Aunt Siobhan. And he guided me in the right direction. That's all I need to know."

"My dear nephew," Siobhan said with a salacious smile. "There's still an awful lot you have yet to learn."

"If you don't mind, I'd like to change the subject."

Siobhan gave a slight nod to his request. But for the rest of the dinner, Mark watched his mother's sister suspiciously. Was there any reason why she was dredging up all the garbage? Perhaps, but Mark needed to consult Roger as soon as he could to find a possible motive.

Chapter 40

The very next evening Roger was reviewing material for the lessons he would give in his classes the next day. It was the perfect time to do it. Beth was busy reading a mystery novel and so there were no sound distractions emanating from the living room television. Nothing but peace and quiet reigned.

Roger was perusing entries made on his electronic notebook when suddenly the house phone rang. The sound startled him to the point of breaking his concentration. Frustrated, Roger yelled to Beth that he would answer it. No sense in disturbing her, too. With a quick greeting, Roger discovered that the caller was his son.

"I hope I didn't interrupt anything important, Dad."

"No. Just going over my lessons. I'm almost finished. What's the problem?"

"It's about Aunt Siobhan."

That's all Roger had to hear. The very thing he'd dreaded was coming to fruition. Siobhan was trying to corrupt Mark's mind with her venomous innuendo. The anthropology professor was fuming over her meddling in Mark's affairs.

"And I'm sorry I couldn't speak to you last night about it, Dad, but I didn't get home until well past nine. I know you have a penchant for going to bed early, so I didn't call. I'm on a break right now at the store. I don't know what to make of her. Is she after something? Maybe you might have some insight. You've known her longer than I have."

"You let me handle her, Mark. Don't let this upset you. I'll talk to you again soon."

Roger hung up the phone. He was seething over Siobhan's instigation. He darted to his cell phone, because her number was listed among recent calls. But Roger didn't want to have Beth hear his tongue-lashing, or the fury directed at his ex-sister-in-law. He moved to a remote part of the back of the house upstairs—a bedroom only used for guests.

Two rings. Finally, there was a connection.

"What the fuck did you say or do to my son last night?" Roger shouted, but not loud enough to arouse suspicion from Beth.

"And a good evening to you, too, Roger. Is that any way to say hi?"

"Never mind the bullshit. Mark called me earlier and gave me all the dirt on your dinner with him last night. This was just the reason why I wanted you to keep your distance. You have a corrupt mind!"

"I just wanted to see for myself what his thought processes were. Congratulations, Roger. You've trained Mark well."

"You've had your meeting with Mark. Now I suggest you stay away!"

"You have no say in this matter! If Mark doesn't want to see me anymore, let it come from his lips! He gave me no indication of that when we parted ways last night."

"That's because he was being polite!"

"A trait no doubt passed down from Maggie, not you." Siobhan paused for a moment. "I assured Mark, as I'm assuring you, I will not bring up sensitive subjects again with him. He made that abundantly clear . . . as did you. Now, if you don't mind, Roger, I must be going. I have a full day planned tomorrow to show some properties, one of them all the way over in Warwick."

Roger heard the loud click on the other end. Still angry that the call had to be initiated to begin with, Roger took some solace in knowing Siobhan wasn't going to repeat another incident like the one that happened in the Providence restaurant. Or so she promised. To Roger, Siobhan was as trustworthy as a snake.

He made his way back down toward the living room. A countenance of rage remained etched on his face.

Beth was alarmed when she heard Roger's loud and harsh words while continuing to read. She had to confront her husband.

"What was that all about?" Beth inquired.

Roger broke his focus. He looked at Beth with raised eyebrows. "You heard that all the way down here?"

"It was pretty loud, dear."

Roger exhaled. "It was Siobhan O'Mara."

"What the hell does she want?"

"That's a loaded question. I wish I knew. She claims I've been keeping Mark from her. Okay, I gave her his number, but with a stern warning not to feed him any garbage. But does she heed my warning? Oh, no! She goes on her merry way and does what she damn well pleases!" Roger slapped his thighs to stress his frustration. He then rubbed the back of his head. "Well, she gave me a guarantee that it won't happen again."

"And you believed her?"

"Not exactly. But I'm going to keep my eye on her. I made that much known before I hung up."

Roger tried to put the episode behind him. He gave Beth a halfhearted grin in an attempt to make her feel at ease. Her raised eyebrows told a different story. But she just exhaled and went back to her police detective story.

He still had to finish his lesson plan. But the calls from Mark and to Siobhan gave Roger serious pause to continue.

166

Chapter 41

The dampness of the bone-chilling rain awoke the mildew demons of the house. Mort Sonnenstein never allowed it to affect him. He was too used to it. Patients, on the other hand, could discern the change. But Mort had no clients coming to see him that day. Just as well. He was still recovering after an overwhelming schedule of patients the day before.

Instead, Mort was lounging in his office, feet up on the desk, chatting away on the phone. He was wearing gray sweats and Sketchers. Papers in need of being filed away lay scattered on his massive desk, some in various groups. With no assistant or housekeeper present, Mort was his own maintenance man. But there was no desperate run to tidy up the place on his part, although there should have been.

Mort was nodding like a dog ornament sitting behind the rear seat of a car. A few grunts of acknowledgement were the only signs he was still alive. Until . . .

"I see where you're coming with this, Roger. But there is no need to stop by."

Mort glanced at his fingernails. He wasn't a bit concerned how manicured they were. It was just passing time before ending the chat.

"Like I said, I wouldn't get too worked up over Siobhan's meddling. She is, after all, Mark's aunt. But let me know if it gets out of hand. Maybe we can talk then. Take care, Roger."

Mort swung his legs off the desk and leaned forward to hang up. As he did, he released a blast of air to dispel the weight of the conversation, sweating from the strain. The exhaling of breath caused several sheets to take flight. Mort slammed them down like swatting a fly, to prevent them from flying over the edge.

Mort rubbed the nape of his neck, causing the back of his hair to become a grotesque cowlick. A call was in order. He flipped through his Rolodex and punched in a series of numbers. Several rings sounded in succession. And after going through the ritual of following prompts, Mort reached his target.

"Hello, Oswald. Mort Sonnenstein here."

Mort began a rhythmic tapping of his fingertips. While he waited for Borshevsky to finish, Mort grabbed a snow globe paperweight, sitting by its lonesome next to a horizontal metallic organizer. He shook it vigorously, causing a blizzard inside the water-filled orb, with cascading snowflakes descending upon the depiction of the quaint village inside. Mort then gently placed it down atop his desk, perhaps thinking of the arrival of winter upon the Providence area. A frown emerged at the mere thought of trudging through several feet of snow and commanding his Lexus to navigate heavily packed, powdered roads.

"Lavoie sounded agitated with his ex-sister-in-law's homing in on his son's psyche. Look, Oswald. I did what you've asked me as a professional courtesy for seeing Margaret, contacting O'Mara and gave her Lavoie's email address. But now I believe it's gotten out of hand."

Mort looked up at the ceiling and sighed while Borshevsky prattled on. Time to get a word in edgewise.

"If you were hoping to rattle Lavoie, then you've succeeded. But personally, I think it was a mistake from the beginning to engage in this experiment of yours, thinking it might cause Lavoie to come forward with the confession you believe he might reveal. Quite frankly, I don't know if that'll occur. I've got to run, Oswald. We'll talk again soon. Bye-bye."

Mort gently laid the receiver down on its cradle. He rose from his seat and made a measured pace out of the room. Just four steps down the hall and a quick left found Mort in the bathroom. A quick flick of the switch illuminated the room. But his purpose for being there wasn't to relieve himself. No, Mort wanted to look in the mirror.

He didn't like what he saw, a saddened vestige of someone who normally comported himself in an upbeat demeanor. Indeed, Mort was troubled by what he'd become: a slave to Borshevsky's obsession of vilifying Roger, causing him to fall into disgrace for sending Margaret to a world of eternal hell. *Not even the anthropology professor deserves that much torture,* Mort thought. The box of twelve meted justice as it saw fit two decades earlier. Give the devil his due. But no. Oswald wanted Mort to play the game as a payback favor for that visit to Crenshaw. The asylum director wanted Roger to pay for the alleged atrocities and Margaret's upkeep the last twenty years. Managing her was no picnic, and Oswald was hell-bent on revenge. Mort became the perfect pawn to execute this master plan. And supplying Siobhan as the perfect conduit to get in touch with Roger was a formality, although her reasons to get under Roger's skin were not the same as one might have thought.

Yeah, Mort took a hard look at his reflection. *How do you like yourself now?* Mort pounded his clenched fist atop the porcelain sink so hard it caused him pain. But this self-inflicted agony was justifiable in his book. Now he was the one seeking psychological help for allowing himself to become trapped in Oswald's scheme.

Mort slumped to the floor. The cold tile was enough to send shivers up his spine, but now the specter of an experiment gone wrong threw him into the deep freeze of guilt. Although he vowed never to be beholden to people like Oswald again, he knew the damage was done. It was irreparable. Mort would spend another five minutes on the floor weeping profusely. How could he betray his profession? A good question, but with no remedial answer.

Chapter 42

It was a week before Christmas. Beth's suggestions for last minute holiday decorations were heeded and put in place by Roger. But much of the heavier artillery was already there. The seven-foot-tall spruce stood majestically in one corner of the living room, adorned with festive lights and ornaments, twinkling at the room's occupants. And it was Beth's creative eye that made everything come together in harmony.

A string of lights hung from the rain gutter across the façade of the house. But they paled in comparison to those of Cal and Francine MacKenzie's, whose front display looked like a Broadway theatre marquee, or the Campbells' house, which gave the appearance of an amusement park, photographed and videoed every year by the local media and those holiday reality shows. But Beth and Roger had no young children or grandchildren to amuse. Their understated display suited them just fine.

A three-inch cover of snow blanketed the front lawn, shimmering in the low-angled but bright sunshine. The barren curbside maple stood with its naked limbs frosted like a birthday cake. There was the high-pitched peep of a brilliant red male cardinal, making its presence known, before taking flight to destinations elsewhere. A black SUV slowly wheeled past the house, its tires and engine noise muffled by the impacted thin layer of fresh-laid white powder.

Mark drove up the shoveled driveway. Although it was a Friday afternoon, he knew his father was home, what with the fall semester coming to a close the day before with the last of final exams administered. Beth, of course, was still at the hospital. This would give Mark and Roger a few minutes alone.

Roger had seen the arrival of his son. He opened the front door gingerly so as not to disturb the magnificent wreath adorning it, replete with carefully inserted pine cones along with a dazzling red bow. Again, all the craftsmanship a product of Beth's handiwork.

"Hi, Dad," Mark smiled as he slammed his driver's side door.

"Hello, Mark. I know you're getting psyched up for the new position, but don't you think that corduroy jacket, sweater vest and scarf could also use a parka to cover them?"

"Hey, it's okay. My car is like an oven when I've got the heat cranked up."

"Well, one thing's for certain. It's a freezer out here. Come, come, come in!"

Roger quickly waved his son inside the house to get out of the early winter chill. But Mark didn't need his father's encouragement. His body was telling him to get inside . . . now!

Once the door was closed, Roger rubbed his hands briskly to generate extra warmth. Despite a brief encounter with the December air, Mark was fine. Roger's offer of a cup of coffee was most welcome.

Mark took a seat on the living room sofa. It wasn't too long before Roger entered the room. With the balance of a tightrope walker, Roger carefully handed the piping-hot mug of joe just as Mark preferred it: a touch of milk and just a hint of sugar to give the French Roast blend some sweetness.

"Thanks, Dad. You remembered."

Roger looked at his son as if he had two heads. "I've only known you take it that way for the past six years. I should hope you'd give me some credit for remembering."

Mark grinned sheepishly, embarrassed over his statement. "I apologize."

Roger chuckled and waved his hand dismissively, as if to let his son know he was only making a joke of the matter. The anthropology professor studied Mark as a sign to move on to other topics.

"I guess you're counting down the days when you'll be saying goodbye to the store," Roger began.

"Next Thursday," Mark replied with a broad grin. "Eight o'clock. Christmas Eve. And then I receive my freedom!"

"Are your co-workers taking you out to celebrate?"

171

"A few offered." Mark looked away for a moment before returning his focus to Roger. "But I told them not to bother. I had that celebration last month, thanks to you and Beth. I just figured with the holidays upon us, it was best for the guys to spend their extra money on gifts for family members and friends. Besides, restaurants have a tendency to jack up their prices now, exploiting the patrons."

"I raised you well, Mark." Roger gazed down at his beige Irish wool knit sweater. He had a little hesitation here, for he needed to ask his son an uncomfortable question, but one that he knew had to be addressed. "Have you heard any more from Siobhan?"

"Oh, we've talked a couple of times," Mark answered with an affirmative nod. "Nothing like the conversation we had at CAV's. She asked me if I could come over for Christmas dinner. I told her I couldn't, but I did tell her I'd stop by soon, briefly."

"I'm sure she must've been miffed. But at least you'll get to spend Christmas here with us."

Mark tugged at the collar of his open dress shirt underneath his crimson-and-gray argyle sweater vest.

"Well, Dad," Mark began clumsily, clearing his throat. "I won't be here for Christmas either."

Roger was blown back in his easy chair as if a gust of wind had smacked him.

"I'm not quite sure I understand."

"I've been invited for dinner over at Rebecca's mother's house. She lives in Greenville."

"I didn't know you were still seeing her."

"Yeah." Mark took another sip of the brew, still fairly hot. "We're going to the Berkshires for a week right after. We'll even watch the ball drop on New Year's Eve from there."

This was getting to be too much for the elder Lavoie to fathom. He looked off to the side to give his son's relationship with Rebecca deep reflection. Roger looked back with concerned and caring eyes.

"You've really been smitten by her, haven't you?"

"Let's put it this way, Dad. When we go up there, I think I'm going to pop the question."

Now Roger was truly floored by Mark's latest statement, and rolled his eyes in disbelief. The veteran professor had trouble digesting this bit of news. Yet he composed himself in order to address Mark.

"You've only known her for not even two months. Are you sure you want to make that kind of commitment so soon?"

"I look at it this way, Dad. I'm moving up to a job next month that will fulfill me not only in terms of a decent paycheck, but will satisfy my desires. I think it's an honor in keeping up the teaching tradition in this family. And it has served you well all these years. Plus Rebecca has a good job herself. I think I'm ready. Besides, I'd like to start a family of my own someday soon."

"That little blond-haired boy of mine now wants to take a wife." Roger tried to absorb the revelation of having a daughter-in-law. "Just let me give you a bit of advice, Son. Before you fully commit to Rebecca . . . by that I mean actually marrying her . . . just pump her with the right questions to make certain she's the one."

"Gee, you make it sound as though I need to interrogate her."

"No, not necessarily. It is, after all, only a month and a half that you've been with her. What I'm trying to tell you is to think about what you want to do carefully. I just don't want to see you hurt. That's all."

Roger didn't want to expand on his statement. That would be revealing matters Mark shouldn't be privy to. Like the real reason Margaret went batty and took up permanent residence at Crenshaw. That was going to remain this guilty father's dirty little secret.

But Roger was also curious to learn how put together Rebecca was. Surely that Thanksgiving meet-and-greet couldn't give him a full answer. And then there was the question of her family members. Was there someone like Siobhan in the Dyer family?

As Mark smiled and excused himself to use the bathroom, Roger remained in his chair. He was hoping his pearls of wisdom might sink into Mark's cranium.

Chapter 43

Mark made the effort to attend Christmas morning Mass at Our Lady of Lourdes Church on Atwell Avenue. He was certainly the square peg in the proverbial round hole. Even Mark had to think hard to remember the last time he attended services. Oh, yeah, Easter. But that was well over eight months ago. Mark was one of the few odd ducks at Mass, as some parishioners stared at him in bewilderment.

He would blame his infrequency to the demands of his job at Best Buy. He had to work a boatload of Sundays. Memories of his last Sunday off from the retailer were a distant recollection. But one thing he wanted to do was return to his childhood religious roots, which went way back to the time when he was an altar server nearly two decades earlier. There was no guilt here. It's just that if he ever took his relationship with Rebecca to the next level he had to set the example of a family man, particularly if and when he became a father. And despite Rebecca's erratic attendance at church herself, Mark was under the strong belief that she might go regularly, if he did.

Rebecca did the honors of meeting the Lavoie clan on Thanksgiving Day. Now it was payback as Mark reciprocated by meeting her family.

He stopped by Rebecca's place at noon to exchange gifts and to jump into her silver Toyota Camry. Mark loved driving except in horrid winter conditions. Fortunately he didn't come across such conditions that day, although a recent snowfall left the smatterings of a blissful white Christmas throughout the Providence metropolitan area. But the driving reins to Rebecca's mom's house in Greenville were ceded to Rebecca. Besides her knowing the route like the back of her hand, Mark didn't want to bother listening to the box lady in his GPS device while concentrating on steering clear of the daft holiday drivers.

Rebecca drove up the snow-packed driveway. As she was pulling up to stop, Mark gave a long study to the charming white Garrison colonial. It was festooned with even more decorations and lights than his father's house, although not quite on the scale of the MacKenzie's arcade. Skeletal frames of electric reindeer bowed to Mark's presence. And a picture of Santa graced the cherry wood front door with a pinecone-laden wreath serving as his crown. But not to forget the true meaning of the venerated holiday, in the middle of the front lawn stood a manger set, with a recently placed figure of the baby Jesus lying in middle of the crèche.

When he exited the Camry, Mark further scrutinized the bedecked home. Fists on hips and arms spread out like wings, Mark beamed at the work and effort that were put into making it so festive.

"Boy, your mother went to a lot of effort in putting this all together."

"What, this?" Rebecca asked, pointing to the arrangement, slamming her driver's side door while locking it up with her remote, the car chirping, letting everyone know the alarm was on. "My mother had nothing to do with it."

Mark raised his eyebrows in curiosity.

"This is all the creative handiwork of my brother Laird. You'll meet him. Oh, by the way, I'm just letting you know, Laird's gay. I think it's best I tell you ahead of time, so you won't think he's strange with the way he acts."

Mark shrugged his shoulders as if to say he didn't have a problem with it.

Rebecca rang the doorbell. In three seconds it opened with Laird welcoming his older sister. There was a noticeable feminine flair with which he greeted her, welcoming Rebecca as though he hadn't seen her in ages.

"Hello, Big Sis!" Laird flung his arms out like a bird readying itself for flight and gave Rebecca a soft peck on each of her cheeks. He then turned to Mark. "Gee, this isn't Logan?"

Rebecca introduced the men to each other. Laird offered a handshake and a subdued smile. Mark reciprocated, but there was a bit of reticence in his returning the favor. Mark knew of a few gay men and lesbian women, but he'd never really associated with them. Chalk it up to the strong testosterone levels he possessed, and the macho bravado associated with that, but Mark preferred to stay away from them. However, the new teacher at Winston put on his best game face to make a decent impression.

Noticing the exchange between them, Rebecca pulled Mark to the side soon after they were inside.

"Don't worry," she advised her boyfriend. "Laird is in a relationship. Besides, gays and lezzies can spot someone straight a mile away. Trust me, Laird and others like him won't hit on you, if that's what you're worried about."

Mark felt a little relief at hearing Rebecca's remark. But perhaps focusing on other matters might get his mind off Laird.

The house tour began and Mark was impressed by the classy interior of the living room. Modern furniture took up the majority of the space, encircling a French colonial table with its glass top. An exquisite Afghan rug padded the base of the table so that the legs wouldn't mark up the glistening stained oak floor. An arrangement of seasonal poinsettias graced the top as the centerpiece.

A quick glance at the fireplace arrested his attention once again. An ivy twine of holly stretched across the mantle, stealing some space meant solely for family pictures during other times of the year. A Monet print accented the wall above it, front and center.

And then there was the Christmas tree, glittering with soft white lights, and suspended ornaments of various sizes clinging to the branches, from the religious to the secular variety. The family preferred a real tree, and it was Laird's responsibility to keep it watered. A huge 54-inch flat screen television was in one corner of the room, but it was kept off. For the special occasion, the family felt no urgency to check out what was on the tube.

There was a high-pitched squeal emanating from one of the back rooms. Mark discerned the voice not to be mature enough for Rebecca's mother, even though he'd never heard Sheryl speak. And his suspicions were correct.

Darting out from what was the kitchen was Rebecca's younger sister Sara. She was the spitting image of her older sibling, right down to her flowing locks of blonde hair and an identical 5'6" height. She was twenty, six years younger than Rebecca, and was in her junior year at UConn studying marine biology. She'd always had a love affair with sea life, and the scientific field was her special calling.

"Hey, hey!" Sara screamed with her arms open a mile wide to receive Rebecca. The older sib was equally elated to see Sara. Their long tender embrace was broken when Sara gave a quick glance to Mark.

"Whoa! New beau, Rebecca?"

"Mark," Rebecca replied proudly, "this is my sister, Sara."

"What a resemblance," Mark marveled. "It's a pleasure."

"To answer your question, Sara, yes, Mark's my new man! Logan's out! Mark's going to be teaching at Winston starting in January."

Suddenly another member of the Dyer family emerged from the kitchen. A woman in her mid-fifties greeted the guests, but with subdued enthusiasm, as opposed to Laird and Sara's. It was Sheryl, who stood about an inch shorter than her daughters and nearly half a foot less than Laird. She wore a conservative chocolate-brown dress, accented by a string of pearls encircling her neck like the moons of Jupiter. Sheryl wore her age well, although a light brown dye with blonde highlights masked those few traces of gray strands in her short hairstyle. She was just a few pounds overweight, but she distributed whatever excess baggage on her body proportionately, not really showing the pounds.

The mother and daughter gave each other a light smack on the lips. Then Sheryl turned to Mark.

"I understand from Rebecca that you're a college professor," Sheryl beamed while shaking Mark's hand.

"Well, that position doesn't start for another month yet."

"Oh, honey," Rebecca interceded. "Could you get the presents from the trunk please? Here are my keys."

Ever the obedient foot soldier, Mark went back outside to retrieve the goodies. Rebecca looked back at him fondly as he exited the front door. But Sheryl wanted to put in her own two cents about Mark.

"I like him, Rebecca. You'd better not lose him."

"I don't plan to. Oh, I thought I might as well tell you, Mark and I are going to spend next week up at the Berkshire East Ski Area over in Charlemont, Mass. We're staying through New Year's Day up there."

"Ooh, that sounds romantic!" Sara piped in.

Rebecca flashed her pearly whites at her sister for the lovely comment. But both Laird and Sheryl looked at Rebecca strangely.

"Since when did you learn to ski?" Laird was inquisitive.

"Yeah," Sheryl questioned with her head cocked sideways. "I didn't know you'd suddenly become a skiing enthusiast."

"Skiing? Who said we're going to spend all of our entire time up there skiing?"

Sara giggled at the sensual suggestion and gave Rebecca a fist bump. Laird wiggled his eyebrows and walked away while holding his head with his hand, his arm supported by his other hand at the elbow. Rebecca wore a smug grin as if to say, *Don't worry, I know what I'm doing.*

Just then Mark reentered the home acting like Santa Claus with two sizeable bags, one in each hand. The family was amazed at the generosity of Mark's benevolence. But the new teacher dismissed it by stating that it was his last hurrah with an employee discount at Best Buy.

"If you could, please, Mark, just leave them by the tree," Sheryl requested. "Thank you."

Sheryl drew a deep sigh. With hands on hips, the family matriarch turned to her adult children.

"I could use some help, family."

Before Rebecca and her siblings began to move, Mark sprang into action.

"Here, let me assist."

Now Sheryl was surprised again at Mark's kind gesture. As he walked toward the kitchen, Sheryl's eyes widened large as saucers with her mouth gaping. She turned to Rebecca, raising two thumbs up, sporting a surreptitious grin as a sign of her solid endorsement.

As he was moving a platter into the dining room, Mark observed an abstract painting in the middle of the hallway.

"That's one of my creations," Laird chimed in before Mark had a chance to ask.

Mark queried, "Oh, so you're an artist?"

"A struggling one," Rebecca interjected.

Laird gave his older sister a dirty look. "I've sold a few pieces at a couple of art galleries in Providence and New-port."

"Well, you're not quite yet in the Jackson Pollock class, but," Rebecca gave careful thought to her words so as not to discourage Laird, "who is?"

The dining room was equally as charming as the living room. A long white linen cloth covered the cherry wood table. And yes, another bouquet of poinsettias served as the centerpiece.

A richly crafted, matching china closet complemented the table. Gold embroidered silk drapes, coroneted by a ten-foot matching valance, were tied back to allow nature's light in. Multiple white wooden frames held the various glass panes in place, filtering in what little warmth of solar heat the low-angled sun could provide.

The entire house was enveloped with the strong aroma of the loin of pork cooking in the oven. And then it became time for the feast to begin. Out from the kitchen came glazed carrots, French-cut string beans with slivers of almonds and bacon bits, whipped mashed potatoes laced with cara-melized onions and garlic with melted stringy mozzarella painstakingly folded in, and of course the meat itself. As a newly self-designated vegetarian, Sara told Sheryl that she wanted no part of the pork. The mother simply sighed and continued to distribute the plates of food with the help of Mark and Laird. Rebecca and Sara brought in the bottles of wine. Much to her delight, Rebecca was pleased to discover that a bottle of chardonnay was among the vineyard variety.

Despite the fact that she was still underage, Sara was planning to imbibe with a glass of Shiraz. There was no harm there, as Sara was staying put for the evening.

Everyone sat down in the high-backed dining room chairs. Sheryl held the head seat, given her status. She indulged everyone in a prayer of grace to be grateful for the display of food and for their general good health.

Conversation was kept on the light side. That was until Mark brought up the fact that Rebecca's father was missing. This was a tender subject that she was hoping to avoid. But Mark wanted to learn more about the absent husband

and father, even if it meant that dirty laundry would have to be aired.

"Besides being an alcoholic, he was abusive to our mother," Rebecca mentioned. She turned to Sheryl. "I know you prefer not to talk about Dad, but I think Mark deserves to know the truth."

"I never really got to know him," Sara lamented. "He left just about the time I was born."

"I'll bet he would never approve the fact that I'm gay," Laird threw in. "I was a little boy when he left. He was a construction foreman. From what Mom has told me about him, Dad was one of those classic macho types." Laird sighed. "I definitely know he'd kill me if he knew I was gay."

"What about you, Mrs. Dyer?" Mark inquired. "If you don't mind my asking."

"Al let the bottle take charge of his life. So much so that I guess he couldn't take the responsibilities of this household. Or maybe it was when I told him I was pregnant with Sara." Sheryl mused over the lemons she was handed when Al Dyer took off. "And like Rebecca told you, he treated me . . . treated his family . . . like shit."

"Mom has a couple of scars on her back because of him," Rebecca mentioned. "I've seen them. I say good riddance he isn't here anymore to inflict any further pain on her. Or any of us, for that matter. And I vow I will not allow that to happen to me."

At that moment, Mark reached across the top of Rebecca's back with his arm and tenderly cupped her shoulder as an indication to her that such abuse would not be tolerated by him either. She leaned the side of her face against his as a token of her appreciation of his kindness and affection.

Sara smiled in admiration of the couple. Laird wasn't fazed by it. And Sheryl had the look that said maybe Mark was a better catch for Rebecca than Logan. But the Dyer matriarch wanted to learn more.

"Rebecca tells me you're going to start teaching math at Winston College. I think teaching is a very noble profession."

"So do I," Mark added. "It also runs in my family. My father is an anthropology professor there."

"Hmm. You said your last name is Lavoie. That's French."

"Yes, it is. But I also have Irish and some Dutch and Spanish mixed in, from what I've been told."

"Where have I heard that name before?"

Mark was hoping Sheryl wouldn't recall. He wanted to keep that ugly chapter in his family's life a dark secret. But Sheryl wagged her index finger at him and peered in his direction with determination in her eyes.

"Now I remember. Your father isn't Roger Lavoie, is he?"

The jig was up. There was no denying Roger's identity. Mark nodded slightly to his interrogator. Rebecca swiveled her head between the two of them in bewilderment.

"Maybe someone can enlighten me on what's going on?"

"Oh, it's something that happened about the same time your father left. It concerns a trial involving Mark's dad."

Mark came to his father's defense.

"Yes, there was a case about my father. But he was acquitted on both counts. He didn't commit murder and my mother went off the deep end over mental issues she was facing at the time. But I also want to clear the air regarding Dad, Mrs. Dyer. My dad has been a tremendous father to me. He's guided me through childhood and adolescence by himself, since my mother was committed when I was seven. And he has been my greatest ally. Even to this day he continues to fight for me. Heck, I probably wouldn't have that job waiting for me at Winston next month if it hadn't been for his vigorous campaigning and fighting for me, especially with the school's chancellor. I owe a lot to him."

"And if I can say something, Mom. I have met Mark's dad on two occasions. And each time he has treated me as if I were his own daughter. He has been extremely hospitable and seems very nice. He shouldn't be condemned, particularly if he was exonerated. Mark's dad deserves reconsideration."

Sheryl sucked in her lips. It was best to drop the subject, especially since her own daughter gave Roger such a solid backing.

There would be no further discussions of skeletons in the closet on either side, while they went on to enjoy the exchanging of gifts and the scrumptious apple cake Sheryl baked from scratch for dessert. And as everyone said their goodbyes, Sheryl pulled Rebecca off to the side before leaving.

"Hey, I really like this guy. Be good to him."

"As long as he's good to me," Rebecca returned with a wink.

Sheryl grinned as she gave a nod of approval.

Chapter 44

The very next morning, Mark and Rebecca wasted no time in traveling up to Charlemont. It took nearly three hours to get there due to a recent blanket of eight inches of white powder. But the ski resort didn't leave anything to chance. The snow-making machines were in full force to ensure all the trails were in peak condition.

Despite this being her maiden schuss down the modest slopes, Rebecca adjusted quickly to her first three trips downhill. Mark had skied before, but was impressed by how well his girlfriend picked up the sport.

The vigorous hillside excursions exhausted them. Mark excused himself from Rebecca who remained in the lounge, taking up every inch of an oversized leather chair. Her limbs were spread out like an octopus in her heightened lethargy, not willing to move a muscle.

Rebecca's eyes danced around the huge room. What chill there was from the subfreezing outside air was quelled by a huge crackling fire in the stone-columned hearth. Coats of arms and even a moose head festooned the otherwise barren walnut walls. A towering, glittering spruce held court in one corner, blocking out nearly all of one of the multi-paned 20-foot windows. Its dazzling lights and decorative ornaments were a sure sign the holiday season was still in full swing. The tree's strong pine scent enhanced the smoky fragrance of the burning embers in the fireplace.

Rebecca watched with fascination as the flames continued to perform a lively dance. Snap, crackle and pop. The fire was in perfect cadence as it licked the interior of the soot-caked brick fireplace.

Whatever cold Rebecca was feeling was further tempered by the ample and thick angora sweater and comfortable woolen jogging pants she wore. She scanned the enormous high-ceiling room and spotted two other couples also lounging on the furniture. One duo was close to her age while the other appeared to be in their late thirties. They smiled at her as she reciprocated the gesture.

Rebecca's gaze then ventured toward the plush Kerman rug, lying in the center of the ivory stone-tiled floor. The intricate and colorful designs were both examples of exquisite beauty and artistic craftsmanship.

Finally Mark showed up. He was holding a large box of Cracker Jacks.

"Boy, I thought you might have gotten lost," Rebecca snorted.

"Who, me? Nah. I just had to get this to munch on." Mark offered the box to his gal. "Would you like some?" Mark even shook its contents to entice her.

"No thanks! Do you know how harmful that is for your teeth?"

Mark shrugged. "That's why God made dentists."

Despite not wanting to indulge in the caramel-coated popcorn-and-peanut confection, Rebecca didn't mind sharing her space on the gigantic chair. She shimmied over to one side and patted the vacant spot for Mark to sit beside her. The teacher-in-waiting took her up on the offer.

Rebecca draped her arm across the top of Mark's back as he reached for her hand. The amorous couple snuggled serenely before Rebecca sighed.

"Just think," Rebecca opened. "We're here right through New Year's Eve."

"More of a chance to break a leg."

"Don't say that! Besides, I was pretty good out there today."

"Don't forget, it was a beginner's course."

"Well, maybe we can tackle a more challenging course before we leave."

"Maybe. But you can't expect to be the next Lindsey Vonn overnight, you know."

"True, but I'd still like to give it a try."

Mark took another handful of Cracker Jacks and tossed it in his mouth. Munching away, he looked around at the holiday getaway display and the patrons enjoying it.

"I'm amazed you were able to get this vacation on such short notice from your company."

"Just sick days I haven't used. I was even more astounded you were able to book this place this week."

"We were on standby. Besides, I hounded this place and a few others to see if a cancellation might occur. We lucked out here."

Mark took another fistful of the candied popcorn. Rebecca was now intrigued by the box.

"If I remember correctly they still have a toy prize in the box, right?"

"Yeah . . . I guess so. Why, do you want to see what it might be?"

Rebecca smiled as she sucked in her lower lip. She nodded as Mark handed the box to her.

Rebecca dug into the box. She looked up absently at the enormous Christmas tree while her fingers continued to feel around for the prize. Much to her delight, Rebecca felt the edge of paper. She yanked the coveted prize out of the box.

"Gee," Mark quipped, "all this for a mass-produced dime item made in China."

Rebecca smirked at Mark. She then looked at the small white paper package. She became puzzled by its taped sides, unusual to be sure. She felt its sides to get an idea of the contents.

"Feels like a ring of some sort," Rebecca suggested.

"Maybe it's some sort of spy decoder ring."

Rebecca ripped the middle portion of the paper. Oh, it was a ring all right. Much to her astonishment, Rebecca saw a one-carat diamond engagement ring in a 14-karat white gold setting. Her eyes sparkled as she gasped at the lustrous beauty of the multi-faceted gem. She then looked at Mark with a vivid smile to match her glowing face. Cracker Jacks never put out anything so dazzling in its boxes before. This was all Mark.

"How about it, Love?" Mark beamed with a huge grin of his own. "Will you marry me?"

Still clutching the ring, Rebecca locked her arms around Mark and squeezed him as if she were sucking the wind out of him.

"Yes!" Despite her happy face, a tear emerged from the corner of her right eye. "Yes!"

The other two couples couldn't help but notice. They gave Mark and Rebecca a loud round of applause. The newly engaged duo beamed back at the others and politely accepted their congratulatory well wishes.

Rebecca gleefully slipped the rock on her left ring finger. She couldn't keep her eyes off it as she was trying to pinch herself to affirm all that was happening to her was real. Mark took hold of his fiancée.

"I don't know about you, but I've suddenly lost my appetite for the rest of the Cracker Jacks." He tossed the box to the side. "On the other hand, I've got a taste for something even better!" Mark then gently nibbled on Rebecca's left earlobe.

"C'mon, big boy," she responded salaciously. "Show me what you got!"

Mark and Rebecca wrapped their arms around each other and made a quick beeline to their room.

Chapter 45

Fueled by the bottle of champagne Mark ordered through room service and buoyed by the dazzling diamond on her left ring finger, Rebecca went to town sexually with her new fiancé. She gave of herself to her beau with such passion that she would still recall the wild ride with him for some time to come.

There was a break when Rebecca couldn't help but text a message to her friend Heather of the engagement. Almost immediately the newly engaged woman received a call.

"I can't believe it," Heather remarked. "Engaged? Shut up!"

Rebecca giggled. "Can you believe it? He teased me with this box of Cracker Jacks and so I went searching for one of those toy prizes they put in it. I pulled out the packet, opened it up, and there was the ring! I know Cracker Jacks doesn't put prizes like this in their boxes!"

"Oh . . . my . . . God! That's unbelievable! Have you told your mom?"

"Not yet. I wanted to tell my maid of honor first!"

Heather squealed with delight after hearing Rebecca's request.

And while Rebecca was giggling with her friend, Mark sat in the chair in the far corner. He was drinking it all in, content with his decision to marry Rebecca, and grinned with delight in seeing her exude so much happiness in her phone chat.

As he continued to enjoy Rebecca's giddiness, Mark's mind wandered. He had hoped Rebecca would accept his proposal. Not only did she accept it, but she was thrilled beyond belief, already making plans for Heather to be a member of the wedding party. And Mark felt a strong sense of really belonging to someone, a woman he could grow old with. It wasn't so much a sense of accomplishment on his part that caused him to feel this way. No, Rebecca was not to become some trophy placed on the mantle. She was a wholesome beauty whose lips tasted so sweet and body smelled so luscious, even without the added boost of an intoxicating perfume.

Rebecca's talk quickly snapped Mark out of his amorous trance. He had to place a call of his own. And like his fiancée, Mark eschewed phoning his closest relative. He planned to get in touch with Roger to be sure, but he had already intimated to his dad his probable intention of asking Rebecca's hand in marriage. What was good for the goose was good for the gander. As Rebecca was sewing up whom her maid of honor was going to be, Mark had to secure his best man.

He pulled out his smart phone and speed dialed the only person he needed to speak with at that moment.

"Hey, Hunter. What's happening?"

"Mark. Hey. I'm having dinner with Kayla."

Mark heard a "Hi, Mark!" in high volume in the background. He chuckled at the greeting from Hunter's girlfriend. Mark shouted back with the same blast and verve. He then waited for Hunter to come back on the line.

"I promise not to take much of your time. But I had to let you know. I proposed to Rebecca and she accepted!"

"No way!" Hunter exclaimed. "Are you shittin' me?"

"No, dude! Not on something like this!"

Mark heard Hunter talking through muffled speech, presumably sharing the news with Kayla. Suddenly he heard a high-pitched squeal indicating Kayla's excitement. Mark's smile deepened. He took pleasure in hearing others were happy for them.

"This is awesome!" Hunter commented. "Do you have plans for the date?"

"Not yet. But rest assured they will include you. I need you as the best man. What do you say?"

"Absolutely! I'm in!"

"You're the best! I won't keep you any longer. We'll talk again soon, Hunter. Say good night to Kayla for me."

And with that Mark concluded his conversation with his best friend.

He sat back in the oversized hotel room chair. Rebecca was still talking a blue streak with Heather, and Mark was relishing every minute of it. But he wasn't looking for a pat on the back. Mark was not one for self-gratification. Quite the contrary. On one of the milestone nights in his life, Mark took pleasure in hearing the joy and exhilaration Hunter, Heather, and even Kayla were exhibiting. But most of all, he reveled in making Rebecca a very happy woman. This was not about him. It was all about the number one woman in his life.

Rebecca ended her chat with Heather, but she wasn't finished with calls. With a perky smile, she held up her index finger to her lover. Mark simply grinned and flashed his palms to let her know he was cool with that.

"Hi, Mom! Guess what!"

Rebecca sang the wedding news to Sheryl. She squealed at hearing her mother's approval. And all the while Mark continued to be captivated by her ecstasy. He admired the way she sat on the desk chair, wearing nothing but an oversized sweater to cover what had to be covered, save for showcasing her sexy, shapely legs.

Her right leg was folded underneath her torso. Each time Rebecca mentioned the exciting news, she curled her artistically pedicured toes inward more and more. As much as Mark wanted to make love to her again and again, he bided his time in allowing the extended conversation.

Finally Rebecca concluded the two most important calls she had to make. She put away her phone and threw a wanton gaze at Mark. She then sauntered back to the bed where she lay on her side, lewdly stroking the satin sheets.

"Ready for the next round, stud?" Rebecca smiled with lust.

Mark nodded as he gently reclined next to her. He then pulled the sweater over her head as Rebecca giggled all the while.

Chapter 46

Their very first day back from Charlemont, Mark and Rebecca went to see her mom. Sheryl greeted both warmly and even celebrated the announcement with a toast of champagne for all. Laird was beginning to get used to the idea of having a brother-in-law, while Sara was thrilled her older sister was getting married. She even gave Mark a hug as tight as her big sister would have given him.

Their stopover at Sheryl's home was brief as they made their way to see Roger and Beth. Whereas Sheryl was made aware of the conjugal pact between the couple ahead of time, Roger was not. The hint dropped by Mark before the holidays was the only notification given to Roger. But it wasn't official.

As Roger opened the door, there to his surprise stood Mark and Rebecca, each bundled up like Arctic explorers to protect themselves from what old man winter was dishing out. The anthropology professor was nonplussed by their arrival, but welcomed them in nonetheless. Beth arrived in Roger's wake and accorded the visitors the same level of enthusiasm.

"Can we get you anything?" Roger inquired.

"No, Dad. We're not going to stay long. In fact, don't take our coats."

Roger was bemused by his son's odd request, but with a shrug of the shoulders he asked if the couple could at least sit down on the divan together. Finally, there was a compromise.

Once seated, Mark smiled at his father and stepmother, but didn't say a word. He wanted to shout out the news, but held back in deference to Roger. Finally the Lavoie patriarch spoke up.

"How was Charlemont?"

"Oh, it was awesome," Mark responded. "Rebecca over here amazed me by how well she schussed down the slopes."

"Ah, it was no biggie." Rebecca modestly grinned, sloughing off the praise.

"Well, that's more than I can say for Mr. Chicken over here," Beth giggled while placing her hand on Roger's shoulder. "He won't even watch downhill skiing on television, let alone attempt it."

"I'm afraid those daredevil days are over for this old man."

Roger's self-deprecating humor got a few laughs, but he wanted to switch gears.

"You'll be starting your Winston career a week from tomorrow, Mark. When will you be seeing Asmundsson? No doubt Edward would like to review your syllabus and your lesson plans."

"That'll be Tuesday, Dad. I have a meeting with him in his office."

"Don't be intimidated by Edward. He's very easy. But he does hold a strict adherence to detail. He'll give you all the guidance and help you'll need."

"And then there's you."

"Yes. Well." Roger looked down as if in embarrassment. "I'll help you, too, Son. But only from the perspective of handling these youngsters."

"Gee, you make it sound as if I'm over the hill. I'm not much older than the students. Not too long ago I was sitting behind the desk."

"You'll be amazed by how much you've matured since graduation, even if you don't realize it."

Mark nodded slightly, hanging on Roger's every word and thinking it all made sense. And like his father, Mark decided to change the subject.

"There's a reason why Rebecca and I stopped by." He turned to his sweetheart with a proud grin. "Maybe you ought to show them."

Rebecca was beaming ear to ear, more than happy to comply. She raised her gloved left hand to eye level, keeping Roger and Beth in suspense. Like a stripper beginning her act, Rebecca slowly started to pull each glove finger one inch at a time until it reached the point where the whole thing could be pulled off without much effort.

When her hand was completely uncovered, it was at that moment Roger and Beth noticed the dazzling gemstone orbiting Rebecca's ring finger. Their jaws dropped as their eyes danced in captivation. Roger and Beth clutched each other as their lips morphed into elation. They had difficulty containing themselves in knowing that Mark was taking the next step toward starting that family of his own.

Now all four stood. Roger gave Mark a hearty embrace to congratulate his son, while Beth welcomed Rebecca into the Lavoie fold. After a crossover reception, Roger happily began to wag his index finger at Mark.

"You told me before the holidays you were considering doing it."

"And I did!"

"I don't know about you two," Beth interjected, "but I think this calls for a little celebration. We've got some wine."

Mark quickly responded, holding up his hand as if to halt the offering. "If it's okay, Beth, I'll pass. We just had a little champagne toast at Rebecca's family's house. Don't want to be pulled over, driving erratically."

Beth closed her eyes briefly and gave Mark an affirmative nod. She then swiveled to Rebecca. "So, how did your parents react to the news? I'm sure they're thrilled just as we are!"

Rebecca sat in silence. She looked at the floor in front of her, questioning herself as to whether to let Beth and Roger in on the family secret. Right then she held her head up with an air of dignity. She worked up the courage to reveal the dark tale. With an air of confidence, Rebecca looked at Beth dead-on and spoke in measured, relaxed tones.

"My mother is the only true parent I have left. My father walked out on us twenty years ago, leaving my mom to raise me and my brother and sister by herself. And she has done a damn good job, I might add. I only hope I can do half of what she does when I have my own children."

Roger and Beth sat back, astounded by what they'd just heard. They were impressed by Rebecca's steely fortitude to make such a bold statement.

There was an eerie quiet in the room as Mark placed his right hand on Rebecca's left thigh, letting her know that he stood beside her. It was then that Mark confessed to Roger what he'd shared with Rebecca.

"Dad," Mark began with a deep sigh, "I told Rebecca about Mom. After what she told me about her father, I had to. I think it's better to be transparent about these matters than hide behind some defensive shield, don't you?"

Roger gave his son a polite nod. But Mark wasn't through yet.

"I know it's way too premature to be thinking about invitations, but I think Aunt Siobhan should be included in the mix. Now that she has entrenched herself within the family again, I think she ought to be notified."

"Good idea, Mark. Why don't you notify her of the great news? It'll sound better coming from you."

Roger wanted no part of Siobhan any longer. Not primarily because his faithfulness was secured with Beth, but rather that he wanted nothing more of Margaret's sister and the devilish past that had returned to him in nightmares. He would just as well like to wash his hands of Siobhan. There was still that lingering doubt that she had something else planned.

The betrothed couple thought it was best to leave at that moment, having made the announcement. A few more handshakes, hugs and kisses were all that was left of the visit as Roger and Beth advised Mark to keep them up to speed on the nuptials.

The front door was closed gently behind them on their way toward the car. And just seconds after getting in to seek shelter from the frigid climes, Mark turned over the engine and cranked up the heat.

Before her fiancé was about to back slowly out of the driveway, Rebecca thought it was the right moment to bring up something she'd been considering for a long time.

"I wish my father had been here today. Of course, I'd have liked to have told him a thing or two, like ask why he walked out on us. But I also would have liked to have told him of our engagement." She looked in the direction of Roger's house. "I would like to have had him walk me down the aisle on our wedding day. I only have my mother, but I know it's got to be a man." Hesitation. "Maybe my Uncle Greg could do it."

"Yeah, maybe."

Mark looked over his right shoulder as he piloted the vehicle back on the road. A shift in gears brought the car forward as Mark aimed at getting Rebecca home.

Rebecca was quiet for several blocks, but she couldn't remain that way. Not with what was still nagging her.

"You have your father to talk to, but you also have your mother. And I don't mean Beth."

Mark's brow furrowed, eyes narrowed. His grip on the wheel became more pronounced.

"What are you getting at?"

"I'd like to meet your mother. You know, talk to her and let her know about us."

Mark slammed on the brakes so hard it almost propelled Rebecca through the windshield, even with the seat belt harness restraining her. He looked at Rebecca with such an evil scowl it provoked deep fear in her. Not even that incident in the strip mall parking lot two months ago had made Mark so livid.

"Now you listen to me! You are not, I repeat, *not* going to see my mother! Do you understand?"

He held up his first finger to make his point. Meanwhile, Rebecca began to shake at hearing his command. Holding up her hands in an attempt to call a truce, Rebecca pleaded, "Okay! Okay! I'm sorry! I didn't mean to upset you! Just chill, bro!"

Mark resumed his driving, though he was still fuming over the suggestion. Rebecca sat quiet as a church mouse, still unnerved by Mark's vitriolic outburst. Mark glanced at his fiancée and felt a little remorseful over the way he'd reacted. With a deep sigh, he attempted damage control.

"I'm so sorry, Honey. I didn't mean to jump down your throat like that, but the whole situation with Mom in that . . . that horrible place just gets me all riled up. I promise not to behave like that again. But if it's okay by you, I'd like to drop the subject entirely. Deal?"

Rebecca recoiled further, perhaps not totally believing Mark's statement. But she accepted his apology nonetheless. This was one area that wasn't going to be brought up again. But then she wondered what else would cause him to go berserk. Did she really know this man who would determine her future?

Chapter 47

Despite his preoccupation with the preparations for starting his Winston teaching career, Mark still took a moment to alert Siobhan of the wedding plans. Thrilled with being included in the family picture once more, she thanked her nephew profusely for her invitation to his big day.

It was still three days away from the start of spring classes. Roger's tasks for lecturing weren't as daunting as Mark's. All he had to do was resurrect the same script he used over and over again. But he also felt compelled to tweak it every semester. And so the veteran professor went at it.

Beth was still at work at the hospital, so Roger had the entire house all to himself. There was nothing to disturb him; nothing except the unexpected ringing of the front doorbell. Roger was startled. *Way too early for Beth. Besides, she has her own key.* Tossing an old lesson plan to the side, Roger rose from his comfortable recliner. When he opened the door, Roger was not pleased to see who was there.

"Hello, Roger. May I come in?"

Siobhan. Roger was almost tempted to slam the door in her face, but thought better of it. There was something devious going on inside her mind, and that, Roger feared. He waved her in, rather than be subjected to any retribution down the road.

Siobhan beamed superficially as she scanned the interior, acclimating herself with the house she hadn't seen in years. She stroked the crushed cotton fabric of the sofa, as if caressing a household pet. And then Siobhan's attention turned toward the elegant glass coffee table. A poinsettia graced its center.

All this time Roger was keeping a wary eye on her every move, as if she intended to swipe something. But it wasn't anything material Siobhan was after. Her presence had an underlying purpose Roger was having difficulty fathoming.

"I see you've bought new furniture since I was here last," smiled Siobhan. "Very nice! Much better than that wretched set before. I wouldn't have given that to a poor family. I hope you burned it after getting this."

"For your information, Beth and I gave most of it away to one of the youth centers in Pawtucket. I know Mr. Manley was very pleased we gave it to him. Plus, Mark has one of the chairs in his apartment."

"Roger! How could you allow your son to have any of those pieces?"

"He didn't seem to mind."

Siobhan raised her eyebrows and flashed her teeth in a feigned smile. With a shrug of her shoulders, Siobhan continued her tour. As she observed the walls and ceiling of the hallway, Roger stealthily moved to within arm's length of Siobhan.

"Were you thinking about putting our house up for sale?" Roger nastily questioned.

Siobhan spun on her heels to face her former brother-in-law head-on. She was bemused by his query as she burst out in laughter.

"Heaven's sakes, no!" Siobhan continued to cackle. "You never cease to amaze me, Roger. I haven't been here in such a long time. I was just trying to readjust, that's all."

"And just why did you come by?"

"To say hello. And to thank you in person for inviting me to Mark's wedding, although the formal invitations haven't been sent yet. I figured this was the best way to do so. I guess I could've sent you an email, but you might have deleted it. As for a phone call, you might not have answered, especially knowing I was on the other end. I couldn't see you personally slamming the door in my face. That would've been so rude. And I was right. Here I am as proof."

"And you knew Beth was at work at this hour."

"Ah, yes. I think she hates me. But that's okay. I'm not fond of her either."

Siobhan lightly brushed a Van Gogh print on the far wall. By now Roger had had enough of her presence.

"If it's okay with you, I'd like to get back to my lesson plans. Classes begin on Monday."

"Does my coming here disturb you, Roger?"

"It doesn't make me feel any better, to tell you the truth. We'll be seeing you in August. That's when Mark and Rebecca hope to be married. And, yes, you will receive the formal invitation. Now, please leave."

Siobhan smirked. She tilted her head back as if in resignation. "I'll go. I don't want to give Beth the wrong impression, should she unexpectedly arrive early. Mustn't remind her of that spark we once had. She'd be jealous."

"You'd be surprised how twenty years can change one's perspective."

Roger didn't utter another word. He calmly walked to the front door and opened it. That was Siobhan's cue to leave. But as she did, she walked by Roger and sensuously stroked his face. A smile creased her lips as she released a muffled laugh, but it was only a front.

The professor waited until Siobhan cleared the driveway before closing the door. He then leaned up against it, trying to come to an explanation for the purpose of Siobhan's visit. Was it to play with his psyche? Or did she have an underlying reason he just couldn't put his finger on? The best remedy was a shot of Johnny Walker Black Label.

A quick toss down the throat of the liquor soon calmed his nerves. But he needed to lie down and expunge Siobhan's visit from his mind. The lesson plan had to wait.

Chapter 48

At the conclusion of his last class the following Tuesday, Roger sent a text to Mark asking to meet him at McGwire's, a pub just off campus where legal drinking underclassmen and teachers often congregated. Mark accepted.

The musty scent of stale beer and grilled hamburgers permeated the dark, rank rathskeller. It was difficult for Mark to spot Roger immediately in the dimly lit and raucous bistro, but he eventually saw his father, hiding behind a pint of Narragansett Bock and a plate containing a brisket-on-rye sandwich.

"Hey!" Mark dropped down his satchel of books. "Were you waiting long?"

"I just got here fifteen minutes ago," Roger responded. He then extended his hand, saying, "Have a seat."

The moment he sat down, Mark was asked by a young waiter for his order. He went with the same drink Roger was having, and grilled tuna on a roll.

The newest addition to the faculty unloaded his backpack, which weighed as though it were laden with mining gear. Mark exhaled in relief as he plopped himself down. After a hand-combing of the strands of his hair across the top of his head, Mark was ready to chat.

"So," Roger began, "is the new job growing on you yet?"

"I have to admit, Dad, it's one hell of a grind. But I made it through my first five classes. The first one was a little nerve-racking. But after that, things went much smoother." The waiter brought Mark his beer, for which he expressed his gratitude.

"That's fantastic!" Roger took a sip of his beverage. "I wanted to talk to you yesterday about it, but I figured Edward had your ear after yesterday's sessions."

"You're spot-on there. We had a good talk. Asmundsson thinks that if I progress well enough now, I might teach calculus next fall."

"And you'll be a married man then."

Mark's smile widened at his father's comment.

Roger took another bite of his sandwich. Not so much because he was hungry, but because he was hesitant to bring up Siobhan's visit the week before. But after digesting the morsel and wiping his mouth, the anthropology professor addressed the subject.

"Aunt Siobhan visited me last week, snooping around. Why? I don't know."

A puzzled expression was Mark's unspoken response. He glanced at his beer.

"I know you're not keen about her, Dad. You've made your point before."

Roger didn't want his son to be left in the dark about his true feelings toward his ex-sister-in-law. A delicate yet honest reply was in order.

"Maybe it's just me. But I think there's something subversive about her. I believe she's up to something underhanded, but I can't put my finger on it. I'm sure it has something to do with your mother. And the funny thing is, she has this smile about her, as if she knows something I don't."

"I'm sure everything will be fine," Mark assured. "She must attend."

The hope of his son changing his mind about Siobhan's invitation was dashed. Roger drew a deep sigh. It was a losing battle. He didn't want to ruffle Mark's feathers since it was important for him to maintain a strong relationship with him, even if it meant acquiescing to allow Siobhan to attend the nuptials.

With the cacophony of the bar patrons rising to a fevered pitch, it was a wonder that the father and son were able to carry on a conversation. That was why Roger set his phone to vibrate so he could feel a call coming in. Heck, there was no way he was going to hear it. And as if on cue, the contraption signaled him that just such an urgent message was coming through. The sensation startled him at first, but he soon regained his composure enough to answer.

Even in the dimly lit bistro, Roger deciphered the call was coming from Mort. The psychoanalyst had become as unwelcome as Siobhan. Roger contorted his face in disgust.

Mark became alarmed at seeing his father turn a beet-red. When asked about his unpleasant visage, Roger confessed.

"Maybe you ought to call him back, Dad."

"What for? To gouge more money out of me?"

"I think you're being a little cynical. Why don't you respond to him after lunch, okay?"

Roger nodded if only to have his son drop the subject. The rest of their time together was spent on tactics effective in getting inside the young minds of the students and Mark's blossoming relationship with Rebecca. Mark even suggested that Roger and Beth come over to Sheryl's house for dinner so that the future in-laws could get to know one another better. The elder Lavoie offered a slight smile and an indistinct nod. But in the back of his mind, the image of Mort was conjuring up unwanted emotions.

Chapter 49

Roger called Mort Sonnenstein after his late lunch with Mark. The very next day he visited the psychoanalyst. The grandfather clock in the living room chimed three times as Mort welcomed Roger like an old friend, asking him about Mark's new job. The feeling wasn't mutual, however, but the professor did respond politely about his son's first three days teaching at Winston.

"Would you like some Earl Grey, Roger?"

"No, thanks."

Mort raised his eyebrows in surprise. But he honored his guest's request as he left briefly to fetch a cup for himself.

In the meantime, Roger sat in Mort's office alone. He was growing pensive, waiting for Mort to return. He cast his eyes toward the bookshelves behind Mort's desk, wondering if the numerous tomes would suddenly sprout legs and jump down at him. Roger swore he could hear them plotting just such an insurgent attack.

The entire time, Roger squirmed in the chair, fidgeting. Finally Mort came back, with a dainty flower-printed cup of the piping-hot, yet soothing tea in hand. A sip of the beverage went down his gullet. He put down the cup and sat in the chair directly opposite Roger.

Mort drew a deep sigh and sucked in his lips. What he was about to say to his guest was unnerving him. But deep down Mort knew it would disturb him even more so if he didn't fess up to Roger.

"How do I begin, Roger?" Mort asked rhetorically. "Well, first off, just like the last time you were here, there is no charge for this visit. But I also must admit your requested presence here was not because of a professional evaluation. Quite the contrary, I asked for you to be here as one friend talking to another."

Roger rocked back in his seat, all the while maintaining eye contact with Mort.

"What the hell is that supposed to mean?"

"Oswald Borshevsky," Mort replied, his voice trailing with each uttered syllable of the Crenshaw director's name.

He peeled back a few leafs of paper on his blotter, thinking of the right words to say next. *Screw it.* Mort decided just to unleash his inner thoughts to Roger as if he were confessing to a priest. Now there was a switch: a psychoanalyst opening himself up to a patient. Of course, Roger had deduced where this chat was heading. He gave a simple nod to Mort and allowed the host to expound anyway.

"Well, I have myself to blame, too. Our first session spiked my curiosity about your ex-wife. I wanted to see her, but I had to go through Borshevsky to do so. In exchange for allowing me access to Margaret, Borshevsky asked a favor in return: that I contact Siobhan O'Mara and give her your email."

"So, you're responsible!"

"Please, Roger!" Mort buried his embarrassed face in his hands. He eventually revealed his visage to his guest, but not without crying mea culpa. "I'm terribly sorry. This has been eating at me for the longest time. But I told Borshevsky I will not do any more of his dirty work!"

Much calmer than he was seconds before, Roger pawed at his beard.

"The trouble is the damage has been done."

There was nothing else that could be said. The professor rubbed the back of his neck as he exhaled a long gust of breath. Mort stared into space, still feeling remorseful over the incident, but relieved finally to get it off his chest. He owed his patient that courtesy.

Tense silence continued. Roger gazed at the open doorway. But leaving Mort's office wasn't on his mind just then. He swiveled his head back at his host.

"I have a confession as well," Roger began. "While Mark's lack of recognition in his ability to work at Winston was a cause of concern for me, it was those flashbacks of that horrible trial that were causing me to have sleepless nights. Beth doesn't even know. And I prefer to keep it that way." Roger gnarled his fingers, much in the same way Mort as did. "Since Siobhan almost knows every step I take . . . and Mark's, for that matter . . ."

Roger nibbled at his index finger. He didn't continue, but that was okay with Mort.

"If you'd like, you can go see Dr. Leon Sliwaska. He's a psychiatrist I network with. He could prescribe Cymbalta or Zoloft to calm your anxiety and—"

"No drugs, thank you!"

Roger was adamant about not wanting his brain to become a prisoner of some mind-altering experience. Mort respected his wishes and backed off, although Roger studied his host's countenance to make certain he didn't have any second thoughts.

Internally Mort wasn't satisfied with the way the informal session was going. Perhaps Oswald had planted a seed in his head that he had to resolve. And that required Mort asking a direct yet bold question.

"Tell me something, Roger. I've been told a lot about you by Borshevsky. But that's his opinion. Did you kill Darryl Haber and torment Margaret into permanent submission at Crenshaw?"

Roger's squinted eyes shot daggers at Mort. His brow furrowed with anger.

"You're not dressed in black!"

"No, I'm not a priest in the confessional box, if that's what you're referring to."

"Either way, the answer is unequivocally no!"

Roger appeared an enigma to Mort. The psychoanalyst shifted his eyes as he contorted his face in puzzlement. Why didn't he want to believe Roger? Had Oswald's opinion taken such strong root in his brain that it was impossible to weed out?

Meanwhile, Roger continued to stare at his host with contempt. Oh sure, the professor's expression clearly demonstrated disgust, but it was an act. Roger was careful not to say anything that hinted at an implication of his guilt.

It became pointless for Mort to continue badgering Roger. Any further antagonizing wasn't going to resolve anything. At the very least, the admission to giving Siobhan Roger's email address had purged his soul of the demons pitchforking him to no end. The cleansing gave Mort a renewed spirit and eased his pain.

Roger also felt the need to harbor grudges against Mort was counterproductive. So with that the two shook hands as they rose from their seats.

"Once again, congratulations to Mark on his new career and best of luck with his upcoming marriage."

Roger forced a slight grin as he made a hastened exit toward the front door.

The moment he made it outside, Roger's phone vibrated. He focused his attention on the screen and saw that Mark had sent him a text.

Spoke with Rebecca. We're on for dinner at her mother's house a week from Saturday. Please tell Beth and let me know if it's okay. Thanks. Mark.

For the first time all day, Roger smiled naturally. Between the collective indifferent attitude of unappreciative students showing disregard toward his passionate lectures, and Mort's disturbing revelation, Mark's text served as a soothing glass of wine to ease Roger's woes.

Chapter 50

"Did you bring the wine?"

"Yes, Roger," Beth said with a sigh. "You've only asked me the same question three times."

"Well, we're almost there."

And with that Roger steered his Maxima onto Sheryl's driveway. Roger brought the vehicle to a dead stop and then cut the engine. Stepping out from the car, Roger gave the Dyer house a thorough scan. Not ostentatious, but it did carry some charm. Even Beth marveled at its quaint simplicity.

The Lavoies made just two steps toward the home when suddenly the rich cherry wood front door swung open.

"Hi!" Sheryl greeted her guests with a broad smile. "You must be Roger and Beth, Mark's parents, right?"

"Nice to meet you, Sheryl." Beth grinned as she shook her hostess's hand. "I love the exterior! And I'll bet that oak tree over there gives this place plenty of shade in the summer."

"Oh, yes, it does!"

Sheryl welcomed Roger the same way she did Beth. But the professor sensed his greeting was contrived. But Roger wasn't looking to win a popularity contest. He nevertheless filed the lukewarm greeting in the back of his mind.

Much to the surprise of Roger and Beth, Mark and Rebecca had already arrived. And while he continued to scan the interior of the house, Roger was relieved not to see Siobhan there. She didn't need to entrench her tentacles further by attending this dinner. This was strictly for the prospective in-laws. In the back of his mind Roger was telepathically thanking Mark for not divulging this engagement to her.

The aroma of the prime rib roast, with its caramelized small potatoes, garlic cloves and onions simmering in its juices in the oven, wafted throughout the home. The sensitivity of one's taste buds was heightened to the max. And the complement of glazed carrots and French-cut string beans added to the highly anticipated feast.

But the moment came to lean on one's thirst for the drink. On weekend break from UConn, Sara gingerly carried around a tray of filled champagne glasses. She instructed everyone to reach for certain ones throughout the distribution so as not to cause any awkward imbalance. Laird was the first in line, so he reached for the center glass.

Once everyone had a glass of the bubbly, Sheryl cleared her throat.

"I'd like to propose a toast," she began, beaming. "To Rebecca and Mark. May the two of you enjoy years of bliss and happiness together."

Their glasses were raised. A collection of tinkling clinks resonated through the living room. Everyone reaffirmed Sheryl's wishes.

The libations over, Roger took refuge on the soft velour divan beckoning to him. Beth joined her husband on the spot next to him, fusing hip to hip. But that left the corner piece of the sectional vacant. With dinner under control so as not to require her immediate attention for the next five minutes, Sheryl seized the opportunity to sit adjacent to the college professor and bend his ear.

"Before that roast of mine beckons me back to the kitchen, I wanted to spend a few minutes with the both of you," Sheryl said as she smiled. "You know, get to know the in-laws better!"

Sheryl couldn't care less about Beth. That was just a front. No, she wanted to probe Roger, fully aware of his brush with the court system two decades earlier.

"I know this is a sore subject," Sheryl began, "but if I recall correctly, you were involved in that murder trial twenty years ago, weren't you?"

Roger fidgeted in his spot on the plush cushion. He was getting uncomfortable with Sheryl bringing up his ugly past. He was a little reluctant to acknowledge her accusation. That was when Beth stepped in to bail out her husband.

"Yes, but he was acquitted," Beth sternly answered.

Sheryl's eyes shifted to Beth, but her face froze. If her expression could utter words, they would be *I wasn't talk-*

ing to you. Somewhat embarrassed, Sheryl released a short chuckle so as not to ignore Beth.

"I didn't mean to be disrespectful, Beth. I was just wondering if that ordeal still bothers you to this day."

"It comes back to me from time to time—in nightmares," Roger confessed. "I'm just learning now how to cope with it. But if you're asking if any lingering negativity will affect Mark and Rebecca, I want to allay any fears you might have, Sheryl. I have shielded my son to the point where he can walk anywhere freely without having that episode blow up in his face. Your daughter will be immune to this, too."

"I didn't mean to put it that way."

"Then what did you mean?" Beth inquired. "Look, Sheryl. My husband went through hell back then. When I met him ten years ago, I didn't look at him as if he were a criminal or some sideshow oddity. I saw his goodness and his loving soul. I just wish everyone saw that and would stop badgering him. Roger told me the head of Crenshaw, where his ex remains, has been on this vengeance crusade for all the years they have had to play nursemaid to Margaret. Let's set the record straight. She had psychological problems leading up to her being committed. As for that murder, the police have a cold case on their hands trying to find the killer. For once I just wish everyone would leave Roger alone."

Beth spent a great deal of energy in defending Roger to Sheryl. So much so that she had to close her eyes. Beth massaged her temples to ease her anxiety.

"I'm sorry for popping off like I did. It just gets to be . . . annoying after a while. I'm sure you'd do the same for your husband."

"Any new one I might have, yes." There was a little hesitation here. "Definitely not my old one."

Roger and Beth looked at each other. Without either one saying a word, they remembered what Mark and Rebecca explained on the situation in the Dyer household. Roger turned to Sheryl and nodded slightly.

The hostess needed an excuse to leave.

"I'd better go check on the roast and the veggies."

And as Sheryl trotted off, Roger stared down at the Afghan rug under his feet. He released a relieved burst of wind from his mouth, all the while hoping to put the conversation with Rebecca's mom in the garbage can.

Just then Laird and Sara walked over to Roger and Beth in a demonstration of cordiality. Roger figured Laird was just gravitating toward training wheels at the time of the trial and Sara was fresh out of Sheryl's womb. And true to his belief, neither of Rebecca's siblings raised the sensitive topic, thus making the rest of the evening incident-free.

Chapter 51

Time passed, and the images of six-inch snowstorms and bone-numbing temperatures became a distant memory, making way for the warmer climes of spring. And as each month went by, the relationship between Mark and Rebecca grew stronger. Their betrothal to each other notwithstanding, the sex they were having together became more powerful and creative, the couple coming up with new experimental positions every once in a while.

Roger was reluctant at first to write down Siobhan's name for the Lavoie side of the guest list. But omitting her name would be tantamount to asking for trouble. There was no telling what scheme Margaret's sister might unleash upon Roger. It was certainly better to include her name on the docket for Sheryl's invitation register. Like needing to have insurance to drive a car, Siobhan now became the necessary evil for Roger to continue his existence relatively worry-free.

It was June, and the weather was already beginning to heat up as cardigans and sweats were long put in mothballs before making another appearance in October. Heather Karinski, in her role as the maid of honor, supervised the female contingent of the bridal party at Rosa's Bridal Shop in Cranston. Her job was to keep Kayla Ling, Amanda Leipzig, and even the bride Rebecca Dyer, in tow. Although she was to be the focal point of her wedding day with Mark, Rebecca understood the importance of having a strong woman like Heather at the helm. Her nerves, in anticipation of the big day still two months away, were too frazzled to run the operation.

Amanda was stunned when she was asked to be a member of the group, although she was a second choice when Tamiqua Barnstable politely declined. Kayla's selection was a natural choice given that boyfriend Hunter Morales was to be the best man. What was also natural about her was the slight protrusion of her midsection. Kayla was beginning to show signs of a baby bump, a direct result of some frivolity when she accompanied Hunter on his Brazilian expedition that February. Condoms were hard to come by in the interior of the Amazon jungle. That and the fact that Kayla had miscalculated her menstrual cycle. In another two months, Kayla's rose satin gown would have to be let out further to meet the increase of her womb size.

Sonja Robles was fluffing out a few places of the lower portion of Rebecca's gown that the crinoline underneath didn't shape. And as Sonja continued, Rebecca stared at her image in the full-length mirror in front of her. Her visage gave one the idea that she was uncomfortable with the look. But that belied her real thoughts.

As Kayla and Amanda took a break, Heather sauntered up behind the bride-to-be. She was concerned over Rebecca's expression. Heather smiled into the same mirror so that Rebecca would catch her reflection. She gently pressed her hands around Rebecca's waist to insist on the latter's attention.

"I think you look beautiful," Heather smiled at Rebecca's image. "You should be happy."

"Your friend is right, my dear," Sonja piped in through her accented English.

Rebecca's glum expression didn't change. Heather looked up at her with concern.

"Hey, c'mon! Cheer up! You wear this dress well. Don't you just love those embroidered pearls?"

A deep sigh of frustration slipped from Rebecca's mouth.

"It's not the dress."

"Well . . . what is it then?"

Rebecca turned to Sonja to enlist her help down from the pedestal. She looked away for a moment before addressing Heather's query.

"I approached Mark the other day and mentioned that it was too bad my father and his natural mother couldn't attend the wedding. The reminder of his mom made him scowl." Rebecca looked down at the carpeted floor, as if she were rifling through vivid images in her mind. "I remember he jumped all over me one time when I brought up the subject of her situation. He nearly threw me out of the car! I love him dearly, but is this the way it has to be?"

Heather offered a melancholy smile. She gently clamped her palms on Rebecca's shoulders.

"Hey, let me ask you something. Has Mark occasionally brought up the subject of your father?"

Rebecca hesitated for a moment. "No. My family and I talked about him at the Christmas dinner table with Mark. But he hasn't discussed it since. Except for the fact that my uncle will be escorting me down the aisle instead of my father."

"Then let it go!"

Just then Sheryl returned from a nature call in the ladies' room. Her eyes widened with a smile to match after taking a glimpse at the gown her daughter was to wear in two months.

"Will you look at that?" Sheryl exclaimed with delight. "I'm going to be so proud of you!"

Sheryl encircled her hands around Rebecca's slender waist, all the while beaming like the Cheshire cat. But the daughter didn't share the mother's enthusiasm. The nemesis within was taking hold of her, depriving her of the joy of the moment and the thrill which awaited her. Rebecca made every attempt to disguise her innermost feelings, but decided it was best to unleash the beast rather than suffer from an ulcer over the matter.

"Mom, I don't know how to tell you this, but I'm beginning to have some reservations over going through with this."

Rebecca immediately noticed a change in Sheryl's disposition.

"Well," Sheryl commented disdainfully, "I'm glad you're telling me this now before I plunk down two grand for this outfit."

Rebecca rolled her eyes and sucked her teeth, not appreciating Sheryl's sarcasm.

"It's Mark and the way he looks at me when I bring up his mother. He's forcing me to watch every step."

"Funny how you feel the way you do about the man you're about to marry while I have reservations about his father."

Rebecca stared at Sheryl as if her mother just stepped out from a flying saucer.

"Well, I don't have a problem with either one of them, Honey," Heather piped in. "Damon has some quirks about him too. But I still love him. Just get over it, Rebecca. All men have a weird idiosyncrasy of some sort. At least Mark's not like Logan, leaving you behind. Mark still loves you."

Ah, Logan Galwyn. It had been eight months since Rebecca's old flame dissed her. But the mere mention of his name by Heather made the August bride twitch. Her eyes became syrupy. She uttered a soft moan, barely audible for Heather and Sheryl to hear. Her attention was riveted to a small corner of the salon as she imagined Logan in her midst, mounted atop a white charger, waiting to sweep her off her feet.

Rebecca! Rebecca!

The pretty blonde was still in a delirium of enchantment. She closed her eyes and envisioned sensuous thoughts, remembering the subtle musk cologne Logan was notorious for wearing. In her state of bewilderment Rebecca imagined the enticing scent wafting through the room and luring her into his arms once more.

"Rebecca!"

The last ring of her name being shouted across the room slapped Rebecca's head like a two-by-four. Her upper body teetered. She stumbled forward. Heather and Sheryl caught Rebecca before her face had a chance to meet the plush burgundy carpeting. Kayla, Amanda and Sonja stared with fright and perplexity.

"Sweetie, are you okay?"

"I'm fine, Mom. I'm . . . I'm fine."

"Maybe you ought to sit down for a while," Heather suggested.

Rebecca scowled at her maid of honor as she stretched out her fingers—her way of saying everything was cool. *Just leave me be, please!* And to further confirm she was in a better state of mind, Rebecca nudged Heather and Sheryl away in order to get one more look at her reflection in the mirror. The bridal gown was very pretty.

"You're right, Heather. It is beautiful. I say we go with it, Mom."

Everyone was relieved that Rebecca had come back to her senses to endorse the dress. But the verve in her approval didn't match her facial expression. Perhaps she was fighting off the last vestiges of her conscience's wicked side to continue to yearn for Logan. Finally it appeared the good side was winning out as Rebecca was accepting Mark for the man he was, not for whom she thought he should be.

Two months away. Better get used to it, Rebecca.

Chapter 52

A beautiful ceremony was conducted at St. Philip Church in Greenville. Mark and Rebecca's big day was met with 83-degree temperatures with nary a trace of humidity.

The reception was held at the Twin Oaks restaurant in Cranston, an expansive and elegant bistro with a breathtaking view of a large tranquil pond from its massive windows. Plush carpeting eased the pain of walking on the floors in dress shoes and heels. And serene paintings christened the well-maintained gleaming walnut walls.

Everyone couldn't keep their eyes off of the pond and the peace it evoked. And it was only right that Rebecca and Mark and the rest of the wedding party had strategically placed their bridal table directly in front of the middle set of panes.

The new Mr. and Mrs. Lavoie were reveling in the festivities. Best man Hunter Morales was keeping a watchful eye on fellow wedding party member Kayla Ling, whose baby bump was becoming more pronounced. They were set to wed in October, just a month before they would become parents.

The band was playing a medley of songs to satisfy both the older generation and the newer set, including the newlyweds. The main course had long been served, but it was still a bit early for the cutting of the cake. Not to mention, Rebecca tossing the bouquet.

This presented a golden opportunity for Siobhan to pry Roger away from his protective wife. Although she'd made the list of invitees, Siobhan was nonetheless placed at a table other than the groom's immediate family. And for good reason. Beth wanted no part of Siobhan's breathing her immediate air space, thus Margaret's sister was relegated to a table full of strangers.

But a strategy like that could backfire. Neither Beth nor Roger would have any control or possess any ability to intervene, should Siobhan discuss Mark's father and stepmom's personal affairs with her tablemates. But the risk outweighed the ignominy of having Siobhan sit within arm's length, and perhaps cause a further embarrassment. Unfortunately, she now could not be contained for the rest of the affair.

Sashaying in a tight periwinkle blue satin gown festooned by rhinestones, Siobhan strutted over to the Lavoie table. With a smile and voice belying her ulterior motive, Siobhan harpooned a question to Beth.

"Excuse me, Beth, but I'd like to borrow that handsome husband of yours for a moment."

Beth glared at her in anger. She would much rather have Siobhan jump in the pond behind the restaurant. Beth cocked her head as another sign of her disdain of Siobhan. Her flaring nostrils accentuated the loathing. But there was no letting it go. And rather than subjecting herself to ridicule by the dinner guests, Beth conceded Roger to his former sister-in-law, if only just to get rid of Siobhan altogether. She tapped Roger on his shoulder. Remaining silent, Beth simply jerked her head in Siobhan's direction. Roger was equally miffed by her request. But with great reluctance, the professor rose from his seat to connect with the devious scoundrel. The corners of Siobhan's lips deepened her dimples with a smile, signaling her satisfaction in stealing Roger away.

Siobhan manacled her hand to Roger's wrist as she whisked him away to a private area, away from Beth, the newlyweds, the band . . . everyone. Roger was peeved at being yanked away into semi-seclusion. *How about an explanation, Siobhan?*

"That music and all the ruckus going on is not exactly conducive to carrying on a conversation," Siobhan explained. "They don't sit well with me. You'll have to admit it's annoying."

"So is that skin-tight dress you're wearing. And for God's sake, what's with the plunging neckline, exposing your cleavage like that!"

"Ah, you still have that testosterone flowing through your body after all! I thought you were brain dead. Or . . . the other kind of dead, if you know what I mean." A snarky smile flashed across Siobhan's face. But Roger wasn't amused.

"Why did you drag me away from my seat? Surely it wasn't to be ridiculed."

"Oh, I wouldn't dream of doing that to you, Roger. One thing has been on my mind, though. By my own admittance, I'm a little too old to stand with Rebecca's single girlfriends to catch her bouquet later. But I'd like the honor of dancing with Mark as a substitute for Margaret."

"I'm sorry to disappoint you, but I'd like Beth to take that dance with Mark."

Siobhan cocked an eyebrow. To confirm her disapproval Siobhan stepped back with a sideways glance at him.

"Surely your penis had something to do with Mark's existence, but he did travel through my sister's vagina. I'm her direct blood relative, you know."

Roger was hotter than the summer sun outside. Siobhan's sniping comments confirmed his original intention.

"Beth is dancing with Mark, and that's final!"

Mark happened to be walking toward the pair. Even the groom needed to take a break from the floor activities. He appeared a bit bemused when he approached them, caught off guard by their commotion.

"Dad? Aunt Siobhan? Is there anything wrong?"

Roger tried to put his best foot forward and not embarrass himself or Siobhan. A deep sigh preceded a forced grin.

"Nothing's wrong. I was just telling your aunt here that you'll be dancing with Beth after Rebecca dances with her uncle, that's all."

Siobhan looked at Mark with arms crossed. A pout of disapproval galvanized her facial muscles. Now the newlywed reached back to massage his neck and he peered down as if the right words were to come forth from the carpet. A confession appeared in order.

"I'm sorry, Aunt Siobhan," Mark sighed. "I agreed to dance with Beth a long time ago. I . . . I didn't think it was going to be such a big deal for you. Had I known you'd . . . I mean . . ."

"Save your breath, Junior," Siobhan decried with raised palm. She then turned to Roger. "Well, I see you won again, Roger. I guess you're like a cicada, always successful every seventeen years. Oops! In your case, twenty-one. I was never good at math, unlike your son. Excuse me, gentle-men. I'd better sit quietly back in my seat like a good little spinster."

Siobhan parted the Red Sea, remaining miffed at the snub. Mark was still dumbfounded over the dancing hul-labaloo. But Roger stood there like the cat that ate the ca-nary. His disposition of satisfaction was not overt so as to gloat. That was under lock and key inside his brain. But Roger took pride in winning this round.

Chapter 53

Eight months had passed since their wedding day. They had withstood a severe winter, highlighted by a succession of January storms that brought well over two feet of snow to the region. They had to adjust to living together, day in and day out, in his Downtown Providence apartment. They had to endure nagging questions by Roger, Beth, and Sheryl to see if that group could become grandparents, exacerbated by the notion that fellow newlyweds Hunter and Kayla Morales were the proud parents of an adorable five-month-old daughter named Emily. Yet through it all Mark and Rebecca became accustomed to their life as husband and wife and ignored the familial pressures to produce a new Lavoie offspring. It wasn't as if they were celibate. Far from it. Mark and Rebecca were enjoying their sexual encounters on a routine basis. They just were being protective. Parenthood was something they had discussed a few times, but both agreed not to rush into it. There were vacations and other activities they had planned to do together without having to worry about an infant tagging along.

The buds on the trees began sprouting as if wakening from winter's hibernation. Flowers emerged, dotting the individual branches, trumpeting the birth of new leaves.

It was still a little cool to hold outdoor farmer's markets. That wouldn't occur for about a month with the much-anticipated and highly popular Hope Street market by Lippitt Park. But it was late April. The only semblance of such a market was held indoors in Pawtucket, just a few miles from the Winston campus.

Mark was spending the spring day working on the final exams for his classes, just weeks away. Rebecca admired his devotion to his work and decided to leave him alone for the day. But she wanted to go a step further. So Rebecca drove up to the Pawtucket market to surprise her hubby with fresh produce for dinner.

She had already selected fresh strawberries and asparagus. Rebecca was carefully examining broccoli, making certain the florets of the stems were perfect. A pursing of the lips confirmed the vegetable passed her inspection.

Rebecca placed the head of broccoli in her plastic carrier. She waltzed over to where the Florida navel oranges were brilliantly reflecting the overhead lights when suddenly she began to smell traces of a fragrance she was familiar with. It wasn't coming from the oranges. Her forehead wrinkled. Her brows dropped over the top of her eyelids. And then she heard a male voice calling her name. "Rebecca?"

Her pupils widened with excitement. Her head swiveled left and right. "Rebecca!" She was both alarmed and anxious as to whom the strange voice and cologne belonged, as if she had forgotten.

"Rebecca!" The voice was becoming louder.

She finally turned in the direction of the speaker. There making his appearance past two other shoppers was none other than Logan Galwyn. He was as handsome as ever with his slim build, prominent cheekbones and wavy hair, as if he embodied the reincarnation of the late actor James Dean. There was that mischievous curl dangling over his forehead. And his eyes. Ah, yes. Eyes that invited women to stare at them, to become captivated by them. Wearing a leather bomber jacket, open collar shirt and designer jeans with stylish boots, Logan looked as though he'd just jumped off the cover of GQ.

Rebecca was stunned at first. She panicked, but was wise not to make a scene in the market. But then her fright gave way to overjoyed relief. Her circled mouth of suspicion began to crease upward at the sides. Her eyes danced with happiness at seeing her former boyfriend once more.

It had been eighteen months since the couple went their separate ways. But that wasn't Rebecca's fault. The blame was totally on Logan.

A lot had occurred during that time, most notably Rebecca's relationship status. The solid gold band on her left ring finger was an indication of her romantic ties to Mark. But if Logan saw it, he didn't say a word. It was time for the two of them to catch up on the times.

"Rebecca," Logan began with an understated grin, "you look as beautiful as ever."

219

Rebecca didn't know how to react to Logan's statement at first. Her body was still quivering inside with exhilaration in the presence of her former beau. She released a slight burst of air while making every effort to tamp down her nervousness.

"Hi, Logan." There was a pause. "Thank you." She searched the market's concrete floor for what to say next. Looking up, she asked, "How've you been?"

"I'm okay. How are you doing?"

"Fine." Her head bobbed twice and she blinked rapidly when she mentioned this. *Fine? No, how about great?* She never thought she would come across Logan again. And then she remembered the taste of his lips. The way his tongue tantalizingly sloshed inside her mouth. And then there were his sinewy muscles holding her firm. There was no mistake. Her left ring finger told everyone she belonged to Mark. As for the rest of her body, Rebecca belonged to Logan. She craved him. She desired him. She wanted him.

Logan glanced into Rebecca's basket and spotted the asparagus. He made small talk and told her that he wanted to make sure he got some for himself before he left. And then she saw him spotting the ring, the one that said Rebecca was beholden to someone else. Logan's eyes were entranced by its shimmering luster. But she knew he also understood its significance.

"I see you're married."

"Yeah," Rebecca chortled, as though embarrassed by it.

"Well, congratulations! I knew someone as fetching as you wouldn't be on the market for long."

Her eyes shifted. "Strange to hear that comment coming from you. You didn't think I was appealing enough to continue our relationship nearly two years ago."

"We all make mistakes, Rebecca."

And with that Logan began to gather his market selections. He flashed Rebecca a sideways grin. But Rebecca continued to gaze at him as if he were a matinee idol. Logan was on the verge of excusing himself to checkout. This was Rebecca's last chance at being with the man with whom she'd shared her most passionate love. The blood was rushing through her body. Underneath her clothing her skin was rippling like waves on the ocean. Logan walked past Rebecca. Fear of not pressing her body against his was etched across her face. Her anxiety was becoming uncontrollable. No, he was not going to pass her up that easily again!

"Logan! Wait!"

As Logan stopped in his tracks and turned around, Rebecca dropped her shopping basket like a hot skillet. With open arms, Rebecca ran to Logan and clutched him like a sack of money fallen off an armored truck. Logan reciprocated with an embrace of his own. This was what she had been missing. This was what she had desired.

Rebecca looked up at Logan through moistened eyes. Her vision was blurred as he played the strings of her heart. And from what she could make of Logan's distorted image, Rebecca could tell he was enjoying it too.

They drew their faces closer to each other. And as they did, their eyelids began to close and lips began to open to receive the other. The coupling of the mouths allowed their tongues to snake their way into the other's territory and perform a shielded hedonistic dance together.

All the while Rebecca stretched her fingers around Logan's head. In her moment of unbridled lust, she kept thinking how beautiful it was to feel his virility again. She broke away to gasp for air, still ivied to his muscular body. Rebecca pressed the side of her face against Logan's chest. With her mind still quite delirious, she heard the soft rhythm of his heartbeat. It echoed in her head like the sound of a drum in a slow jazzy song.

Rebecca's lips craved seconds. And so she and Logan engaged in another lip-lock. She moaned with pleasure. No one had ever kissed Rebecca like Logan—not before, and not since.

She couldn't care less if all the vendors and shoppers were gawking at them. Rebecca had Logan once more and that was all that mattered. But this was just the appetizer. The betrayal had just begun.

Chapter 54

It had been eighteen months since their last heated passionate encounter. But the gap didn't cloud the idiosyncrasies that each remembered and tolerated—no, enjoyed—with the other. It was the moment to reminisce on old times and so Logan brought Rebecca back to his Providence high-rise apartment. Apparently his prominent job with the local city government had paid off.

Logan quietly closed his front door. He wanted to be a hospitable host and offer something to his guest. But there was only one thing on Rebecca's mind and it wasn't coffee cake. No, it was cake of a different sort: beef cake.

He tossed his keys on the modest dining room table then suddenly felt what seemed like a bear paw clamp down on his right hip. He spun around like a top until he faced Rebecca head-on. Forget the cordial foreplay. They went right for the heated jugular.

In the privacy of his pad, Logan and Rebecca resumed their passionate kissing begun in the market, only this time with a little more heat. His fingers moved up and down her sides, from her graceful neck to the tops of her thighs. Rebecca broke for air. She was gasping as she tilted her head back, eyes closed, with a soft cry of ecstasy. Logan skimmed his lips over her neck and began to taste her luscious skin with his tongue.

Rebecca began to open her eyes. It was a narrow opening, but the mere slits of her exposed pupils spoke volumes. Her eyes darted up and down over Logan as if he were a package to be inspected. Her mouth was ajar with lust on her mind. Rebecca couldn't contain herself. She clutched his jacket and peeled it off. Next came his shirt, which she pulled over his head without any resistance on his part. His well-defined torso was irresistible.

Logan returned the favor by slipping Rebecca's insulated jacket off her shoulders. Purposely he slid his long, thin fingers under the sides of her sweatshirt and slowly lifted it over her head, all the while rolling his tongue around Rebecca's gums. And unlike Mark on his first sexual encounter with Rebecca, Logan had no trouble unbuckling the back strap of her bra, allowing the undergarment to drop to the floor. Logan gazed at Rebecca's exposed breasts and sported a salacious grin. He remembered her chest area being firm, the nipples inviting his fingers to fondle them. And as Rebecca gazed downward she noticed they weren't the only body part becoming enlarged and stiff. She clamped down on Logan's crotch, not wanting to let go. And then came the unbuckling of his belt. It wasn't too long thereafter that they'd shed every stitch of clothing they had left.

Seeing Rebecca's scintillating naked body brought back great memories. But Logan's sensibility wasn't lost in gawking at it and stroking her silken cover. He had the presence of mind to use a condom.

Logan maneuvered his head between Rebecca's legs, all the while whispering his approval between each lick. And as he slowly and sensuously wigwagged his tongue along the insides of her thighs, Rebecca's orgasmic moans grew louder until they came to a crescendo at that moment of utter coital nirvana. The climax soon followed, and it was all over.

The pair was gasping for air as if they'd just run a 10K race. Despite perspiring heavily, they still engaged in one more heated lip-lock.

"You were amazing," Logan said, smiling.

"I just hope your neighbors aren't home next door," Rebecca answered. "They might call the police!"

Logan broke out in laughter at the thought. Rebecca joined him briefly before suddenly switching gears.

"I'd better be going. Mark is going to wonder why I'm gone so long."

Logan chortled and nodded to concede to her wishes. She grabbed her clothes and asked to use the bathroom before she left. Logan simply raised his arm to indicate its direction.

While Rebecca was washing up, Logan pulled up his boxers and then donned his jeans, leaving his slim, chiseled upper frame exposed for Rebecca's pleasure. Inspired, he bolted to a work desk in his living room. Logan opened a small white box by his laptop. He pulled out one of his business cards and selected a nearby pen. Logan glanced at the closed bathroom door. Knowing who was on the other side caused his smirk to deepen. The lascivious encounter encouraged him to write a personal note on the back. Satisfied with the intimate inscription, Logan gingerly slipped it inside the right pocket of Rebecca's jacket.

The door then opened. Just in time, too. Logan picked up Rebecca's jacket and helped her on with it.

"Well," Rebecca began as she zipped up. "I'll see you sometime soon."

"You mean there's going to be a next time?"

"Sounds like you're dissing me again."

"No, no. Not at all. I mean . . . what about Mark?"

"You know you were the only one I ever wanted. You just don't want to admit it."

"I'll confess. You're right. But how will we contact each other?"

"Give me something to write on."

In his haste, Logan took another of his business cards and handed it, along with a pen, to Rebecca. She glanced at the front, impressed with the raised lettering and title of his name.

"I've got tons of them," Logan mentioned off-handedly.

Rebecca smiled and began to scribble her name and mobile number on the back of the card. Like holding a winning lottery ticket, Logan took the card and stared at her penmanship with admiration.

And with that Rebecca gave Logan one last sensuous kiss before she departed.

Chapter 55

Mark was agonizing over the preparation of the spring term final exams. Every cell in his brain was waffle-ironed in his constant challenge to reinvent the wheel. With three semesters of college teaching under his belt, one would think Mark would've gotten the hang of it. But even his father and Dean Edward Asmundsson remarked that they still had to sweat it out when it came to assembling tests.

His eyes were transfixed by the monitor. Mark gaped at one problem for a solid minute. It was a contest as to who would blink first. The problem won. Mark threw up his hands in disgust and erased the equation off the screen. To further heighten his angst, Mark ripped the top sheet of paper from his legal pad where notes were displayed and angrily balled it in rapid fashion. He fired the crumpled paper across the room at an open trash can, but missed. *No multi-million-dollar contract with the Celtics,* Mark mused. But then the mere suggestion by his subconscious tempted him to take a break and catch a few innings of the Red Sox game on TV.

Mark rose from his seat and was about to give the exam a rest. But then an inner voice told him to sit his butt back down in the chair and finish it. When seated, Mark simply reclined with hands folded behind his head, waiting for inspiration. His mind flat-lined. Perhaps the baseball game might prove to be a much-needed diversion from stressing over the exam after all.

Before he had a chance to move another muscle, Mark heard the front door being unlocked. His beautiful wife had returned from shopping. Mark catapulted himself from the chair to give Rebecca her due.

"Hey!" Mark lip-smacked Rebecca. "I was wondering where you'd gone."

"I'm sorry, Honey. Heather called me and she wanted to spend a few minutes together for some gelato. I couldn't say no to her."

"Still a little cool for that, don't you think?" Mark countered while assisting Rebecca with the bags of produce.

"What can I say? She knows my weakness."

Feisty crawled out of a hiding place to greet Rebecca. The tabby had grown to accept Mark and his new surroundings. But it wasn't until Rebecca came home that the cat would materialize.

"Hey, little guy! Did you miss Mommy?"

As Rebecca fussed over Feisty, Mark came from behind her and bandaged his muscular arms around her. He gave her such a bear hug it was impossible for her to move.

"Gosh, what's gotten into you all of a sudden?" Rebecca asked with a giggle in her speech.

"Is there any reason why a guy can't show his irresistible woman some affection?"

Rebecca released a short burst of laughter as Mark gave her a soft pat on her ass.

As he unleashed her from his captivity, Mark sensed a different fragrance in the air. For dramatic emphasis, Mark made a couple of loud sniffs. His forehead wrinkled, but he couldn't place the scent.

"Do you smell something unusual?"

Rebecca at first didn't answer. Her back was turned to Mark and it was just as well. Her eyes widened with her realization of the true explanation. But Rebecca came back with a careful rejoinder. She spun around and switched faces.

"It's the produce, silly!" Rebecca smiled. "Here, take a whiff."

Mark wasn't convinced, but played along regardless.

"Everything was super fresh, and the snow pea pods are really crisp," Rebecca continued. "How about being my hero and putting them away in the fridge?"

"Well, I've got to get rid of any rotten tomatoes first."

Rebecca laughed with Mark as both recalled the incident the day after they first met.

As Mark performed his task, Rebecca was about to peel off her coat. She rummaged through her pockets to make sure nothing of significance was left inside them. Rebecca felt something strange in the right pocket. Something thin. Something with hardened edges. Stumped over what it could be, she pulled out the curious item. Much to her shock, it was Logan Galwyn's business card. She didn't put it there; Logan did. Then she discovered the handwritten note on the back:

Dearest Rebecca, The sex we had today was just the way we left it. It was awesome. Call me. Let's meet again soon. L.

While Mark was still carefully placing the fruit and vegetables in the refrigerator, Rebecca's face became ashen with fear Mark would find it. There was no time to rip it up. She quickly crumpled the card and tossed it in the kitchen receptacle before Mark knew what was happening.

Mark closed the refrigerator, but not before taking one of the bananas Rebecca had purchased earlier. He turned toward her, peeling the fruit as he walked. By this time Rebecca had gotten rid of Logan's card. She took a glance at the trash can before excusing herself to hang up her coat.

The young teacher made quick work of the banana. Mark opened the kitchen trash can to dispose of the discarded skin. He didn't think anything of the other contents of the can while tossing away the peel at first. But after closing the lid, Mark stopped in his tracks. His face contorted like a Picasso masterpiece. There was something inside the receptacle he'd glanced at that required a second look. Lifting the lid revealed Logan's mangled card. Mark picked it up and read Logan's note.

Stunned. Bewildered. Angry. Saddened. All applied to Mark when he read Logan's message. A sudden headache came on as he massaged his temples, but nothing like the pangs in his heart. A few tears emerged. Mark's face suddenly scrunched as rage was building from within.

Rebecca returned to discover her husband's reddened visage. She seemed bemused by his appearance, but Mark deduced it was an act. An explanation was in order . . . now!

"What the fuck is this all about?" Mark yelled, raising the crumpled card. "Huh? Huh! What is this shit?"

By now Mark was violently waving the card in Rebecca's face. She'd never experienced Mark's full-blown fury. Even that moment in the car, when he told Rebecca in spades that she was not to see or discuss his mother Margaret, paled in comparison. Frightened out of her wits for not knowing what Mark was capable of doing, Rebecca was forced to come clean.

"Please! Please!" Rebecca screamed as tears began to stream down her cheeks. "I'm sorry! I'm sorry! It won't happen again!"

"I don't fucking believe you for one second! And do you want to know why? All you've ever talked about was fucking Logan since I've known you! I was afraid this might happen if you ever came across that bastard again! You wanted him to fuck you again, didn't you?"

Rebecca was backed up against the kitchen wall. Mark wanted to interrogate his prisoner even further. She held up her hands against him to fend off his advances.

"No! I mean, it was just that one time! I didn't put that card there! Logan did!"

"When we got married last year, I thought that it was just the two of us . . . you and me! Maybe a baby or two! I am telling you right now: I am not sharing your body with that asshole creep!"

Rebecca was still trembling. But this one-way diatribe could only go on for so long before driving her mad.

"What about those women you've talked about? Marisa! Stephanie! Natalie! Cara!"

"Oh, no! Don't get me started! Do not go there! Okay? I've had the decency to put all those chicks in my rearview mirror! Do you know what that means, Rebecca? It's called settling down! But, no! Apparently you haven't finished sowing your wild oats!"

"Stop bullying me!"

"I have every fucking right!"

Rebecca broke away from Mark's pinning her down. She darted for the bedroom closet with him in hot pursuit.

"Wait a minute! We haven't finished yet!"

"Well, I'm done!"

With anger racing through her veins, Rebecca violently yanked a suitcase from the closet. The carry-on piece was always a struggle for her to lift. But the adrenalin was flowing so feverishly through her body that the weight of it was just an afterthought.

With a little embellishment, Rebecca hurled the luggage on top of the bed. Her pace to and from the closet was with purpose. Every metered step was accompanied by a sweatshirt, jeans, slacks, a few tee shirts, underwear and footwear. It didn't matter how the clothes got into the suitcase so long as they could fit.

Meanwhile Mark was observing Rebecca's antics, but it was pretty obvious what her intentions were. It did, however, beg the question from which simple logic could be drawn.

"What the hell are you doing?" Mark asked, rhetorically.

"What the fuck does it look like?" Rebecca countered. "I'm packing up my main essentials and I'm heading to my mom's place in Greenville. I'll bring the rest in due time."

Mark turned away and released a short burst of outrage while looking up at the ceiling. "Oh, my God! If this doesn't beat everything. You freakin' cheated on me and you're reacting as if I were the guilty party."

"You need to leave me alone, okay?"

Rebecca crammed as much as she could into the carry-on. She looked around as if she forgot something. Out of nowhere Feisty walked in and gave her a throaty meow.

"Oh, baby," Rebecca cried as she peered down at the cat with tears in her voice. "I can't forget you!"

She immediately grabbed the pet carrying case and promptly nudged the feline inside. Once Feisty was secured, Rebecca glared at Mark. "You're liable to poison him! I don't trust you!"

Mark was so enraged by her accusation that he had to vent. "Go! Go. Take your fucking cat and your fucking clothes! See if I care! Just don't come back! Not until you're serious about apologizing!"

"Fuck you! I'm outta here! C'mon, Feisty!"

And with a firm grip on the luggage and Feisty's cage, Rebecca stormed out of the apartment. To emphasize her disgust, a not-so-subtle slam of the front door resonated through the flat.

Mark was left alone to wallow in his pity. He slowly recoiled like an accordion, slinking to one of the kitchen chairs. The life had been sucked out of him. No, his heart had been sucked out of him. He sat disconsolately with droplets forming mini rivers from his eyes, running down the landscape of his face.

Mark looked one more time at Logan's crumpled business card. He stared at it for a solid fifteen seconds. Utter sadness was morphing into hostility and thoughts of revenge. Trembling with anger, Mark heaved volumes of air in and out of his lungs. With clenched teeth, he vised the ends of the card and was ready to tear it into shreds.

Then Mark studied the card once more. His eyes narrowed as he leaned in closer. *Maybe I should pay a visit to this scumbag,* Mark mused. A fiendish grin appeared. He wanted so desperately to settle the score. But that was when the better part of his conscience kicked in. Was it worth going to prison for a crime of passion? Mark drew away from the table to think this through carefully. Finally he dropped his head. It was a clear indication that Mark wasn't seeking a bloody vengeance.

He needed advice on the subject. But to whom could he turn? Hunter? Kayla probably had him changing Emily's diaper. Lane? He was at some fantasy/science fiction convention in Hartford. No. There was only person Mark could truly rely on in this moment of crisis. He grabbed his smart phone and put it to use.

Chapter 56

Beth was enjoying one of her favorite hobbies out in the backyard: gardening. She was busy planting the gladiolus she'd bought at a local nursery that morning.

Her arthritic knees were crying for her to stop. But the few moments of agony were worth it for the months of pleasure spent admiring her floral display. And the mere sight of her tulips, daffodils and crocuses beginning to make their vernal debut made Beth smile, though she was still grimacing from her aching joints.

Beth was nurturing one of the plants, packing the topsoil around it, when she heard the sound of an engine approaching. She lifted her head to spot Mark driving up. Beth tossed her garden shovel down as her body slowly turned from question mark to exclamation point. Straightening herself out took a little time as her fifty-plus frame needed a major adjustment to do so. With her knees still throbbing, Beth hobbled over to Mark as he stepped out of his car.

"Well, this is a pleasant surprise," Beth remarked as she removed her thick cloth gloves. She kissed Mark on his right cheek as he reciprocated.

"I called Dad a little while ago. Is he inside?"

"Yeah, I think he's going over the final exams he's preparing for his classes. Did you finish yours?"

"Not quite," Mark said with a stiff smile, "but I'm getting there." Mark looked at Beth's horticultural handiwork. "Looks great, Beth."

"Thanks! This gives me joy, but oh, am I going to pay for it later."

"Yes. If you'll excuse me, please?"

"Go on ahead. In fact I think I'll join you. I could use a break."

Roger was ruminating over potential questions when Beth and Mark made their entrance. He was too engrossed in his work to notice them.

"Look who came to visit, dear!"

Startled by Beth's announcement, Roger swiveled his head in their direction. He was pleased to see his son, but he'd known he was coming. It was time to take a respite.

Roger stood erect to welcome Mark. Beth, ever the good hostess, offered Mark a drink, but the young teacher declined.

"I received your call, Mark. You didn't sound well. What seems to be the problem?"

Mark was hesitant. He sheepishly grinned as he glanced at Beth for a quick second. Perhaps he was embarrassed to say what was on his mind in front of her. Beth's facial expression was one of a troubled friend.

"Perhaps I'd better go back to my gardening," she suggested.

"No," Mark counteracted. "It's . . . it's okay, Beth. Please. Stay."

She was hesitant, but decided to concede to Mark's request.

He had an audience of two, but like the nervous speaker in front of a huge gathering, Mark was fumbling for where to begin. All Mark could do was snort. He finally threw up his arms and allowed his hands to slap his sides.

"There's no beating around this," Mark sighed. "Rebecca cheated on me and now she's run off to her mother's house."

Roger and Beth stood in shock. Their mouths dropped to allow the harsh reality to sink in. Roger slowly retreated to the sofa, all the while trying to fathom the disturbing news. Meanwhile, Beth snapped out of her catatonic state to comfort her beleaguered stepson.

"Oh, Mark! I'm so sorry!"

Beth gently wrapped her arms around Mark. He appreciated her concern as he patted her on the back to thank her.

As Beth broke away, Roger continued to sit in silence, still numbed by Mark's announcement. He pawed at his beard as if in search of how to guide his son and offer advice, but nothing was forthcoming.

"This is the bastard to blame for all this." Mark retrieved Logan's dog-eared card. He first offered it to Beth, who quickly handed it to Roger in disgust.

"I hope he rots in hell!" Beth exclaimed.

Roger studied the card intently. He then looked up at Mark with his reply.

"I'm so sorry you're going through this, Mark. Perhaps she might come back. That is, if you'll forgive her."

"I don't know, Dad. This really hits low. I put my ex-girlfriends behind me. Why can't she do the same with her exes?"

"That," Roger sighed, "is a question only Rebecca could answer. I'm just saddened that you can't enjoy the bliss Beth and I have."

Roger reached out and gently clutched Beth's hand. She admired the way her husband treated her and was enchanted by the way Roger affectionately kissed the back of the proffered hand.

Mark was delighted to see his father and stepmother still happy to be in each other's company. But that didn't eradicate his dilemma. Roger then pivoted.

"I know this might not sound appropriate at this time, Mark, but I wanted to share with you some ideas for my final exams. I know you only deal with numbers, but the same thought processes are in effect. The information is on my PC. Will you excuse us, Beth?"

Beth left the house to return to her gardening chore. The two men were alone, but the topic of tests was never brought up again.

"I wanted to vent a little more about your predicament, Mark," Roger began while examining Logan's card. "But without Beth around."

"I don't know where to go with this. Maybe I can talk to Heather. I see her every day and she's Rebecca's closest friend."

"Yes, and she's finally graduating from graduate school." Roger then gave a long look at the card. "But let me see what I can do first."

Chapter 57

Two weeks had passed since the fallout between Mark and Rebecca. Final exams were over. Now came the point of bringing closure to the spring term.

Mark had seen Heather many times during that period. He'd hoped that Heather might intervene and act as a liaison between the warring factions. But there was only so much she could do. Even though Heather was more in Rebecca's corner in terms of their long-standing friendship, she shook her head over why Rebecca would stray from their marriage to have another go at the man who dumped her like yesterday's fish a year and a half before.

The Saturday after the finals had Roger in an unusual spot. He sat for two solid hours parked a half block away from Sheryl Dyer's home.

Roger knew Rebecca was living with her mother. He also was hip on the tryst between Rebecca and Logan Galwyn. But he didn't have a clue how Logan looked. What Roger's intentions were with Logan didn't include his apartment. Besides, that would have meant going through a concierge who might have prevented Roger from going up in the first place.

The temps climbed to near 70 degrees that mid-May day, yet Roger wore a long-sleeve black turtleneck, black pants, and a black ski cap. If the cap were pulled over his head, he'd have the look of a Ninja warrior.

Roger knew Rebecca was home by seeing her Camry parked in the driveway. He was only hoping Logan was with her.

Nearly three hours had elapsed since Roger had parked his Maxima. Frustration was building as he grew tired of waiting. He decided to give up the ghost as he reached for the key in the ignition. Just as he turned the engine over, Roger looked one last time at the house. *At last! Paydirt!*

Roger spotted what looked like a male figure standing next to Rebecca just outside the Dyer home. He picked up his binoculars to get a better look. The male sure wasn't Laird Dyer. It couldn't be, as Rebecca gave the young man a luscious tongue kiss. *You don't do that to your brother.* And Laird was gay to boot. It had to be the infamous Logan Galwyn.

Logan's every move, Roger carefully observed. Roger spied as Logan climbed into a champagne-colored Buick Enclave SUV. The anthropology professor scribbled down the license plate of the vehicle. He studied Logan's features and filed the description in his brain. Roger was excellent at storing details. It had much to do with his profession as a college instructor.

There, that settled it. Now Roger not only knew where Logan lived, but also what vehicle he drove. It wouldn't be long before the next phase of his bizarre scheme would take place.

Chapter 58

Rebecca was experiencing her typical Monday morning doldrums at her accounting job at Templeton's. It had been sixteen days since Roger spotted Logan leaving Rebecca's mother's house in Greenville. But there was more to it than that. Rebecca was supposed to spend the past weekend away with Logan. The plan was to go to Cape Cod and do a little antiquing there. But they didn't. In fact, Rebecca hadn't heard from Logan in four days. She even went so far as to go to his Downtown Providence high rise that Sunday, only to be told by the concierge that Logan wasn't home. To make matters worse, she was told that Logan hadn't been seen in a few days. It wasn't like Logan's occupation required him to travel out of town unexpectedly. And even if it did, they had plans. For sure Logan would've told Rebecca if complications stemming from his job or perhaps some personal or family situation arose.

She rang his cell phone almost hourly that whole weekend, only to get his voicemail. After leaving three messages, Rebecca was resigned to hanging up once she heard his greeting.

Rebecca was going through the motions of her occupational functions. But in the back of her mind, there lingered that concern for Logan. His unresponsiveness clouded some of her judgment.

Torey from the mailroom suddenly stopped by her cubicle. In his hands was a six-inch square box, enveloped by sanitary white wrapping paper, but tied with a pretty red silk ribbon and matching bow on its top.

"G'morning, Rebecca. This package just came for you."

Rebecca sat staring at it in bewilderment. Her eyebrows went in different directions. Her lips were pursed. At least she had the awareness to thank Torey for the package.

She waited for the mailroom man to leave. After all, the contents of a beautiful box such as this were meant for

Rebecca's eyes only. There was a small envelope held by the ribbon with her name written in what could be script drawn by a professional calligrapher. She lifted the package up to detect the trace of Ralph Lauren perfume. That brought a dramatic change to Rebecca's visage. For the first time all day there was a hint of a smile.

Rebecca delicately removed the envelope. She opened it and retrieved the tiny matching card inside. On it was a message in exquisite penmanship.

> Dearest Rebecca, I'm so sorry I couldn't be with you this weekend. But rest assured my heart is with you. Love, Logan.

Now Rebecca's excitement was heightened about what was inside. Maybe a charming pearl necklace, or perhaps a diamond-studded woman's watch? She couldn't wait any longer as she tore through the lovely packaging to get at the box inside.

There it was—the box. It sat there proudly like a religious idol to be adored. Rebecca was anxious, yet there was that hint of trepidation running through her veins. *Oh, what the hell,* she thought. Rebecca carefully opened its lid. She rifled through the tissue paper and discovered the prize. It was actually Logan's heart, complete with ventricles and torn capillaries. The aorta was severed as what remaining blood there was oozed out of small pockets, badly staining the tissue below. No wonder the box was scented. The perfume was to mask the stench of the macerated organ.

Rebecca's eyes bulged out of her head. Her face lost its color. Shattered nerves were setting her off into convulsions. She wanted to scream, but there was that inner sense of hers that told her not to make a scene in the office. Still she fastened her hands over her mouth to create an air-tight seal.

Her first priority was to regain her composure and control her hyperventilation and shaking. The second was to close the lid. Rebecca didn't need to have any of her co-workers snooping. And the third was to head straight to the police. As she gathered the box and her dress coat, Rebecca had to notify her boss on the way out. She dared not reveal the true reason why she had to leave lest she'd alarm everyone. Rebecca approached the office door of Brett McLellan with trepidation.

Brett was scouring his emails. He was well liked in the office because of his fairness and honesty. The forty-something family man held his medium-brown goatee in his hand as he squinted at his laptop screen. Nothing could have pulled Brett away. Nothing, except a hard knock on his door. At first startled, Brett jerked his head toward the doorway.

"Oh, hey!" Brett smiled. "What's up, Rebecca?"

Despite her frenetic state, Rebecca swallowed air just to settle her nerves. She had to come up with an excuse. And then she realized the simple way out.

"I'm not feeling well, Brett."

"Yeah, I can see that. Let me call an ambulance and have you taken to the emergency room."

"No! No!" More hesitation. "I mean, I can handle it my-self, thank you. I do need to see a doctor right away. If you don't mind."

"No, go ahead. Just please, keep me posted."

Rebecca feigned a smile to throw Brett off track. She was almost in the clear until . . .

"What's in the box?"

Rebecca froze. She had to improvise once again. She couldn't ignore Brett's query. She pirouetted with a ficti-tious grin.

"Oh, it's just a small vase I ordered from one of those cable shopping networks."

Thankfully Brett bought Rebecca's story without seek-ing proof of evidence. He then reminded her to keep in touch regarding her so-called medical malady. Rebecca modestly nodded and quickly hurried out of his office.

As she was heading toward the bank of elevators by the reception desk, Rebecca clutched the box and its grizzly contents, guarding something with her life that ironically had no life left in it. All the while her eyes darted back and forth, as she was praying not to be accosted by a fellow employee with twenty questions and a much harder to beat curiosity than Brett's.

But it wasn't until she stepped foot off the elevator on the ground floor that Rebecca could breathe a little easier. Unfortunately her day of surprises had only just begun.

Chapter 59

It was only half-past twelve. Rebecca had spent just ninety minutes in the nearest police precinct, yet it seemed like an eternity. She filled out endless sheaves of paper, gave the sob story to a clerk, a desk sergeant and one of the detectives. To calm her nerves, Rebecca was offered coffee; black, with no sugar. It wasn't the way she normally preferred it, but then the turn of events that morning were certainly anything but normal.

She sat in a glass-enclosed room looking down at the floor, numbed by what had occurred. Rebecca was searching for answers, wondering what to make of all this. The only explanation she could come up with was that Mark had to be exacting his revenge.

Every once in a while Rebecca would stare through the glass. People of all types scurried by. Uniformed police officers, detectives, admins, and other interested parties made up the kinetic frenzy of the department. But Rebecca could almost feel the eyes of these individuals peering down at her. *I'm not some fucking lab specimen!* she wanted to shout out at them. The problem was she couldn't. She was told someone of special interest would stop by soon. Soon. Hah! That seemed like eons ago. Yet there she remained, still in her seat, silent and alone with her fear acting as a grim consolation.

The doorknob turned. The sound startled Rebecca. She jumped nearly a foot. The door opened wide. Making his way first was the desk sergeant Rebecca had met earlier. He apologized for frightening Rebecca.

In his wake were two plainclothes men in suits. The first was middle-aged. His face was that of a bulldog—his jowls sank around pouting lips. Circles had formed under his eyes from years of on-the-job fatigue-induced insomnia. He wore his cheeks like the parched earth stemming from a severe drought. Waves of silver and gray swam through what black hair he had left. Rebecca gave the man a good study. All she could think of at that strange moment was her father, whom she had last seen at the tender age of seven. In an odd way, the man symbolized the father figure Rebecca had been missing for over twenty years. The officer exuded a relative sense of calm. It was almost like Rebecca wanted to reach out and hug the man as she sought out comfort to soothe her frayed psyche.

The second man was much younger. He was extremely handsome with his Matt Damon good looks. But despite his choirboy appearance, he had a small scar above his right eye, no doubt as result of one of his more pugilistic encounters in his earlier years. Rebecca gravitated to the second man, too, but not in the same way as the first. If he had asked her out for dinner, she wouldn't hesitate to accept.

"Mrs. Lavoie?" the paternal man asked.

Hmm. Mrs. Lavoie. It had been eight months since Rebecca and Mark tied the knot, yet she was still having difficulty getting used to being called anything other than Miss Dyer. But Rebecca gave a modest nod to acknowledge him.

"I'm Lieutenant Detective Vincent Calabrese, Providence Homicide." The elder man flashed his badge and picture ID to back up his claim. "This is my partner, Sergeant Drake Nowak." The Damon lookalike flashed a subdued smile.

Rebecca didn't respond. At seeing them, she was not as fearful of what Calabrese and Nowak would do with her as she was of the frightening experience she'd had earlier at her grisly discovery.

"We were brought down to investigate the possible murder of one Logan Galwyn and—"

"Possible murder?" Rebecca interrupted, looking at both men incredulously.

Calabrese gave a side glance to Nowak.

"Well, here you are. Walking in here with a box you received at your job. A box with a note I think we can all assume was not written by Galwyn. Or maybe not. A box containing a heart, supposedly that of Galwyn. Or is it?"

Rebecca's jaw dropped. "I can't believe I'm hearing this."

"For all we know, Mrs. Lavoie, the heart could be that of an animal. It could be Galwyn's way of kissing you off, although I grant you, it's a little sick."

She appeared as though she were about to catapult over Calabrese by throwing herself at him, but Rebecca's invisible guardian pulled her back to the chair.

"I came into this stationhouse three hours ago, trembling, numb, and sobbing like a frightened child. Now the both of you are acting like this is all a big joke. A big, fucking joke! Where's the compassion you're paid to have? Huh? Where's the empathy? Or is that just bullshit you cops like to advertise?"

"Let's just say that we're leery after all the crap people have pulled on us through the years," Nowak replied. "You have no experience in dealing with the dark side of humanity. We have, okay?"

"Well, maybe you ought to change your attitude!" Rebecca yelled back.

"Hey! Don't tell me how to do my job, you little—"

Calabrese swung his left arm at Nowak's chest to refrain him. He told his partner to cool it. Nowak quickly realized that discretion was the better part of valor. And so the younger detective stepped back. A little fence mending was in order.

"Please forgive us, Mrs. Lavoie," Calabrese humbly sighed. "We've seen it all." He turned to Nowak. "Hey, Drake. Give her some water or coffee or something, will ya?"

"No! No, I'm . . . I'm perfectly fine, thank you."

Calabrese pawed at his chin. "How did that package arrive, and what time was it?"

"Torey from the mailroom delivered it at around ten-thirty."

"Did he say who dropped it off? I mean, was it a postal employee? UPS guy? A messenger?"

"I was so overwhelmed by seeing the pretty package at first that I didn't think of asking him before he left. And I came straight here from my office, bypassing the mailroom entirely."

"I want prints taken on the wrapping, the envelope, everything. Got that, Drake?" Nowak nodded. Calabrese then took a different tack with Rebecca. "Suppose you tell us about your relationship with Galwyn."

241

Rebecca was ashamed. Calabrese's question was simple enough, but her answer was complex. The interrogation caused her to hunch over as if shivering from the cold, but it was the mere thought of answering it that made Rebecca feel like the detective had denuded her. There was no way out it. With a constriction in her throat, and muscles beginning to galvanize, she finally conceded to his query. Rebecca jerked her head up and faced the policemen.

"Logan and I were lovers at one time, until he broke up with me about two years ago. Just after our break-up I met Mark Lavoie. Mark proposed to me during the holidays and we eventually married last August. A few weeks ago I was at farmer's market in Pawtucket. Who do I find there but Logan? We went back to his Downtown apartment and made love to each other. I eventually came home, hoping that Mark wouldn't suspect anything. But he found Logan's personal handwritten note on the back of one of his business cards, thanking me for the sex. Mark was irate, and then I thought it might be best to leave and head back to my mother's home in Greenville. I . . ." Rebecca paused a moment, bowing her head to screen her face. "I've seen Logan a few times since, but not this last Thursday. I was both puzzled and hurt about why he didn't show up, and why he never called me back when I reached out to him." Her eyes drifted. They fixed on an electrical outlet near the far corner. "Now I know why," Rebecca whispered.

Nowak was drinking in the story. Perhaps he might have been captivated by the carnal activity between Rebecca and Logan. Who could say? But he was curious by the look of his upraised eyebrows.

"You mentioned your husband was irate after you confessed to him about your tryst with Galwyn. What kind of person is Mark?"

Rebecca's eyes looked through Nowak in thought. "You think he may have killed Logan?"

"Nobody's making any such accusation. We don't even know yet if Galwyn's been murdered." Rebecca was ready to jump at him. Nowak quickly held out his palms. "Please, let's not go there again!"

"If you could, please," Calabrese interjected, but with a slight pause and his voice ratcheted down a few decibels.

"Rebecca, do you think your husband is capable of committing murder?"

She looked away, waiting for the answer to scream at her. Her lids closed as she began searching her memory banks for any abnormal acts by Mark.

"Mark is normally easy going, good-natured to a fault. I can only remember one time he jumped down my throat about visiting his mother, who's been locked up in a mental institution for over two decades. That and, of course, our falling out four Saturdays ago."

Amid scribbling a few notes, Calabrese released the grip of his 99-cent special ballpoint. His glazed look warranted a side explanation.

"Lavoie." Calabrese's head tilted left. "Lavoie." The light bulb must have lit for the veteran detective, instantly riveted his attention back toward Rebecca. "Your husband's mother wouldn't happen to be Margaret Lavoie, would it?"

"Yes, why?" Rebecca's face contorted in fear.

Now Nowak seemed just as curious as Rebecca. But only Calabrese, who was near the age Roger was, knew the significance.

"Oh, nothing really," Calabrese smiled. "We need to investigate Logan Galwyn first and see if what you experienced this morning adds up to what you think it is. Do you have his home address?"

Rebecca freely dispensed the information. It was a sign leading toward closure. Nowak jotted down the address and then offered a sucked-in smile at Rebecca. The attraction toward him was almost back to where it was before. Rebecca's eyes softened as she allowed a smile for Nowak.

"Here are our cards," Calabrese muttered. "We'll be in touch with you, Rebecca. But don't hesitate to call if something else occurs that may be suspicious. Oh, and tell this Torey guy we may need to question him on that delivery."

She uttered a barely audible thank you. Nowak, having mellowed a bit himself, offered a kind gesture.

"Listen, if you'd like, we can drive you home to Greenville."

"No thanks," Rebecca firmly replied. "I drove here from my job and I was a heck of a lot worse then. Besides, I don't have that," she hesitated for a split second, "box sitting on the passenger's seat next to me."

The detectives thanked Rebecca for her cooperation and began to leave. Rebecca was free to exit too. But somehow that box and its contents held her prisoner.

Chapter 60

No fewer than ten minutes had elapsed since their questioning of Rebecca when Calabrese and Nowak slammed the doors of a late model, fully equipped Chevrolet Caprice. The young detective exhaled deeply through puckered lips. Calabrese just stared through the windshield, still trying to absorb Rebecca's twisted tale. They remained that way for nearly a minute.

"This is a weird one," Nowak stated, opening the dialogue. "What do you think, Vince?"

"About the story or the girl?"

Nowak shrugged. "Both."

Vince Calabrese pouted. "The possibilities are endless. For all we know Galwyn could still be alive and this may be his sadistic way of breaking up. You remember Rebecca told us he broke up with her two years back. Maybe he had his own conscience to deal with, having screwed a married woman, albeit someone he had sex with God knows how many times long ago."

"Yeah, but this?"

"Hah, I don't know." Then Vince looked at the address for Logan that Rebecca gave them. "It all starts with his place."

Drake Nowak snorted, but with a trace of a silly grin behind it. He gazed off into the distance.

"I can't understand why Galwyn dumped the girl in the first place." He paused, appearing to be deep in thought. "Man, she is a looker. A guy would have to be out of his mind if he thought he could improve upon her. I can understand why Galwyn or any other straight guy would want to fuck her."

"Hey, keep it on the QT, okay? You're a fucking professional! Act like one!"

"Don't get so excited, Vince! I'm only stating the obvious."

"Juanita and I have a daughter just about Rebecca's age."

"Ah, the specter of dear old Dad is kicking in with his fatherly protection."

"All right, just cut the bullshit! I can break you down the ladder, Romeo! Remember that!"

Drake zipped the lips. If it weren't for Vince, he might still be walking a beat in uniform. A little gratitude, with a dash of humility, was in demand. Staring at the squad cars outside the precinct, Drake relaxed his head back to review the details.

"If Galwyn is dead, maybe the girl's husband may have done it out of revenge."

"Or maybe someone else in that family did it," Vince countered.

Drake's forehead furrowed. He wasn't following Vince's supposition. Vince decided it was time to connect the dots and give his protégé a little history lesson.

"Twenty-two years ago, a man named Roger Lavoie, I'm presuming that's Rebecca's father-in-law, was on trial for killing the man who was having an affair with his wife Margaret. But that wasn't the only crime. Apparently Roger took the dead guy's body parts and one by one sent them to Margaret, driving her insane. Lavoie was acquitted on both counts. It was a big story, made all the headlines."

"Sounds like he's at it again, only this time he's fighting his son's battles."

"I don't know. It's a nice theory, though. But I'm sure Rebecca knows of the story and the trial, if not from discovering it on her own then maybe her parents informed her. But we've got our work cut out."

Vince turned over the engine. The soft hum of the motor was the sole indication the vehicle was ready to pull out. His meaty right hand enveloped the gear shift handle like a tarantula. But before switching to drive, Vince gave his partner instructions.

"Do me a favor. Get a hold of Scarpone. I want him to run a check on Galwyn, Roger and Mark Lavoie and, yes, the girl. I trust no one. Also, have him check to see if any family member, friend or co-worker has filed any missing persons on Galwyn in the last seventy-two hours. I also want a DMV check run on his vehicle, if he has any. I want

Lowery to go to Templeton's main office and ask this Torey guy in the mailroom who delivered that package. And have Hanlon ready in forensics. If Galwyn is missing, I want to gather any piece of clothing or anything that has his DNA on it and check it with the tissue of that heart Rebecca brought to the precinct. And we need for him to step it up. Do you have that photo the boys took of Rebecca earlier?"

"Yep."

"Okay, then. Let's go!"

Chapter 61

The fears and suspicions over the disappearance of Logan Galwyn were beginning to take hold. Upon arrival at Logan's residence, Vince and Drake interviewed both Antonio, the chief concierge; and Alex Zorpitsky, the superintendent of the building. Each corroborated the other's story. They hadn't seen Logan for nearly four days.

Without asking any questions, Alex brought the two detectives to Logan's apartment. He jingled out a huge ring holding just about every key under the sun. Several had spots of paint on them, each varied, in a plethora of colors. Each color represented the opening to specifically designated doors throughout the building. Only Alex, with his uncanny knack for knowing which apartment matched which colored key, knew immediately which key to use.

"Like I said," Alex began in his heavy Russian accent, "the last time I saw Mr. Galwyn was Thursday."

"Do you see him on a regular basis?" Vince asked.

Alex shrugged as he was in the process of unlocking the door. "Just about every other day. Nice guy. You tell me he's missing? That very big surprise. Is not like him."

Success was achieved at last as Alex finally managed to open the door. Vince and Drake scanned Logan's flat from the doorstep as if it were a foreign land. Neither stepped inside immediately. Not that they were expecting trouble from the get go, but their years of police work advised them to proceed with caution.

After a nominal wait, Vince finally ventured in with Drake in his shadow. They were deliberate in their approach as Alex remained by the threshold. The super needed to leave to oversee other matters that were pressing on his schedule.

"If you excuse me, officers, I must tend to other chores."

Alex was about to make a hasty retreat when Vince iced him.

"Do you happen to know if Galwyn owns a car?"

"He owns a Buick Enclave SUV. He keeps it in our underground garage."

"What's the space number?"

Alex couldn't remember. He radioed Antonio at the front desk, since he had access to a great deal of information on the tenants on his computer at the console. A few quick exchanges later resulted in the desired answer.

"S2-079; that means is on second level down from street, 79th space."

"Besides the photo of that woman I showed you downstairs, to the best of your knowledge, did Galwyn have any other visitors in the last few days?"

"No. We keep accurate records of who sees who at front desk. As I showed you, Mr. Galwyn had no visitors."

"Does Galwyn have a history of people occasionally visiting him?"

"Beside that woman, no. He is, how you say, a recluse."

Although he had nothing to hide, Alex was growing nervous, and was tired of the interrogation. But like the obedient public servant, he remained available until Vince and Drake were through with him.

"Okay, Alex," Vince climaxed. "Thanks. We'll lock up. And if you can think of anything else, give either of us a call."

Vince and Drake handed Alex their calling cards. Alex studied them for a brief moment before dashing off to the next crisis in the building.

The detectives were left to themselves. Wearing gloves, they began to scour Logan's apartment for anything that seemed unusual. Drake was impressed with Logan's collection of Blu-Ray DVDs and CDs. Some brought a smirk to his face as he couldn't believe Logan's taste when it came to entertainment.

Vince was more focused on eyeballing every pertinent detail. He was looking for any sign of struggle, indicating Logan had become a victim here, surrounded by his creature comforts. He closely scrutinized the area rugs, wood flooring, tiles in the kitchen and bathroom, furniture and walls for anything out of the ordinary such as blood stains and damaged corners, but he was coming up empty. Vince then rummaged through the medicine cabinet and drawers for any sign of illicit drugs, but he was scoring a zero there too.

A bath towel was draped over the shower curtain rod in the bathroom. Drake carefully pulled it down and folded it into a huge manila envelope marked "Evidence." Opening up the medicine cabinet, Drake stumbled upon Logan's razor. Much to his delight, there were several hairs on the shaver from his facial growth. There was the possibility that Logan's DNA could be found on the towel and razor and they could then match it with the heart Rebecca was given.

Vince opened the refrigerator, not that he was hungry. Vince was starving for critical minutia to explain the life and times of Logan Galwyn. Much to his surprise Vince found the fridge well stocked. He summoned his partner.

"Take look at this, Drake. For a bachelor living by himself, Galwyn sure has a healthy supply of food."

"Not the sign of someone who decided to vanish, leaving all this behind."

Vince reached for a quart-size plastic container of orange juice. He held it up in front of him for closer inspection.

"Expiration date is in two weeks." Turning to Drake. "Do me a favor. Empty it and seal up the top. I want it brought in too."

"Are we that desperate, to have to scrounge for food back at headquarters?"

"Don't be an asshole. How many guys living alone do you know that drink OJ from glasses?"

Vince shoved the container into Drake's midsection. And as the younger detective executed the task, Vince rose up from his crouch before the fridge. They were done here. For now at least.

But as they walked toward the front door, Vince suddenly froze. He eagle-eyed a business card lying atop a glass end table in the living room. Narrowing his stare for a closer look, Vince studied the phone number and address of Logan's workplace.

After he finished taping off the apartment, Drake walked over to see what Vince had found so intriguing.

"Galwyn's job," Vince surmised. "I'm surprised no one from there inquired as to his disappearance over the weekend."

"Well, I don't see a landline phone anywhere. Must just have a mobile."

"What say you and I pay a visit to this city agency where he worked? But first, I want to check out that parking space."

It was nearly three o'clock. Vince was aware that a number of agencies close at four. With the items taken from Logan's apartment secured, Drake shadowed his boss to the elevators.

Chapter 62

Their most-feared suspicions came to fruition. Vince and Drake noticed Logan's underground parking space was conspicuously vacant. It had rained heavily that past weekend, yet Vince couldn't detect any trace of wet tire tread marks on the pavement. All indications pointed to Logan's Buick Enclave not having been there for a few days.

Before leaving the complex, Vince told Alex and Antonio that he would like a copy of the garage exit surveillance tape to gain an accurate time fix for when the Enclave was last seen. Alex vouched for the staff, shareholders, board and management company, assuring Vince that they would lend their full cooperation to the Providence PD.

Drake made the call to Scarpone to verify the disappearance of Logan's Enclave. No one from his immediate family or close circle of friends, outside of Rebecca, had filed a missing persons report with the authorities.

He was on to the next destination: the Department of Traffic. There Logan worked as a road and street safety engineer, or so said his business card. The thought of it caused Drake to come up with a quip as they rode the elevator.

"Street engineer, huh? Where did Galwyn go to college, Tulane?"

Vince frowned at his younger partner. "Do me a favor. Don't give up your day job."

Vince opened the door to the modest fifth-floor office space housing the agency. A young woman of olive complexion sat at the front desk. The scent of her heavy perfume was overwhelming, making her a walking bouquet. Clickety-click was the repetitive sound of her finely manicured fingernails striking the keys in her data entry. Her mahogany eyes were transfixed on the screen, making the appearance of the detectives seem like an afterthought.

The senior detective cleared his throat. For a moment the woman froze as if in pose. She swiveled her head and offered a hint of an apology with a side order of a suppressed smile. Vince just wanted to get on with the investigation, so he flashed his hardware credentials. The woman made a call and then relayed a message that someone would be coming out to greet them.

Vince and Drake decided to remain standing rather than ensconce themselves in the deep-pocketed chairs. They surveyed their surroundings, but weren't amused. Only a potted fern offered color to the vanilla environment.

"Can I help you, gentlemen?"

The voice was male. And when Vince and Drake turned around, in their midst stood a man of average height with a slender build. He wore dark, thick-lens glasses, which overshadowed his close-cropped receding red hair and matching beard. A taciturn expression was his disguise.

"Lieutenant Vince Calabrese, Providence Homicide," the elder detective declared, flashing his badge. "This is my partner, Sergeant Drake Nowak. And you are?"

"Greg Koppelman. I'm the director of this agency. What's this all about?"

"You have an employee by the name of Logan Galwyn working here?"

"Yes, he's one of our street and highway engineers."

"When was the last time you saw him?"

"Thursday, I believe."

Vince exhaled a breath of frustration. "Mr. Koppelman, today is Monday. It's almost three-thirty in the afternoon. Has it ever occurred to you to wonder why Galwyn didn't show up for work today? Or earlier, on Friday? Aren't you at least a bit curious what might have happened to him?"

"Lieutenant, let me explain. Logan is one of our engineers here. But these engineers are often out in the field. Their time in this office pales in comparison to the time they spend outside."

"Yes," Drake broke in. "But they have to be accountable for their time, don't they? I mean, doesn't a guy like Galwyn have to at least check in with your office? Or how about your office, don't you contact him?"

"This is not the gulag, sergeant. We don't keep running tabs on the engineers. Yes, they must report in, but we don't hold it to them if they skip a day."

"Or two," Vince interrupted. "No wonder citizens are always crying about where their tax dollars are funneled. It goes to no-show jobs like your agency has here."

For the first time, Koppelman began to show he had an emotional side after all. "I take exception to that remark. For the record, Logan Galwyn is one of our most dedicated and hard-working employees. I can unequivocally declare that nearly one-third of Providence's streets are improved because of Logan's diligence. Please don't sell him or this agency short."

"Relax, Mr. Koppelman. Taxpayers pay us too, you know." Vince released a sigh before continuing. "Did Galwyn maintain an office here?"

"Yes. Right this way, please."

Koppelman led the detectives through a cubicle maze before reaching Logan's office. For someone who had a decent-paying job, at least one to pay for a nice high-rise flat, Logan's workspace was humble. Then again, as Koppelman mentioned, Logan didn't spend much time in the cramped quarters.

The walls were sterile like the rest of the agency. Only a corkboard and a print of a tiger in the wild broke up the monotony. Drake opened the drawers of Logan's desk. Nothing out of the ordinary. Just office supplies paraphernalia, files on several street projects, personal notes of insignificance, and the occasional widget. Logan didn't keep personal pictures on his desk, which might be attributed to his lack of time spent in the office.

Vince examined the drafting table near the window, with a few blueprint sketches. To the detective the drafts were as noteworthy as a comic strip, although to Koppelman and the agency they carried a more pertinent meaning.

While Vince and Drake continued to scour the office, Koppelman stood by the doorway, acting as a policeman in his own right. He was concerned the detectives were going to tear Logan's place apart. But Vince and Drake were drawing a blank here. The senior detective couldn't help but notice Koppelman's presence, which begged a question.

"When Galwyn worked in here, did he receive any visitors?"

"None. Oh, we'd get the occasional representative from the mayor's office, but they would come to the conference room. Logan and the others would join us there."

"Well, look, Mr. Koppelman. Here's my card. Also ask around if any of your employees can think of anything to contribute. Thanks."

A handshake exchange then followed as the detectives made their way out of the agency. It wasn't until they were completely out of the building that they felt comfortable enough to discuss what had just transpired.

"That Koppelman guy was weird, Vince."

"Ya think?"

Vince released a suppressed laugh through his nostrils. Even the seasoned detective wondered if all intelligent architects of systems and roadways possessed an obscure persona as countless designs swam through their heads.

They were heading to the Caprice when Vince's mobile suddenly went off, the ringtone belting out the theme from *Law & Order,* Juanita's way of amusing her husband. The corners of his mouth curled up when he read the display. It was Scarpone.

"Okay, Pauly," Vince answered without so much as a hello. "What've you got?"

Vince whipped out his handy notepad and pen and began jotting down the critical minutia coming from Scarpone's lips. Only a few grunts and an occasional *yep* indicated Vince's acknowledgement of the information Scarpone was dispensing to him.

"Where did they find it?"

Drake's ears perked up when hearing that line. Perhaps Logan's Enclave was found. Meanwhile Vince continued scribbling more data with a few "uh-huh" mutterings as his responses.

"Great job, Pauly! Now, listen. I want you to dispatch a department flatbed to impound the vehicle. I'll be there in, say . . ." Vince stopped to look at his watch, "forty-five minutes. I want to have the vehicle examined up and down, back and forth, but without the people living there gawking at us and asking 10,000 questions. Got it? Oh, and I want Maszukevich assisting Lowery on the case. Speaking of which, did Lowery talk to that mailroom guy yet? Uh-huh. Keep me posted. I will talk to Lou later about his involvement. And for God's sake, I want someone from Hanlon's department to retrieve that heart the Lavoie dame brought in to the first district precinct this morning. Nowak and I have DNA samples from Galwyn's apartment. I want to get Hanlon cracking on this ASAP. And have a glass of Chianti on me tonight. Thanks."

Vince hung up the call. He scribbled down a few more details from his conversation with Scarpone. Then he tucked the phone away. The notepad he slipped into his suit jacket pocket.

"They found Galwyn's Enclave at 43 Kenyon Street. Apparently some nosy neighbor spotted his SUV as early as Saturday. He decided to make a case about it and called it in to the traffic department."

"As if he had nothing else better to do," Drake remarked.

"Yeah, but it did save us some time in locating Galwyn's wheels." Vince glanced once more at his Citizen watch. "C'mon. I want to take a firsthand look before the truck gets there."

The whirlwind afternoon adventure continued for the boys from homicide. The Caprice was earning its keep in mileage.

Chapter 63

It wasn't difficult to spot the Enclave. Its champagne fuselage gleamed in the late afternoon sun.

As Vince and Drake were examining the vehicle with stealth precision, one of the neighborhood denizens was cooking up a storm. The aroma of barbecued chicken wafted through the air. Even a hint of garlic could be detected. Drake's stomach was roaring like a lion. A stale donut and two cups of over-brewed coffee was all the junior detective had to eat that day. He commented to Vince that he was hoping to get an invite for the outdoor feast. Vince shook his head, pointing to the SUV.

Vince was astounded by how immaculate the interior was. There wasn't so much as a folded newspaper or a beverage bottle in the cup holder.

Suddenly there came a rumble of thunder on this cloudless day. The genesis of the sound came from a flatbed tow, which made its clangorous appearance on the otherwise quiet block. In its wake was a Providence PD squad car. The whirling blue and red lights atop the cruiser, along with its shrieking siren, were a signal to all to keep back.

The sights and sounds also caught the attention of Vince and Drake, both of whom flashed their credentials to let the blues know they were on their side. The uniformed officers came out of the car to greet the detectives, but neither group said a word. Vince was the one who began giving out orders.

"I want tow boy over there to get this Enclave to HQ, PDQ. Detectives Lowery and Maszukevich and their team will be fine-tooth-combing it. Got it?"

A simple *yes, sir* came from the officers.

Knowing that the vehicle was in capable hands, Vince and Drake could focus their sights on why the car was there to begin with. Vince retrieved a folded piece of paper from his jacket pocket.

"Sam Aponte, 61 Kenyon."

Vince cast his eyes in the direction of the house. Drake interceded.

"Is that our rat?"

Vince frowned. "*Informant.* Aponte was not an accomplice to any crime." Then Vince gave pause to reconsider his words. "Although one can never be too sure."

As the flatbed driver maneuvered his vehicle into a position to easily hoist the Enclave, Drake took a photo of the SUV with his smart phone. The intention was to ask the neighbors if they had witnessed anything or anyone associated with it. But the first person to question was Aponte.

"I don't get it, Vince. We went through Galwyn's apartment earlier. There we found no drug paraphernalia of any kind. And this street is still a mile away from Lockwood and its problems."

"Who knows? For all intents and purposes the vehicle may have been left here just to throw us off. C'mon. Let's go visit Aponte."

Drake tailed Vince like a puppy does its master. But as he kept up with Vince's brisk pace, Drake couldn't help but comment on the SUV.

"That's another thing that's puzzling. The Enclave is as clean as a whistle. If Galwyn was murdered, it doesn't appear he was killed in his vehicle."

"Unless he was killed by asphyxiation. Hopefully Donny and Lou and their men will shed some light on the subject."

Vince stepped up to the front porch of the modest white clapboard home of their target. Although the outside structure was fairly well maintained, the same could not be said of the entryway. The porch's floorboards were warped and begged to be repaired. Every step taken resulted in an ear-splitting creak as a red flag screaming for help.

The main metal front door was open, but the screen door in front of it was locked and closed, although it offered little protection from a potential home invasion, since anyone with average strength could easily tear it down. The closed screen did allow cool breezes to filter through the house on the warm late spring day.

A series of high-pitched yips sounded in the background. No need to ring the doorbell, not with Sparky on patrol. Suddenly from out of the dark interior, the figure of a man began to emerge. He was scrawny and wearing nothing but his underwear, which consisted of a sleeveless tee and a pair of red and gold-striped boxers. An anchor tattoo stretched itself over what was once an imposing right bicep, now atrophied to wrinkled weakness. He sported a pencil-thin black mustache mixed with a few strands of gray. Just a few wiry strands of hair encompassed his otherwise bald peak with one bulging right eye while the left appeared almost shut. The invisible dog continued its yaps until its owner yelled back at it to keep quiet. He then refocused his attention on the visitors.

"Yes?" he asked, with a gravelly voice to match his senior age.

"Sam Aponte?" Vince asked.

"Yeah, what do you want?"

"Detectives Calabrese and Nowak, Providence PD Homicide. May we come in?"

Aponte was so shook up about the police knocking on his door that he allowed them to enter without any resistance.

Vince entered first. Aponte's living room was a mess, no doubt due to the old man's lack of help to assist him in keeping the place neat. Newspapers and an occasional cardboard box occupied most of what could pass as furniture. There was a heavy scent of garlic and cooking oil, as if Aponte had just fixed himself a simple dinner.

Meanwhile, the dog continued to bark from behind a closed door in the next room. Aponte commanded the animal to keep quiet once more.

"Ah," Aponte groused, waving his hand in the direction of the room. "She's my wife's dog. A little, what do you call 'em . . . a shih tzu. My wife died two years ago and I got stuck with her. My kids, grandkids and even great-grandkids don't want her. Drives me nuts."

Vince offered a feigned smile. He wanted to make their visit as short as possible.

"Mr. Aponte, my partner and I are here to check out the disappearance, possibly the murder, of a fellow by the name of Logan Galwyn." Vince showed Aponte the photo of Logan that Rebecca had given the police earlier. "He was last seen last Thursday and he drove a Buick Enclave, the same vehicle you told the PPD was oddly out of place on your street."

Aponte gave a long look through his good eye. "I never saw the guy," he replied, handing the picture back to Vince.

"According to the report, you called in at three-thirty-two Saturday afternoon about the emergence of the vehicle. Had you seen the Enclave at that spot earlier?"

"I first noticed it Friday. Didn't think anything of it. Then I saw it was still there Saturday afternoon. I never saw it before. And I know my neighbors don't have anything like that. And they hardly get visitors. Kind of like me." Aponte looked off into the distance. "The only time I get family here is when my daughter picks me up and wheels me somewhere else. Nobody wants to stay here."

Despite the hardened edge sewn into his skin that came from too many murder cases in his lifetime, Vince was feeling a little soft toward the forgotten old man. But there was the matter of the crime yet to be solved.

"Did you ever notice anyone getting in or leaving the vehicle for any reason, Mr. Aponte?"

"No."

"Did you speak to any of your neighbors about the vehicle?" Drake chimed in. "Perhaps they may have seen someone associated with it."

"Nah. Nobody seen nothin'."

Vince saw he was getting nowhere. He gave his business card to Aponte with the hope the diminutive man might recall an important fact or two sometime later. The senior detective then jerked his head toward the door to let Drake know it was time to leave.

The men were back on the street. Vince gazed in the direction where he and Drake left the officers and the flatbed. He was relieved to see the Enclave had been taken away. Meanwhile, Drake posed with his arms akimbo, with an expression that read, *where do we go from here?*

"Let's question a few of the neighbors to see if they recall anything," Vince began. "Just the immediate ones, those closest to where Galwyn's car was parked."

"And then?"

"We'll head back. And with the help of Scarpone I want to put together a list of people and interested parties to be contacted, starting with Galwyn's immediate family."

"How about Rebecca's estranged husband?"

"Him, too." Vince paused for a second, scanning the street block. "And his father."

Vince's phone rang. He noted the identity of the caller: Captain Borromeo.

"Now what?"

Chapter 64

Mark Lavoie had just arrived back at his apartment. His cell phone never rang while he was out. But he was hoping Rebecca might call him. Despite her brief infidelity, Mark was willing to forgive her if she just got rid of Logan.

He reached into the fridge to pop open a cold one, perhaps to make him forget he'd married her or to wallow in his sorrow. Mark had exhausted all possible ways of contacting her except to call her mother's home. But it had been three weeks since the blow-up and there was only so much a man could take when apart from his beautiful bride. Winston was closed down, save for a handful of courses being conducted for the summer. And there was no reason to seek out Heather Karinski. Besides, even Mark thought it was shameful of him to keep placing Heather in the awkward position of having to choose between him and her lifelong friend. Plus, Mark didn't want to impose upon Hunter Morales any longer, what with his new responsibilities as a father and wife Kayla, who was growing annoyed by Mark's numerous calls. And Lane Pascale had little enough time for himself, let alone lending an ear to Mark's tales of woe.

Mark flipped through a magazine sent to him in the mail the day before. Just then his cell began to ring. Startled but unfazed, Mark recognized the number, signifying Rebecca was calling him. He flung the periodical across the room to concentrate on the urgency of the call.

"Rebecca!" Mark exhaled a short blast before his lips creased to a smile. "Oh, it's so good to see your name on my ID display! I never thought I'd hear from you again! Listen, I'm willing to overlook that fling you—"

"You murdered Logan, you bastard!" Rebecca interrupted, screaming at the top of her lungs.

The accusation floored Mark like a two-by-four. He was at first speechless, but soon gathered himself in order to address her.

"What the fuck are you talking about?"

"This morning," Rebecca replied, gasping for air in her frantic state, "I received a box containing Logan's heart! You killed him! You sent that package to me!"

Mark had intended to turn the other cheek when Rebecca called. That changed in a heartbeat. "I never sent you a package! I don't even know what this Logan character looks like!"

"Well, I've already talked to the police!" Rebecca's voice was quivering at this point. "Be expecting a call from the homicide detectives I notified! They are coming after you!"

And with that Rebecca abruptly disconnected her line. Mark wanted to rebut the accusation, but never had the chance to do so. He dropped his mobile without realizing it.

Mark continued to sit with his mouth open. As much as it would've been enticing to get drunk on the beer, the intoxicating beverage no longer appealed to him. Just the thought of sending a body organ to someone gave Mark the creeps. But then the wheels in his head began to spin. Suddenly thoughts Mark had been fed and what he read in the past began to take up occupancy in his cerebellum.

There was only one person he had to turn to, especially with the startling revelation by Rebecca. Mark reached for his phone.

Chapter 65

A full year of teaching takes a toll on any instructor. But at sixty, the professor of anthropology found the last year exhausting. So much so that Roger Lavoie was looking more and more toward retirement.

Beth was still a half hour away from home, but Roger already had chicken roasting in the oven, complementing it with wild rice and spinach. The rice was resting on top of one of the burners and earmarked to be ready by the time Beth arrived. The spinach was still a few minutes away from being finished.

With dinner under control, Roger was going to relax for a few minutes and savor what little time he had before the next round of activity. But that hope was dashed suddenly by the ringing of the house phone.

"Dad, I just got a call from Rebecca."

"Oh? Is she begging for forgiveness?"

"Hardly. She was screaming bloody murder. She claims that Galwyn guy was murdered, and she accused me of being the murderer. But to top it all off, she blames me for sending her his heart, cut out from his body. Can you imagine that?"

There was no sound for several seconds before Roger responded with an almost silent *no*. He looked off into the distance, but there were hidden thoughts behind his poker-faced veneer, accompanied by his momentary silence.

"Dad?"

It took a while, but Roger answered his son. He sensed something else was coming.

"Look, Dad. I . . . I know of those stories from the past, you know, your trial, Mom being committed, and that guy who was murdered back then. I know you were acquitted and all, and I realize you've steered me in the right direction since I was seven. And I'm still grateful for the teaching job at Winston you and Professor Asmundsson helped me land. But I have to know something. I heard Rebecca's rants and cries and all I could think of was what had happened twenty-two years ago. I want you to level with me. Did you kill Galwyn? And did you kill that man twenty-three years ago?"

"I'm outraged to hear this coming from you, Mark! After all I've done—"

"Just hear me out! Please!"

Roger remained silent to allow Mark time to speak.

"I'm not accusing you of anything. I just asked a question or two. I . . . I hear this shit from Rebecca, and then all these ideas come swimming in my head. And then I also remember you telling me you'd take care of things after I told you Rebecca left me three weeks ago. Was this what you had in mind?"

"Did it ever occur to you that perhaps it might be Sheryl Dyer?"

"Rebecca's mom? How did you come up with such a farfetched idea like that?"

"Think about it, Mark. Sheryl was never crazy about Galwyn. She admitted it. Maybe with Galwyn out of the way, her daughter would come back to you."

"But with the same set of circumstances as you were involved in?"

"I don't think she may be too fond of me either. She is old enough to remember that trial way back when, and perhaps she thinks repeating those crimes might make me a likely target, and throw the authorities off her scent."

"I owe you everything. But so help me, if all this truly points to you, I mean the situation now and also what happened decades ago, I will renounce you as my father."

There was a soft click on the other end. But for Roger it pealed like a clanging church bell.

Roger ejected himself from the lounger to hang up. He thought about every syllable of Mark's words in reflection. But then he stiffened, as if given a jolt. *No, there is one more thing I must do, my son. It is only for your benefit. I must crack that whore, and make her pay for her libertine ways. She has caused you great suffering. Please don't begrudge me this act of justice.*

Roger was resolute in executing the next step. But then he snapped out of his daydream to tend to dinner.

265

A torrential rain from an incoming system hugged the East Coast like a sex-starved rogue the following morning. Vince and Drake were its soaked victims as they made a mad dash through the parking lot of the PPD's main head-quarters. The smell of damp granite permeated the grounds. Dogwood bushes held in every teardrop from the sky.

They made their way to the second-floor office of Police Chief Ralph Heimler. There waiting for them was Heimler's admin, Fiona Flannery. She was in her early 50s but her permed hair was a fiery red. Her skin was fair and speckled with freckles. Fiona's rounded face was the map of Ireland. An immigrant from County Kerry at sixteen, Fiona was well adjusted to American life, particularly the New England version.

As Vince and Drake came into view, Fiona's cheeks plumped up like a chipmunk's. And her smile was as radiant as a fire in the hearth.

"Well, if it isn't Detective Calabrese!" Her brogue was as thick as Killarney. "Hello, Vincent! 'Tis grand of you to stop by again!"

"Ah, Fiona! You're about the only face I look forward to seeing when coming here!"

"Surely you don't mean that. The chief trusts your wisdom."

"Sometimes I'm not so sure. Oh, you know Sergeant Nowak."

"And what a fine specimen of a man he is! Tell me, Drake. Have you ever settled down with anyone? 'Tis sure you could steal a sweet colleen's heart!"

Drake bowed his head in bashfulness. But a wide grin advertised that he wouldn't mind the company of a young woman in his arms.

Fiona rose from her chair. Although just a few pounds overweight, Fiona carried her extra baggage well. She was proportioned acutely and strutted like a runway fashion model.

"Would you like some coffee, Vincent?"

"If you're making it, I know it's got to be the Irish variety."

"Heaven's sakes!" Fiona laughed boisterously. She waggled her right index finger at the senior detective. "You could be a bad influence, Vincent! You know darn well we can't have alcohol on the job!"

"But if you could, I'd bet it would be Jameson!"

A few chortles filled the room as Fiona prepared Vince's cup. Even though he wasn't a regular visitor to Chief Heimler's office, Fiona had a photographic recollection of how Vince preferred his coffee. But she needed a clue for Drake's version. "Same, please."

"Well, that was easy."

Fiona turned to hand over the prepared brews. But her attention was suddenly drawn to an angular figure, almost taking her breath away. Her flummoxed expression swiveled the heads of Vince and Drake.

"Relax, everyone," the tall, uniformed man offered.

Captain Frank Borromeo. He was head of detectives for the PPD, namely the direct boss of Vince and Drake. But the relationship they had with him was amicable. In fact, Vince and Frank grew up together when rising through the ranks of the department and shared similar lines in their respective families. Like Vince, Frank was also pushing himself toward retirement. He was well past the mandatory twenty for a full pension, but there was something about "the job"—police slang for the occupation. Both Vince and Frank loved their line of work, complete with all its foibles. There was always a challenge, something you couldn't get anywhere else.

"Hello, Frank." Vince smiled, shaking his superior's right hand. "I guess the word got out about that heart Rebecca Lavoie brought in."

"Yeah," sighed Frank, with his oscilloscope smile. "Chief wants an update on what you've got. He's even called in Debra Vogel."

"His press secretary?" Vince questioned with a contorted walnut face. The seasoned detective reclined further in his seat, still holding the coffee Fiona gave him. His free hand massaged his chin, as he sat looking off in an absent stare. Vince's enigmatic expression had him pondering in deep thought. "It's still a little early, Frank. My team is still sifting through all of this. How the f—" Vince caught himself in order not to cuss in front of the church parishioner Fiona. "What am I going to say to Ralph?"

"Give him whatever you have at this point. Oh, and DA Noreen McCarron will be here too."

"Great! And all we have is that heart and Galwyn's SUV, which is proving negative. God knows how long until Hanlon and his boys can come up with a DNA match. I've also got Scarpone, Lowery, Maszukevich and others working on this. But I really don't have much else."

"C'mon, Vince! Just tell the chief and McCarron that you're still working on a lot of loose ends. They know what goes on."

"Yeah, and now he wants the media involved in this, starting today. You and I both know those TV and paper bloodhounds ask too many questions, hindering our case. I'm telling you, it's just too soo—"

"Sorry, boys, for being a little late."

Enter Ralph Heimler. He was a giant of a man whose ruddy complexion might give one the impression he frequented the bar too often. But if he were there, it'd be no surprise if he paid for your beer. Everyone knew, though, never to cross Ralph, for even in his mid-sixties he was still quite capable of knocking you into the next room.

Ralph was never one for chitchat. For him, it was all about getting to the point. And his tardiness made all the better reason to speak in bulleted responses.

Noreen McCarron was all business. The late-forties woman hid her feminine side from everyone, sometimes even from her husband. If you rubbed her the wrong way, she wouldn't hesitate to kick you in the nuts.

"You all know Debra and DA McCarron. Let's go into my office." Ralph turned to Fiona. "Unless the mayor or the lottery commission calls about my winning numbers, I am not here." He winked at Fiona as a confirmation that she caught his drift.

Fiona closed Ralph's door so the entire group could exchange ideas.

Everyone took a seat. Although the chairs in Ralph's office were quite comfortable, sitting on a splintered park bench would've been more pleasant, given the circumstances.

"Let's get on with this."

Ralph opened a manila folder containing a few sheets of paper, as did Noreen. He scanned through them quickly as Debra sat off to the side with her legal pad, pen, and laptop at the ready to jot down the minutes of the session and translate them into some plausible press release.

"At twelve noon, there will be a press conference to be held in the media interview room down the hall. Mayor Kincaid will be on hand to offer a brief opening statement before deferring to me. I will embellish it regarding the subject matter of the heart brought in to the first precinct by Rebecca Lavoie. And then I'll incorporate the input of Captain Borromeo and the lead detective on the case, Lieutenant Calabrese. Debra will prepare a release and will confer with and email her counterpart at the mayor's office. Being that we have just under two hours to make this announcement, I suggest that we open the discussion about any significant facts to include. Let's start with you, Frank."

"At about eleven am Monday morning, Rebecca Lavoie walked into the first district precinct with this box, allegedly containing the butchered heart of Logan Galwyn. As soon as I got wind of this, I dispatched Lieutenant Calabrese and Sergeant Nowak from homicide to interrogate Mrs. Lavoie."

With his fingers fanned out over his mouth and chin, Ralph's eyes darted to Vince and Drake.

"Sergeant Nowak and I questioned Mrs. Lavoie at length. She's married to the son of Roger Lavoie, the same guy twenty-odd years ago who was on trial for the murder of Darren Haber and frightening his then wife Margaret sufficiently to be committed to an institution, and I believe she's still there."

"So, you think Roger Lavoie may have repeated the same dismemberment crime?"

"It's just a hunch. But the same sadistic pattern has repeated itself. Margaret Lavoie had an affair with Haber, he gets killed and his body parts are sent to her one at a time. Rebecca, by her own admission, had an affair with Galwyn, an ex-boyfriend of hers. From what I gather, I don't think her husband Mark had anything to do with it. But it may be that Dad is fighting his son's battles here."

Ralph quickly turned to Debra to remind her that was just Vince's opinion. Meanwhile, Noreen was intrigued by Vince's supposition. It wasn't intended to be used as a fact, and it was understood that all judgment on Roger should be withheld until evidence proved otherwise. The police chief then gave a nod to Vince to continue.

"Drake and I went to Galwyn's apartment. Neat as a pin. If he were killed, it wasn't there. But we did gather a few items for DNA testing to match that heart."

"Did you speak with anyone there?"

"We spoke with the chief weekday doorman and the head of maintenance. The last time Galwyn and his vehicle were seen was last Thursday. Surveillance cameras backed that up. Before leaving his apartment, I spotted a business card of Galwyn's. He worked as an engineer for the Department of Traffic. What was very strange was the lack of emotional concern at that place of employment over his absence. Then I got the call from Detective Paul Scarpone about the appearance of Galwyn's Enclave on Kenyon Street. Drake and I questioned the guy who called it in plus a few other neighbors. No one saw anyone parking or leaving the vehicle."

"Anything on the vehicle?"

"I had Hanlon's team check for fingerprints. They told me this morning that only Galwyn's came up."

Ralph drew a deep breath. "What do you think is the next move?"

"Well, besides working with Scarpone and the others last night, Drake and I came up with a list of people we should investigate. Obviously, Mark Lavoie, for one. I think we can eliminate Galwyn's family members, to whom, by the way, Scarpone began reaching out. But there are others . . . especially Roger Lavoie. Personally, I'd like to get a search warrant for probable cause, Mrs. McCarron."

"Permission granted," Noreen declared.

Ralph sucked in his lips. There wasn't much else to discuss at that point, although he admitted the door was always open.

"As I said, Mayor Kincaid will attend the press conference with the rest of us. I want to make certain that Detective Scarpone contacts Galwyn's next of kin before we go to the press. For now, we will treat Galwyn's case as a missing persons until forensics bails us out. I will be reciting the facts as you stated, Fred and Vince. But that's all. Any reference to persons of interest in the investigation, especially Roger Lavoie, is pure conjecture, as I'm sure Mrs. McCarron will attest."

Noreen gave a slight nod.

"In that event, we will give them our patented answer, 'We cannot make that determination as this time. It's still under investigation.' Got it?"

The meeting was adjourned until all were to reconvene in less than two hours. But as he made his way out of Ralph's office, Vince felt a firm tapping on his arm.

"We need to put this case to bed early, Lieutenant," Noreen commanded. "This department suffered a disgraceful blow twenty-two years ago. I was just out of law school then, but I remember some of the dynamics involving the case against Lavoie. If you and your team assist us, I'll make sure these charges stick and not allow the jury to have second thoughts on it."

"Hopefully you'll have a different prosecutor."

"That's assured. As I recall, Claire Torelli is now in semi-retirement, teaching tort law at Brown Law School. Judge Sylvia McCormack died six years ago, and Lavoie's attorney Vance Beckwith made a fortune in real estate out in Arizona somewhere. He won't be back, either."

"Hmm, a fresh slate. Well, we're going to give it our best effort."

A smug smile creased her lips. Vince's affirmation was like music to Noreen's ears as all parties went their separate ways.

Chapter 67

The press conference went on without a hitch. Debra Vogel started the event by giving a brief introduction to members of both print and electronic journalism. Whirrs of cameras serenaded the opening remarks as bulbs flashed like dance club strobe lights. TV camera crews were at the ready with their own glaring beams.

Mayor Travis Kincaid was the first to speak. He was a clean-cut individual, whose 6'1" height gave him a presence. A seasoned politician, having cut his teeth in the Rhode Island state assembly and as a former three-term US congressman, Kincaid gave a brief overview before deferring to Chief Ralph Heimler, DA Noreen McCarron, and Vince.

Just as Ralph had instructed everyone, each gave the standard no comment response, as the matter was still under investigation. And at no time was that reply stressed any further than when a member of the press corps brought up the similar set of circumstances of Roger's trial when the name Lavoie was aired. No comment.

At the conclusion of the media circus, Vince and Drake headed back to their office to sit down with the investigation unit. Seated around the conference table were fellow detectives Paul Scarpone, Donny Lowery, Lou Maszukevich, and Soma Montero.

Paul was the most innocuous of the group. With the appearance of a tax accountant, Paul was nicknamed *Friar Paolo*, due to his bald dome and ring of dark hair around the back of his head giving him the looks of a monastery monk. And his benign display matched the demeanor he had in his family life. He was known as quick to share pictures of his family, consisting of his wife and two teenage children. The entire family looked about as average as Paul. Yet despite his humble looks, Paul was more than capable of handling a Glock.

Donny was the womanizer of the group. With two failed marriages behind him and three children to show for it, Donny came to the realization that he was no longer the marrying type. He was resigned to spending his time off checking out strip joints and bars, not that he was totally successful in finding female company. And there were times when his children sorely missed him. If only he had reciprocated.

Lou always had cold feet about totally committing to someone, which explained his seven-year relationship with his girlfriend. There was only one thing he was married to: his job. Lou took his job seriously. Not that the others didn't, but he would talk shop whether at a family get-together or a department social gathering. If he were to become serious with his gal, she would have to accept his chatting about police work morning, noon, and night.

And then there was Soma, added to the group by Vince for her ability to relate to the women they would need to seek out. That and to keep a wolf like Donny away from them. Soma was married with two children. That combination, together with her stressful line of work, placed a strain in her relationship with her husband, a sanitation worker, and curtailed her time spent with her twelve-year-old son and eight-year-old daughter. But she made the best of it in balancing her work and family.

Vince didn't want to make the meeting as extensive as the photo op with the reporters. Drake distributed some handouts on the case, complete with all the updates.

"Gee," Paul said. "Is there going to be a quiz on this later, Drake?"

Drake smirked as he continued passing out papers.

To break the monotony Donny made a comment on Lou's recent visit to the barber.

"Hey, great cut, Lou. Who's your stylist, John Deere?"

A couple of chuckles echoed through the room at Lou's expense.

"Man," Donny continued, "you're never going to catch any fucking pussy with a buzz like that."

"Hey!" Vince yelled. "There's a lady here, you know!"

"That's no lady, Lieutenant. That's only Montero."

Soma raised her hand up to stop Vince. "It's okay, Lieutenant. I can fight my own battles." She then turned to Donny, peering at him through squinted eyes. "Cut the bullshit, bendejo! One of these days I'll rip off your balls and you'll be Detective Donny Eunuch!"

A couple of the other detectives released a couple of *oohs* while clapping for Soma's assertion over Donny. The womanizer even pushed out his lower lip and nodded in acknowledgement to Soma for her stinging comeback.

But now it was time to act as a team. Vince gave everyone a brief recap of the sideshow with the press. He looked each detective in the eye as he forged ahead.

"We need to address all the key players. And we need to act wisely. It's my gut feeling that Roger Lavoie ought to be the main focus. That's why I asked DA McCarron to get me a search warrant. That's not to say others might not be under investigation. Drake and I will handle Lavoie personally. We'll also check out Margaret O'Mara, Lavoie's ex-wife."

"Isn't she in that nuthouse, Crenshaw?" Lou inquired.

"Yeah, but as Drake and I are dealing with Rebecca Lavoie, I want to know something about the circumstances surrounding the first victim."

Soma tilted her head. "Do you think she'll open up to you?"

"Not us," Drake interrupted. "We'll bring a psychiatrist to see where Margaret's head's at, preferably a woman. Less intimidating that way."

Vince turned to Paul. "I need you to focus on Galwyn's family members and any friends he may have had. Personally, I don't think we'll find anything there. But we gotta cover all the bases."

"And I'll put some pressure on Hanlon's guys in forensics."

"Good man." Vince smiled as he slapped Paul's left shoulder in admiration. "Oh, any luck on those prints on the package, bow, ribbon and cards?"

"Except for Rebecca's, none. Whoever put that package together must have used latex gloves."

With a frown from Vince, he then zeroed in on Donny. "Mark Lavoie is your guy. Also, I want you to question those associated with him such as friends or even people at Winston, like his boss, for instance. And, did you question that mailroom guy at Templeton's . . . the one who delivered the package to Rebecca?"

"Torey Willis? Yeah. All he remembered was seeing the back of the delivery guy who left the package. According to Willis, the guy wore a grey short-sleeve shirt and had a Patriots' baseball-style cap on backwards. Never saw his face. When he asked him if there was anything to sign, the guy muttered in a Boston accent there wasn't any."

"Well, keep at it and follow the guidelines I've given you."

Donny nodded as he scribbled down a few notes.

"Lou, I want a little more insight on Big Daddy. Maybe his former sister-in-law, Siobhan O'Mara might open up and give us some dirt on him."

"Heck, I might get a little from Lavoie's first victim's sister too," Lou remarked.

"You won't get anywhere," countered Drake. "I did a little research on the original case. Chloe Haber-Doyle died thirteen years ago of a heroin overdose. The murder of her brother took its toll on her. Even broke up her marriage. She lost custody of the one child she and her ex-husband had together. She fell off the cliff and hasn't surfaced since."

"Which brings us to you, Soma," Vince said. "While Drake and I put the squeeze on Lavoie, I want you to question his current wife thoroughly. I understand she works at a hospital. I also don't want to rule out Rebecca's mom, Sheryl Dyer. By her own admission, Rebecca said Sheryl was never crazy about Galwyn. Perhaps she could have bumped him off so that her daughter could reconcile with her husband. She may have viewed Galwyn as a cancer that had to be eradicated."

The meeting was adjourned. Each one had their assignments, and Vince made it clear that his squad was going to conduct the thorough investigation he had pledged to do for DA McCarron earlier.

Drake and the others rose from their seats as Vince headed to the half pot of coffee still on the burner in the room. He was tempted to have a cup of the half-day-old swill to keep him active. But the sheer excitement of this particular case, not to mention the possibility of righting a nearly quarter-century-old wrong, was all the veteran lawman required to keep the juices flowing.

Chapter 68

By two the word had gotten out. Every local television station in Providence had carried the press conference live. Radio stations began exclusive coverage. And various news information websites were plastering their homepages with news of the story. Rebecca wasn't aware of it until a fellow employee brought it to her attention. And that was when her countenance revealed her despair.

She first covered her face in embarrassment and asked to be left alone for a brief moment. When left to her solitary confinement, Rebecca ran her fingertips down her face until they just covered her mouth.

Her phone began to ring. It was a local reporter, of all people. How in the world could they have known where she worked? Rebecca had mentioned her employer when she walked into the precinct the day before, and perhaps it was divulged at the press conference. But this shouldn't have been a tale about the person who reported the crime as opposed to the story of the crime itself. Perhaps one could chalk it up to great investigative senses and journalistic instincts, but Rebecca preferred to have nothing of it. Now composed, Rebecca politely told the reporter she wasn't interested in spewing out the details of her ordeal.

Only a minute had passed after she hung up with caller number one when the phone rang once more. Again, another reporter was intruding on her turf. Rebecca once again refused to answer any questions, only this time she gave the inquisitive journalist a piece of her mind.

In order to prevent any more annoying media calls from going through, Rebecca told the company switchboard not to pass anyone from the press through to her. They were instructed to give a brief apology, and politely warn them not to try again.

Brett McLellan also learned of the press conference and asked Rebecca to see him in his office. She was rumored to replace Brett, and the thought of the media circus cascading on Templeton's headquarters wasn't a good idea toward that end. Rebecca agreed and explained that she had already told reception to turn them away. With tears in her eyes, Rebecca conveyed her sincerity as enough evidence that she didn't want this to happen. She was also steadfast in her resolve to perform her functions. His slight nod was his consent.

When Rebecca arrived home, the first to greet her was a local TV reporter with a cameraman and soundman in tow. She shielded herself with her arms around her head to cover her face.

"Mrs. Lavoie, may I have a few minutes with you, please?"

"No, I want to be left alone!"

The moment she stepped inside her mother's home, Rebecca slammed the door behind her. She spread her arms and legs out against the door as if barring any intruders from entering, especially snooping reporters. Her facial expression said it all. Rebecca closed her eyes and appeared to be gasping for air.

Despite her daughter's agitated state, Sheryl came to Rebecca's aid to comfort her. Ever the doting mother, Sheryl pried Rebecca away from door while caressing the fallen woman's face. Sheryl pulled Rebecca to her and slowly escorted the distraught daughter to the divan in the living room.

"Sit down, Rebecca," Sheryl said in whispers. "Let me get you something."

"I'm all right, Mom." Rebecca's eyes were clamped down, in her efforts to wish her anxiety away. "It's not necessary."

Laird entered the living room, puzzled over what was going on.

"What happened?"

"What do you think happened?" Sheryl snapped at Laird, still comforting Rebecca while pointing out the obvious. "Your sister is being hounded by the press. I'll bet it's because of that news conference with the mayor, the DA, and the police."

Rebecca was slowly regaining her composure. She gently pushed away her mother.

"I'm okay. I'll . . . I'll be fine." She searched for an explanation. "I wouldn't doubt if the press got hold of Mark when the bulletin went out. He probably told them where I live."

"I'm not defending your estranged husband," Sheryl countered, "but didn't you tell the police that you're living here for now? Maybe they released that information?"

Rebecca's head jerked up as she looked into Sheryl's face. A scowl and narrowed eyes displayed her displeasure at her mother's logic.

"Why are you sticking up for him?"

"For God's sake, Rebecca, it's just a theory."

Laird broke away for a moment, but he returned seconds later with a box wrapped in brown paper.

"I forgot to tell you, Rebecca," Laird began, "but I found this package at the doorstep when I came home this afternoon."

"Why didn't you tell me that earlier?" Sheryl asked her son.

"Because it wasn't addressed to you."

Rebecca looked at the package suspiciously. Trepidation ran through her veins, for she suspected what the contents might be. The sadistic prank was escalating to the next level.

"I . . . I need a pair of scissors, please."

Laird went to fetch the shears while Rebecca began to tremble. She was in no condition to handle a sharp instrument. That was why Sheryl took the scissors from Laird as she prepared to cut open the package.

Before one incision in the paper was made, Sheryl inspected the package carefully. Although there was a printed label bearing Rebecca's name and the Greenville address, there was no return address. Plus the package didn't contain any postmark, nor was there a shipping label from any recognized courier.

With the wrapping discarded, all that was left was a corrugated box. A small envelope was taped to it with Rebecca's name beautifully scripted in calligraphy. Sheryl vised Rebecca's right arm for support. The daughter opened the envelope. The message inside was written in the same artistic penmanship.

278

Here's to getting your foot in the door for that big promotion.

Outside of her family, only Mark, along with his father and stepmother, and Heather knew of the possibility of Rebecca taking over Brett's position. And she feared what was coming next. Rebecca began to tremble. Tears emerged as she girded herself up for the expected grisly gift.

"Go on, dear," nudged Sheryl. "I'm right beside you."

Even Laird sat across from them, more as a curious onlooker than a concerned brother.

Rebecca firmly held the sides of the box lid. She rapidly lifted it, but kept her eyes closed. In one way she wanted to get it over with, but that other side of her was refusing to accept its contents.

"It's just tissue paper," Laird muttered matter-of-factly.

Rebecca opened her eyelids and confirmed Laird's statement. A swallow of air was her only way to move on. Now Sheryl barnacled to Rebecca as the Templeton's worker gingerly peeled away the layers, ultimately revealing the box's darkest secret. And there it was, presumably Logan Galwyn's right foot. It was almost ashen in color, having been deprived of blood circulation for several days. What blood there was, had caked at the toes of the appendage. It was a cut worthy of a butcher. No, it was more of a surgeon's incision, clean and straight across.

Rebecca couldn't take it anymore. She cried hysterically as Sheryl pulled the troubled woman into her arms. But even the steely nerves of the mother came undone as she could no longer gawk at the hideous contents. Laird's mouth soured as he released a gasp.

"Cover the box up, Laird!" Sheryl commanded her son as both she and Rebecca refused to take one more glance at the unnerving sight. Laird executed the task, but not without treating it as if it were radioactive material.

The lid was on. Rebecca gently pried herself away from Sheryl's grasp. Trying to gather her wits, she began to open up.

"I . . . I," Rebecca began stuttering, shaking as if from fever, "I n-need to m-make a phone c-call."

Chapter 69

Just a half-hour later, Vince, Drake, and Soma arrived at the Dyer house. The moment they had received the call from dispatch, the three detectives raced over to Greenville.

Rebecca was still trembling with fear as Vince and Drake donned latex gloves to examine the alleged foot of Logan. Meanwhile, Soma was observing Sheryl for any outward sign of a slip-up that the mother might demonstrate.

Vince and Drake exchanged a few whispers. Rebecca and Sheryl cocked their heads as they tried in vain to listen in on the detectives' hushed conversation. Finally Vince looked up at the two women, clearing his throat.

"Well," Vince began, "we'll be taking this back with us to forensics. Check it with the heart you brought in. Even though technically this falls under the Greenville jurisdiction, our office will contact the local authorities to allow the Providence PD to oversee this matter."

"Do you think this might speed things up?" Rebecca inquired.

"In dealing with this particular science, solutions don't appear overnight. Sometime it takes days, even weeks. But one thing's for certain. We might make a match on footprints. Galwyn was born down in Warwick, so he's a Rhode Island native. That helps in making a match quicker when you're at least dealing with the same state records. Plus, footprint matches produce slightly quicker results than DNA matches. But let me caution you: Don't expect quick answers."

"I noticed you and your partner were taking a long time looking at that—" Sheryl flicked her hand, "that foot."

"Detective Nowak and I noticed some significant amount of dirt under the toenails. I'm not inferring that Galwyn, or whoever this foot belonged to, didn't follow proper hygiene. But we're under the assumption that this foot was buried in the ground somewhere. The dirt looks like topsoil. But we're going to have Bobby Hanlon and his forensics team run additional tests."

"Maybe they dug up someone's grave," Sheryl reasoned. "I mean, I know it sounds morbid, but then again look at the act of depravity in sending that box."

"I don't think so. Despite its graying color, this looks fairly fresh. Plus, morticians drain the blood of the cadavers they work on. Not to mention it's a pain in the ass for someone to dig up a grave, open the coffin, take what they need, and then seal it up and cover it. No, this has all the earmarks of an impromptu grave, probably in a backyard or some other local secluded area."

"You said your son first noticed the package, Mrs. Dyer?" Drake asked.

"Yes. Let me call him down."

As Sheryl went to retrieve Laird, Vince's phone rang. It was Paul Scarpone. The veteran detective excused himself from the others to take the call in private. This gave Soma a chance to ask Rebecca a few questions.

"On the way down here, Detective Nowak told me that your mother wasn't that keen on Logan. Is that true?"

"They didn't exactly see eye to eye, if that's what you mean," Rebecca responded. "She was never crazy about Logan, even before I met Mark. In fact, she was thrilled when he broke up with me about two years ago. I don't know, maybe she saw a little of my father in him. He abandoned us over twenty years ago."

"I'm sorry." Soma bowed her head, clearing the way for the next salvo. "Rebecca, do you think your mother could have sufficient resentment toward Logan to do something like this?"

"I'm not feeling very comfortable with your insinuation, Detective."

"I apologize. But I'm trying to put the pieces together, much as my cohorts here are."

Rebecca looked off in thought as she replied to Soma's accusation.

"No. But there remains one man on this earth that my mother wouldn't mind hitting with a two-by-four." She hesitated slightly. "Or a gun. And he's in parts unknown as he has been for the last two decades."

An eerie silence filled the room as both Drake and Soma became aware of the bitter pill of frustration Rebecca and her family had been forced to swallow when Al Dyer took a flyer.

Suddenly Sheryl returned to the living room with Laird in her wake. Drake questioned Laird about when he first noticed the package and if he had seen anyone dropping it off before he approached the house. Four-twenty, and no.

Vince reemerged from his sequestered call.

"Good news. McCarron's office gave us a search warrant for Lavoie's house."

"Great!" Drake exclaimed. "Let's get a couple of units with us and pay him a visit after we get the warrant."

"Not so fast. His wife might be there. I want this kept between us and him. Besides, we need to get that box to Hanlon ASAP." Vince turned to Soma. "But I want you to question Beth Lavoie tomorrow. I have the name of the hospital in town where she works."

Soma gave a modest smile in compliance. But as she rose from her spot, the detective turned to Rebecca.

"Do you have someone you are close to?"

"Well," Rebecca replied, "there's my good friend Heather Karinski."

"I'd like to speak to her, if you don't mind. May I have her name, address, and phone number?"

While Vince and Drake wished the clan as pleasant an evening as possible under the circumstances, Rebecca complied with Soma's request. She wasn't going to question Soma's authority as she freely gave the information Soma sought. But as Rebecca began scribbling away, Soma was keeping a watchful eye on her mother. She was waiting for any twitch, facial expression, or body language Sheryl might exhibit to raise the suspicion that the Dyer matriarch could have had a hand in Logan's presumed demise. Soma was so zeroed in on Sheryl that she was oblivious when Rebecca tried twice to hand her the slip of paper. She snapped out of her fixation to join the others outside.

There were still a couple of stragglers, media reporters, parked on the front lawn. They soon spotted Drake carrying the box with its ghastly contents. The snoops were barraging Drake with a battery of questions.

"It's my birthday today, okay? I got a new pair of Nikes."

Drake shook his head in frustration at the persistence of the reporters. Finally Soma emerged from the house as she flew into the backseat to keep the foot company.

"I'll call Captain Borromeo on this one," Vince began while cranking the engine. "Tomorrow we're going to hit the ground running. And I'm going to have everybody hit their assignments hard. Plus, we're going to see firsthand if Lavoie cracks."

Chapter 70

While Bobby Hanlon and his forensics team had begun working on the foot specimen the night before, Vince's group began their fevered quest to interrogate all persons of interest. Vince gave his squad last-minute details before each detective was to fan out over the county.

Before hitting the streets, the detectives viewed the latest press conference that morning, this time focusing in on the divulgence of the foot found at Rebecca's doorstep. Mayor Kincaid, Chief Heimler, DA McCarron and Vince's direct boss, Captain Borromeo were all there in front of the reporters and cameras. Vince had his time in the spotlight the day before. That was enough for him. He was more hands-on in solving the case soon, rather than into posing for a photo op.

Donny Lowery trudged up the stairs to Mark's apartment door. Before knocking, he made sure he had the right frame of mind to ask the questions he needed. After all, he was dealing with a jilted husband in a romance triangle that might have resulted in Logan Galwyn's death. With a deep sigh, Donny was ready as he ever would be.

Mark opened the door slightly in response to Donny's rap. Only a meager chain prevented it from opening any further. It was Mark's way to ensure members of the press corps weren't breathing down his neck. Donny flashed his badge and announced his name. The young college teacher had no other recourse but to unhook the chain.

Donny walked in as if the flat were booby-trapped. His eyes darted left to right, up and down. Mark gave the detective a quizzical look as he decided to break the silence.

"Would you like something to drink?" Mark asked his visitor.

"No, thanks," Donny replied. "This isn't a social call."

Donny did sit down at Mark's modest kitchen table. All the while he kept quiet for nearly thirty seconds as his head and eyes did a 360 in hopes of spotting something unusual.

"I know why you're here, Lowery. You think I may have had something to do with Logan Galwyn's disappearance."

"The thought did cross my mind."

"Well, put it to rest. As much as I hated that home wrecker for causing a rift between me and Rebecca, murder is not in my DNA, okay?"

Donny snorted. He was aware of the story surrounding Mark's father years before. Not believing that the trait to kill is necessarily passed on in genes to the next generation, the detective nevertheless found it amusing for such a line to be coming out of Mark's mouth.

"Forgive me for chuckling."

Mark was unforgiving. The downward curve of his lips was a dead giveaway of Mark's disapproval. He would've liked to have thrown Donny out on his right ear. But prudence took hold of the college teacher as he allowed the detective a little slack. And whereas Donny was in no need for refreshment, Mark decided to help himself to a brew, if only to calm his combination of anger and fear.

"Look, Mark, right?" Donny asked boyishly in his cool approach. "I don't personally think you might have had anything to do with Galwyn's disappearance . . . or murder. Oh, sure, there's a motive behind it, but I don't think you're the type. From what I gather from my bosses who saw your wife last night, I understand you're still holding a torch for her and hope she will return to you."

The reference to Rebecca caused Mark to perk up. He jerked his head toward Donny with saucers for eyes.

"They were with Rebecca last night?" Mark looked down at the floor to work up the courage for the next question. He then lifted his head. "Do you think they can help the two of us get back together again?"

"We're police detectives, not fucking marriage counselors. Anyway, let me ask the questions. For starters, where have you been since last Thursday?"

"Pretty much in town. I went to see a friend of mine on Saturday. His name is Hunter Morales. He and his wife Kayla have a baby girl. He'll vouch for me."

"I'm sure," Donny replied wryly. "What about your bosses?"

"Most of the campus is closed for the summer, except for a few courses held here and there. Professor Asmundsson, he's the Dean of the Math Department I'm a part of, is away in China with his wife. Aside from the Chancellor, there's hardly anyone else there that I know of."

Donny didn't want to stay much longer, and Mark was only too willing to oblige. The college math instructor scrambled for a pen and paper and swiftly jotted down Hunter's name and address as well as Dr. Valen Pagano's name. In haste, Mark dashed off the slip. Donny gave it a glance before folding it and slipping the information into his left breast pocket.

The detective didn't come away with everything he'd sought, but he did get names to confirm Mark's whereabouts. Donny rose from his seat and headed for the exit. But before leaving, he wanted to give Mark something to chew on.

"Thanks for the names. And how's your father doing?"

"My father?" Mark scrunched his face in confusion. "What does he have to do with this?"

"Oh, nothing. Take care."

Donny closed the door behind him with his rather smug attitude quite evident. He would've liked to have seen Mark's face at that moment. But discretion proved to be more prudent. Still, Donny had to feel satisfied for planting the bug in Mark's head. Just maybe either the younger Lavoie or the elder might slip up.

Chapter 71

Siobhan was running late that morning for a meeting with a potential home buyer. Yet despite her tardiness, it was crucial for Siobhan to look her best. She had just completed the finishing touches on the mascara and began to apply her rose-colored lip gloss. Siobhan gave herself a kiss in the mirror, partially because of her inflated ego, but mostly to make certain the application remained even.

The real estate agent was about to top everything with a spritz of Calvin Klein when she suddenly noticed a navy-blue Toyota Corolla pulling up in her driveway. Her face scrunched in trying to decipher who she knew that owned one, let alone who would visit her at nearly ten in the morning. Siobhan became so focused on learning the identity of her visitor that she forgot to splash on the fragrance.

She continued to gawk at the long drink of water emerging from the tiny vehicle. All at once Siobhan closed the blinds to her bedroom. She had seen enough of the visitor as he continued to swivel his head to check out her house. *A cop,* she thought. *Who else would wear a suit that's too drab and short, not to mention sport a haircut that would make a Marine master drill instructor proud?*

There was no getting around pretending she wasn't home, not with her shiny cherry-red Mercedes sitting in front of the Corolla. Siobhan drew a deep sigh and conceded to facing the music.

Without giving the guest a chance to ring the doorbell, let alone knock, Siobhan opened the front door to welcome him. The game face required here called for one of her trademark spurious smiles.

"Good morning, may I help you?"

The tall man flashed the metal.

"Lou Maszukevich, Providence Homicide. Are you Siobhan O'Mara?"

"Why, yes," Siobhan answered, her grin deepening, forcing out a slight chuckle to add a semblance of good humor.

"Miss O'Mara, I'm sure you have read or have seen on TV the story about a missing Providence man in his late twenties named Logan Galwyn. The department is entertaining the suspicion that Mr. Galwyn may have been murdered."

"Oh, my!"

"May I come in?"

"Well, I was just on my way out the door. I'm trying to close on a deal on a property in Johnston."

"This won't take but a few minutes, I assure you."

There was no wavering by Siobhan. Lou's bullish insistence matched his tight end physique. It was useless for Siobhan to refuse the detective, and so entered Lou.

His eyes continued to dart to and fro, as if he were trying to spot the location of a hidden camera. Siobhan was getting the jitters. She offered the visitor a cup of coffee, not so much to relieve Lou's anxiety as it was to settle her frayed nerves.

"No, thanks."

"Huh? A cop refusing coffee. That's tantamount to a Texan refusing an offering of barbecued ribs."

"I know it sounds crazy, but it's the truth."

Siobhan giggled, although there was an edge to it. She understood his rationale to be there, and it was best to expedite the interrogation by feeding the detective words.

"Look, Mr. Mash—"

"Just call me Lou. It's a lot easier on the tongue."

Siobhan just deepened her smile. "I've heard many of the details on the case. It's about the split-up between my nephew and his wife. She finds body parts sent to her and you make the connection between my nephew and his father: Lavoie."

"Mark Lavoie's father, Roger, was married to your sister, Margaret, is that correct?"

"Yes, but I have nothing to do with Roger."

"When was the last time you saw Roger?"

"At Mark's wedding last August. Haven't seen him since. As for Mark, I stopped by his place about two months ago. He and Rebecca appeared to be the ideal young couple.

All this talk of her cheating on him, and Mark allegedly getting even by possibly killing that Galwyn fellow, is making my head spin."

"No one is accusing your nephew, Miss O'Mara. At least not yet. But we do have our suspicions about Roger Lavoie. The modus operandi is strikingly similar to what happened to Darren Haber. You remem—"

"I know who Haber was," Siobhan interrupted, eyes closed, palms raised.

Lou grabbed the back of his neck. He began to rub it in a nervous fashion. Siobhan could easily see Lou was wishing he were somewhere else, just as Siobhan was hoping for the same. But Siobhan knew Lou had a job to do.

"Look, I know it's been almost twenty-five years since the Haber murder and your sister being committed and all, but can you recall anything about that case involving Roger Lavoie that might show some sort of link to this case?"

"To be frank, it's been so long ago that I have mentally blocked a lot of those horrid details from my mind."

Siobhan closed her eyes for a brief moment, as if to emphasize her point. But when she reopened them, Siobhan found Lou looking at her quizzically.

"What seems to be the problem . . . Lou?"

"I don't know. Call me weird, but I find it rather odd that even with the talk of your sister being sent to Crenshaw, possibly because of what her ex did, you don't seem to have any anger or fury at Roger Lavoie."

"Time heals all wounds. Besides, Roger was found innocent by the jury, if I remember correctly."

"The judicial system has its flaws, Miss O'Mara. Even letting rats like Roger get away scot-free."

Lou slapped his hands on his lap as a signal of waving the white flag. Both he and Siobhan rose from their spots and proceeded to the front door. But just as he was about to leave, Lou handed Siobhan his business card.

"Call me if you can give us any insight."

Siobhan said nothing in response. She just offered a wide grin as to assure Lou and the PPD that she was ever the cooperating citizen.

But just as soon as Lou and his Corolla disappeared from sight, Siobhan's grin morphed into a subtle devious smile. There was something she wasn't willing to reveal to

Lou or anyone else concerning the principal characters in the investigation that might have a significant bearing on her. This hidden agenda remained safely tucked away.

Chapter 72

It was another monotonous day in the bullpen at the Providence Journal. That was where newspapers place young, unproven talent. Call it the minor leagues or a glorified internship, but everyone here had to weather this humble beginning.

Gina Chaudhary was just another face and name in the crowd. Four years removed from receiving her Bachelor's Degree in English from UMass and two from getting her Master's in Journalism from Rhode Island, Gina was pigeonholed, as most college grads are when breaking into the industry. She was filtering agate-type newsfeeds and attempting to make sense of these esoteric newsflashes worthy of only a select few. Gina grew exasperated, wondering if she'd ever actually be given a chance to prove herself and demonstrate her talent as a journalist.

As she went through the motions of looking to post another single column tidbit, Gina sensed she was being watched. The emergence of a shadow began to eclipse the fluorescent lighting from above. Perhaps not feeling a sense of imminent danger, but rather a definite concern, Gina moved her eyes toward the source.

"Ooh!" Gina gasped as she looked up at the perpetrator.

"Sorry!"

A young man close to Gina's age apologized for scaring the wits out of her. He was Scott Menken, whose outward appearance of dark, thick-framed glasses, and unruly hair badly in need of a trim, made him seem innocuous enough. His approach to say hi left something to be desired.

"Geez, Scott," Gina replied bitterly. "Why can't you just say hello like everyone else instead of scaring me half to death?"

"Christ, Gina. I said I was sorry. I think you may have too much coffee in your system."

"For the record, I don't drink coffee. I drink tea. And it's decaffeinated. It's been a tradition in my family for many years, even decades."

"Right. Your family's from Mumbai."

"It's New Delhi. And one more thing, for the record, I was born in Walpole, as in Massachusetts."

"Thanks for the MapQuest lesson."

Gina sighed as she continued her mundane scouring of news bits to be reformatted for the next edition. Meanwhile, Scott frowned to see his cohort looking miserable and acting even worse.

"What's eating you, anyway?" Scott begged the question.

"What do you mean?"

"You've been sour lately."

"Don't you feel the same way? I mean, here we are, the two of us, languishing at our jobs."

"Languishing. I like that! So you do make the most of your English major in college. Your parents must be proud."

"Oh, come off it. You know what I mean."

"Well, I don't appear as hung up about it as you do. You're trying to earn the Pulitzer before you're thirty."

"I feel I'm underutilized. I know what I'm capable of writing."

Gina paused for a moment. She picked up that day's edition of the Journal. After a quick glance, Gina held up the front page to Scott.

"This is what I'm talking about," Gina explained.

Scott studied the headlines and immediately snorted.

"Oh, that's deep. Instead of trying to work out a walk like any other rookie, you want to swing for the fences."

"This story involving the disappearance of Galwyn is huge. That's all anybody's been talking about in this town for the last twenty-four hours. And that name Lavoie: The father-in-law was involved in that murder case several years ago."

"Yeah, that was when you and I were wearing Pull-ups."

"I'm serious, Scott. I bet I can contribute something to this story, maybe not so much as by covering the main topic, but perhaps contributing by some underlying story."

"Like old man Wasserman back there is going to allow you that opportunity."

Gina glared at Scott. With a glint of determination, she slammed the newspaper on her desk. Ignited by her strong will, Gina shot up from her seat and pushed Scott to the side. And as she passed him, Gina noticed Scott's eyebrows were raised.

"Someone has to speak up," she looked back at Scott. "It might as well be me."

Gina marched through the maze of cubicles until she finally came across the windowed office of Editor-In-Chief, Fred Wasserman. The headman was busy studying pieces being funneled through to him by the various department editors.

Fred was more than twice Gina's age. He was looking to retirement soon enough, and spending quality time with his third wife. But there was something about the energy of the newspaper business that made him want to continue. It was the adrenalin rush the chief editor received for being at the heart of developing news stories, not just in Providence, but those coming from across the nation and around the world.

He was sucking on the back end of a pen. It was a trait he had recently developed. A reformed chain smoker, Fred needed the security blanket of something in his mouth. Since cigarettes were no longer an option, Fred went for the pen as his pacifier. That and the convenience the practice offered to allow him always to have his pen at the ready to sign or write something.

Gina stood in Fred's doorway, but wasn't getting any notice. She cleared her throat, but Fred wasn't budging from his intense scrutiny of other reporters' work. Gina had to resort to other means to get his attention.

"Excuse me, Mr. Wasserman." Gina was ever so sweet with her delivery as she lightly knocked on his door.

Fred's head jerked up. It didn't seem possible at first with his focus on the computer monitor, but the chief editor pivoted in his comfortable executive chair toward her.

"Oh, hi . . ." Fred snapped his fingers several times, trying to jostle his brain to sputter Gina's name.

"It's Gina Chaudhary. I'm in the bullpen with Scott Menken and Moira Clemens."

"Oh, yeah. What's the matter?"

"Well, I've been with the paper for nearly two years now. And I know I shouldn't be so forward with this, but I'm beginning to wonder if my skills as a journalist are being appropriately utilized."

Fred gave Gina a sideways look. "Go on."

Gina sighed. "I'd like the opportunity to write stories that are noteworthy. You know, hard-hitting. Something that people would want to read, and not some tidbit about a farmer in Iowa growing some new crop of hybrid corn."

"Just what did you have in mind?"

"Oh, I don't know. How about a side story concerning the Galwyn/Lavoie case?"

"Whoa!" Fred threw up his hands while shaking his head as if to clarify what he'd just heard. "You suddenly want to be up there with the big boys?"

"Look, Mr. Wasserman. I'm not taking anything away from Cameron, Eisen, and Petrie. They're seasoned journalists. All I'm asking is to write a pertinent piece that might be of some relevance, but something they may not be willing to write or are overlooking."

Fred stuck his pen back in his mouth. He shook his right index finger at the young woman.

"I like you, Chaudhary. You've got chutzpah. Not to mention drive, and I like that trait in my reporters. Tell you what I'm going to do. See Suzanne Dresner. She's the City Desk Editor. Tell her I said you can contribute a story to that case, so long as it doesn't interfere with Cameron and the others. Let's see what you can come up with."

Gina flashed a broad grin and thanked Fred profusely for the chance. She wasted no time in seeking Suzanne, dashing from sight in haste.

Chapter 73

Roger enjoyed a sip of lemonade. He was relaxing in the home alone; Beth was at work. As much as he wanted to cuddle with his wife, Roger also enjoyed moments of solitude. A good book while listening to classical music, or watching an old classic film, were his companions of relaxation sans Beth.

As he read a passage from a John Grisham novel, Roger began to hear a stir of sound outside the home. Suddenly the suspense story didn't appeal to him any longer. He was experiencing his own bit of drama firsthand.

Roger gently put down the book, leaving the page open to where he had left off. With a cat burglar's instincts, Roger crept around the living room, his ears tuned in to everything as an extra sensory antenna. It was broad daylight. In fact, it was high noon. What or whom could be lurking on the property at that hour? Certainly not anyone aimed at pillaging the place. Or could they be? Roger didn't want to take any chances. With the sound of a whisper, he stealthily opened the front door closet. Keeping his eyes darting to and fro, Roger grabbed the handle of his trusted Louisville slugger. He wasn't in a position to sock a grand slam. Rather, Roger was hell-bent on giving any intruder a barrel full of heavy ash to the side of the skull.

He tiptoed to the front door, where he began to hear the muffled voices of individuals talking. Roger looked down at the glistening wooden floor by the front door. He didn't know what to make of the muted conversation, which caused him to pause for a second. Conventional wisdom compelled Roger at least to open the front door peephole and get a handle on who was darkening his driveway at the height of day. Two men he recognized, in suits. And a patrol car across the way. Roger put two and two together. With the news of Logan Galwyn's disappearance continuing to be a lead story item, Roger suspected it was only a matter of time until the police would come knocking on his door.

The first thing Roger did was put away the DiMaggio special back in the closet. Second, he took a deep breath. There was no telling what was to come next, so Roger had to be prepared for whatever he might face. *Act cool,* he kept reminding himself. *Deflect any hint of suspicion.*

The doorbell rang. That was expected. The police weren't going to break the door down. Roger tapped the top button of his open-collared shirt and proceeded to greet his visitors, unwelcome as they may have been.

Swinging the front door open, Roger came across the nattily attired gentlemen.

"Roger Lavoie?" the older man asked, verifying his identity.

"Yes," Roger meekly replied.

"Lieutenant Vince Calabrese, Providence Homicide," he countered. "This is my partner, Detective Drake Nowak. We have a search warrant."

Roger's forehead rippled, in part as an act. But then the anthropology professor didn't actually suspect Vince to have reason to turn his domicile upside down. Still, he demanded an explanation.

"We suspect you might be the reason why Logan Galwyn vanished."

"Who?"

"Let's not play dumb, shall we? Your daughter-in-law Rebecca had an affair with Galwyn. Although your son had a motive, we don't think he was responsible. As a matter of fact, this has all the makings of your handiwork."

"That's history," Roger scowled. "And I was exonerated by the jury! Your boy here probably wasn't eligible for Little League when that happened."

"No, but I was a young detective back then. And I remember that case vividly. Your suit-for-hire did a pretty good job. But you and I know you did it. If we can't get you on the Haber murder, perhaps we'll get you on Galwyn. Oh, I'll need your car keys so we can search that too. I'd hate to have one of my guys resort to using a slim Jim. It might scrape the paint."

With great reluctance Roger reached into his pants pocket for the keys to his Maxima. He handed them to

Vince, who offered a smug smile in return. The professor kept his thoughts to himself. He knew there was nothing Vince's men could discover. But he was also praying that they would do their work quickly so he could return to his book.

As a two-man team from Bobby Hanlon's forensic office continued to search with the aid of a couple of blues, Vince and Drake made their way inside the home, much to Roger's disgust.

"If I knew you were coming in, Lieutenant, I would've made a fresh pot of coffee for you and your friends."

Vince's stoic response was a tipoff that he was not amused by Roger's sarcasm. As all three sat on the living room furniture, Vince motioned to Drake for the manila envelope he was holding.

"I want you to take a good look at these photos." Vince purposely wanted Roger to touch both. "Do you recognize that man?"

Roger scrunched his face. "I've never seen him before," Roger said and shrugged.

"What about that SUV? It's a Buick Enclave. Owned by Galwyn; incidentally, that was his picture I just showed you."

"I'm afraid I don't recognize that, either."

Vince took back the photos from Roger, but not without a look of disbelief.

"Galwyn was last seen in his apartment building at 71 Broadway, Downtown. Were you around there, say, last Thursday?"

"I can't say I was," Roger replied.

Drake tag-teamed on the next question. "What about 60 Kenyan Street this past weekend?"

"For the final time, no. Look, gentlemen. Can we end this witch hunt of yours? It's gnawing on my nerves."

Vince rolled his eyes. There was nothing else he and Drake were going to pry from Roger's brain. The three men continued to sit while the others foraged through the home for anything that might hold any hint of suspicion.

For the next quarter hour Roger was under close scrutiny. It was becoming a psychological game of chess to see who would blink first. The professor was beginning to squirm a little, this being the time when he might have conceded at least a hint of the crime. But Roger was soon saved when one of Hanlon's men came to Vince.

"Any luck, Dougherty?"

"No, Lieutenant. We tossed this place upside down, including the basement and upstairs. Kliegmann had no luck with the Maxima either." Dougherty's eyes shifted to Roger, but continued to address Vince. "Mr. Lavoie apparently is in the clear."

"Not even a firearm?"

"Nope."

Vince's frustration was evident when the corners of his mouth dropped down. Meanwhile, Roger was both relieved and satisfied that the search had ended . . . for now. But as he rose from the sofa, Vince gave his chief suspect a stern warning.

"I'm not through with you," Vince decried, wagging his finger at Roger. "So help me, you're going to make a mistake, just one little slip-up. And when you do the PPD will be ready for you."

Vince, Drake, and the others filed out of the house. But as he was about to leave, the seasoned detective gave Roger pause.

"We'll be watching you, Lavoie. Good day."

Roger stared at them with contempt as they left in their vehicles. And after the last of them was out of sight, Roger slammed the front door shut. He leaned against it, scanning his living room for a solution.

He began to slide his hand up and down his left leg. Roger felt a protrusion. Upon further examination he realized it was the precision scalpel he had stolen from the hospital where Beth worked. A deep sigh of relief ensued. Roger was lucky that Vince and Drake didn't frisk him or search his pockets. That would have ended the game right there.

The phone began to ring, probably another reporter, Roger surmised. This was all reminiscent of what he had experienced before and during the Haber murder trial. Roger was a much younger man then. But was he up to the task at sixty? Were there second thoughts clouding his mind? Suddenly that suspense novel couldn't hold his interest any longer. Roger was living his own real-life drama.

Chapter 74

Gina was taking copious notes on items she was reading off the internet. Her legal pad was indecipherable to the average person. The scribbling resembled a complicated full-page mathematical formula in astrophysics. Yet if you were to ask Gina for a specific, salient point on the subject matter, she wouldn't hesitate to spot it. Oh, it's right here, two-thirds down the page to the right.

Scott waltzed by looking at some copy to work on. He stopped in his tracks when spying Gina. She looked up at him and his contorted look.

"What's up?"

"I was going to ask you the same thing," Scott shot back. "What the fuck is going on? Why are you doing this on company time? Ol' man Wasserman's not going to like that."

"And what if I told you he gave me the green light to proceed on a side story surrounding the Lavoie/Galwyn situation?"

"What? No way!" Scott rubbed the back of his neck, still bewildered as to how Gina managed that coup. "Okay. What did you do? Promise him that you'll—"

"Don't go there, Scott!" Gina interrupted him, pointing at Scott to drive her meaning home.

Scott raised his left eyebrow and smirked, but not another word was uttered. Satisfied that she had Scott's respect, Gina revealed her formula for winning over the big boss.

"If you must know, I simply walked into Wasserman's office and pleaded my case to break this story. He liked my sassiness so much that he told me to see Dresner at the City Desk."

Scott folded his arms and gave Gina an incredulous look.

"Do you really believe they're actually going to publish your piece?"

"Well, that all depends upon me, doesn't it?"

Scott stashed any petty jealousy he still harbored. He gazed over Gina's shoulder.

"Just what exactly are you angling for anyway?"

"I'm curious about the husband she cheated on, Mark Lavoie. Very interesting. Did you know that his maternal grandparents had a great deal of money stashed away? A big insurance policy paid off huge dividends. I'm curious how much he was awarded."

"Well, let me ask you something. Unless this Logan Galwyn guy came from more money, what was the incentive for Lavoie's wife to stray if big bucks were coming his way?"

"That's what I intend to find out. According to the article, Mass Mutual was the insurance company for the policy. I think I'll give them a call."

Scott folded his arms again while Gina picked up her desk phone. As she began to dial the number for Mass Mutual, Gina glanced up at him. She wasn't pleased he was still there.

"Don't you have more small-town items to edit?" Gina emphasized her point by waving her left hand dismissively, as if to shoo him away.

Scott drew a deep sigh and raised his arms in frustration. He knew he wasn't welcome any longer as Gina was taking her assignment very seriously. And after various automated greetings, Gina finally spoke to someone live.

"Hello, I'm Gina Chaudhary with the Providence Journal."

Chapter 75

Fresh out of an administrative meeting at the hospital, Beth Lavoie was dead tired. Dealing with Chief Administrator Dr. Kirk Mehrens was bad enough. But throw in the chief surgeon, the head of the nursing staff, the head of the custodial staff, and other parties of interest, and it became an aggravating chore.

Just being back in her office seemed to provide an oasis from the everyday chaos associated in running a medical facility. Beth told her admin Felicia to hold all calls for the next twenty minutes while she unwound before tackling the next project.

Beth decided to surf the net. She was an avid online shopper, and she wanted to get in on the latest sale items of sites she frequented. Just as she immersed herself in what Kohl's was offering, Beth got buzzed.

"Yes," Beth responded testily, annoyed at being interrupted.

"I'm sorry, Beth," the woman responded through the phone speaker, "but I have a detective out here wanting to ask you a few questions."

Beth stared into space for a moment, her mind a blank. The story about her stepson's problems with his wife was spreading like a forest fire. There were even times when Beth had to field a few questions from fellow employees, including those that attended the meeting moments earlier. And now Beth wasn't sure what to say to the police on the matter. But there was no way this Q & A session could be avoided. She took in a deep breath. If ever Beth was ready it was right then.

"Let him in."

Beth sat up in her seat, and as the door opened, much to her surprise, Beth saw a woman enter. She raised an eyebrow as even she, with her feminist beliefs, was stunned to see someone of her gender in a profession that is male-dominated. But this was Soma Montero, who could hold her own with just about any man on the force. A few pleasantries were exchanged, but then Soma got down to the real purpose of the visit.

"As you are fully aware, Logan Galwyn, an engineer with the city traffic and highway department, is missing. Supposedly Galwyn had an affair with the wife of your stepson, Mark Lavoie. While any act of revenge might seem to be a motive for Mark's getting rid of Galwyn, Police Headquarters believe that your husband may be responsible."

Beth sat back and folded her arms.

"For years I've had to defend Roger, many times in the past, telling people he was acquitted of any wrongdoing to Daryl Haber and his ex-wife Margaret. I thought that was all behind us. Maybe we could live a normal life together. Now this happens and everyone suspects Roger because of the similar set of circumstances. Even the staff members keep asking me about it. But they'll sugarcoat it by asking how I'm holding up. Well, I'm telling you, Detective Montero, that I've had it up to here. Your presence only exacerbates the issue."

"Have you noticed any strange behavior exhibited by your husband?"

"What do you mean?"

"Well, let's see," Soma replied. "Were there any unusual heightened bouts of anxiousness, or have you experienced any unexplained trips Roger made or prolonged absences?"

"No to all of your questions."

Soma stared at her fingernails. It wasn't so much as to appreciate the most recent manicure her nail salon gave her as it was to decide how to bring up the next topic delicately. With a sigh of resolve, Soma brought her eyes back to Beth's.

"How much do you love your husband?"

Beth replied with a tilt of her head.

"What kind of question is that? Just what are you getting at?"

"Oh, I don't know," Soma answered as she finger-dusted the front edge of Beth's glistening cherry wood office desk. "Some wives may go to great lengths to shield their husbands." Soma zeroed in on Beth. "Oh, men do it too if they need to hide something about their women."

302

Soma laughed at the irony of her disclosure, but Beth didn't find it amusing.

"I love Roger dearly. But I can assure you I am not hiding anything from you or anyone else, because there's simply nothing there to protect."

"Did you aid or abet your husband in anything nefarious that might be connected with the investigation?"

"What?"

Soma shrugged her shoulders as if this were an easy question to understand.

"You heard me. Did you aid or abet your husband in anyth—"

"No!" Her emphatic rebuttal put a stamp on where she stood on the subject. But Beth's reddish complexion and her protruding neck veins stood as the exclamation point to the interrogation. Class dismissed!

"Okay," Soma pouted. "But if you are an accomplice to anything that may link your husband to Galwyn's disappearance, let me assure you that the law will come down hard. Enjoy the rest of your day."

Soma's signoff was about as meaningless as that, *have a nice day,* routine police officers tell you after handing you a summons. No way was Beth going to be at peace after that exchange.

There was no handshake. Soma casually rose from her seat and sauntered out of Beth's office. The moment the detective left, Beth slunk down in her high-back executive chair.

Soma's questioning caused Beth to reflect on her marriage to Roger. She gazed at the band of gold on her left ring finger and began to massage the area. Beth fondly recalled their wedding. It wasn't as ostentatious as Mark's marriage to Rebecca, but that was okay with her. It was Roger's second trip down the bridal path, and Beth respected his wishes for a more low-key event. Beth remembered the honeymoon in Hawaii, the funny but sweet instances during the trip, and how much Roger doted on her. Even to the present day, Roger continued to show his affection toward Beth.

But then this series of events came to the forefront. Her happy face was history. Beth began to wonder, how many more lies could Roger be hiding? One more glance at that cylindrical reminder that consummated your vows, please.

Beth began to wriggle her finger until the ring finally came loose. She focused hard on the band. As much as she tried to allow the happier times to fill her mind, the ugly talk of the Galwyn disappearance and her husband's possible involvement took center stage. Beth's throat tightened while her lips puckered in disapproval. Finally Beth's face became one of rage. The clenching of her teeth was the clincher.

The raging volcano within her caused Beth to take aim at the far wall with the ring. But as she made a hurling motion to fire it, Beth didn't release. Why spoil a nice piece of jewelry? No, Beth took one more look at the only thing that was keeping their union intact. She needed answers, and she wasn't going to wait until six o'clock to find them.

"Felicia, I'm not . . . feeling all that well."

"Why don't you have one of the doctors check you out?" Felicia answered, without missing a beat.

"I'm not going to trouble them. Besides, they'll just give me a quick probe before dispensing medication I probably have at home. No, I'm going home to rest. That might do me good. I should be okay in the morning."

Felicia acknowledged with a simple, "Okay."

Beth was actually fine, except for the migraine that was coming on. Perhaps a little venting at hubby might be the best tonic for what ailed her. No, make that a lot of venting. A quick dousing of the table lamp light and Beth was set to go interrogate Roger.

Chapter 76

Gina was sifting through more material on the case involving Mark. She was so zoned in on the subject that even Scott didn't bother her anymore. But that could be attributed to some petty jealousy Scott might have harbored for not going up against Chief Editor Fred Wasserman first with an idea for a backstory to the media frenzy the case was taking on.

As Gina was skimming over some notes, her desk phone rang.

"Gina Chaudhary."

"Hello, Miss Chaudhary. My name is Forrest Getters with Mass Mutual. I understand you're doing a piece for your paper concerning Mark Lavoie."

In her excited state upon hearing back from anyone in the big insurance firm, Gina nearly knocked over her iced latte drink on the papers near her desktop keyboard. The sudden panic caused her to shout out an expletive.

"Did I call at a bad time?" Getters inquired.

"No," Gina responded nervously. "Sorry. Thank you for calling me back!"

Getters began to dissertate on the inheritance case, with Gina taking copious notes and asking the occasional question for further clarification. When Rose O'Mara passed away six years earlier, it marked a windfall inheritance to any direct living blood descendant of her and her husband Padraig, who died fifteen years before. The total amount was $746,872.00, and the money was to be divvied up between all living direct blood descendants of Rose and Padraig over a ten-year period. That included their two daughters, Siobhan and Margaret.

Siobhan had legally established herself as guardian over Margaret, since the latter could not think clearly for herself in her present condition. Through her attorney, Siobhan informed Mass Mutual that she would entrust herself with Margaret's share of the windfall, which was to say she'd horde everything. But lawyers from the insurance firm cited that Mark, Margaret's son, should also be entitled to a cut. This came to a head about two years before, when the insurance firm threatened to cut off the annual payouts of the policy unless Mark was given a share. Siobhan stalled Mass Mutual by promising them she would provide full disclosure to Mark. The insurance firm was still waiting.

"Her sister I can understand, although I still find that a little greedy on Siobhan's part," Gina reasoned. "But that's still a quarter of a million Mark Lavoie is being denied."

"Yeah," Getters replied. "Nearly twenty-five thou a year. I'm sure he could've invested that money."

"Do you think Siobhan O'Mara is purposely hiding this policy from Mark?"

"Strictly off the record . . . yes."

Gina scribbled down some further notes, but promised she wouldn't quote Getters on his last remark. They exchanged several additional questions and answers before their chat came to an end. Gina thanked Getters for his information.

Gina sat back in her chair and stared at her notepad. Scribbles of every shape and size ran all across the page. Yet Gina was able to decipher it all. She began looking at her scrawl and admired it as a work of art. For something that was a pure lark compared to the main focal point, Gina knew she was sitting on a story that might pull her away from the bullpen for good. She wasted no time in moving forward on her laptop. Gina was ramping up on several possible headlines and opening lines to herald the release of the newsflash.

Chapter 77

Nearly three hours had passed since Lieutenant Detective Vince Calabrese, Detective Drake Nowak and a team of other suits and blues descended on Roger's house like flies to cow dung. It was not quite four-thirty, and Roger was still dealing with the search by the PPD. But he also needed to start preparing dinner for Beth. Something light was in order on the menu, given the 75-degree temperature and his coming to terms regarding the earlier visit.

Roger rummaged through the refrigerator looking for the ingredients he needed. He found plenty of romaine lettuce, tomatoes, and red, yellow, and orange peppers. Toss in cubed pieces of grilled chicken and Caesar dressing and he had the makings of an easy-to-fix healthy pre-summer salad.

His hands were full as Roger was ready to set down much of what he would use. No sooner had he set out everything than he heard the front door opening. And then being slammed! This was very odd.

Roger raced out toward the living room. Much to his surprise Beth stood there, a solid two hours early from her usual six-something arrival. Roger was extremely curious about why his wife had arrived so soon.

"Hello, dear," Roger began. "What a surprise to see you at this hour. Were you not feeling well?"

But Beth said nothing. She just remained there in the living room with her arms folded, her leather purse flung to the sofa. Beth gave her husband a *What the hell did you do* look. She cocked an eyebrow while Roger regarded her strangely. And then it finally struck the sixty-year-old professor. Beth was probably aware of the investigation on Galwyn by the police. But Roger was shrewd not to let on unless the wife opened up first.

"I received a visit by a Detective Montero at my office this afternoon."

Roger licked the side of his mouth. He looked down, not wanting to face the missus. Oh, who was he kidding? Better to tell Beth about his encounter as well.

"I had company a while ago, too," Roger sighed. "I had the boss of that detective you saw, along with a bunch of others, swarming the place. They had a search warrant, thinking they were going to come across something incriminating. But they didn't. Still, the embarrassment of them being here with all the neighbors to see—and they were here for a good solid hour, mind you. I was infuriated that they were here to begin with, but I played their fucking game!"

Roger was allowing his elevated blood pressure get the better of him. A pang surged through his chest as he tried to rub it away, as if that was actually going to work. He collapsed on the lounger and winced at the discomfort.

Meanwhile, Beth was getting tired of standing. She sat down on the sofa, all the while glaring at hubby. Beth locked her legs together, giving the impression that she was about to leap on Roger if he so much as sneezed the wrong way. A strong hint of suspicion was written across her face as Beth was about to apply similar pressure to Roger like what Soma had given her earlier.

Roger was getting over the last of the tingles electrifying his chest. It was as good a time as any for Beth to begin her probing.

"I'm going to ask you a direct question," Beth opened. "I expect a direct answer. Did you have anything to do with that man's disappearance?"

"Confound it, Beth! Not you, too! Jumping on their bandwagon?"

"I'll ask you again: Did you have anything to do with Galwyn's disappearance?"

"No! Goddamn it! No! Everyone is making that hideous connection. They read and hear about that guy missing. Then they hear about the heart being given to my daughter-in-law. And then the name. Ah, yes, the name! Lavoie! And suddenly I'm accused of this crime, like the one I was acquitted for a quarter century ago! That's why we were getting all of those media calls! How do I feel about this, Beth? Well, I'll tell you! I've had it up to here!"

For emphasis Roger held his hand level to his throat. Beth observed his theatrics by resting her elbow on the sofa, and in turn propping her head up on the fist of the same bent arm.

"When we first met, Roger, I was willing to look the other way from what most others thought about you. I was of the minority who didn't think you had anything to do with Haber's murder or your ex-wife's psychiatric problems. I stuck by you as a matter of trust. Do you remember that, Roger? That long talk we had about trust? When we were married, we made a pact together on several things. Devotion and love are two of those things. But trust was the most important, and with that, honesty. I hold that as more sacred than the others; especially when considering the hell you had to go through. But if that trust were to be broken, then all bets were off. So, as a matter of trust, honesty . . . and our marriage, did you have anything to do with Galwyn?"

Roger was uncomfortable about answering Beth, with the way she placed it as an ultimatum. But she needed absolutes. And as much as he was hesitant to approach this, Roger owed that much to Beth. His head began to shake back and forth.

"For the last time," Roger replied, but in a hushed tone, "no."

Beth reclined on the sofa, her legs more relaxed.

"Good. But heed this little chat as a stern warning. Now if you'll excuse me, dear, I'm going to take a nap. This afternoon took its toll on me."

Roger allowed Beth her rest. But as he retreated to the kitchen to begin his dinner preparations, Roger was compelled to feel the same hidden compartment in his pants, which held the precision scalpel he'd deftly cloaked from the authorities.

To deceive the police was one thing. But to deceive Beth? This was not going to go down easy.

Chapter 78

Vince gathered with all of the detectives on the Logan Galwyn case the next morning in the war room. All were present with the exception of Paul Scarpone, who was suddenly called away to see Bobby Hanlon in Forensics. Perhaps the long-awaited break was finally coming through in Hanlon's group.

He was about to imbibe his second cup of coffee when Vince felt a little hunger pang. The seasoned detective opened the box of donuts, hoping there might be one left. Vince saw a glazed prize sitting by itself, screaming out to him, *Eat me!* But the confection wasn't alone in there. A cockroach suddenly emerged from underneath the confection. *Damn it!* Vince pounded the multi-legged creature out of its misery. So much for his appetite. With the creature exterminated, it was back to business.

"Let's get down to brass tacks, shall we?"

Vince shuffled a few papers. He distributed them to all the attendees, a brief overview of the latest events.

"Drake and I will be heading to Crenshaw once Dr. Olivia Rosano arrives. You did set it up for us to meet with them, right, Drake?"

"We're seeing the head man, Dr. Oswald Borshevsky. He's even going to bring in the analyst Lavoie has been seeing. That might be illuminating."

"Maybe we might get somewhere by learning a little more about Margaret O'Mara." Vince turned to Donny. "What about you, hotshot?"

"Sat down with Mark Lavoie," Donny opened. "In spite of what that little vixen of a wife did to him, he still holds her close in his heart. That's his heart, not Galwyn's. But nothing is ironclad. Lavoie did give me the names of two people. One's the chancellor of the school where he teaches, some guy named Valen Pagano. And the other is a friend of his, Hunter Morales. I'm seeing Pagano in a couple of hours. I'll hit Morales tonight."

"His friend may defend him regardless," Vince replied. And then the lieutenant turned to Lou.

"I sat down with Siobhan O'Mara yesterday, you know, Roger Lavoie's former sister-in-law? Well, let me tell you. She is one strange bird. I tried everything to stir some animosity toward Lavoie, but she was more forgiving, even after seeing her sister head off to Crenshaw. It was like she was carrying a torch for him. I just don't get it."

Vince was at a loss as well. Just where did Siobhan stand in the whole sordid case? But there were other matters, too. Soma was next up.

"I met up with Beth Lavoie at the hospital where she works. I grilled her to see if she knew anything peculiar about her husband and if she were involved in his antics. She flatly refuted my suggestions. I then asked her if she still loved him." And it was at that point that Soma released a sly smile. "You know what? I think I planted a bug in her ear, caused her to take pause. Nothing like injecting a little dissention within the ranks to break people down, eh, Lieutenant?"

Vince grinned back. He agreed with Soma's tactical method of causing disharmony in the Lavoie household. And then Vince and Drake droned on about their unsuccessful search through Roger's house. But in the back of his mind, Vince was agonizing over his failed attempt to get the goods on his prey. This was developing into a chess match with his adversary. Who could outwit the other in the sordid mind game that they were acting out?

To break up the routine, Paul returned with company. It was Bobby, Mr. CSI himself. He might not have been suave or possessed the sophistication that Donny Lowery had. But that was okay with Bobby. He was a walking encyclopedia when it came to crime scene details. That was why he was hired by the PPD. With his hair out of place, which was standard for him, Bobby brushed his thin moustache and stood silently, waiting to be cued. Paul made a brief statement as a prelude to Bobby's major announcement.

"Hello, friends," Bobby began pedantically. "First of all, I have some interesting news about the heart and the foot that Rebecca Dyer Lavoie was sent. Usually it takes several days, even weeks, to get a DNA match. But due to the heightened awareness of this rare high-profile case, our department and the state lab we work with have been at it around the clock. I think I've lost count of how many cups of coffee I've consumed. But hard work and sweat, plus the drive to get the right answer swiftly, has paid off. Both the lab and the Forensics department have come to the same conclusion. With the materials that Lieutenant Calabrese and Detective Nowak were able to obtain from Mr. Galwyn's apartment on Monday, we were able to achieve the desired answer we had hoped for. The heart and foot are indeed those of Logan Galwyn's."

A low rumble of murmuring like shockwaves resonated throughout the room, although the match between Galwyn's personal effects and the body parts was not exactly a surprise. The assumption of everyone present was that the discovery was a foregone conclusion. This just confirmed it, so that the guys in the suits couldn't debate it in a courtroom. But if there were any doubt, Bobby put those notions to bed.

"One more thing, the footprints taken also matched Galwyn's records."

Vince instructed Paul to inform Logan's next of kin at the conclusion of the meeting. The period for Logan's family to grieve over his loss was about to commence. Then Donny raised an issue that needed to be addressed.

"I wonder if Roger Lavoie has the body parts buried in his backyard."

"The answer is a flat no," Drake piped up. "Vince and I had a team of people scour Lavoie's premises thoroughly yesterday. The thought of Lavoie burying Galwyn's body parts in his lawn did cross our minds. But there was no indication of that, none whatsoever, no sign of digging of any sort having taken place on his property for quite some time, except for a small plot of ground. But it's too small to use as a grave."

"I would like to make a comment on that, if I may," Bobby interjected. "I was examining the dirt under the toenails of Galwyn's foot. I found evidence of perlite."

Everyone looked at each other with confused faces. *Okay, Bobby. Perhaps an explanation is in order.*

"It's those white crystals you see in potting soil. It has low water retention, thus filtering water to the soil for plants and shrubbery. It does eventually break down."

"What's the significance?" Vince asked.

"Well, our friend Mr. Galwyn had his body parts buried in an area where fresh soil was placed. No doubt the perpetrator used a spot where the ground was easier to manipulate and dig. And judging by the expansion of the perlite or lack thereof, I'd say this soil was put there no more than a month ago."

Vince sat back with his hands behind his head. He was stumped like the rest. And then he went back to a notion that Sheryl Dyer could still be the person they were looking for. "Lou, I'm going to have one of McCarron's judges issue a search warrant for the Dyer property. I want you and some blues to check it out. Say it's a follow-up to the foot that was left at their house Tuesday. You need to tie a few loose ends up over there. When you get it, high-tail it out to that house in Greenville and scan the grounds. She still could be a possible suspect. Mrs. Dyer was the last to leave from what I gather that Tuesday morning and may have left it there for her son to discover."

Ever the good soldier, Lou nodded and scribbled some notes. Vince turned to Paul for another assignment.

"After you contact Galwyn's next of kin, notify Captain Borromeo and Chief Heimler of a press release. Then I want you to find out from Parks and Recreation when and where they put down the newest soil. Also check for any excavation in these parks. If Sheryl Dyer is eliminated as a suspect, then there's no doubt in my mind Roger Lavoie is behind this. And I'm sure he didn't ask some friendly neighbor if he could stow away body parts in their yard."

Paul replied with a simple, "Yes, sir," as he continued to scribble notes.

Bobby's appearance was no longer necessary, so the head of Forensics left to perform studies on lesser known cases. No sooner had Bobby left when a woman in her mid-thirties appeared. She wore thick-framed glasses and had her hair pulled back in a barrette. The woman appeared homely with a lack of glamour in her dress and aspect. But that didn't stop Donny Lowery. A lascivious smile creased his lips; no doubt the man was envisioning what the woman would look like with her hair down and glasses removed, not to mention the removal of the business suit she wore.

"Excuse me," the woman began. "I'm looking for Lieutenant Calabrese."

"That'd be me," Vince said as he smiled. "You must be Dr. Rosano."

Olivia grinned back with a simple confirmation. Vince wanted to get cracking at Margaret O'Mara and advised Olivia and Drake to be ready in five minutes for the trip to Crenshaw.

Vince adjourned the meeting with the other detectives, but not before reminding them of their responsibilities. The next phase was ready to commence.

Chapter 79

The Winston Campus, normally bustling with students and faculty darting in different directions during the main school year, was a veritable ghost town in early June. Graduation ceremonies had just concluded two Sundays before. The summer hiatus was about to head into full swing as only a mere handful of people pockmarked the sprawling grounds.

Ruth Wojteka was at her keyboard clicking away while sitting at her work terminal. There would be no vacation for the septuagenarian, at least not until after the July fourth holiday, when she would be able to go away for two weeks. And then it would be a return to the old grind, with perhaps one more year before officially calling her work career over.

Donny Lowery opened the office door. He looked around the rich reception area and marveled at its cherry wood walls, books aligned in rows on shelves. The detective easily spotted Ruth at work. To the gumshoe, she appeared older than his mother. Not on his hit 'em up for a date list.

She might have appeared to have been too engrossed in her work to notice him, but much to Donny's astonishment, Ruth's strong sixth sense acknowledged his presence.

"May I help you, sir?" Ruth asked while still focusing on her screen.

"Hah," Donny chortled. "Multitasking! Love it!"

Ruth turned toward the visitor with a *spare me with your ill-fated attempts at humor* glare. She continued her deadpan expression while shuffling paper into a neat collection for the printer.

Donny decided charm wasn't going to win over Ruth's affections. The serious side of him took over as he handed Ruth his card. The admin glanced at it. If Donny thought she would be impressed by it, he had another think coming. Her reticent visage spoke volumes. The detective was simply told to have a seat while she called the chancellor. Donny sucked in his lips as he was sequestered in a corner chair.

A couple of Monet prints caught his attention until the moment came when Donny heard his name called.

"You must be Dr. Pagano," Donny answered as he catapulted from his wooden barrel-back seat. He tried to shake Valen's hand, but the chancellor was even colder than Ruth, if that were possible.

"You might want to do something about that grease stain on your tie, Detective Lowery. But please forgive me. Won't you come in?"

Valen's apology for criticizing Donny's wardrobe appearance was about as sincere as a congratulatory call from someone who'd lost an election to a victor. But Donny's sole purpose for being there was to pump information from the pompous iconoclast, not to win a popularity contest.

Like Roger, Mark and many others, Donny felt a tad uncomfortable with Valen's sardonic attitude. Everything from the oversized desk to his huge executive chair was a statement. *You may be the authorities, but this office is my realm. Don't forget it.* Donny was happy just to ask a few pertinent questions and then flee.

"I'm not going to take much of your time," Donny began. "No doubt you've been following the news concerning the disappearance of Logan Galwyn and the connection between him and one of your teachers, Mark Lavoie."

"I have," confessed Valen. "His father teaches here, too."

"Yeah, I know. Roger Lavoie. When was the last time you've seen either of them?"

"I haven't seen them since late March. Let me explain something to you, Mr. Lowery. I don't go to great lengths to be seen with any of the faculty, except perhaps for a photo op where warranted. My time is spent with the donors and benefactors who support this institution. Tuition only goes so far. I make it a point to be with those who have a favorable bankroll for an endowment or two. Professors like the Lavoies don't have that income."

"What are your impressions of them?"

Valen sighed deeply before addressing Donny's query.

316

"I told the elder Lavoie and to a lesser extent his son that there is a code of conduct to which every employee of this university, be they a professor or a nightshift janitor, must adhere. They were warned of this."

Donny shrugged his shoulders. "Does this count as an offense?"

Valen didn't respond. He simply told Donny that he had some *pressing engagements* to which he had to attend. But Donny could tell the chancellor was not pleased when the detective pressed him. Nervous habits, such as reaching for the knot in his necktie, rhythmically tapping his fingers on his desk, and twirling his executive pen several times, were dead giveaways that Valen'd had it up to here with the badgering. The man who was better suited to grilling potential candidates for teaching at Winston was not at all at ease being on the receiving end of an interrogation, for a change.

The detective's main purpose was fulfilled. Like Soma had done to Beth Lavoie, Donny got under Valen's skin to give the chancellor pause. A simple handshake was exchanged before Donny departed Valen's office.

The detective gave Ruth a simple smile as he passed her desk while Ruth nodded. But as he was walking through the doorway, Donny heard Valen on speaker.

"Ruth, can you please bring me the files on both Roger Lavoie and Mark Lavoie? Thank you."

Donny began to smirk. The once-fortified foundation of the veteran anthropology professor was beginning to crumble.

Chapter 80

Vince had been patting his knee for God knows how long, counting the days until his eventual retirement. The adrenaline rush Vince had at the beginning of the current phase of his career was exhilarating, but it seemed that buoyant surge had subsided. Oh, he'd give the same patent answer that it sure beat rocking in a chair on the front porch, waiting for the mailman to arrive, and timing when the kids went back and forth to school every day. But even his own Juanita had hinted to him several times how fun it would be to fly off to exotic destinations for weeks, at a time, instead of only days. That only happens when you put your 9mm into mothballs.

Meanwhile, Drake was busy playing a video game on his smart phone. Judging by his facial expressions, Drake wasn't proving very successful at it. Vince watched as Drake got frustrated, which begged a question: Why do they call them smart phones when they allow stupid games to piss you off when using them?

As for Olivia, she was engaged in a psychology trade magazine article. As Vince observed her, he was thinking how smart he was to send Donny Lowery to question Valen Pagano, instead of dragging him down with the three of them. There was no doubt Donny would be staring at Olivia's shapely legs rather than the periodical she was reading.

A pretty woman came walking along the narrow corridor and introduced herself as Crystal Cambridge.

"Hello," Crystal announced with a smile, "you're here to see Dr. Borshevsky?"

"Yes," Vince answered, coming to his feet, with the others rising as well.

Crystal walked with the grace of a model. Perhaps she might have been just that in a previous occupation. Crystal certainly had the well-defined facial features and thin frame to pass for one.

They finally arrived at Oswald Borshevsky's office where the director of the facility was waiting. Mort Sonnenstein was also present for the occasion. No doubt Vince and Drake were interested in hearing from the analyst who had seen Roger on a few visits. Olivia had made it known on the way out to the facility that she wanted to learn the inner workings of the mind of the number-one suspect, in addition to probing Margaret O'Mara's psyche. With handshakes and introductions exchanged, it was time to get down to business.

Vince sensed that Oswald wasn't exactly keen on seeing the police here in his inner sanctum. Maybe it was because of too many speeding tickets. Or perhaps it was a little mistrust he had for the men in blue. Still, Oswald didn't flinch in agreeing to see Vince and the others. That could have been because of the magnitude of the case. Of course, having a fellow psychiatrist like Olivia with them didn't hurt.

As for Mort, Vince found him to be a little too friendly. But the detective reasoned this was how Mort always welcomed visitors to his own office.

Vince detected a hint of incense, probably a practice of Crystal's, no doubt. It wasn't overwhelming. Just enough to clear the stale air and give the place a welcoming ambiance.

The group exchanged a little small talk. Oswald seemed fascinated by Olivia's credentials and the school she attended to achieve her degree. Vince was growing impatient. *Cut the bullshit and let's get on with the investigation, for Christ's sake.* Oswald must have heard Vince's thoughts, for the director finally moved on to the real purpose of the meeting.

"I know you're all interested in Margaret," Oswald opened. Then he turned to Olivia. "Especially you, Dr. Rosano, but I don't want you to get your hopes up. She is completely withdrawn. We have tried everything to help Margaret improve and assimilate back into society. But we have met with strong resistance from her. It's been two decades and we're still stymied."

Olivia asked for the list of medications Oswald and his staff had been administering to Margaret. One caught her attention, causing her to jolt back in her chair and open her eyes even wider.

"One hundred-twenty milligrams of Fetzima? Rather excessive, don't you think, Dr. Borshevsky?"

"It has reached that point, doctor. Like I said, we're trying everything. The Fetzima at the high dosage helps Margaret, but only for so long."

"And what about her length of time here? Twenty-three years! Don't you think that's also rather excessive, Dr. Borshevsky? Patients, even the most severe cases, don't stay that long in a place like Crenshaw. Most of these places prefer a fairly quick turnaround, especially when dealing with how much insurance companies are willing to pay."

"Margaret is a special case. The insurance, now being supplied through her sister Siobhan O'Mara, is covering part of her stay. Plus we are receiving grants from the state as we're a non-profit entity. The state is looking at Margaret's situation with a lot of scientific curiosity. That and the fact that Margaret poses a danger to herself . . . and possibly others, all these considerations have convinced us that she's safer here."

"Forgive me for sounding naïve, Dr. Borshevsky," Vince questioned, "but I am an outsider when it comes to evaluating the minds of people and what keeps them under control when they're, you know, whacky."

Vince circled his hand around the side of his head to dramatize the term he used. But it was a statement and gesture that wasn't appreciated by the psychologically trained individuals present.

"I think I can speak on behalf of Doctors Rosano and Sonnenstein by saying that a better phrase to use is *unstable*," Oswald argued.

Vince sucked in his lips in embarrassment. He wanted so desperately to hide in the corner for his ill-fated attempt at using a layman's phrase. Thank goodness he had Mort to question instead.

"How many times has Roger Lavoie visited your office?"

"Three times," Mort responded.

"How did he behave?"

"Well, he took exception to a couple of suggestions that might have gotten under his skin, but I get that from many patients. Roger didn't let it get to him. He even invited me to attend a party he hosted when his son Mark was hired to teach at Winston nearly two years back."

Vince sat back to absorb Mort's comments. The seasoned detective's intuition told the rest of his brain that Mort was holding back on something. Perhaps he was nervous in the face of Vince's questioning, but rubbing his necktie and stroking his blazer were telltale signs that Mort had more to reveal. In that regard Vince was on par with Oswald and the others in reading body language. He'd earned his own Master's degree in psychology. That's what years of cases and running into people like Mort time and again will do to you. Best education ever, in Vince's book.

"Just what prompted Lavoie to get upset?"

Mort hesitated for a moment. He looked at Oswald for a quick second as Vince followed the sight trail. *This is getting even more interesting,* Vince thought.

"Dr. Borshevsky made an arrangement with me. He accorded me permission to see Margaret O'Mara while he had me contact Margaret's sister, Siobhan. She wanted me to give her Roger's email address. That was the bargain I had to make."

Now all eyes were on Oswald.

"I don't care what you think of me, Lieutenant Calabrese, but let me make one thing clear. I despise and loathe Roger Lavoie! I'm of the opinion, and I know I don't stand alone on this, that he was responsible for what happened to Margaret and in doing away with Darren Haber. And I wouldn't be surprised if he did something with Galwyn and sent his body parts to his daughter-in-law. The man is sick and disturbed!"

"He's also very cunning," Vince jumped in. "Look, Dr. Borshevsky. I think you and I are on the same wavelength on the chain of events then and now. I'd love nothing more than to put away Lavoie. But Drake and I took a team of fellow officers and detectives with a search warrant to ransack Lavoie's house yesterday. Came away with nothing, but I know he did it. What's stopping us is our inability to come up with enough evidence to put Lavoie in the slammer. That's how the judicial system works."

There was nothing else left to discuss, at least for the moment. It was time to pay Margaret a visit as all five vacated Oswald's office for Margaret's private room on the fourth floor.

Chapter 81

The walk along the fourth floor corridor brought back memories for Mort. Not necessarily good ones. His head swiveled as if in search of someone. Oswald looked at Mort with some amusement. But the director had to tell Mort the truth.

"If you're looking for Melanie, Mort, she's not here anymore," Oswald disclaimed.

Mort's face registered his concern. "What happened? Did she pass on?"

"No, thankfully. We deemed her fit to be released. She's now living with her younger sister and her niece. And by the way, before she left, she had her hair trimmed. You wouldn't recognize her if she walked down this hall right now."

Mort chuckled at the thought. He remarked how great it was that Melanie was back to assimilating with society, while the same could not be said for the person they were about to see.

Vince was as curious as the others to get a glimpse of Margaret, and perhaps be able to ask a question or two to learn what a scheming prick her ex-husband truly was.

As Oswald was about to reach for the doorknob to her private room, he cautioned everyone to stay outside until it was safe. That was meant for all concerned. Margaret was very much a recluse. The smallest disruption might cause her harm. She was much like a frightened animal. Even the smallest of creatures has the instincts to fight off its foe when cornered. That was the message Oswald was conveying to everyone. Do not gather around or charge Margaret, for like the helpless critter, Margaret would spring forward and cause anyone some serious damage if in her fractured mind they were out to hurt her. Just ask Rocco and the rest of the orderlies. As imposing a giant Rocco was, even he wanted to keep his distance from *that O'Mara lady,* as he called her.

Oswald reached for the knob and turned it with the stealth of a nighttime home invader. With equal precision, Oswald slowly opened the door. As he entered the room Oswald looked back at Vince and Drake, advising them to keep quiet and to remain behind him. Vince was upset with being relegated to the rear of the bus, but then reason grabbed hold of him. Oswald was a familiar subject for Margaret, and she'd developed a tepid relationship with him. As for Mort and Olivia, well, they were the psychological experts much like Oswald. They already had a free pass and now were given professional courtesy.

The door swung open without a sound. Little by little, Margaret's isolated room appeared there for all to see. There was a question of whether to have windows in her room. But a windowless room had been tried before, and the idea was met with disastrous results. Margaret became extremely belligerent. If there was any hope of rehabilitating her, it would have to be in a room where the light of day was permitted. But the institution didn't want to take any chances. The glass was bulletproof, similar to that found in banks. It allowed Margaret to keep an eye on the world, or whatever she could make of it in her compromised state. And there was an overwhelming scent of disinfectant to mask any accident Margaret might have had.

Oswald did a quick scan. It didn't take him long to find Margaret. She was sitting on the floor near one of the windows with her knees drawn up to her chest. A powder-blue gown covered much of her body. Only her shins and hands were exposed below her neck as Margaret cowered, with her Rockports supporting her feet.

Her hair appeared a little matted, although a female aide would help her into the shower every day to help Margaret maintain some decent level of proper hygiene. As for her locks, the staff would occasionally trim them, but they first must sedate her. There was that one time when the beautician held a pair of scissors in her hands for Margaret to see. That set Margaret off, bringing back the horrible nightmares that caused her to take up residency at Crenshaw initially.

Oswald looked back at Vince and the others. He whispered one more warning not to say a word unless he directed them to do so. With a mutual understanding of the ground rules, Oswald made himself known to Margaret, who up to that point was strictly focused on the outside world.

"Margaret," Oswald began in a pleasant offering, spoken softly, but loud enough to be heard. Or so he thought.

"Margaret," Oswald repeated himself.

This time she turned around to face the director. But the company surrounding him caused the disturbed woman to scuttle back against the farthest wall. Vince could see that this was not going to be easy. And was he still bent on questioning such a distraught person? Yeah, he was. But he had to allow Oswald to conduct the session and bide his time. Meanwhile, Oswald had to go into spin control to pacify the subject.

"It's okay, Margaret. It's all right."

Somehow Margaret found that hard to swallow. She continued to cower in fear in view of the strangers. Her one-time visit with Mort didn't exactly constitute him as a dear old friend. But Oswald's experience took over.

"You remember Mort, don't you?"

Mort offered a smile, but Margaret gave him a *deer in the headlights* stare. She simply shook her head, not recognizing him. Undeterred by Margaret's lack of recognition, Oswald moved on.

"Margaret, this is my good friend, Olivia. She would like to become friends with you, too. You know, just as I am, and the rest of the staff here."

"Hello, Margaret," Olivia beamed to show her benevolence. "I'm here to help you, just as Dr. Oswald has said."

Olivia opened the palm of one hand to Margaret. It was a sign of showing the frightened patient Olivia had nothing to hide. Margaret eyeballed Olivia up and down. The fact that Olivia was also a woman made it a little easier for Margaret to accept the psychiatrist's token gesture. At first Margaret was tentative in her acceptance, afraid to move a muscle. But eventually she reached her arm out toward Olivia. Finally the two hands met as the veneer of anxiety on Margaret's face started to dissipate. In fact, Margaret seemed relieved in her bonding with Olivia. She closed her eyes and exhaled a deep sigh.

While the professionals seemed thrilled that Olivia was able to win Margaret over, there was still one person who was hoping to get to the crux of the matter. Vince was getting fidgety in his eagerness to learn a little more about Roger Lavoie and his methods of sadism from the person that knew him best. He stepped over to Oswald to express his anxiousness, but the director angrily hissed at the detective to conduct himself in a more dignified manner, given Margaret's propensity for withdrawal.

And no later did she hear the heated exchange between Vince and Oswald than Margaret pulled her hand away from Olivia's gentle grasp. She began to cower once more, all the while looking at Vince with deep fear. Olivia glared back at Vince. *Nice work, Lieutenant!*

"Margaret," Olivia smiled awkwardly. "I'm sorry. It won't happen again. The man behind me is a police detective. His name's Lieutenant Vince Calabrese. He's really a good man." Olivia then continued, but looked back at Vince when doing so, saying, "Sometimes he gets carried away with his assignment."

Vince didn't care for Olivia's comment, but even he might have conceded he was a bit over the top. Margaret was about as stable as a radioactive isotope. Before Olivia yielded to Vince, she reminded him once more of his inept handling of the situation.

"Hello, Margaret," Vince grinned, as if that was going to change Margaret's fear of him. "I'm with Providence Homicide. That's my partner back there, Detective Drake Nowak. I believe you and I are of similar age. I remember what happened to you many years ago. Drake over there was still in Little League, about ready to discover girls."

Vince's aim at invoking a little humor didn't seem to crack the ice with Margaret. She was still petrified. *Okay,* Vince thought, *let's go for the jugular.*

"There's been a horrific murder that has been committed. It involves your son and your daughter-in-law."

Margaret stared quizzically at Vince. For the first time during the session, she started to move her lips, much to everyone's astonishment.

"My . . . son . . . Mark? Married?" Margaret looked away for a moment before returning her stunned gaze. "He's . . . he's just a little . . . boy."

"I thought you said Mark visited his mother on occasion, Dr. Borshevsky?"

"He does. But it is sporadic, and he does keep his distance. Margaret wouldn't recognize him. It's difficult putting together the continuing changes of a face throughout the years, especially in Margaret's condition."

Vince pouted while looking at the floor, pondering his next move. He finally mustered the courage to face Margaret again.

"Yes, your son is married. But his wife had an affair with someone who was later found dead. Well, that's what has been proven when the deceased's body parts started to show up at her doorstep."

"No! No! No!" Margaret screamed. "Roger did it! Roger did it!"

"Great job, Lieutenant!" was Olivia's cutting remark to the detective.

At last Vince was on to something, but it came at a price. He didn't need Olivia's commentary, but he did have it coming. Margaret became so hysterical at the mere mention of body parts that orderlies were quickly sent in. Her arms and legs were flailing every which way. Rocco and his team went into action to restrain her physically. Then the nurses came in.

"Get me 600 milligrams of Lithobid! Stat!" Oswald screamed at them.

It didn't take the nursing staff long to come up with the medication to control Margaret's violent behavior. No, the ordeal was in how to get it down her. And it took every ounce of strength by the staff to execute the action.

Several minutes passed, and Margaret finally succumbed to the medication to the point of it making her drowsy. The staff helped Margaret to her bed where she soon slumbered off into dreamland. With the ordeal behind them, Oswald turned to Vince and Olivia.

"I'm afraid the show is over," Oswald stated. "There is no way you're going to get much out of Margaret now, Lieutenant. And dare I say, maybe never, with her compunction for flying off the handle when being reminded of that crime. Or even anything similar to it."

"But you heard it yourself," Vince argued. "She was beginning to open up about Roger. I may have been on to something!"

"Inasmuch as I think Lavoie is a piece of shit, do you honestly believe that a jury is going to give credibility to a deranged woman, who's been locked up in a mental institution for over twenty years? Think about it."

There was no counter to Oswald's logic. Vince hit another dead end as he, Drake, and Olivia soon departed from the facility.

Chapter 82

The news conference involving Chief Heimler, Mayor Kincaid, and Captain Borromeo was conducted at about the same time Margaret O'Mara gave Dr. Oswald Borshevsky and the Crenshaw fourth-floor staff a workout. If you missed the live feed, you would've seen segments of it as part of the lead story on any of the local TV stations' early newscasts. The news was out that the heart and foot sent to Rebecca Dyer Lavoie did indeed belong to Logan Galwyn.

As painful it was to disclose the information, so too was it agonizing for Ralph Heimler not to have made an arrest. They thought Roger Lavoie was behind it, but Vince came away with an empty bag from his efforts the day before.

Soma Montero had been planning to visit Heather Karinski ever since she was given her name by Rebecca two days earlier. But the timing when the pair could get together was always a problem.

After rapping on Heather's apartment door a few times, Soma was delighted that the door swung open. Heather had already changed into her shorts and her *Think Green* environmentalist tee shirt.

"Miss Karinski? I'm Detective Montero from PPD Homicide. We spoke on the phone earlier. May I come in?"

"Yes, please," was Heather's pleasant reply.

Soma surveyed the apartment. It had a décor that reflected a feminine touch, but wasn't over the top. It was just right for someone Heather's age.

"Would you care for something to drink or eat?"

"A glass of cold water would be fine, thank you."

On Heather's return, she offered Soma a seat on the sofa. But the detective decided to sit on the upholstered chair instead. From a psychological point of view, it was much better that the person being questioned be more relaxed than the interviewer. That was Soma's little secret, and it made sense. And there was no argument from Heather.

Soma and Heather exchanged a little light-hearted chitchat. The detective even complimented Heather on her acquisition of a small modern metal sculpture on the latter's bookshelf. But then it came down to the main purpose for the visit. Heather had firsthand knowledge on the subject matter, and she'd learned of the identity of parts of the remains of Logan. But it was the underlying layer of information Heather might have that Soma was interested in.

"How long have you known Rebecca and Mark?"

"Rebecca and I go way back to when we were freshman classmates in high school. As for Mark, I've known him for about two years, but I've known his father for at least six."

"Given your age and Rebecca's, you've known her for half of your life, as opposed to Mark for just a fraction thereof. That would place Rebecca more favorably in your mindset, wouldn't it?"

"Although Rebecca and I have gone through a lot of crap in our time together, that doesn't necessarily dictate I coddle favoritism for her. I think Mark is a super guy. I introduced Rebecca to Mark, and urged her to date him. Heck, if I hadn't already had a boyfriend at the time, I might've wanted to go out with him myself."

Soma raised an eyebrow. So much for loyalty and friendship. She needed to break the tension and change the direction of the interview. What better excuse than to take a slurp of the aqua pura in the tumbler. Soma's sip was slow and deliberate; all the while the wheels in her brain were spinning, contemplating the next question. Even the placement of the glass was calculated. To draw out the drama even further, Soma feigned a cough, and then took another sip.

Heather cocked her head, staring at Soma's odd delays. She began twirling the bottom of her tee into a knotted circle, anticipating Soma's next line of questioning.

"We haven't made any arrests yet in the case, because the DA's office doesn't have sufficient evidence to pin anyone, although our emphasis had been on Mark's father, Roger Lavoie, due to similarities of a case a while ago. But we haven't ruled anyone else out. Mark is the most obvious: the jilted and angry husband. Someone suggested that

Rebecca might be behind this, wanting to get rid of Logan and save the marriage, but that seems a bit of a stretch, at least to me, personally. What do you think?"

"You want my honest opinion, Detective? I don't know who or what the fuck to believe any longer. Ever since they broke up, I've been used as a go-between. 'What did he say, Heather?' 'You've got to give her that message, Heather.' A ping pong ball in a bingo game machine, that's all I've been for the last month. I might need to see a shrink myself. How do you think I feel, Detective? Do you really want me to choose? Seriously?"

Soma curled the corners of her lips downward.

"And what do you think of Roger?"

"I don't have any beliefs that he might be behind this either. I'm sorry."

This wasn't getting Soma anywhere. It was best to fold up her tent as she thanked Heather for her time. Another roadblock, another detour leading to nowhere. Vince wouldn't be too pleased with the big zero Soma came away with. But that was all part of the job. Nothing gets handed to you. Sometimes you get the lucky break you're looking for, and other times you hit a brick wall. As she walked toward her car on the street, Soma hoped maybe some of her co-workers might strike gold. That would bring closure . . . and maybe a little vacation.

Chapter 83

Donny Lowery had the distinct pleasure of being chosen to quiz the last person on the list: Hunter Morales. Similar to Mark, Hunter, his wife Kayla and their infant daughter Emily lived in a modest flat in the Valley District of the city.

Donny climbed the stairs to their third-floor flat. With each step he took, Donny carefully scanned the surroundings, as if he were about to be ambushed. But this was the ever-cautious side, one that in his job would often take over his other senses.

Apartment 3C. There was a little hesitation at first. Maybe he wanted to make sure it was the right apartment. Donny looked at the drab paint. Heaven only knew when the walls were last given a fresh coat. A dank odor suffocated the corridors. Donny could easily guess what each tenant was having for dinner. A forest-green door was the portal to Hunter's abode. It wasn't one of Donny's favorite colors. But the detective had to get on with his assignment.

He was about to rap on the door when Donny heard the sound of a baby crying. Then came the voice of a woman trying to quiet it down, while alternately yelling for a third person to get something to help pacify the young child. Perhaps Donny wanted to wait until the deed was accomplished. But there was no telling if the child would settle down, without him seeing for himself. Besides, it was a long day, and the detective wanted nothing more than to enjoy a ribeye and a cold one back at his own place.

Donny sucked in a gulp of air as he knocked hard three times. The woman was now instructing her cohabitant to answer.

"Who is it?" the male voice inquired.

"Detective Donny Lowery, Providence PD Homicide."

The door opened a crack. First an eyeball emerged from the other side, and then the sliver of a face. Donny flashed his shield and credentials as evidence for who he declared himself to be and to assure the occupants he meant no harm. Questions were his only ammo. The crack widened into a crevasse.

"Hunter Morales, correct?"

Hunter nodded like one of those bobble-head dolls. He welcomed the visitor inside.

Donny scanned the apartment. Some things were in need of repair. But that was up to the landlord. Besides, Hunter was a scientist, not a graduate of Tool Time.

Then the detective spotted Kayla holding young Emily in her arms. The seven-month-old girl was crying as Kayla was trying everything to pacify the child. If Kayla were by herself, Donny would have one of his moments of licentious thoughts. But seeing her holding a screaming baby with her husband present was a direct turn-off for the woman-izer. Grandma Ruth would've been more appealing to him.

The young family had just finished dinner. Kayla pre-pared chicken for Hunter and herself and fed little Emily strained beef, carrots, and peas. Although she'd just got her first tooth, Emily was far from her first adult meal.

Hunter looked out of place with an apron tied around his waist. But that was the deal for this evening—Kayla cooked while he washed and dried the dishes, glasses and utensils. The geologist offered Donny a seat.

Donny was about to start his line of questioning, but Emily was still making her presence known. Kayla gently rocked the baby in her arms as she took the little one into Emily's room where a soft crib and warm blanket welcomed her. Kayla's coddling seemed to do the trick as the infant fi-nally quieted down. The detective felt relieved that he could conduct the inquiry in relative peace.

"I'm not going to take too much of your time, Mr. Mo-rales. It's late. Your daughter needs her rest. And I dare say that goes double for you and the missus. I questioned Mark Lavoie the other day. Kind of a mixed bag, he is. He has hatred for Galwyn, yet holds out forgiveness for Rebecca to welcome her back."

"That's my impression about Mark, too, Detective," Hunter replied.

"Personally, I'm of the opinion that Mark didn't kill Galwyn. A lot of my fellow detectives feel the same way. What's your take?"

"I've known Mark since we were in grade school together. This is not like him. I just can't fathom Mark sending that . . ." Hunter paused for a second, but not without fluttering his fingers to dramatize the point, ". . . heart! Sure, he would've liked to smash Galwyn's face up; I would, too, if that happened to me. But Mark is above all that."

"Don't be too sure!" was the remark of a higher-pitched voice in the distance.

Donny and Hunter raised their eyebrows as Kayla reappeared in the living room, now that Emily was beginning to sleep like a . . . well, baby. Although his chief reason for being there that evening was to interrogate Hunter, Donny extended his hand to Kayla, encouraging her to elaborate.

"The both of you make Mark out to be some innocent victim in this mess," Kayla affirmed. "What makes you so sure he is?"

"Honey," Hunter answered, "I've known him for over twenty years. This is not like him. He may get a little opinionated, but he is even-tempered."

"Oh, so you think Rebecca staged all of this, huh?"

"I didn't say that. Please don't put words in my mouth."

Donny remembered what he had told Mark the other day. He wasn't a marriage counselor. But he saw a storm brewing between Kayla and Hunter and felt the need to butt in.

"If I may interject," Donny interrupted. "Have you seen Mark since all this happened, Hunter?"

"No. I've been quite busy with my work. And then there's the baby. Besides," Hunter paused to look over at his wife affectionately before addressing the detective, "I don't think Kayla wants to have Mark come over anyway."

"But you've had chats with him since Monday?"

"Yeah, we spoke a couple of times. Even exchanged texts and emails. Mark wants nothing more than to have Rebecca back. If he's hiding anything from me about Galwyn, he's doing a damn good job of covering it up."

"Well, I still don't trust him," Kayla snorted.

Donny looked up at Kayla. There was nothing more he was going to be getting from Hunter. In fact, if he stayed any longer, he might have to go into Jerry Springer mode and break up a fight between Hunter and Kayla. Donny thanked them for their time. Hunter's goodbye was sincere. Kayla's was cold and distant.

But as he left the flat, Donny did glean something from the skull session. He was becoming more convinced that Mark was not the prime suspect that Kayla might have thought he was. His next call was to Vince.

Chapter 84

The following morning was brimming with sunshine. The ten-room Tudor-style house up in Pawtucket, not far from the Winston campus, was high on Siobhan's hot list to sell. She had three families lined up for her to show the property, all of whom were eager to buy it. Siobhan salivated over these situations. She knew she was in the driver's seat, psychologically pitting one against the other to see who would blink first to buy the home at the higher price she was looking for, thus upping the ante in her commission.

Before stepping into the shower, and then dolling up her hair, and putting on her best Andrew Marc outfit, Siobhan sat down at her kitchen table for juice, coffee and toast with strawberry preserves. Her daily morning routine included burying her head in the headlines of the Providence Journal, courtesy of the paper delivery man Corey MacPherson, who was supplementing his income as a middle-school custodian to help make ends meet.

The big story was the confirmation that the heart and foot were once part of Logan Galwyn, no longer classified as a missing person, but now a murder victim. Siobhan twisted her lips as she read the article that weighted Mark in suspicion. Instead of displaying anger or sadness at the story, Siobhan had the look of contentment. It was as if the downfall of her nephew might not be such a horrible thing after all, at least according to her.

But all that disappeared when Siobhan turned to page five. One screaming headline said it all: LAVOIE AUNT WITHHOLDING INSURANCE FORTUNE. Siobhan's eyes bugged out. Her hands began trembling, barely holding onto the paper. Gritting her teeth, Siobhan began to read the story. When she was through, Siobhan flung the journal across the room, pages flying in the process.

In her rage, Siobhan clenched her fists, attempting to suppress her anger. But it was no use. Too much hatred and animosity was building from inside, like a volcano about to erupt. It was no wonder that she lost interest in breakfast. Her dirty secret of withholding money from Mark was now open to the public. So went that possible added income.

"Who the fuck does she think she is? Whose dick did she suck to get to pry into my life?"

Siobhan scrambled to find again the page bearing the story. Her eyes narrowed to slits as she studied it to discover the writer's name. Gina Chaudhary. As anxious as Gina was when snooping into her life, so too was Siobhan, in wanting to know more about the journalist.

Siobhan raced over to her PC. She first went to the Providence Journal's website, and then followed numerous links until she finally stumbled upon Gina's profile. Siobhan glared intently at Gina's picture for several seconds, and then read her mini bio outlining her journalistic qualifications and experience, as thin as it was.

Time was running out. There was important business for Siobhan to tend to up in Pawtucket. But the problem of Gina wasn't going to be dismissed so easily. Siobhan printed the page. When she ripped it away from the printer, Siobhan decided to study it a little more.

"You're going to pay for this, bitch!"

As pissed as she was, Siobhan had the wherewithal to realize she had to get ready for a big day. A lucrative payday was in the offing, and it was extremely important that Siobhan remain focused. But the realty agent placed Gina's dossier in her briefcase, folded up so that Siobhan wouldn't have to look at it until it was absolutely necessary.

But how exactly was Gina going to pay for the incriminating article? What sort of retribution did Siobhan have in mind? Tucked away in a sly and devious corner of her cunning mind was the answer.

Chapter 85

Mark didn't grab that morning's edition of the Journal. Had he done so, he might have become just as incensed as his Aunt Siobhan was, only for slightly different reasons.

He decided to clear his head of the entire Logan Galwyn murder story, now confirmed by the police and promoted by all the local news outlets, print and electronic. A spirited fifteen-minute jog was the panacea to cure these media blitz ills.

Despite the warm June morning, Mark decided to don a winter ski cap, with no team insignia or corporate logo blazed across it to draw attention to him. A navy-blue nondescript pullover was also part of his ensemble to avoid recognition. He was about as inconspicuous as the next guy.

His morning exercise ended, Mark went home to brew some Starbucks coffee and munch on the two scones he'd bought on the way back. As his Keurig was warming, Mark opened his laptop for the latest email. Some messages he was looking forward to reading, others not. He had received a variety of hateful remarks on his Facebook page, especially from people he didn't know. They were just spewing their venom at him, referring to that week's chain of events.

One email he received was from the Chancellor, Dr. Valen Pagano. This raised an eyebrow. Any notice from the taciturn chancellor was about as common as finding gold coins in the sand on a beach.

Without hesitation, Mark opened the email. He wished he hadn't. Mark's jaw dropped as he read the following:

Dear Professor Lavoie,

If there's anything that anyone should glean from a Winston College education it's that he or she has not only received a sound education useful in the real world, but also developed a respect for time-honored traditions and a dedication to proper conduct and high morals. Winston prides itself in its alumni achieving success in the fields of medicine, science, mathematics, engineering and the law. And, yes, education. And a number of those Winston graduates who have chosen this field, have taught at Winston or are currently doing so, such as you and your father. We prefer to hire our graduates who excel at teaching for they truly know the character we seek, and will uphold our high standards.

We are all mortal men, replete with attendant flaws and shortcomings. But however egregious our missteps may be, there is still that high threshold of integrity that each of us must maintain.

As I had outlined to both you and your father some time ago, we expect these standards to be upheld. However, in light of the tragic events surrounding the demise of Mr. Logan Galwyn, which implicated your family name, I see that the trust between you and the school has been breached. Therefore, it pains me to inform both you and your father that you have been suspended immediately from teaching in our classrooms. We will continue to compensate you through August nineteenth of this year. On that day your status will be reviewed by the Board of Trustees as to whether or not to reinstate each of you, so my recommendation to you both is to keep a low profile as the investigation by the authorities continues.

I regret sending you this notice, but there are levels of decency to which our faculty members and all employees of Winston must be held accountable. Thank you.

Sincerely,
Valentino R. Pagano, PhD
Chancellor
Winston College

A look of utter disbelief filled Mark's face. He reclined in his seat, trying desperately to wish the letter away, or at the very least make it simply an aberration. But after star-ing absently at the walls of his living room, Mark glanced back at the screen. Valen's email was still there.

At first Mark's hands began to tremble. There was a huge pit in his stomach as if he had just received a suck-er punch. There was sadness, despair, and anguish. But those feelings quickly morphed into bitterness and anger.

Mark began to think of all those horrible stories he had heard about his father years ago. Could they actually be true? Did Roger kill Darren Haber and send Margaret to Crenshaw? And just what did Roger mean when he had told Mark that he would *take care of the matter* upon learning of Rebecca's infidelity? Did Roger kill Logan, too?

Clenching his fists, Mark gritted his teeth. His com-plexion turned a beet red. He couldn't contain the rage within much longer. There had to be a release button. And what better way was there than to confront his father, the source of his pain?

Chapter 86

Roger was working feverishly on one of the kitchen chairs. Woodworking was a hobby with him, so nursing the seat to health with his Dremel and sander was more a labor of love than an exercise in futility.

As Roger was buffing one of the spokes, a harsh screech resounded in the driveway. The shrill sound caused the professor to drop what he was doing to investigate the genesis of the noise. He'd walked but two steps before he discovered that Mark was responsible for disrupting his sideline passion.

Roger was baffled by Mark's penchant for theatrics. But there was a red-hot streak of it in his son which made him uncomfortable. Yet despite his disapproval, Roger was curious to get to the root of the heated display of anger, even if it meant further incurring the wrath of the younger Lavoie.

The veteran professor wiped his hands clean of resin. He removed his shop goggles so that he could peer into Mark's eyes with the aid of just his normal set of spectacles. What he saw made him ill at ease, but it warranted an explanation.

For a solid minute Mark continued to glare at his father. His eyes followed Roger's every subtle move, as innocuous as they might have been. It finally came to the point where the elder Lavoie had enough of the cold silence.

"What's the matter, Mark? You look like someone just stole your lunch money."

"Did you look at your email today?" Mark asked testily.

What an odd question to ask, Roger thought. With a brief look away to center himself, he addressed Mark's question head on.

"I looked at it earlier this morning, around seven."

"Then allow me to enlighten you on what I was sent by the Chancellor, probably about two hours ago."

Mark angrily threw the page he had printed in his father's face. Roger adjusted his glasses to get a good look at it. Fifteen seconds into the reading Roger began to raise his eyebrows. But then his forehead furrowed. Roger did a double-take at seeing Valen's message. He pushed the paper away to an extended arm's length, trying to come to terms with Valen's foreboding decree.

Roger dropped his arm, still disbelieving the letter. What was he to do now? And what of his son? But worst of all, how did everything go so wrong?

The veteran professor turned to his son. He was at a loss for words. What could he say? Was he willing to come forward, admit something he had held back from Vince and the PPD, even his wife Beth—and now Mark?

"Let me ask you, Dad. That night I came by and told you and Beth that Rebecca had that affair with Galwyn, you took me aside and told me you wanted to see where you could help first. Was killing Galwyn what you had in mind? And then driving Rebecca insane?"

"Mark, you're believing those stories and vicious rumors from the past!"

"Seriously? Vicious rumors?" Mark screamed in defiance, nearly raising the garage roof. The young man raised his index finger at his father. "I'm giving you one chance, Dad! Just one! Come clean with me or forget we ever knew each other!"

Roger looked away, weighing his options. There was no chance to keep things secret any longer, at least not with Mark. If he wanted to save face with his own flesh and blood, he had to fess up.

The elder Lavoie looked down at the concrete floor, searching for the right way to begin. His heart was pounding and his head was throbbing. Roger was beginning to gasp for air as if he had just finished a 10K race. A gentle wave of his hand was a start.

"All right," Roger commenced, in much softer tones than those Mark had used. "But you have to understand that I did it for you. Yes, I killed Logan Galwyn. Because I saw what he did to you was what Darren Haber did to me. They fucked our wives, Mark! That's your mother we're talking about here! They were nothing but fucking home wreckers! And they deserved their comeuppance!"

"It's strange how you're talking about Mom so reverent-ly, seeing there is no doubt that you drove her to Crenshaw. She's afraid of her own shadow! And now you're doing the same to Rebecca!"

"Don't you see, Mark? They had to be taught a lesson! I wanted to bring justice to each situation!"

Mark gave Roger a bizarre look as he tried to absorb his father's illogical and crazed explanation. Now the son was shifting his beliefs to what Borshevsky, Vince, and the vast majority of Rhode Islanders had taken as fact: Roger was a madman.

This was getting to be too much for Mark to handle. Yet despite the sheer incongruity of Roger's twisted logic, Mark wanted to ask only one question.

"Where have you hidden Galwyn's body parts? I know they're not here. The police would have found them the oth-er day. Where are they?"

"Up in Wanskuck Park. They're hidden in the ground, the area where they recently placed new soil. They're be-hind a dogwood bush next to a big oak tree. I painted the trunk of the tree with a white spot as a marker."

Mark was about to turn away and leave when Roger grabbed him by the arm.

"Please, Mark. Don't turn me in! You must under-stand!"

Mark threw off his father's grip. He just glared back in disgust. "You make me want to puke!"

The son hightailed it out of the garage and sped off. Roger was left alone. Suddenly the chair project didn't seem so important.

Roger began to seethe. Next came the hyperventilating. His eyes narrowed as he began to grumble.

"I'll get you, Rebecca! If it's the last thing I do!"

Chapter 87

Infuriated by his father's confession, Mark called Donny Lowery and spilled his opinion on the truth behind Logan Galwyn's murder. Although it was his day off, Donny thanked Mark for coming forward. And realizing that in the business of police work there is never a true day off, save for sickness or attending Aunt Millie's funeral, Donny apprised Vince Calabrese of the phone call.

As much as Vince was eager to talk with the younger Lavoie, something in Donny's eerie description of Mark's story compelled the veteran detective to take the extra steps to put Rebecca's safety first, even if it meant delaying another showdown with Roger. If the cunning professor was ever going to try anything with her it would be immediate. Vince called Rebecca at her job and asked if he and Drake Nowak could meet her for lunch. Their seeing Rebecca at her workplace would have been too distracting, thus the call was to meet at a neutral spot. Mark's estranged wife conceded.

Rebecca chose Angelo's as a place to convene. It was a spacious bistro where the three of them could sit quietly and discuss matters. And because it was a self-serve establishment, there wasn't the annoying interruption of a waiter barging in every so often wondering if you'd like a refill of the beverage you were downing.

Twelve-twenty-two, unusually early for Rebecca to be indulging in lunch. But then again, this was no ordinary encounter. It wasn't long before the fetching blonde spotted the detectives sitting at a table trying to pick at sandwiches that each could have polished off in a few minutes. She was still a little uncomfortable meeting them, but coupled with that was the assurance that they were on her side.

The first to welcome her was Vince, who stood to give Rebecca a handshake. Drake rose simultaneously. He had been sitting opposite Vince while they waited for Rebecca, but now sat next to his boss so the two detectives could ask their questions directly at her.

"I'm glad you could meet us so soon," Vince began, to open the dialogue.

Rebecca was laconic and just offered a simple smile in return to the gentlemen. Vince pressed forward.

"We've had our detectives interview several key persons of interest in this case. One of whom has spoken with your husband. Well, my man received an unusual call from Mark about an hour and a half ago, so bizarre that it made us all sit up and take notice. Mark is of the strong opinion that his father Roger may indeed have murdered Logan."

Rebecca became puzzled. "Then why don't you arrest him?"

"It's not so cut and dried as you might think," Vince countered. "We searched Roger's property with a fine-tooth comb, inside and out, on an earlier day, but found nothing that would make us suspicious or seem associated with foul play. But it's still our belief that Roger is the chief suspect. We just have to catch him at the right moment."

"What is disturbing is the way Roger acted toward Mark in a conversation between the two this morning," Drake chimed in. "We have reason to believe Roger may want to go after you again. And I don't mean by only sending you another of Logan's body parts; perhaps worse than that. The man is definitely deranged."

As if on cue, Vince reached inside the breast pocket of his blazer. He pulled out an electronic tracer, about half the size of a smart phone. On it were two buttons.

"The green one activates it," Vince explained. "Keep it on whenever you leave your home, even at work. That light you see is an indicator that it is active. The battery inside should keep it going for a very long time—hopefully until this case will be over. If you sense any danger, press the red button and hold it down for at least five seconds. I have the receiver, which I will keep on me at all times, even in the middle of the night. Once you depress the red button I will receive a signal, which also ties into my Samsung Galaxy. It'll pinpoint where you are by satellite navigation, sort of a GPS. Besides issuing a dispatch of police vehicles, I will send you a text message, based on where you are at the time, and instruct you on where to go so we can corner Roger."

Rebecca examined the device as if it belonged to Luke Skywalker. Satisfying her curiosity enough to be comfortable with it, she then swiftly tucked it away in her shoulder-strapped bag.

"What Drake said before about your father-in-law is true. He might be at the point of trying anything, perhaps even trying to kill you. We have reason to believe he's done it before, and he may attempt it again."

"Another thing," Drake cautioned. "Don't try to be a heroine and lure Roger into a trap. You're asking for trouble if you do. Have we made ourselves clear?"

Rebecca sucked in a breath and nodded her head vigorously, indicating the detectives got their point across. She then zeroed in on Vince.

"What are you going to do about Mark in the meantime?"

"We want to speak with him as soon as possible. Mark may hold some key answers. Is there anything you'd like us to tell him?"

Rebecca became pensive. She looked up at the ceiling of the restaurant and released a sigh that rippled the bangs of golden hair covering her forehead.

"Tell him . . . tell him I sincerely apologize for my egregious lapse in judgment. I'd like to reconcile. But also tell him that, if he is truly forgiving, he won't hesitate to tell you all the secrets he knows about his father. Mark should not withhold anything from you if he wants to bridge the gap."

Vince twisted his pursed lips and gave Rebecca a nod. They all rose in unison and departed in separate ways: Rebecca to her job, and Vince and Drake to the next rung on the ladder to the top.

Chapter 88

Gina Chaudhary's story on the exposé of Siobhan O'Mara was a hit at the Journal. The veteran journalists covering the Galwyn murder congratulated her on putting together such a fine piece. Members of the local electronic media picked up on the story and used it as a sidepiece to the main headliner. And best of all was the praise Gina was given by Editor-in-Chief Fred Wasserman. That was the ultimate stamp of approval.

Of course, there was the most personal endorsement of them all, that by fellow bullpen writer Scott Menken. Perhaps there might have been a little envy on his part, but Scott nonetheless hailed Gina for a job well done.

And there was Gina's rise in her social media status. The story garnered more likes on her professional Facebook page in one day than she'd had in the entire year. Scores of people began to follow her on Twitter. Gina's popularity spiked big time.

Her parents and best friends called and emailed to congratulate her on her groundbreaking story. She was asked by her parents to come up to Walpole that weekend, but Gina had to tell them she was working that Saturday. "Let's do a raincheck," she'd said.

Before Gina left the building, she was called into Wasserman's office once more. He briefed her that she might get a crack at other big stories very soon. And all Gina could think of was trading in her bullpen spot for her very own cubicle, leaving her ally Scott behind. But any reservations she might have had in pulling away from her most trusted co-worker were quickly replaced by the idea that she was on the fast track to making a name for herself and writing her own ticket to fame.

It was six-o-five. The sun was still brilliant on the early June evening as Gina hopped into her Hyundai, hoping that her newfound success could lead to a bigger and better vehicle. A simple turning over of the engine and Gina was out of the parking lot.

Gina was heading east on Broadway. The traffic was modest as most people had already made an early beeline, an exodus from the midsize city, toward more spacious places elsewhere. Pre-summer weekends tend to fuel the urge to get away.

The traffic light at the intersection of Almy Street turned red. Ever the responsible driver, Gina slowed to a crawl and then waited for the light to change. While biding her time, Gina felt a slight push from behind. The surprise bump startled Gina. If it weren't for the seatbelt harnessing her in the seat, Gina's face might have kissed her steering wheel. Shaken but not stirred, Gina looked in her rearview mirror. All she could see was a red sedan behind her. Then there was the emergence of the driver's left hand sticking out, giving a gesture that appeared to be apologetic. Gina was a little miffed, but decided to dismiss it.

The light turned green. Gina continued her journey until another red light at Knight Street impeded her progress. Just like before, Gina was bumped from behind by the same red sedan, only this time a little harder. Now Gina was fuming mad. She unbuckled herself and got out of the Hyundai to give the other driver a piece of her mind.

Her face was furrowed in anger. Gina looked at the vehicle. It was a Mercedes C-Class sedan. If Gina was supposed to be impressed by it, she wasn't. She tried to get a good look at the driver, but the elegant tinted windows made that difficult. Still Gina wanted the driver to get out so they could have a facedown.

"What the fuck is wrong with you?" Gina yelled.

She approached the driver's door even closer, but then the light had turned green. Now Gina was the target of the other, now angry motorists. Gina was pissed off at the entire world. She gave the other drivers the middle finger salute. It was best for the journalist to get back into her car and lead the caravan of vehicles. But before she did, Gina shook her fist at the Mercedes driver and gritted her teeth. As an outward sign of her fury, Gina kicked the fender of the Mercedes before getting back in her Hyundai.

Gina resumed her path along Broadway. She had only gotten two blocks past Knight Street when she felt another bump from behind by the Mercedes. That was followed seconds later by a more vicious shove. By now Gina's countenance of anger had morphed to fear. She didn't know what to make of the Mercedes driver, or why she was being targeted.

Her first reaction was to contact Scott back at the paper. But even in her panic she dismissed the idea. All Scott would have done would be to question her on what was happening to her and then decide on the appropriate course of action. No, Gina needed to skip the fluff in her search for immediate help.

Through her iPhone, Gina voice-activated a call to 911, and then felt another hard bump from the Mercedes. Anxiety was setting in as Gina began to sob in fright. Finally an operator came on.

"Please! I'm being driven off the road by some madman!"

"Calm down, ma'am," the operator replied, with coolness in her voice from being confronted with situations like Gina's many times over in the past. "Now where are you?"

"I'm traveling east along Broadway! I'm approaching the interstate! Please! I need the police now!"

"I'm dispatching the request to them right now, ma'am. Can you make out the type of vehicle, the plate and perhaps its driver?"

"I couldn't see the driver! But it's a Mercedes sedan! Yes! And it's red!"

"I realize you're in danger, ma'am, but I need some information from you and a description of your car."

"My name is Gina! Gina Chaudhary! I own a gray Hyundai Sonata, Rhode Island pla—"

Another nudge from behind caused her to scream hysterically. The operator was trying to help Gina maintain her composure, but Gina was way beyond frantic at this point. She was so deep in her delirium that Gina paid no attention to the red light in front of her as she approached the southbound service road. And that was when an eighteen-wheel tractor trailer, which had the right of way, was about to hit her broadside. In her panic, Gina took a quick glance at the oncoming rig. In a split second Gina realized her young life was about to end.

The truck driver first beeped furiously with his heavy resounding horn as he tried to slam on the brakes. But Gina was a goner. The Hyundai caved in like an accordion on impact. Debris from both vehicles flew in various directions, narrowly missing other cars, trucks, and passersby by inches. The rig came to a screeching halt, pushing the mangled wreckage in its path. For certain, no one in that car could've survived such a smash-up.

Fellow motorists stopped driving to lend assistance. Pedestrians even tried to lend a helping hand until emergency vehicles could eventually show up on the scene. The driver of the rig was so devastated by the accident that he got out of his smashed-in cab and began to bawl profusely. Others came to his aid to console him, while the rest made 911 calls of their own to report the tragedy.

But there was one driver that didn't feel a bit of emotion over the horror. It was the driver of the red Mercedes sedan. When the driver brought the car to a halt like everyone else had done, the driver began to emerge. First to appear was a pair of very shapely legs. The rest followed.

It was Siobhan. She looked at the accident with a smug expression on her face. She stuck her nose in the air as a signal to everyone that she was not to be messed with.

She would've liked to have hung around to absorb her retaliatory triumph. But Siobhan then heard the sudden emergence of sirens from police cars to ambulances to fire engines. That was her cue to leave. And for her, it would be the end of anyone probing into her personal affairs, or so she hoped.

Chapter 89

News of the tragic deadly accident that claimed the life of Gina Chaudhary was the lead story of the eleven o'clock newscasts, putting the Logan Galwyn murder on the back burner. Now there was something else for Rhode Islanders to talk about. But there was the ironic connection to Roger Lavoie, serving as the common denominator to both major stories.

Saturday morning finally arrived. It was time for Rebecca to run a few errands. She got into the driver's seat of her Camry and rummaged through her handbag. Rebecca bypassed a small wallet, a hairbrush, and two tubes of lipstick to retrieve the prize she had been looking for: the device that Vince gave her in the restaurant the day before.

Rebecca looked at the contraption like another new gizmo that required extra reading of the operations manual. Trouble was there was no such manual that came with it. Only a green on/off switch and a red button to alert Vince and the rest of the PPD, should she run into any danger. Taking some comfort in it, Rebecca placed the instrument down on the front passenger seat.

She was traveling east into the city from her mother's Greenville home. All seemed to be going well. There was the threat of rain, but that didn't deter her journey. Nothing seemed out of the ordinary. Nothing, that is, until she reached the Providence city limits and just happened to notice a particular vehicle in her rearview mirror. Rebecca's brow furrowed as she glanced up again to get a better look. There was no doubt what she saw. It was Roger's navy-blue Maxima.

Suddenly the thought of the horrific chain of events she'd seen on the newscast last night surrounding Gina's death flashed in her mind. But unlike Gina, who didn't know the identity of the Mercedes bumper thumper, Rebecca knew who was stalking her. Plus she had something that Gina never had: a device to connect with the PPD immediately and track her down.

Her heart began to throb. Rebecca promised herself that she wasn't going to act like Chicken Little or the Boy Who Cried Wolf, but she knew the identity of the driver behind her. Still feeling hesitant, Rebecca then reminded herself that she wasn't going to suffer the same fate as Gina. She grabbed the device and flicked it on. A deep breath was followed by a nervous gulp. Rebecca pressed the red button.

Chapter 90

Vince and Drake made the call to Mark and agreed to meet at the younger Lavoie's apartment that Saturday morning. Ever the hospitable host, Mark offered coffee, but the detectives politely declined. The point of being there was strictly business, not to have a coffee klatch.

Vince scanned the modest apartment that Rebecca once shared with Mark, until that fateful fracas between her and Mark. The long-tenured detective opened the dialogue.

"First of all, I want to let you know that Rebecca is deeply sorry for that affair she had with Galwyn. She wanted you to understand that."

Mark closed his eyes and nodded.

"Secondly, we got a call from Detective Lowery who told us of your conversation with your father. From what I gather, things did not sit well with you."

"No." Mark sighed as he toyed with a spoon on his kitchen table.

Mark would not make eye contact with either Vince or Drake. Instead, the math prof covered his mouth to signal nothing more needed to be said about the exchange.

Vince and Drake traded quizzical looks while Mark seemed more interested in his Maytag range. To Vince, Mark appeared to want the world to know of his anger, his disgust, and his frustration with Roger. But on the flip side, Mark wasn't communicative. *Perhaps he's holding back,* Vince thought. *Could he be? Is there any last shred of that father-son connection that Mark doesn't want to sever, especially after so many years when Roger cared for him?*

"Did your father confess to you that he killed Galwyn?"

Again Mark was hesitant. But he came to the point where he couldn't hold back.

"Yes," Mark replied softly. "And he also told me that he did send those body parts to Rebecca." Mark paused for a moment before releasing a short chuckle of irony. "It's strange how you hear about all of those stories, and I've heard them all ever since I was a boy. But you force yourself to disregard them, especially the way my father has cared after me ever since my mother was committed. Now I look back and realize how it was all a façade, one big illusion my father cooked up to mask the truth. And I'm possibly out of a job because of him. The same job he fought so hard to get me. How's that for a kick in the head?"

"What do you mean?" Drake asked.

Mark looked over at the questioner strangely and then shrugged.

"The chancellor at Winston sent me and my father an email stating that we are both suspended with pay until August. That's when the board of trustees will vote on our fate. Trust me, I don't hold out much hope."

"I would think your chances of being reinstated would improve dramatically if you helped us pin the goods on your father, Mark," Vince voiced. "For one thing, did he tell you where he hid Galwyn's body parts?"

Mark threw up his hands and mentioned some sort of field, but not much else.

"I've dispatched a detective, along with a few officers, to check out several areas where Parks and Recreation recently turned over the soil. Some potting soil samples were found on the foot sent to Rebecca a few days ago."

Just then the receiver Vince had, which was tuned in to Rebecca's device, began to beep. She was in trouble. Vince and Drake jumped up from their seats.

Mark heard Vince and Drake exchanging banter, something to the effect of dispatching backup and tracing Rebecca's whereabouts on the GPS tracker. The math teacher wanted to contribute.

"Wait! I could be of use to you."

Vince and Drake eyeballed Mark.

"You're right, especially if we have to negotiate with your father. C'mon!" Then Vince held up his right index finger. "But you'll sit in the back and only get involved when we need you. Got it?"

Mark nodded as he joined the detectives for a possible showdown with Roger.

Chapter 91

It was a full minute since Rebecca signaled for Vince and the cavalry to come to her rescue. She continued to check her rearview mirror. Roger was still tailing her relentlessly. Even when Rebecca skated through a traffic light before it turned red, hoping that Roger might get stuck there, she discovered to her astonishment just how dogged Roger was in his pursuit, risking both a ticket and perhaps a nasty fender bender.

She was making every effort to remain cool under pressure. But Rebecca's stomach was filled with butterflies. Her heart raced. Her skin began to crawl. Her forehead began to perspire, despite the full blast of the Camry's AC.

To quell her anxiety, Rebecca decided to turn on the radio for background music. Just her luck, it was the top of the hour. That meant the airing of a brief news report. And as fate would have it, the announcer spoke of the horrible accident that killed Gina Chaudhary. In light of the circumstances, that was the last thing Rebecca needed to hear. She quickly turned off the radio. So much for that idea.

It had been a full five minutes since Rebecca signaled for backup. And there she was, still driving aimlessly through the streets of Providence. She had wanted to head farther into Downtown, but she was heading east, not focusing on her planned itinerary. Being chased clouds one's thoughts. And that was when she received a text message from Vince: PROCEED TO THE POINT STREET BRIDGE! NOW!

Rebecca was heading east on Point Street. She heard the sound of sirens in the distance, not knowing in which direction they were going. Mixed feelings were overwhelming her. A sense of relief comforted her with the belief that help was nearby. But then, she mused, perhaps they weren't meant for her. Some other crisis might be occurring without her being center stage.

She was motoring across the Point Street Bridge when she spotted a barricade of cruisers some 200 yards ahead, not permitting access to the other side of the Providence River. It was the end of the line.

Rebecca brought her Camry to a screeching halt. She was experiencing a sense of ambivalence. On the one hand, she took solace in knowing that the guys and gals with badges and weapons were in front of her to protect her. But there was that sick feeling of not knowing how brazen Roger would be in spite of the heavy police presence.

Quite shaken and fraught with fear, Rebecca got out of her Camry. Her head was on a swivel, trying desperately to decide where to go first. At the same time Roger got out of his Maxima. Never mind that three cruisers waited in the distance. He seemed hell-bent on confronting his estranged daughter-in-law and exacting his vengeance.

Rebecca stumbled over to the side rail of the pedestrian walkway. A portion was missing as a pair of orange traffic cones, mounted by flashing yellow warning lights, and several lines of caution tape were the only means of preventing anyone from falling into the river below. She had to catch herself before tumbling through the flimsy barricade. And that was when she looked up and saw Roger.

The veteran professor sported a satisfied smile as if in his warped mind he had won, having her cornered. In his hand was an oversized white postal envelope. Roger took just two steps toward Rebecca, causing her to lose her balance and slip, falling against one of the warning cones. Again Rebecca was able to brace herself before heading into the drink. She quickly glanced down in fright and scanned the angry currents of the river. Suddenly she heard Roger begin to speak, refocusing her attention on him.

"So," Roger began, "we meet again, Rebecca. You thought you were going to continue your affair with that bastard? You ruined my son Mark! Do you know how depressed you made him?"

"I'm . . . I'm sorry! I didn't mean to! It was just . . ."

"Just that home wrecker you still had feelings for! That's it, isn't it? Why did you marry my son if you still held a candle out for that bum? Why did you destroy Mark?"

Rebecca was speechless. She was too frightened to think clearly to respond, and too frightened to utter a

sound. And that was when Roger opened the postal envelope. He pulled out a plastic bag and showed its contents
for Rebecca to get a good look. It was the greyed, shriveled
penis that once was Logan's.

"Here! This is what you were after all along, wasn't it?"

It wasn't long ago that Rebecca had lustily welcomed
that same appendage inside her body. Now the mere sight
of it caused her to shriek. Tears streamed down her face as
she pleaded for mercy, but Roger was unforgiving. And that
was when he reached into the envelope once more. He held
out another plastic bag, this one containing presumably
Logan's right hand.

"Maybe your lover can save you from falling into the
Providence River! Here! I'll lend you his hand!"

Roger tossed it at Rebecca, causing her to sidestep it,
not allowing the packaged hand to touch her. Once again,
by dancing away from the bag, she bumped into the same
traffic cone, impeding her trajectory toward slipping over
the edge.

Just then, three cruisers and Vince's Caprice, all wail-
ing away with their sirens and flashing lights, came up from
behind Roger. There was no place for either Rebecca or Roger to turn. Every vehicle came to a screeching halt, with all
four strategically positioned so as not to allow anyone to
gain access to the scene.

Vince and Drake jumped out of the Caprice. They gestured to the uniformed officers with them to fan out. Each
blue held his or her weapon drawn, pointing directly at
Roger. The hope was that no one would have to fire a shot.
That would be the last resort.

"Step away from Rebecca, Lavoie!" Vince commanded,
keeping a thirty-foot distance from Roger.

Roger looked back at Vince and the others briefly before returning his focus to Rebecca.

"You keep out of this, Calabrese! This is between Rebecca and me! I have a score to settle with her!"

"I said step away from the girl! Now! I want you to come
Downtown with us . . . quietly!"

"No!"

Mark was sitting in the backseat of the Caprice while
the intense drama in front of him unfolded. Despite Vince's
stern warning to stay put, Mark felt compelled to intervene.

He got out of the car and headed toward Vince and Drake. His presence caught the eye of the seasoned detective.

"What the fuck are you doing out here?" Vince roared. "Who told you to get out? Now get your fucking ass back in the car and stay put until I say differently!"

"Please, Detective! Let me at him! I can reason with my father better than anyone else!"

Drake overheard Mark's plea. He nodded slightly to Vince. The lead man was still a little uncomfortable in allowing Mark out there at that moment, but he finally conceded. Vince gestured to the officers to hold their fire. But each uniform knew he or she could relax only so much. Each one would have to be at the ready in the event of this becoming a dangerous altercation.

Mark approached Roger, seemingly calm. He was the only one that prevented the officers from shooting at his father. A tall order to be sure, but Mark was desperate to stop the showdown from escalating into something even uglier.

"Dad! Please! Leave Rebecca alone! Please come with the police before it's too late!"

"Hah! Now you're on their side? After all I did to protect you? To protect you from this whore?"

"It's not worth it!" Mark was now sobbing along with Rebecca. "Please! We had our differences! I . . . I just don't want anyone else to die! Not Rebecca! Not you! Not anyone!"

"First, your mother ruined me! Now, this tramp is ruining you! I'm going to put a stop to her machinations!"

"I won't allow it!"

Mark began to struggle with Roger in his attempt to subdue him. But the elder Lavoie used every ounce of strength in his body to fend off his son. He heaved Mark away, causing the latter to topple backward. And whereas Rebecca was able to prevent herself from slipping and plunging down into the river, Mark was not as fortunate. He broke through the flimsy caution tape and fell over the walkway.

Rebecca screamed in horror as she saw Mark drop. Roger was in complete shock. In his descent, Mark's head struck one of the protruding wooden pilings under the midsection of the bridge. One might have the impression that the glancing blow knocked Mark unconscious, as his shout of fright was silenced. Mark hit the water hard and then disappeared completely.

Roger was in disbelief.

"Mark! No! Mark!"

What once was a glazed look of disbelief on his face was now one of complete rage. Roger turned his focus back to Rebecca. His eyes bulged out as he turned beet red in the face.

"Forget about scaring you to death, I'm going to kill you!"

Roger quickly reached into his hidden side pocket in his pants leg for the sharp scalpel, the same one used to cut up Logan. Rebecca backed away in terror. She hoped not to suffer the same fate as Logan by the scalpel, or Mark by tumbling over the bridge to the rushing water below them.

"Freeze, Lavoie!" Vince ordered. "Don't make us shoot!"

"She must die!"

At the very moment Roger lifted the surgical knife above his head, one of the officers fired, striking Roger on his left side. Undeterred, Roger staggered toward his target. He began to spit up blood. But he was determined to finish off Rebecca. Roger made a feeble lunge with the scalpel before three more shots were fired at him. Roger stopped in his tracks. He dropped the scalpel. With his petrified daughter-in-law reeling from the turn of events unfolding before her, Roger looked up at her for the last time. He then collapsed on the walkway and expired.

Vince, Drake and the officers approached the lifeless body of Roger with caution. But with each closer step it was evident that the anthropology professor was dead. For good measure, Drake tried to get a feel for Roger's pulse, both in his wrist and in his neck. There was none. Vince ordered a sergeant to call for an ambulance from the city morgue to remove Roger's body. He then turned to Drake to order a couple of police boats with divers to comb the river in an attempt to recover Mark, also presumed to be dead from both the concussion and fall.

Rebecca was still shaking and sobbing as she stared first at Roger's corpse, and then down at the Providence River, wondering where Mark was in the vast torrent. That was when Vince stepped in.

"I can have Drake drive your car and take you home," Vince said softly, a far cry from the hair-raising shouting he'd done minutes ago. "It's all over, Rebecca."

Rebecca nodded in agreement. But an ordeal like this just doesn't go away. It comes back and haunts you in nightmares, just as it did to Roger when he relived the interrogation and prosecution decades later. And even Vince had a difficult time believing his own words.

Chapter 92

While the surrealistic drama was being played out on the Point Street Bridge, Siobhan O'Mara was applying the finishing touches of her mascara and eyeliner. She had re-scheduled two of her three appointments for that Saturday after she came up with some lame excuse for why she couldn't keep them the day before. She wasn't feeling well, she had told them. Perhaps she wasn't. But it was Gina Chaudhary's scathing article that made her so ill she couldn't work. It made her so uneasy that she had to stalk Gina until the right moment came along to do away with her, taking up the entire day.

Siobhan was all set to grab her shoulder-strapped bag when she spotted a vehicle and a squad car outside her house, one of the few not called upon for the episode over the Providence River. She recognized the navy-blue Corolla and its driver Lou Maszukevich. But who was the Latina riding shotgun with him?

The real estate maven had a strong intuition about why they had showed up. It had something to do with the tragic accident from the day before. Siobhan cocked her head while she inhaled deeply for strength. She reached for the doorknob to greet her unexpected guests.

"Well, well, well, Lou," Siobhan smiled superficially. "Fancy seeing you here again." Siobhan then glanced at the woman. "And I see you brought your girlfriend, how nice!"

"Detective Soma Montero, ma'am," Soma replied as she flashed her shield and ID. "I work with Detective Maszukevich in PPD Homicide."

Siobhan released a forced chuckle.

"Of course, of course! I should've known. I suppose you have more questions concerning my ex-brother-in-law."

Lou explained "The purpose of our visit this morning has nothing to do with him and everything to do with you."

Siobhan gave them a quizzical look. "I'm afraid I don't understand."

"Where were you at about six-eleven last night, Miss O'Mara?"

"I had several phones calls to make during the day. Then I went out to eat at around that time."

"Do you have witnesses to back up that claim?"

"Yeah," Siobhan testily responded. "Now can you two get to the point? I have a property to show and I'm running rather late, if you don't mind!"

Soma was as miffed at Siobhan's disposition as the realtor was annoyed at their barrage of questions. The policewoman twisted her lips and narrowed her eyes. She wasn't buying Siobhan's story, not for one second.

"We understand Providence Journal reporter Gina Chaudhary wrote a very unflattering expose looking into your handling of an insurance policy payout distribution, whereby your nephew Mark Lavoie, and his mother, your sister Margaret O'Mara, were denied their legal payout."

"I read the story," Siobhan snapped. There was a slight pause before she continued. "Yes, I was a little pissed at it. But Margaret's state of being is compromised. As for Mark, well, I was going to resolve that."

"You won't have to worry about any more scathing articles about you by Miss Chaudhary," Lou countered. "She was killed in a car accident last night at the intersection of Broadway and the west service road. A tractor trailer slammed into her as she ran a red light. I'm sure you've heard of it. It was the lead story on all the evening newscasts as well as the main headline on the Journal's front page."

"I'm aware of the misfortune. I was very sad when I first learned of it."

Soma began to rake her hair with her fingers, trying to convince herself that Siobhan had even an ounce of remorse over Gina's death. But her time was valuable, as was Lou's and the two officers'. It was time to cut to the chase.

"Miss Chaudhary had a very clean driving record," Soma stated. "No speeding tickets. No accidents. No running of red lights. Yet all of that was erased in less than a minute. Strange, coming from a model driver. But here's the kicker. Miss Chaudhary called 911 just before she was killed. We have the full tape and I have a copy of the transcript of her call to the operator with me. Let's see."

Soma opened to a portion that contained explicit details. She quoted two lines from Gina's frantic transmission.

"Here's the first. 'Please! I'm being driven off the road by some madman!' And now the second. 'I couldn't see the driver! But it's a Mercedes sedan! Yes! And it's red!'" Soma closed the transcript before taking a long look at Siobhan's car, which matched the description in the transcript. She and Lou then stared at the real estate lady to wait for what was about to come out of her mouth.

"Oh, come now," Siobhan scolded. "I'm sure there are other red Mercedes sedans out there."

"The motive was there, Miss O'Mara," Lou argued. "Revenge can be cruel. And sometimes deadly."

Just then one of the officers called Lou and Soma over to him. There were a couple of very distinctive dents in the front bumper. Lou stooped down to scrutinize the damage

"These gashes look fairly fresh," Lou said. "Were you in any recent accident?"

"That happened a week ago," Siobhan answered nervously. "I was showing a property up in Pawtucket when some idiot backed up into my car in a strip mall."

Ever the consummate professional, Lou pulled out a small plastic Ziploc bag. He then reached for a pair of eyebrow tweezers he kept for just such an occasion. Lou began to pluck away paint chips of a different color. He gave the chips a good inspection. They were gray, just like the color of Gina's mangled Hyundai. Holding the bag in his grip, Lou looked up at Siobhan.

"We'd like to take you Downtown for a few more questions, if you don't mind."

There was no weaseling out of this dilemma. Soma opened the backdoor to Lou's Corolla and motioned Siobhan to sit in the back with her . . . quietly. Siobhan wasn't going to keep her appointment at eleven. And judging by the situation, it was rather doubtful she was ever going to be able to make it up.

Epilogue

It had been over four months since the ordeal. Four months since the incident on the Point Street Bridge. Four months since Rebecca Dyer-Lavoie kept looking over her shoulder for Roger Lavoie to arrive with a new Logan Galwyn body part. Four months since Roger met his own Armageddon with Vince Calabrese and the police. Four months since Gina Chaudhary met her end by way of a barreling semi. Four months since Siobhan O'Mara was booked on suspicion of third-degree murder, involuntary manslaughter, and reckless endangerment, to name but a few of the charges. Four months since Rebecca would be considered a young widow, even though Mark's body was never recovered. The strong currents of the Providence River might have washed Mark out to Narragansett Bay. Perhaps he might have gone as far as the open waters of the Atlantic.

The last of the gold, orange and crimson leaves were leaving the trees with Halloween fast approaching. It wouldn't be too long before Old Man Winter would make his howling debut for the year.

Rebecca walked into Brett McLellan's office, or what used to be his. Brett was kicked upstairs to assume his new role of VP of Merchandising for Templeton's. What became of his previous position as head of the accounting area? That had become Rebecca's new responsibility.

Her coworkers congratulated her on her new duties. Simone Henderson got along well with Rebecca and was extremely happy for her. Tiffany Zadrozny, Aaron Reinhardt, Elba Soriano, and Dustin Kramer all chipped in with Simone to surprise Rebecca with a box full of delectable pastries from a local bakery. Even Brett came down that Monday morning to wish his successor well.

Rebecca was all smiles as she thanked everyone for the kind wishes and warm thoughts.

"You guys are just tremendous," Rebecca began. She bowed her head briefly and then paused to choose her next set of words carefully. "I've had to endure some disturbing events this past year. Yet through it all, you have stood behind me. For that alone I am eternally grateful. I couldn't have made it without your strong support. And I vow to make this team shine. Thank you."

A round of applause went up with a few cheers added in.

"You know, Rebecca," Simone chimed in, "we actually wanted to get you rum cake, but I don't think Brett and the company would've approved!"

A roar of laughter filled the office.

"Well, you can all do that at Tommy's after work," Brett replied. "But seriously." He raised his coffee mug to her. "This moment belongs to you, Rebecca. Here's wishing you well in your new post."

A few of the workers clanked their cups with hers. Rebecca was heartened by the generous appreciation she was receiving.

As the celebration was winding down, Torey from the mailroom walked in. A box covered in brown wrapping paper with a label bearing Rebecca's name and the Templeton mailing address, computer-written, was in his hands.

"Excuse me, Rebecca," Torey politely interceded, "but a special package just came from you by a mail carrier."

Torey's presence may have seemed like a bad omen, but Tiffany was trying to be upbeat. "You have a well-wisher, Rebecca!"

"Hopefully it doesn't have a severed finger or other appendage," Aaron whispered to Tiffany. That got him a slap and a dirty look.

But Brett was curious about who might have sent the seemingly ordinary package. He carefully examined the box and noticed the name of the sender: Dr. Valentino Pagano. Brett was dumbfounded by the name. He gave it a quizzical look before looking up at Rebecca for an explanation.

"Do you know the guy?"

Rebecca had to think hard for a moment. And then it dawned on her.

"He's the Chancellor at Winston College. That's where Mark and his father worked."

Still harboring some fear, Rebecca took the package from Brett and began to open it. Inside was another ordinary box with a letter attached to it. She unfolded it and began to read aloud.

Dear Mrs. Lavoie,

I'm so sorry about the loss of your husband. He was a far better man than his father and deserved a better fate. But I'm sure he would be glad knowing that you're continuing on with your life.

Sincerely, Valentino Pagano, PhD.

Rebecca carefully removed the lid. Its contents were there for all to see. It was the decaying skull of Logan Galwyn. His flesh had turned gray and was flaking off. The hair was stiff and brittle as straw. Logan's teeth had become more prominent than any smile he could've given when he was alive. And his eyes, oh, that was the best part. They jumped out at you through the sockets. The whites were bloodshot and the brilliant blues that were once his were now almost completely black. But there was a bonus. A small off-white maggot was wriggling its way through the middle of the left one, gorging on what little living tissue remained.

Tiffany screamed. Elba fainted. And Aaron vomited up his jelly donut. The rest tried to regain their composure as best they could. All except Rebecca. She retreated to a corner of the office and dropped to the floor. Rebecca grimaced and convulsed, holding her hands to her ears and trying to forget all of the other times she was exposed to Logan's body parts.

Everyone began to come to Rebecca's aid. But that wasn't how she saw it. There was Torey's sneaker in her sight, but she saw the flashback of Logan's severed right foot. Dustin's chest was in view, but that brought on the flashback to the heart. Simone reached out to try to comfort Rebecca, but that revived memories of Logan's hand. And then there was Brett, trying to look Rebecca in the eye, but that brought on the view of the head in the box.

"Please, Rebecca," Simone cried. "Let me help you, baby!"

"Get away from me!" Rebecca yelled. "Don't you touch me! Don't you touch me!"

Brett looked up at Torey and Dustin. "Someone call nine-one-one! She's flipped!"

Rebecca had gone over the edge. She was now ready to become roommates with Margaret O'Mara and take up residence at Crenshaw, possibly for a long time.

As for the sender of the package, the chances of Valen Pagano sending it were about the same odds as of hitting the lottery. Valen didn't even know of the existence of Mark's wife before that horrible week in June.

But then who could have sent it? Roger Lavoie, the architect of both the Darren Haber and Logan Galwyn grisly murders and the twisted episodes that followed each, had his ashes sitting in an urn in a simple plot in Moshassuck Cemetery. Beth Lavoie was still oblivious to Roger's sadistic secrets. She couldn't have done it. And as for Siobhan O'Mara, she had her own legal problems with the numerous charges leveled against her after being indicted in connection with the Gina Chaudhary death.

That left Mark. He was told by Roger where the Galwyn body parts were hidden, although he didn't tell Vince Calabrese and Drake Nowak when questioned. But how could that be? Surely his time had come on that fateful day on the Point Street Bridge. His body was never found and he was never heard from again.

. . . Or did he survive?

About the Author

I'm a graduate of St. John's University and have been writing ever since 2009. A proud father of three, I am happy to refer to my loving companion Connie as my guiding light and true soul mate.

WEBSITE: https://www.molloyauthor.com
TWITTER: https://www.twitter.com/AuthorMJM
FACEBOOK:
    https://www.facebook.com/molloyauthor